A
BREAK
IN THE
STORM

A
BREAK
IN THE
STORM

ARNOLD
SIMON

Except for known historical events and figures, all events and persons portrayed in this novel are fictitious, and any resemblance to actual persons, living or dead, is purely coincidental. In addition to such universally known persons as Hitler, Churchill, and Einstein, historical figures mentioned include Field Marshall Haig, Generals Blomberg and Gamelin, Premier Sarraut, Foreign Ministers Flandin and Eden, Ambassador Clark, Ernst Röhm, Léon Degrelle, and scientists Hahn, Röntgen, Wien, von Laue, Heisenberg, Fermi, and Meitner. The actual historical events described, including those in Dinant of August 23, 1914 and those of March 7, 1936, have been set forth to the extent that they affect the lives of the fictitious characters. The statements attributed to the participants in the French cabinet meeting of March 7, 1936 are set forth in substance only, but are consistent with what is known to have taken place at that meeting. The contacts between Exenby and Churchill are obviously fictitious, but are consistent with the activities in which Churchill and some members of the Foreign Office were engaged at the time.

Published by:
Noldan Publishing
Los Angeles, California
www.abreakinthestorm.com

Copyright © Arnold Simon 2004
Library of Congress Control Number: 2004101753
ISBN: 0-9749312-1-7

Book Design by Dotti Albertine
www.albertinebookdesign.com

For Nancy

ACKNOWLEDGMENTS

Thanks to my editor, Robin Quinn, for her always-perceptive work, and to Margaret Sobel, Emily Shaffer, and Tom Simon for their valuable comments on the manuscript. Thanks are also due to the Faculty of Physics at *Ludwig-Maximilians Universität* and to Mainau Gmbh for their kindness in supplying me with historical information. Above all, I thank Nancy Simon for her fine judgment and her steadfast encouragement at every step of the way.

There is a tide in the affairs of men
Which, taken at the flood, leads on to fortune;
Omitted, all the voyage of their life
Is bound in shallows and in miseries.

—JULIUS CAESAR. ACT IV, SC. III

1935 - 1936

PROLOGUE

The truck turned off the highway and started down a side road into some woods. It was night, and the headlights revealed a dirt road. After a few minutes the vehicle stopped. By now they were deep into the forest. The driver turned the headlights off.

Walter, who was the one in charge, spoke. "Get out, Yid."

They pushed Grunberg, and he half-fell, half-jumped out the back of the truck. Then the rest of the men got out. Everyone had become quiet.

In the total darkness, Erich Behrndt at first saw nothing. As his eyes began to adjust, he noticed figures standing at a little distance in what seemed to be a clearing. He also saw several other trucks.

The men were in two groups. About twenty of them stood in a loose clump. Some were carrying rifles or pistols, whose glint pierced the darkness. Facing them were ten men standing in a row. Behrndt understood that these were the Jews.

Walter grabbed Grunberg by the throat and shoved him back; Grunberg nearly fell, then recovered his balance. He stood, looking at Walter, and made a sound as if to speak. However Walter broke in first.

"Get back there, swine," Walter ordered, pointing to where the Jews were lined up.

Grunberg turned and walked to the line.

By now Behrndt realized that the clump of men facing the Jews really consisted of two groups, one consisting of members of the SA, the Storm Troopers, all of them in uniform, and the second of men who, like Behrndt himself, were in street clothes. Looking at them, Behrndt decided that this last group must be the recruits that he had been told they would send him out with.

When he had been instructed to come here, they had said it would be for "training." Erich was not in the SA, nor in any other uniformed service. What he didn't understand was what value this training could possibly have for a civilian government employee like himself.

Many developments had led to this episode in Behrndt's life. Part of it was his childhood. His father had been killed in 1914 in World War I when Erich was only two, and later his mother had died at an early age in poverty and misery, a victim of the draconian and devastating conditions imposed on Germany after the war by its enemies. Erich had little recollection of his father, but his mother had always kept her husband's memory alive, frequently mentioning him as a great man. Erich's father became a constant presence in the young boy's mind. When Erich misbehaved, he was told that his father would have disapproved; when he did well in school, he was told that his father would have been proud of him.

To his surprise, Erich learned after his mother's death that out of her meager earnings she had, over the years, managed to put aside enough money to make it possible for him to enter a university. Her great sacrifice heightened his resolve to avenge the wrongs that had destroyed both his father and his mother. But Erich did not know how he could do this.

Then one day his university friend Helmut Stangl had taken him to hear Hitler speak.

Erich had been overwhelmed by the scene. The immense field overflowed in every direction as far as the eye could see with hundreds of thousands of human beings. The whole mass was parted down its middle by a wide, clear passage that led the eye to an area near the far side packed with thousands of men arrayed in military formations. Throughout the whole flew the *Hakenkreuz*, the swastika, in its white circle centered on the red field of hundreds of large Nazi flags, many so huge that they dwarfed the human beings below them. Hitler spoke from a high platform, both separated from and towering over the military formations and the crowd. It was a long oration, with Hitler's guttural tones swelling in tribute to Germany's greatness, rising into a crescendo of hatred at its foreign enemies, and culminating in a storm of invective against the great masterminds of it all, the Jews. In response, the crowd exploded into ever more deafening screams of approval.

At that moment Erich had heard Hitler's promise: Follow me and I will take this great people out of the abyss and restore Germany to prosperity, to honor, and to glory. Here was someone who deeply felt the sacrifices made by Erich's father and mother, the agony of the German people, someone who had a vision of greatness and knew how to avenge injustice, someone who could turn that vision into reality...if you followed him.

Within a week Erich had joined the Nazi Party. Although it was not required for mere Party members, his enthusiasm was such that he had insisted on taking an oath of absolute loyalty to the person of Adolf Hitler, the same oath that would later become mandatory for members of the armed services.

As he grew up, Erich's respect for his father and obedience to his perceived wishes had broadened into respect and obedience to authority in all its forms. But what was happening now, this man whom Erich had seen dragged away from his wife less than two hours ago in Munich after the glass on their storefront business had been smashed into jagged shards, and who now stood quivering in pain and fear, and what Erich now realized they would do here in the forest, none of this was what Behrndt had expected or even imagined. He did remember a Jewish woman, a poor neighbor who owned a small farm, who had given his mother some work to do when none was to be found anywhere, but he had no particular feelings about Jews one way or the other. His enthusiasm for Hitler was for what he promised to do for Germany, not what he said about the Jews; Erich was willing to accept the latter because of the former. He had no particular objection to Jews being removed from positions of influence, but he had no wish to see wanton brutality directed at them, much less take part in such brutality himself. But he knew that, civilian or not, he had sworn obedience to Hitler before being accepted as a Party member and later being employed by the Government. A wave of cold sweat and nausea now swept over him.

Walter had a gun in plain sight in his holster, but now he pulled out a second one which had been hidden in a pocket. He handed it to Behrndt.

"Behrndt, you get over there," he said, pointing with his raised chin in the direction of the recruits.

"It's time for you to have a little fun," Walter said, addressing all the recruits. "You each have a weapon. You get to choose. Understand?"

"Yes," said several of them.

"We'll soon see if you do. If you fail, it will not go well for you." He pointed at one of the recruits.

"You. Choose."

The recruit walked part of the way towards the lined-up men, but stopped and looked back at Walter.

"Choose!"

The recruit took another step in the direction of the Jews.

"We don't have all night."

The recruit then walked along the line of men, looking at each face. Halfway along he stopped again and looked back at Walter.

"Please, tell me which one."

"You insolent coward. I'll tell you all right." He walked up to the recruit and put a pistol to his head.

"Kill or be killed."

The recruit fired, at the nearest man. The man fell. He was bleeding, but he was still moving.

"I said kill him."

The recruit leaned down and fired again, this time into the man's head. More blood spurted out. Then Behrndt saw the life go out of the man's body. He was dead.

Everyone was quiet for a moment.

Walter picked the next recruit, who seemed to have no trouble choosing his victim and killing him; the process continued, until it came to Behrndt's turn. Two Jews were still standing. All the rest, including Jacob Grunberg, had been killed.

"All right, Behrndt. Your turn."

Moving close up to the two Jews, Erich saw that the one on his left had one eye swollen shut, and blood on his face. His breathing was a sort of gurgle. The other man stood bent over forward, and what Behrndt could see of his face was swollen and bruised. Behrndt realized that everyone was looking at him. He felt numb. He had never held a gun in his hand before in his life, let alone fired one. He was paralyzed.

"Are you afraid? For God's sake, it's only a Jew."

Behrndt was terrified now.

"This is your last chance!"

Still Behrndt could not move. He turned cold with sweat and started to tremble uncontrollably. He bent over to one side and vomited.

For just a moment, which seemed to last forever, Walter kept staring at Behrndt, as if he couldn't believe what had happened and was trying to make up his mind about something.

"Come here, scum," he ordered.

Behrndt walked up to him. Walter put his pistol against the side of Behrndt's head. Behrndt had no illusions; he knew he was going to die. He only hoped it would be quick. He found himself wondering if he would actually hear the shot.

An eternity passed. Then, without moving the gun, in a voice so low that none of the others could hear, Walter said, "I should kill you, but I was told I'm not allowed to do that."

He paused again.

"You can be sure this will go on your record," he said, loudly now.

With the gun he jabbed Erich in the ribs, shoving him forward.

"Get back in the truck," he commanded. Behrndt got in.

Erich was now seized by a new wave of terror. But overriding the terror, and much stronger than the terror, was self-loathing and shame, a deep, crushing shame. He had let the Party down. He had let his country down. He had let his father down.

Behrndt swore to himself that he would never let them down again.

CHAPTER *1*

THESE EVENTS IN THE FOREST still lay in the future. At this moment on the train to Brussels, Behrndt was sensing that good fortune was smiling at him. Things were going well. Erich felt the train begin to slow down. He glanced briefly outside. A light rain was trickling down the compartment window. Here, inside, he felt comfortable. He went back to reading his newspaper. He was still reading when the train stopped in the Belgian city of Liège.

In the two years since Behrndt had joined the Party, while he completed his studies at the University, certain higher-ups within the Party had kept their eye on him. They liked what they saw. They had no doubt about Behrndt's dedication and his loyalty to Adolf Hitler, who in these two years had become the absolute ruler of Germany. But what pleased them the most was that he combined this loyalty with personal qualities that were rare among the dedicated, yet essential for the diplomatic job in Brussels they had in mind for him. Behrndt offered education—normally what the Party wanted was men of iron, not intellectuals—and charm, a gift for communicating with people, in addition to the good looks and the "pure Nordic" racial features that were so prized.

He had been living in Brussels less than two weeks. He was returning there now from a business meeting with his superior, Josef Steeg. Although Steeg also used a small office in the German embassy in Brussels when he was there, this particular meeting had been held in Steeg's regular office, which was in the German city of Münster. Because that city is a considerable distance inside Germany, this required Erich to make a trip of several hours by train from Brussels, each way.

The train was almost full. There was one empty seat in the compartment, next to Erich. A woman appeared at the door window, peered in through it, saw the empty seat, then slid the door open and stepped in. Behrndt had the newspaper wide-open and was paying no attention, but as she went past him her coat brushed the paper slightly. He looked up. An unusually pretty young woman. She was holding a purse in one hand and a suitcase in the other. She had a raincoat on. She put the suitcase down for a second, the purse on the empty seat, then leaned down and started to lift the suitcase. It was a medium-size suitcase; when she started to lift it, he saw that it was just heavy enough to make his help useful. Behrndt jumped up.

"Permit me," he said. Although Behrndt spoke excellent French, he was surprised to hear himself say this in German instead of French, since they were now in Belgium. It was probably because they had crossed the border from Germany and entered into Belgium only a short while before, or perhaps just force of habit.

"Thank you, that's very kind of you," she said, in equally perfect German.

He put the suitcase on the rack above her seat and went back to his paper.

The ride from Liège to Brussels was not long, about an hour. When the train stopped, Erich was still reading the newspaper. The woman walked past him, suitcase already in hand, and was out the door before he stood up. There were porters on the platform, but, as was his custom, he carried his own bag out of the terminal.

It was early evening. Outside the station, the Gare du Nord, people were waiting for taxis in the pouring rain. One cab was driving by as Erich reached the sidewalk. The cab stopped there for a moment, its way blocked by the traffic ahead. Erich saw that there was already one passenger in it, although in the dark he could not make out who it was. Erich tapped on the window. The driver opened it slightly.

"Can you take a second passenger?" Erich asked.

The driver turned around to look at his passenger. "It's up to you," he said. The woman hesitated for a moment, looking from the driver to this man standing in the drenching rain.

"Not at all," she finally said, speaking French without any foreign accent.

The driver got out; Erich handed his bag to him and got in. Then he saw that it was the woman from the train. He had put her out of his mind and was surprised to see her, but not unhappy with the coincidence.

Another woman stood outside the cab. She was middle-aged. She had no umbrella and the rain was pouring off her hat. "Are you free?" she asked the driver.

"I can only take two, *Madame*," he said.

Now Erich hesitated. The young woman next to him was pretty, but his natural politeness won out.

"*Madame*," Behrndt said, as he got out of the cab.

"Oh, thank you, *Monsieur*, you are very kind," the second woman said.

She had no luggage. The driver went back to the trunk, took Erich's bag out, and put it down next to him on the sidewalk. Erich soon got another cab. There was no other passenger this time.

When Behrndt got to his house, the driver jumped out, took the suitcase out, and put it on the sidewalk. Erich paid him, picked up the suitcase, and started for the front door. However, something, he was not sure what, perhaps a difference in the heft of the bag, perhaps some barely-perceived difference in its appearance, made him put it down and take a good look at it. The bag was not his.

This was not a minor matter. Usually Erich carried nothing in his bag other than a few clothes and a shaving kit, but this time it was nearly filled with the papers Steeg had entrusted to him. These were important papers that were needed the next day and were irreplaceable. At that moment, the driver closed his cab door. Erich heard the clunk of the transmission as the car went into gear. He shouted at the top of his lungs.

"Stop! Stop! My suitcase!"

The taxi had started moving, but there was a squeal of brakes. It stopped. The driver hopped out and met Erich alongside the cab.

"Yes, *Monsieur*. What is it?"

"You gave me the wrong bag."

"That is not possible, sir. It's your suitcase."

"No, there is a mistake."

"I will show you." The driver walked back and opened the trunk. "You see, it's empty."

"Well, this is not my suitcase." Erich had to admit that the bag was remarkably similar to his.

"I could tell you the whole story," Erich said, "but I'll just say that I was in the cab in front of you."

"I know. I saw you get out."

"You see, there was a mixup. There was another person in that cab. She obviously got the wrong bag. What a mess!"

"I'm sorry, *Monsieur*, but you see, I had nothing to do with it."

Erich thought for just a few seconds.

"Look, have you ever lost an important paper, one that could not be replaced, and that you had to have?"

The driver said nothing. Erich knew that Steeg had fought in the war. This man looked about the same age as Steeg. Erich had nothing to lose by asking.

"Were you in the war?" Behrndt asked.

"Yes, at Ypres. But I never talk about it, you understand."

"Well, tell me. Can you imagine being somewhere,

separated from your comrades, all alone, an enemy soldier coming at you, and having lost your rifle?"

"Yes, but what has that…"

"What's inside that suitcase means that much to me."

The man looked puzzled. Then he seemed to be mulling something over.

"I know that driver," he finally said.

"What driver?"

"Of the taxi you got out of."

"You know him?"

"Yes, that's what I just told you. We work together. Always at the station. He'll be back soon."

Although Brussels was a city approaching a million inhabitants, its traffic was much lighter than it would become in later years, and even lighter now since it was nighttime. The man drove like a maniac all the way to the Gare du Nord. When they got there, the rain had stopped, and the large Place Rogier in front of the terminal was almost deserted. There were only three taxis waiting in line. No, the driver said, his friend's cab was not here. But he had no sooner said it that he shouted out, "There he is! That's him!"

Yes, the other driver said, there had been two passengers in his cab, both ladies. One of them had no luggage, but the other, the younger one, had a suitcase. No, he didn't remember what it looked like, he saw so many every day. But yes, he remembered the address. Yes, of course, he would be glad to take *Monsieur* there.

✢✢✢

When Lise got back to the apartment she shared with her friend Suzanne, she changed from her traveling clothes into something more comfortable, and then sat down in the living room with Suzanne. They chatted about Lise's trip, an overnight visit to an old school friend. Then Lise went back to her room to unpack the suitcase, but the key would not turn in the lock. She tried it numerous times with the same result. Lise thought that perhaps she was using the wrong key, but she wasn't. Then she looked at the suitcase more closely. It was very similar to hers, in size, style, and color, but it was not hers. For a moment Lise was puzzled; she had carried the suitcase herself and seen it go into the trunk. Then she remembered. Someone had boarded the taxi and then got out. A young man, the same one who had helped her on the train. She had not paid much attention to him. Another woman had entered the cab after he left. Lise didn't know which of these two passengers was the owner of this suitcase, but whoever it was would soon realize they had the wrong one. She could only hope they would return it to the Lost and Found at the station soon. The only thing she could do was to take this one there and see if hers had already been turned in. She phoned for a taxi. When they asked for the destination, she said the Gare du Nord. They said they would have a taxi at her apartment in about ten minutes.

The doorbell rang promptly ten minutes later. She knew it had stopped raining, but in Brussels that usually did not last long; she draped her raincoat over the arm that was holding the suitcase.

The sidewalk was several steps down from the front door. When she opened the door, a young man stood at the foot of those steps, looking up at her. She had assumed it would be the taxi driver, but then she noticed that he was holding a suitcase and recognized him as the man who had briefly been in the taxi with her. She was mystified.

Erich looked up at her. Before, on the train, she had been encased in a raincoat, which she had kept on throughout the trip. Now she had it draped over the arm that was holding the suitcase, and what she wore was much softer-looking—a yellow cardigan over a buttoned blouse open at the neck, and a light-brown wool skirt. Peering down at him, she leaned slightly forward, and as she did, the ends of her tresses, which were let down, swung forward towards him. She was smiling at him.

"I think this is your suitcase," he said, smiling back at her.

He didn't look like a remorseful suitcase thief. Also, Lise had hardly paid any attention at all to this man earlier, but she had a good look at him now. Tall, with broad shoulders, a great build, well-dressed, and a look that was at the same time youthful and self-assured. And that smile! He was beautiful.

"Yes," she said. "Thank you."

"And I think that's mine," he said, pointing to the one at her side.

"Of course," she said, as if that had to be obvious.

They exchanged suitcases at the base of the stairs, then just stood there for a moment. Erich pointed behind him and said, "The taxi..." as a way of explaining how he got there.

"Yes. How did you know which apartment?"

"Your name. It's German. One of the other names there was Flemish, but that's different."

"Yes, that's different."

"And you spoke German without an accent. On the train. So I figured you might be German."

"Yes."

"I work at the German embassy. My name is Erich Behrndt."

"Yes, I see."

"Good night, then."

"Good night. And thank you again."

Suzanne had already gone to bed. The next day, Lise thought briefly about the incident. The day after that, she thought about it again, several times. The following day, she thought about it some more. He was so good-looking! The few contacts she had had with men had been disappointing, but she sensed that he might be different. Lise was not so much taken by him as curious. Before leaving for work the next day, she called the German embassy. She asked if a Mr. Erich Behrndt worked there. The

operator said yes, she would ring him. Lise said no, that would
not be necessary. She left for work a few minutes later. As she
was leaving, she noticed that there was something in the mail-
box. She opened it. It was a note from him.

✝✝✝

The moment *SS Hauptsturmführer* Josef Steeg saw that
Stoeffler was holding a file folder in his hand when he entered
Steeg's office in Münster, he got a familiar uneasy feeling in his
stomach. Steeg did not know what the problem was going to
be, but he knew there would be a problem. Up to now, the only
files that ever arrived in his office were applications for admis-
sion to the SS, Hitler's "elite" Shock Troops, and Stoeffler
always handled these himself. Stoeffler knew the requirements,
made the decisions, then simply handed Steeg a form, which
Steeg always signed. Yet here was Stoeffler, standing before
him, a file in hand.

"I don't want the fucking file," Steeg said. "You know my
standards, my requirements, and you know my orders." Steeg
waved his hand at the proffered file. "And you know not to
bother me with these applications. That's what I have you here
for."

"This is not an application."

Steeg thought for a few seconds, as if hoping it would go
away.

"Well, what is it?"

"It's the man they are assigning to Brussels." Stoeffler
knew this would displease Steeg, particularly since the Brussels
assignment was the very one Steeg coveted. Stoeffler was right.
For a few moments Steeg said nothing, as if lost in thought.

Steeg was over forty years old. Like others of his generation
in the SS, his appearance bore little resemblance to that of the
young men with tall, lithe bodies, fresh faces, and smooth skin
who now formed the mass of the organization. His body, while

still powerful, was shorter and heavier than theirs; the glow of youth in his face had long since been replaced by the almost doleful appearance of a disillusioned man desperately hoping to recapture his youthful dreams of power and success. The eyes, however, bore a complex message: toughness, arrogance, even cruelty, yet at the same time the look seemed almost reassuring, perhaps the result of aging.

This was an ambitious man. He wanted to be recognized, to play an important role in the great Nazi revolution, but things had not gone well for him. Steeg had been waiting for a promotion for several months, so far in vain. Some time before Hitler's accession to power, Steeg had learned from certain Party insiders, whom he made a point of cultivating, that the day when Hitler would become the "Führer," leader, of Germany was not far off. These Party members had told him of plans to maintain a "presence" in several countries abroad, which Hitler saw as one day joining in his great mission. The purpose would be to encourage sympathetic circles in those countries to help bring that day about.

Steeg also knew that the plan included posting selected members of the Party in some of those embassies. When he had heard about these new positions, Steeg had formed an image of the type of man they needed, someone mature, experienced, and with proven loyalty to the Party, the Führer, and Germany, in other words someone like himself. He visualized himself in this new job as a military attaché, or perhaps wearing civilian clothes and being to all appearances a civilian. He did not realize it, but the type of man the Party actually wanted for the job was not a hard-bitten man like him, but someone who, while made of iron at the core, would come across as educated, smooth, well-spoken, and attractive. In a word, they were looking for someone who was "diplomatic," and preferably young as well, attributes which Steeg was totally lacking.

Steeg's overtures through his contacts in the Party had been met with the message that, while he was appreciated as a loyal

SS officer, it would be best for him not to set his own expectations too high, and specifically, that these positions abroad were out of the question.

"I don't need to see the file," Steeg said. "What is the man's name?"

"Erich Behrndt."

"What's his background?"

"University-educated..."

"Don't they realize that what the Party needs are men who are willing to serve the Führer, to die if necessary, not intellectuals. Adolf Hitler himself never..." Steeg let the sentence trail off.

"What's his age?"

"Twenty-three."

"Twenty-three? Are you playing some sort of a joke on me? Because if you are..."

"*Herr Hauptsturmführer*, there is no joke."

"But such a critical position surely cannot be put into the hands of an intellectual, and a mere youngster still wet behind the ears at that?"

Stoeffler knew when to keep quiet.

"Between you and me," Steeg said, "I still don't understand this way of thinking." He laughed. "I suppose they'll be appointing Jews next. Of course, there is nothing I can do about it. If that's the kind of person the Party wants... it's really not my business."

This was, of course, true. But the whole thing rankled Steeg, and he could not resist going on.

"Well, we'll see. I suppose he was subjected to the usual thorough investigation."

"He was."

"The results?"

"Ranked in the top twenty percent on the evaluation of racial features."

"I see."

"Pure Nordic."

"Well, that's something. What sorts of people has he been associating with. Any Jews?"

"None, sir."

"Close friends?"

"He has many friends, makes friends easily. He first came to the Party's notice through a fellow student, Helmut Stangl, who has been a Party supporter for some time. Behrndt had had a number of discussions with Stangl, the usual students' talk. Behrndt had never heard much about *Herr* Hitler. But once he heard him speak, well…" Stoeffler extended his hands up and out.

"Naturally. Does he drink?"

"Just the usual students' drinking parties. But he's never been seen drunk."

"That's better than the drunken rabble that fills the SA."

"Yes, *Herr Hauptsturmführer*."

"One more thing, Stoeffler. How is this Behrndt with women?"

"Oh, they are all over him like bees around sugar. I should be so lucky. Plus there was one girl that he slept with for a whole year."

"Why only a year?"

"She finished her studies and moved away."

"Good. At least he's not a homosexual."

Steeg's demeanor throughout this exchange had not revealed the full depth of the jealousy he had instantly formed towards Erich Behrndt. This jealousy stemmed from the simple fact that Behrndt had everything that Steeg coveted but did not have, including youth, good looks, personal charm, a gift for communicating with people, and now, evidently, the very job in Brussels that Steeg had applied for.

Steeg was consumed by two passions. The first and stronger of these was the desire for power and success. The second was lust, not the simple kind of lust that could be satiated by prostitutes—he had long ago lost interest in his wife, and had to settle most of the time for prostitutes—but a lust that demanded nothing less than copulation with the most exquisite sort of mistress, in fact, as Steeg dreamed of it, with a goddess. Prostitutes, common ones, and the women he craved were to him the same, yet paradoxically completely different. They both took you from A to B, but oh, the trip was all the difference! In Steeg's imagination, the one was as different from the other as sitting up all night on a hard wooden bench in a crowded third-class train compartment was from the blue *wagons-lits* he had glimpsed speeding by in the night where people slept on luxurious sheets in opulent private compartments and dined on tables set with linen, crystal, and expensive silver.

These two desires, of power and of lust, did not reside in separate parts of Steeg's brain. His sexual ambitions were merely another aspect of his craving for power; women to him were not there to be cherished, but to be mastered.

It galled him particularly that the job Behrndt was slated for would be such a sinecure. It would mean living in relative luxury, and in Belgium of all places. Some of Steeg's proudest moments had taken place in Belgium during the war. Steeg also knew that the job in Brussels would mean women, the kind of women he wanted.

Although Steeg had not known until a few moments ago that Behrndt even existed, he already hated the cocky young swine.

✝✝✝

Steeg did have one consolation. Even though Behrndt would be supervised by regular Party superiors, Steeg also managed to be assigned to supervise him, albeit part of the time from Steeg's regular office in Münster, Germany. Such dual oversight was deemed desirable because of an institutional predilection for having one informer cross-check on the other.

Steeg had served his country with distinction in Belgium before; that experience would serve him well. He would be rendering a valuable service to the Party by reporting his observations. This work would also require Steeg to spend some of his time in Brussels. This also meant—just as he had hoped might happen—that throughout this entire assignment he would wear civilian clothes at all times and in all places, both in Belgium and in Germany, and to all appearances be a civilian. And on top of all that, there was always the possibility that Behrndt's inexperience would cause him to make some blunder or other. This might give Steeg some unexpected power over the upstart. And if there was one thing Steeg lusted after even more than exquisite women, it was power.

✝✝✝

Before leaving for his assignment in Brussels, Erich was summoned before SS *Hauptsturmführer* Josef Steeg. This meeting was the first opportunity Steeg had to actually see Behrndt. At the sight of the young man, Steeg's face took on a peculiar aspect, caused by the fact that his dislike of Erich mingled pleasantly with the knowledge that he now held considerable power over him.

"So you are Behrndt, the prodigy," said Steeg.

Behrndt was slightly surprised at what he correctly took as hostility, but said nothing.

"They tell me that you are wanted abroad. Important work."

Again, no answer was called for; Erich gave none.

Steeg paused for a moment.

"Now, you will be given instructions by others than me. But there are a few things you should know. For one thing, you will be working for the Party, at least its operations in foreign countries. Do you understand that this means you will be reporting to members of the Party?"

"Yes, *Herr Hauptsturmführer.*"

"And, for reasons that are none of your concern, you will also be under my supervision. That means you'll have two different superiors. Now I don't know what your superiors within the Party organization will expect from you. But whatever it is, if I hear that you fall short of their expectations, you will answer not only to them, but also to me."

"Yes, *Herr Hauptsturmführer.*"

"That's not all. Being under my supervision will be the hardest part of the assignment. Do you know why?"

"No, *Herr Hauptsturmführer.*"

"Let me make it clear. You must have some good friends in certain places. I don't know what you did to get them, but I must tell you that if I had had anything to do with it, you would never in a thousand years have been given this important assignment. As your supervisor, I will be watching you. If you fail in the slightest to live up to my standards, you will bear the consequences."

"Yes, *Herr Hauptsturmführer.*"

"That is all."

Steeg was treating Behrndt as if he were just another of the military recruits who were his usual subordinates. But Behrndt was neither military, nor a recruit, but someone whose sole purpose in volunteering was a desire to do his part to right the wrongs that had been committed against his father, his mother, and his country. To achieve that, Behrndt was prepared to accept hardship. Like most German youths, he had grown up with an enormous respect for authority. It would never have occurred to him that there was anything wrong with what Steeg was telling him; Behrndt saw these threats and conditions as simply part of what he was assigned to do. He accepted them without question.

✝✝✝

Party *Gauleiter* Otto Primmer's headquarters office was enormous, two stories high. Just as the Party, and specifically Hitler, had by now seized control of this land, so had many of the Party leaders appropriated the symbols of its venerable power. This building had obviously once been the home of some wealthy industrialist or other titan. An oak parquet, inlaid with the figure of an eagle, wings outspread, a fawn gripped in its talons, covered the entire floor. Oak wainscoting surrounded the room, its intricate carvings echoing those of the massive coffers that formed the ceiling. The walls from the wainscoting to the ceiling were entirely bare, except for an immense *Hakenkreuz* that filled one entire side wall, and on the facing wall, an equally large photo of Hitler, in full uniform, his arm jutting out in the Party salute.

Gauleiter Primmer briefed Erich on his assignment.

The Party official started by telling Behrndt that even though Erich was a civilian, his oath of unquestioned loyalty must remain foremost in his mind at all times. Then Primmer launched into some background.

There was in Belgium a political movement, or at least the makings of a political movement, which was sympathetic to Germany's plight and could, if properly encouraged, help to further the Party's long-term goals. It was headed by a young Belgian, a writer named Léon Degrelle. That movement believed that the Treaty of Versailles had been unjustly punitive, that Belgium had in the past been exploited by the other Allies, and that it was in Belgium's interest to support Hitler's new order. Adolf Hitler had decided that fostering this movement was of crucial importance to his country, and that only the most loyal members of the Party could be assigned to the task.

The mission to which Behrndt was being assigned was not an intelligence operation in the usual sense: the only thing to be reported back was the progress being made by this political movement. It was important to avoid any impression that the movement was in any way being directed from the outside. Behrndt would, of course, also perform any other duties he might be given from time to time.

"Our work there is going very well, very well indeed," said Primmer. "The Belgians are not such bad people, once you get to know them. They are simple people, nowhere near as sophisticated as we are, of course. They made the mistake of showing great hostility to us in the war. It would have been much better if they had welcomed us into their country, instead of trying to fight us. They fought hard, I must admit, at Liège among other places."

Erich thought of his father, killed at Liège at the very start of the war.

"Of course," Primmer went on, "they never had any chance of stopping us in those first days, when it was just the few of them against our mighty army. They were obstinate. And this attitude didn't just come from their military. As you know, it was unfortunate, but we had to shoot civilians in a great number of towns and villages to get the people to respect us. But I stray. As I say, our work now is going very well. The movement there admires us for the new order we are going to bring about. It's going to restore to Belgium its historic pride and independence."

The things Primmer was saying echoed Erich's own beliefs. He was impressed.

✝✝✝

Within two weeks Erich was in Brussels. The embassy had located an apartment for him. It was in the attractive quarter called Uccle, on a height with a view. On one of his first days at the embassy, Erich was pleasantly surprised to find his old friend from his university days, Helmut Stangl, working there. The two quickly resumed their friendship. However, within less than a week, Helmut was transferred to Munich, where the

Party headquarters were located. But he and Erich promised to keep in touch.

+++

Erich's note to Lise was nicely written. His handwriting was cultured-looking. In the note, he had addressed her as "Miss Hermann." Of course, only her last name appeared on the small tag next to the doorbell button. But Lise felt sure that he would have used this more formal means of address in any event. Erich had seemed polite, a gentleman. Since he worked at the German embassy, Lise thought of him as a diplomat. Diplomatic was in fact what he had been throughout their whole encounter. She sensed gentleness in Behrndt.

The note said that Erich had enjoyed meeting her, however briefly, and that he hoped she did not think him too bold to ask her to answer back, either in writing or by phone. Erich wrote that he would enjoy hearing from her and hoped she would be pleased to receive his note.

She discussed all of this with Suzanne. Lise could talk with Suzanne about everything, without restrictions or judgmental answers. Suzanne was the older sister of one of Lise's classmates; they had quickly become close friends. Although she excelled in science and had wanted to go on to become a scientist, Lise had been forced to prepare for bookkeeping work instead. When she graduated from high school two years earlier, she had had to settle for part-time work, which did not pay enough to live on. Lise had moved in with Suzanne. They shared the grocery expenses. Lise would pay Susanne what she could for rent, when she could.

After she had told Suzanne how she had met Erich, and of his looks and sweet manner, she confided that she was hesitant to respond to his note; after all, he was a total stranger.

"Obviously you want to see this man," Suzanne said. She laughed and added: "Frankly, from your description of him, I wouldn't mind seeing him myself! But I think you're wise to be careful. Someone you meet on a train, in a taxi, at your front door."

"You're right. I know nothing, next to nothing, about him. But that thing about the suitcase; it's amazing. He was so kind."

"Maybe. Remember, he was looking for his own suitcase. Do you think he would have brought you yours otherwise?"

"You're right. But I'd like to know."

"Why don't you write him a note? Tell him he can call you. Tell him at what time to call. Then you can see if he does. If he does, he will obviously say he wants to see you. You can tell him you will meet with him, but in one of those big cafés on the Boulevard Émile Jacqmain or someplace like that. Just for coffee. And if you're worried, ask him if it's all right if your friend Suzanne comes along. That will make it perfectly safe for you."

"I'm not that worried. What is he going to do in a café?"

"You're right. I just thought I might like to see this supposed Adonis myself. I might be interested, you know."

"I saw him first. And you already have a boyfriend."

"I'm just joking."

"I know."

"So you'll write to him."

"Yes."

"When?"

"As soon as I can get my hands on my notepaper."

✛✛✛

Erich called at the exact time she had mentioned.

"I'm glad you answered my note," he said.

"I thought it would be the polite thing to do."

He didn't take this as a brush-off. Erich had never experienced rejection anxiety when it came to women. "I suppose it was. We met so briefly, I thought it might be good to talk some more in person. If you would like."

Lise was afraid that it would not give the correct impression, or rather that it would, if she accepted too quickly. But Erich jumped right into the gap.

"Just for a drink, or coffee. We could meet somewhere." He paused. "That way you would be safe."

"So would you."

"Should I be worried about that?"

"I really don't think so."

He suggested a café on the ancient Grand'Place. It would be better than the big boulevards.

"How about Saturday," he said, "at three?" That was two days away.

"That would be fine."

"Good. I'm glad. Until Saturday then."

"Until Saturday."

✠✠✠

It wasn't at all unusual for a woman to be sitting alone in a café for a few minutes, but Lise was just young and inexperienced enough to feel uncomfortable doing that; she didn't want to get there first. She arranged to arrive at least five minutes late. Even then, Lise planned to stand at a point from which she could see into the glassed-in terrace of the café from a distance in order to spot him.

Although the weather was warm, it was winter. In place of the flower market that at other times of the year filled the square, a few enterprising merchants had set up to sell hot-house flowers. Erich saw her as she was still making her way among the bright colors of their blossoms. He was on the terrace, sitting at one of the small, round, marble-topped tables. He had already taken the silver drip top off his coffee, and was pouring cream into the steaming glass.

Lise had never done this before, met a man in such a place. For that matter, she had only met a handful of men in the two short years since she had left high school. During the four years between her mother's death and her graduation, her only contact with adults had been with the nuns who ran the school. Lise now felt the same mixture of anticipation and fear of being disappointed that she had experienced as a child each year before opening the package handed to her on Saint Nicholas Day, the day children received their gifts. Through the glass enclosure of the terrace, Erich seemed to her like a large male doll seen through the cellophane window of a gift box. As a child Lise had often wished for one of those long-eyelashed dolls but had never had one; she did not know what this one would be like once she lifted the lid. Lise did not want to betray how eager she was to find out.

She started towards him. As she came through the door Erich broke into a big smile and stood up. She smiled back.

"Hello," she said.

"Oh, there you are."

Lise ordered coffee, and they each ordered a *bolus*. He did not know about these Belgian sticky buns; she loved them.

They started with chitchat, the surprising coincidences that had brought them together.

"I'm not sure why I spoke to you in German," he said, "but I was surprised when you answered in such good German. Did you grow up in Germany?"

"No. My mother and I moved here from Germany after the war. But you, you are German?"

"Yes." This pleased her.

Lise told him about herself, how it happened that she lived in Brussels, that her father had been killed in the war.

"I'm so sorry."

"I never really knew my father. I have only a hazy recollection.

"My mother wanted me to receive a Catholic education, so

when she and I got here, she put me in a Catholic boarding school. My mother died when I was fourteen."

"I know how you must feel. I was two when my father died. Also fighting for Germany. I don't remember him at all. But my mother spoke to me about him often, every day it seemed. He was a great man. He died for a great cause."

"I never heard the death of my father put that way. I've always known he died, but my mother never spoke of his actual death. She never mentioned that he died for a cause. He was just dead."

Erich said he loved Germany, that it had been a proud nation until the Allies had brought it to its knees. He then mentioned Germany's new leader, Adolf Hitler, a name that Lise had heard but that meant nothing to her. Erich told her what great things Hitler was doing for Germany.

The idea of seeing the personal tragedies of his father and hers in the context of an even greater tragedy that had befallen Germany itself was new to her. Erich expanded on the idea. His serious subject surprised her, but his face showed no anxiety, his speech was free of tension, and what he said did not disturb her. He was passionate, yet seemingly without anger. Lise supposed that was what made him a diplomat. At the same time, while the other men she had known had been inconsiderate and insensitive, he seemed gentle and thoughtful. Lise was impressed and moved.

"How long have you been at the German embassy?"

"Just a few weeks."

He didn't give any more details than that about his work, but that didn't bother her; it just made him more interesting.

They had sipped more coffees, and had finished their second *bolus*. The flower vendors were starting to pack up their displays. It was Saturday and Lise had the rest of the day free. However, the conversation had reached the point where she felt the need to say she had really enjoyed meeting him but had to leave. The problem was that Lise was afraid he would not call her. If Erich didn't, she could call him, but under the conventions of the time that was not done. And with this brief meeting their first connection, she was too proud to want to be perceived as trying to force herself on him. Erich was charming and attractive, but at the same time she sensed something too vague to identify other than as a sort of coolness. What she detected seemed to place a barrier, a thin veil, between them. Lise did not feel love for Erich, not even the stirring of love, but she did feel a sharp, yearning curiosity, like that of a traveler briefly seeing an enchanting mountain village in the distance from a speeding train, knowing that its image would always be remembered, but the village never seen again, its promise lost forever. She knew she did not want to let him get away.

"I've really enjoyed meeting you," he said.

This was it, the goodbye, she thought.

"Me too."

"I was wondering," he said. "It's short notice, but by any chance would you like to have dinner tonight? We could spend the rest of the afternoon together." Erich briefly waved his hand towards the gilded façades of the centuries-old buildings lining the square. "Perhaps we might spend a little time walking around here first. I love this area."

Erich was charming, but Lise was cautious. For just a moment she hesitated.

"Yes, it is short notice," she said, "but I would love to."

✞✞✞

Although women had invariably found his combination of physical beauty and personal charm completely irresistible, Erich had never before devoted his opening gambits with them to such serious subjects. He was not sure why he had been impelled to do so with Lise; maybe it was simply that she was a fellow-German in this foreign country, or that they had both been victims of an identical tragedy. But by the time Erich felt they had to say goodbye, he was sure he had bored her and that she would decline to see him if he called. He had often wanted to see women again after first meeting with them; he could not remember any of them ever turning him down. But with Lise—he could not have said why—he didn't want to take the chance. Erich decided that he to make the move then, while Lise was still here with him, at this small table.

✝✝✝

After dinner that night they went to a nightclub. Erich was a marvelous dancer. While they danced, he spoke very little, as did she. To Lise's surprise this did not produce awkward silences, only an unexpected sense of closeness that made her feel at ease. Erich also seemed to be at ease, as he had in the afternoon. Now, seated at a nightclub table, they both talked. It soon became clear to her that he was more educated and sophisticated than any of the other men she had known. Erich didn't talk only about Germany and the war. He was familiar with the latest films and plays. He also seemed knowledgeable about sports, a subject, however, in which she had little interest. Erich apparently could talk on almost any subject. Lise was charmed.

She was not a virgin. However, although Lise had been eager to have a sexual experience, until a year ago she had never even gone out with anyone. When she had first become aware of the blossoming of her own body, she had begun to be aroused by unexpected longings. Lise had not accepted the nuns' implied message that sex was inherently sinful. It was obviously part of creation, part of God's work, not the devil's. She had expected that the experience of sex would be as natural and full of wonder as the rest of nature. The result was that during this short year Lise had slept, or at least briefly been in bed, with a few men. But all of those encounters had been terrible disappointments.

The first man was Henri, a *futbol* player who had been introduced to her by Suzanne. When he started his overtures, eager as she was, Lise did not pull back or stiffen. After two glasses of wine and some kisses, the embraces became passionate. Henri had no way to know that she was a virgin; he did not realize that her innocent compliance was not the result of having gone through this before, but precisely of not having done so, and of wanting to be led tenderly through the act of love.

Within minutes he had placed her on the bed, half-naked. He was not in any way rough, but wasted little time, as if he had done this with her many times. As he started to roll on top of her, she felt a surge of panic. Lise had a sense that it all was going too quickly, that what up to now had been pleasant and exciting might take a disagreeable turn, although she could not have described what that would consist of.

"This is my first time," she said, suddenly.

Henri jumped clear off the bed. "Oh, I'm sorry," he said, "I had no idea..."

"No, it's all right. I thought you should know."

He stood frozen.

"Me too," he said.

"You're joking."

"I mean with a woman who has never..."

"Oh."

Henri's eyes gleamed with desire, but he still didn't budge.

"It's all right," Lise said finally. She was looking into his eyes, smiling. "I don't want you to stop."

He didn't, but he calmed down, or at least seemed to at first. It seemed initially as if he didn't quite know what to do; Lise had no idea that there might be anything she could suggest. Then he entered her, gently enough, but soon began moving fast, without any apparent concern for what she might be feeling, and came quickly.

For a moment Lise didn't realize what the sudden slumping of his body, its dead weight on her, meant. Then she understood. She had expected some pain; there had only been a very little. But not much else; tension, just up to a particular point, and then this. Nothing. She felt let down, all expectation of pleasure, even ecstasy, shattered.

Henri was now on the other side of the bed. Lise suddenly felt that she wanted to be comforted. If he would just hold her tight, make her feel secure, that would be enough; it would, in fact, be marvelous. "Hold me, please," she said.

There was no answer. Henri was breathing deeply, sound asleep.

Suzanne had given her the pick of some other men she knew. She went out with one of them, then another. They all seemed cut from the same cloth. Nice looking, no great intellect, pleasant enough. But in the end, it was clear that what they wanted was a quick, easy lay.

Lise now knew that Erich was different as a person, and she felt he would be different as a lover. They kissed in his car after leaving the nightclub, and she responded warmly. She realized she was being impulsive and reckless—the reality was that he was someone she had just met almost literally on the street—but if he had suggested going to his place, she would have immediately agreed.

He did not make the suggestion she was thinking of. When Erich dropped her off at her place, he told her he would like to see her again. She said she would enjoy that. He said he would call her.

As Lise walked into the apartment, she thought of how ironic it was that where all the others had hardly been able to wait to rush her into the bedroom, with Erich she was the one who couldn't wait. It was not that she was falling in love with him—she found him exciting but despite her youth knew the difference—but that she felt that his lovemaking would give her tenderness. She wanted to find out. She felt it was too early to assign complex motivations to Erich's restrained behavior, as she perceived it, tonight. Lise thought that it was most probably just the result of his natural politeness. In any case, Erich had said he would call her.

✝✝✝

Although Lise had no way to know this, it was Erich's custom to bed the women he met at the first opportunity. This was usually almost immediate. And in fact he desired Lise as much as any woman he had ever known. Yet where with other women he had never hesitated, this time he had found himself holding back. He himself wondered why, and he concluded that it was simply because of her apparent innocence.

Erich called the very next morning, a Sunday. He picked Lise up at her apartment, and they spent the afternoon and evening together. Erich and Lise saw each other twice again that week, including once at his apartment for dinner. They kissed and held hands, but did not go much beyond that. Lise fully understood that this unhurried approach was considered perfectly normal and acceptable in the usual case. However, she did not see this as the usual case, not only because of how exceptionally attractive Erich was, but also because his gentleness was the very reason she felt he was the one who could fulfill her longings.

They agreed to have dinner again at his apartment. She decided that this was the night when they would make love.

Erich's apartment was on a height which afforded a wide view of most of Brussels. The living rooms and both bedrooms all faced this view. It was a clear night, and the lights of the city below filled the living room windows. After dinner, coffee, and drinks, they again started kissing and embracing. Although these episodes had become longer and somewhat more involved with each passing day, Lise had no reason to suppose that Erich had any intention similar to hers on this particular night, so, at one point, she stood up and said, "Almost midnight. It's time to go to bed." She took hold of his hand for just a moment, then headed for the guest bedroom. In her other hand she held the large purse she had brought with her. At the door, she looked straight at him, said, "Knock on my door in five minutes," and went quickly into the room, closing the door behind her.

The large window of her bedroom was open slightly, and the light curtain over it was billowing gently, backlit by moonlight. After she had undressed and put on the light, flowing nightgown she had brought in her purse, she opened the curtain wide and looked out. The city lights were dimmer by now, but there was a nearly-full moon.

There was a knock on the door.

"Come in," she said.

He opened the door, and stood in the doorway. She went up to him and looked at him for what seemed a long time. Neither of them spoke.

"Do you want me now?" she said.

He said nothing, but reached out for her.

"You'd better go take off your clothes," she said.

He disappeared instantly. When he came back a moment later, she was standing at the window in the bright moonlight. He walked over to her. His clothes were gone except for his shorts. They kissed. They stood without a word, looking at each other. He reached for one of the shoulder straps of her nightgown. She slipped both straps off her shoulders, letting the nightgown fall to the floor.

Her body was a study in deep shadow and moonlit glory. Lise was even more splendid than he had imagined.

Erich wrapped his arms around her. A wave of excitement swept through Lise. As he held her against him and her breasts first touched his chest, she started to tremble. This had never happened to her before.

"Are you cold?" he said.

She was looking at him and smiling. "It's not that."

They lay down on the bed. She had thought they would lie there for a while, just embracing and looking at each other in the near-darkness. But to her surprise, Erich moved fast. Nevertheless, when his experienced hands touched her, Lise shivered with unaccustomed pleasure. As he continued, she could not have explained why she was so quickly filled with increasing delight and heightening anticipation. In that moment, knowing didn't matter to her.

Lise found herself overcome with an excitement she had never experienced. After a while she suddenly wanted him inside her, and although nothing was said he seemed to sense the moment and entered her. Soon she was seized with a tension which rose to a nearly unbearable pitch, then suddenly broke into splendid waves which crested into the most delicious pleasure she had ever felt, and did not cease until she felt glowing but utterly drained. Only then did he come.

After that Lise wanted him to keep her in his arms; she had hoped they would hold each other, that they would speak some tender words, that they would drift into sleep clinging together. But none of this was to be. After only a few seconds, he rolled away from her and was soon asleep. Lise lay awake a long time, her body fulfilled, but not her soul.

When she awoke in the morning, Erich was still sleeping. She lay in the bed looking at him for a few minutes, then got up and went into the living room, closing the door quietly. She drew open the curtains. Brilliant light flooded in, a change from the frequent rains. Below her, the city spread out in the bright sunshine. As she sat admiring the view, she thought about the previous night.

In many ways it had been marvelous. Erich was a master at lovemaking. Even now, hours later, her body still felt pleasantly limp. Yet, as experienced as he obviously was, why had he gone so fast once they had started? Why hadn't he even looked into her eyes afterwards? Why hadn't he held her? Why hadn't he said even one loving word, when he was always so facile with language? Why hadn't he sensed her needs?

She wondered if she was not being too critical. Many women would have been happy to be in her place; she was certain that many had been. But Lise felt there must be more to love than this. There must be more to fulfillment than this. There must be more, even to passion, than this. Something that she needed was lacking in him. But she didn't know why.

✠✠✠

With minor schedule variations, Lise and Erich made love, or more accurately had sex, every night that week. She stayed for the night each time. She usually arrived at his apartment shortly after he did; sometimes they took dinner in a small neighborhood restaurant, then returned to the apartment and made love. Other nights the passion seized them as soon as she got there, and they went out for dinner afterwards, then came back and resumed their lovemaking, which on those days they referred to as "dessert."

But things stayed the same: physically spectacular, devoid of tenderness. Erich was a good conversationalist, as he had always been, and charming, but he did not express affection or speak of love; on that subject he was uncharacteristically tongue-tied.

Behrndt's behavior was influenced by the way it had been between him and the women he had had before Lise. The first of these was a certain Greta Heidecker, whom he had met when he was at the University. She was also a student, but one obviously more advanced than him. Upon meeting Behrndt, she had taken him almost directly to her place, which was just a room barely larger than the bed it contained; this room sat in a building full of such rooms, all rented to students. Under her guidance Behrndt had rapidly learned to have sex that was passionate, or more accurately lustful, and overwhelmingly exciting for both of them. This continued every day for a year, until Greta's studies were completed and she left. As they parted she displayed no grief, only gratitude; and the same was true of him. They never met again. During the remainder of his university days, Erich had affairs with various other young women, one of whom, although her name was Christine, turned out to be half-Jewish; there were also affairs with several older women who were not students. All of these encounters, and all of his later encounters up until Lise, had been brief and equally devoid of emotional involvement.

As for Lise, she did not feel love for Erich, so she did not think there was anything for her to say on the matter. She was quite willing to continue enjoying things this way, for the time being.

The first time Lise came home, after being with Erich, Suzanne, whom Lise had kept generally informed, rolled her eyes up, grinned, and said, "Well, I take it the accommodations were satisfactory!"

Lise ignored it.

"This looks serious," Suzanne said later.

Lise didn't respond.

"Something must be going on."

"Obviously, something is going on. But I'm not sure how serious."

"Lise, I know you well. I think what's happened is that you have found sex. Am I right?"

"You certainly are."

"But what you want is love."

"Yes."

"And he doesn't love you."

"I don't know whether he does or not."

"But do you love him?"

"I'm not sure. No, I don't think I do, but..."

"But it could happen?"

"I suppose it could, but I'm not even sure of that."

✝✝✝

The phone was ringing in Steeg's office in Münster. Steeg picked it up. It was Conrad Leist. He was in town on some business unrelated to Steeg, and he was taking the opportunity to make a brief report to Steeg.

"Nothing unusual to report. The people you've asked me to keep an eye on seem to be behaving themselves."

"What about Hauser?"

Hauser was the name they had agreed to use for Erich Behrndt. Leist knew that Steeg was particularly interested in Behrndt.

"Not much there either. Oh, one thing, he has acquired a girlfriend. I've started checking her out, just as a routine matter."

"Good. How often has he seen her?"

"Well, she has been sleeping with him."

"What else?"

"The name is Lise Hermann. She's German, both parents German, Aryans."

"Good."

"Has been living in Brussels since childhood. Speaks fluent French, and German. Works as a bookkeeper."

"Anything else?"

"No. Other than that she's a beauty."

Steeg's heart jumped. "Oh?"

"A goddess."

Steeg was stunned by the use of that word. Leist had not heard it from him.

"And it goes on every night."

"I see. By the way, how did you find all this out?"

"Our man occupies the downstairs apartment. He knows everything that goes on."

1915

$\mathcal{S}$TEFAN'S BED was about midway down the hospital ward. Against both of the long walls were dozens of other beds, all occupied by other wounded German soldiers. Also each day more wounded had been brought in, and beds, cots, and even stretchers had been added. Now the beds were crowded together; some had even been positioned lengthwise in the space between the two opposing rows, and sometimes men on stretchers had been placed in the spaces between the beds. The whole place was permeated with the smell of disinfectant.

Like most of these German soldiers, Stefan had been wounded in the 1915 battle which was still raging in Champagne. This battle would later be dwarfed by the much larger ones at Verdun, at the Somme, and other places. But in less than three months of fighting in Champagne alone, with virtually no ground gained by either the French or the Germans, the casualties to both sides totaled over four hundred thousand men. The doctor told him later that anyone with injuries like those Stefan had incurred in battle usually died. However, much to the surprise of the nurses and doctors, he was now recovering from his injuries and from the surgery for them, although he was in constant pain, despite the morphine. The doctor also told Stefan that he would remain in the hospital for some months. The numbness in his legs should gradually go away with the treatments and with exercise, and there was every expectation that he would be able to walk again, but not soon, nor as well as before. Yet Stefan was one of the lucky ones. And obviously, he would never be able to return to the front.

For a long time, the world around Stefan had been partially hidden as if by a fog which dulled both sights and sounds. One of the first things he remembered hearing was the voice of a nurse.

"Well," the voice had said, "it looks like we're awake."

Stefan could not make out who the voice was talking about.

"Stefan Mueller?"

It was definitely talking about him.

"There is a letter for you."

That was interesting.

"Would you like me to read it to you?"

"Yes," he heard his voice say.

"'Dear Stefan, I have wonderful news for you. Today Catherine gave birth to a beautiful baby girl. She is perfect. You should be proud. I am writing this in a hurry, as I want to get it off to you right away. More details later. We were happy to learn that you are recovering nicely, thank God, and we hope that you will soon be home. I embrace you, Emma.'"

"Thank you," his voice said.

"You're a lucky man."

✝✝✝

Stefan had no clear idea how many days had gone by, but it seemed to have been a long time, as if he had come back from a long voyage. He was sitting up. He saw his father-in-law Johann almost as soon as this relative came through the door at the end of the ward. The fog had nearly cleared up. Stefan was feeling stronger, and he had begun to be aware of things around him. Johann looked old. But as he got near Stefan's bed, Johann broke into a smile.

"Ah, there you are, Stefan! You look well! You are sitting up like a prince!"

Stefan wondered why Johann had come. He had never liked Stefan. Johann had in fact hardly ever spoken to him.

"I got Emma's letter."

"Yes. You should see the baby!"

Stefan turned and looked at the photograph of Catherine in its silver frame next to his bed.

"Is Emma staying with Catherine?"

"No."

That was Johann, all right, always holding back, as if teasing you. What in hell did just "no" mean?

"What?" Stefan said impatiently.

"Well, it wasn't possible."

"What do you mean, it wasn't possible? Is Emma sick?"

"No. Well, I was going to tell you…"

"For God's sake, Johann, tell me, is Catherine all right?"

The smile was gone from Johann's face. All that was left was the devastated face of an old man.

"Johann?"

"Stefan, I'm sorry to have to tell you…"

"Oh God!"

Johann just stared at him.

"Oh God in Heaven!"

"I'm sorry, Stefan."

✝✝✝

Emma and Johann had decided that the only way to handle it was for Johann to go see Stefan in person. A letter would be too complicated, and it couldn't explain things the right way. If it had only been to tell him Catherine had died giving birth to the baby, a letter might have done, hard as that would have been. But not for the rest of it.

They were in their house, not far from Munich, in the same room and in the same chairs they had sat in almost every evening since Catherine herself had been a child. They called it the living room, though the actual living room was at the front of their small house and was used only on special occasions. The room where they sat was smaller, less fancy, and further back, just off the kitchen. Johann was smoking a pipe as he did every evening. They sat in silence for several minutes.

"I don't see how we can keep the child," Johann said suddenly. "It will have to be adopted. There's no other way."

"How can you say that? Our own grandchild," Emma said.

"Emma, who's going to take care of it? Stefan certainly is not going to be able to do that. He'll be in the hospital for months, and when he gets out he may not even be able to walk. The idea is absurd. We're both over sixty. We're too old."

Emma began to cry.

"How unfair! To lose first one's only child, and then one's only grandchild!" she said between sobs.

She continued crying. Neither of them said anything for a while.

Emma regained her breath.

"She's all we have left," Emma said.

"We can't just think of ourselves. We have to think of the child. What kind of a life could we give her? How much longer will we be around? It wouldn't be fair to her. And there's no one else. Stefan's father is all alone, and he's old too. What the baby needs is a good solid, loving home with parents who are still young. A couple who can give her a good life."

More silence.

"Let me think about it," Emma said.

†††

Emma couldn't get the situation off her mind. She was awake most of that night. The next day, Emma told Johann that she had thought about it, and that he was right. It was the only solution. She had also had another thought.

She and Johann had always been good Christians, and they had raised Catherine the same way. So they had been shocked and disappointed when Catherine had announced that she wanted to marry a man whose mother was Jewish. True, Stefan Mueller was an educated man, a university professor, but in their eyes he was still a Jew. Besides, many Jews were well-educated, and that did not make them any less undesirable. Actually, it was quite the opposite, with all the power the Jews had. The thought of having a Jew in the family appalled both Johann and Emma. They had used every argument possible to try to dissuade Catherine: appeals to reason, appeals to her religious conscience, pleading, angry words, but all to no avail.

"At least we can make sure the child is given a Christian upbringing," Emma said. "We can make sure her parents are Christian."

And so it was done. Stefan was almost totally undone by the death of his beloved Catherine, especially coming as it did at the precise juncture of their daughter's birth and his own incapacitation. But Stefan was a rational man, and he was able to see beyond his grief and frustration, to the unavoidable conclusion, the only possible conclusion, that it would be best for the child to be raised by a suitable family. Nevertheless, it devastated him.

Stefan was also satisfied with his in-laws' intention to put the baby in a Christian home. Although his own mother, who had died some years ago, had been Jewish, his father was a church-going Protestant and Stefan had always considered himself a Christian.

The adoption was arranged through a lawyer. Through the attorney, Johann and Emma, and Stefan, were supplied with information which, although general in nature, included assurances that the baby's new parents, who were childless, were of good character and in good health. They learned that the husband, who was about eight years older than Stefan, was an educated man, and that they were Germans and good Christians, who would raise the child as a Christian. Emma made a particular point of this last requirement, which she considered essential. True, the adopting parents were Catholic, not Protestant as Emma would have preferred, but the lawyer said that suitable adoptive parents were hard to find, particularly with the war going on, and that it was not advisable to insist on too many qualifications. Comparable information was supplied through the lawyer by Johann and Emma, including assurances that the family the child came from was entirely Christian. Emma felt totally comfortable with this lie. After all, it was in the child's best interest.

The new parents lived in another city, also in Germany but some distance away. Everything was handled with dispatch and great discretion. Neither side learned the other's identities.

By the time the child was actually handed over to her new parents, she was less than three weeks old. It was agreed not only that she would never be told that she was adopted, but also that no one else would ever know either. The birth was registered to show her as having been born to her new parents, and the lawyer fixed things so that there was no indication of any adoption.

The new parents asked what her Christian name was. They were informed that the child had not yet been baptized, and that her family felt that it would be most appropriate for her to be named by the new parents. The adopting parents said that they had thought about this and had decided to name her Lise. The new mother handed the lawyer a letter she had written. It did not reveal the adoptive family's identity. She asked that it be passed on to Stefan. The letter told him how happy the couple was to be adopting his child and assured him that they would love and care for her as their own.

1935 - 1936

CHAPTER 3

_L_ISE HERMANN had been filling Steeg's dreams by night and his fantasies by day ever since Conrad Leist had told him about her, and tonight was the time when he would meet her. Steeg was not clothes-conscious—until his present assignment, he had not worn civilian clothes in over twenty years—but tonight it was crucial to make the right impression. He wore the best suit in his new wardrobe, which happened to be a blue serge, and a red silk tie. When he stepped out of his Brussels hotel, the evening sky was clear. The restaurant was not far from the hotel. Steeg decided to go on foot.

This was a business trip, of course, part of his supervisory duties over Erich Behrndt. But there was no rule that said Steeg could not enjoy his work. He had arranged to have dinner with Behrndt—it was important to observe him in a social context—and two women. Behrndt had made no particular effort to conceal the fact that he had a lady friend; and without disclosing that he knew anything more than that simple fact, Steeg had asked Erich to bring her along, together with a dinner companion for himself. It would make for a pleasant evening for the four of them, Steeg had added in his most genial manner.

As Steeg made his way along the boulevards and thought about the coming evening, he congratulated himself on his ability to get the assignment of supervising Behrndt and to set this evening up. He had been delighted when Leist had

mentioned that Lise was racially pure; however as further protection, Steeg had ordered Stoeffler to make a complete investigation of her, including where she worked, her background,
what her views were concerning Germany—in a word everything. It was to be handled in complete confidence. Even the
fact that it was being run at all was not to be disclosed, and
Stoeffler was to report the results directly to Steeg and to no
one else.

The restaurant was one of the finest of the many fine
restaurants in Brussels. Although Steeg had never been there
before, he was greeted at the door like a valued guest, which
was the way this restaurant treated all its customers. The décor
was elegant and cheerful, not gaudy or overstated. The tables,
chairs, and other appointments were what one might have
expected to find in a tasteful private home; indeed it all looked
as if the owner had deliberately tried to give the guests the feeling of being in such a house. This was in the splendid era
before canned music, and although the restaurant had the services of a small orchestra available for those occasions that
called for it, on this night, as on almost all other nights, the
only music was the soothing murmur of dozens of conversations, punctuated by gentle laughter and accompanied by the
light and inviting tinkle of silverware and china.

He saw Behrndt and the two women almost as soon as the
Maître d'Hôtel started to lead him to the table. The two
women were seated on either side of Behrndt. Both of them
were attractive, but one of them was outstanding. Erich Berndt
stood up and made the introductions. The gorgeous one turned
out indeed to be Lise Hermann. She wore a pale blue wool
dress that flattered her figure, and it did not need any flatter-
ing. Her blond hair was swept upward into a mass of curls,
baring her neck. Lise was looking at Steeg as he sat down. As
her eyes lingered on his for just a moment afterwards, Steeg
noticed that the pale blue of her eyes seemed to color the black
of her pupils dark blue. Her gaze was almost imperceptively

myopic, slightly out of focus yet looking straight at him, an imperfection so slight that its very existence accentuated her perfection. At the sight of her Steeg felt his breath stop and his heart skip a beat. She was indeed the goddess Leist had said. For a moment the look in her eyes brought back some memory from a long time ago, but Steeg could not pin down what or when. It didn't matter; he now knew what the word "captivated" means literally, because that had just happened to him. Religion was totally foreign to Steeg, but now he prayed. He prayed that Lise would like him.

✝✝✝

Steeg ordered a bottle of wine, while making it clear that he only drank the finest French wines. Erich was already starting to get bored with him.

When Steeg had ordered him to arrange the evening, Erich had told Lise that Steeg was someone higher up than him who worked at the embassy some of the time and was coming to Brussels for a few days. She invited a woman she had met through Suzanne. The woman's name was Yvonne.

Yvonne, who was older than Lise, turned out to be a German who was on a visit to Brussels. She had started to make small talk with Steeg. She seemed to be very much at ease.

"Mr. Steeg..." she was saying.

"Please, call me Josef."

"All right, Josef. Is this your first visit to Belgium?"

"Oh, no, not at all!"

For the rest of his answer, Steeg turned to all of them, but mainly to Lise. "Oh no, I've been here before. I love the Belgians. We Germans love Belgium."

"Oh?" said Yvonne.

"Of course. Would you like to know why?"

"No, tell us."

"Why, we love the ladies here." Steeg exploded with laughter.
"Josef, you're just teasing us."

"Not at all. I must say I have never met such charming and beautiful women."

The first bottle of wine was now empty; Steeg ordered two more, which were in turn quickly consumed, mostly by him. He had become even more voluble. As he did so, Steeg found himself almost unable to take his gaze off Lise, even when what he said was addressed to all three of them.

Lise at first did not know what to make of Steeg. She had never been out with an older man before or run into anyone like him. She noticed a small but deep scar on his left cheekbone. Lise had heard that such scars were sometimes the result of duels fought between certain young men in Germany in their youth; putting that together with Steeg's age, Lise now fantasized that this scar was the result of such an encounter. It also fit the general impression Steeg was making on her. It seemed to her that he exuded power. Lise had never experienced that before; she was impressed by it. Also, Steeg clearly dominated the conversation; while someone else might have found his talking boorish and out of place, Lise found it in a way very interesting. She was absorbed in his tone of voice, his apparent self-confidence, and his unrestrained manner, though she paid little attention to what he was actually saying. Lise assumed that Steeg held a prominent position in the diplomatic corps. Although she had never experienced anyone this loud or unrestrained, she was not put off by it. At the same time, Lise found his tipsiness, if not outright charming, at least somewhat amusing, and certainly innocuous.

As the evening went on, Steeg paid more and more attention to Lise. She did not mind.

As the dinner ended, Steeg suggested that they go to a nightclub he had heard about.

✝✝✝

At the nightclub, with Steeg again in the lead, they had several more drinks. Lise was actually surprised when Steeg asked Yvonne to dance first. When Lise and Behrndt got to the dance floor, Erich said: "I have to ask for your forgiveness."

"What for?" Lise asked.

"His behavior. It embarrasses me."

"Why? What about it?"

"Don't you find it annoying?"

"Not at all. Should I?"

"He's had too much to drink."

"He seems to handle it well enough."

"But doesn't it bother you? The way he goes on?"

"Erich, I think you are getting a little jealous."

"Really, Lise, you know better."

"I don't. Not at all."

"I just thought that intellectually…"

"Sometimes I enjoy not getting too intellectual."

"I've noticed."

"I do think you're jealous. Erich, he must be twice your age. But I like him. I think he's a very powerful man, but quite harmless."

They went on dancing, but said nothing for the next minute. "But still…" Lise finally said.

"Still what?"

"Still I'm glad about the suitcase."

He didn't answer. "Aren't you?" she said.

Erich pulled her closer to him; she reciprocated.

"Yes," he said, "I am glad."

After they got back to the table, Lise had hardly sat down when Steeg asked her to dance. She found him a bit heavy-footed as a dancer. She didn't know whether all the wine in him was a factor, but decided that his dancing style matched what she took to be his personality, a little rough and unpolished, but not disagreeable, in fact gently amusing. The band was playing fox-trots, which Steeg could manage well enough, but after a few more numbers, they switched to tangos. Steeg had never run into the tango before. Lise tried, very cheerfully and taking care not to bruise Steeg's ego, to help him out. It was no use; he soon got completely lost. Fortunately, Steeg took it all in good spirits, and they ended up laughing. He didn't seem to mind his dancing fiasco. Lise didn't either.

✠✠✠

The next day, Stoeffler was in Steeg's local office at the Brussels embassy.

"Well, what have you found?" Steeg asked.

"She's twenty years old," Stoeffler said. "Works as a part-time bookkeeper. Born in Germany during the war. Her father was killed at the front, mother and daughter moved to Brussels after the war. Her family on both sides were Christians. Aryans all the way back."

"One can tell by looking at her. But it never hurts to check. Anything else?"

"No, that's all. As a precaution I'm double-checking everything, looking for any loose ends, but I don't expect to find anything different."

"Good work, Stoeffler."

Steeg could hardly contain himself with joy. After Stoeffler had left the room, he got up and did a little dance.

✠✠✠

André Laroche entered the German embassy. There was some paperwork he had to take care of. Although André regularly did business with Germany from his office here in Brussels, this was the first time he had been in the local German embassy. As he was walking down the hall, something about the man walking ahead of him caught André's attention.

The man was about ten meters away. For the briefest moment there was only a vague feeling, a horrible memory, just below André's consciousness. Then it all came back in one quick jolt. The fellow was wearing a suit, not a uniform. But the walk. The swagger. It surely was him. But André had to make sure. He had to see the man's face. Just then, the man, still the same distance ahead, turned and disappeared to the right into a hall or doorway.

The man had evidently entered the wrong room, because seconds later he was back out and headed in André's direction. This happened just in time for André to catch a glimpse of him head-on; it was enough. The man looked much older—it had been over twenty-one years—but André recognized the small, deep scar on his left cheekbone. The man also looked shorter, but André realized that this was because in those years he himself had grown from an unformed youth into a tall, strong man in his mid-thirties. Most of all, André recognized the eyes that he had seen thousands of times in his mind since then. They had become much softer, the look almost benign, but to André it brought back again the cruelty, the arrogance, the total lack of mercy. A wave of revulsion swept over André. For a moment he felt weak and thought he would vomit. Then anger took over.

The man walked right past André, certainly unaware of the reaction he had aroused.

✝✝✝

When they had agreed to meet for lunch, André had told Raoul Maartens that his embassy business might make him a few minutes late. As it turned out, the business was taken care of promptly, and André arrived at the restaurant on time. Raoul looked up at André as his friend approached the table.

"You look as if you've seen a ghost," Raoul said.

"I have."

As André sat down, Raoul didn't ask the obvious question, but just kept looking at him. André was thirty-six, Raoul a good five years older. They had been in the war together. The two had been such close friends for so many years that they could almost read each other's thoughts.

André was seated by now, saying nothing; Raoul continued to gaze at him. André's face was still white.

"What happened?"

"I saw him."

"Dinant?" It was in the form of a question, but Raoul was not really asking; he knew.

André nodded.

"Are you sure?" Raoul asked.

"I'm sure."

"But where? What happened?"

"While I was in the embassy." André was usually self-controlled, but his voice was trembling. "He was in front of me. It was odd; he was walking in the same direction, with his back to me, yet I knew right away. I didn't actually, of course. I mean, I couldn't be sure, but then he turned and came back in the other direction and I saw his face. Just for a moment, but then I knew."

"But how can that be?" said Raoul. His voice rose; it was not curiosity, but outrage. "How can it be that he is alive, running loose, here, in Brussels, of all places? I thought that was long since over. The trials. The sentences." Raoul emphasized the word "sentences."

"I never paid attention to all that. I've never even known his name. I had heard there were some acquittals, but…"

"Yes."

"…surely not him."

"Surely not."

André and Raoul sat there, saying nothing, both of them thinking the same terrible thought.

"Surely not him," said Raoul, again.

"Maybe they never even tried him…" said André.

"The bastards!"

"I have to find out," André said.

"Of course."

"But Raoul, we don't know his name."

They both paused again.

"Maybe the newspapers," said Raoul. Now that Maartens had said this, it was obvious, but Raoul was the one who had come up with it, not André. It was almost always like that.

"Yes. Maybe if we look in the papers. Yes, let's do that."

"And there must be some records, somewhere."

"Yes, records."

André could still hear the shots.

1914

*I*T WAS AUGUST 23, 1914, twenty days after the first German soldiers had stepped on Belgian soil, starting World War I, the Great War. As the German armies advanced, Belgian cities along the Meuse River had begun to fall. But in many places, civilians harassed the Germans with sniper fire, obstruction of roads, and similar activities.

The Germans had their response ready: kill civilians, the guilty and the innocent. They had massacred, and were continuing to massacre, civilians in town after town throughout this small country. Today was Dinant's turn. It was the Germans' official policy, *Schrecklichkeit*, "frightful terror." The idea was to punish any resistance so frightfully that the enemy would submit.

It was almost noon, and after scouring the few streets of Dinant, the troops had so far collected only a couple of hundred civilians. Like the other young officers in charge, Josef Steeg knew that this would not do. He was standing with his back to the Meuse River, looking up at the onion-shaped steeple of the ancient Church of Notre Dame. Its door was closed, but he could hear the organ playing inside. Steeg had ambitions of promotions.

He turned to a sergeant standing near him.

"Inside the church," Steeg ordered.

"But sir, it's Sunday."

"Neatly lined up in their pews." As Steeg said it, he smiled, as if recalling some pleasant memory. Then, without warning, his face turned to fury. "Get them out!"

The sergeant acknowledged the order, saluted, and marched off. In a few minutes he was back with a small contingent of soldiers. At that very moment, a long line of additional men and women, held in check by other German soldiers, rifles in hand, appeared from the far corner. There were children among the men, and some of the women held younger children by the hand. One or two mothers held infants in their arms.

The sergeant was now facing Steeg. He was thinking that now they wouldn't need to go into the church, but the sergeant was not about to mention this. He just stood looking at Steeg.

"Well, idiot, get on with it."

The sergeant opened the door to the church, and the organ music, now much louder, spilled out. Then it stopped in midphrase, replaced by shouts and screams of women as the worshipers were driven out the door. The shouting continued outside, and some of the women in the long line also began shouting. The German soldiers shouted back and attempted to keep order, but the clamor only got louder.

Steeg did not like the way things were going. He knew he could easily give orders that would control these people, but it would look much better for him if this went quietly and without actually using force. After all, this was only the time to round the civilians up.

By now about fifty people had come out of the church. "Halt! That's enough," Steeg shouted to the sergeant, and with his hand he signaled to cut the line coming out of the church at this point and to leave the rest inside.

✝✝✝

From a small dormer in the attic of a nearby house, fifteen-year-old André Laroche watched the scene in the main square.

Word of what the Germans had done in the other towns and
cities had quickly spread; the great fear was that it would be
repeated here. André was well aware of this, and he knew that
his father, Albert, had intended for their family of four to
escape town. However, they had waited too long. Albert had
said that he hoped at least to save his wife and children. That
morning, Jeanne had gone to church, taking their small daughter with her. Albert had taken his son to this house, which
belonged to friends who had passed along the key before
escaping town.

On the way to the house, Albert and André had passed one
of the officers who seemed to be in charge. It was Steeg,
although they didn't know his name. The officer glanced at
them as he came within a few meters, but he seemed preoccupied and moved right on. Just the same, the man frightened
André. There was a small but deep scar on his left cheekbone,
but that was only a detail. He had a peculiar walk, a certain
swagger, like that of other German officers André had seen, but
more pronounced. What most frightened André was the cold
arrogance in his eyes; they seemed to André devoid of humanity. Years later, in Brussels, he would not be sure whether his
recollection of this first glance was not influenced by what had
happened later the same day, but it really made no difference.
The fact was that from the moment he first saw the man,
André was engulfed by a wave of dread that drowned everything out of his soul.

From this attic, André now saw his father enter the square
and almost immediately walk out again. He saw an officer in
the square. He recognized him as the man they had seen earlier. André saw the long line of civilians being herded and
shoved into the square. Then he saw his mother and his small
sister among them. He kept watching.

✝✝✝

It was now near sundown. The Germans had gathered over six hundred civilians by this time. The soldiers made them line up along both sides of the square. There were still children and small infants in the crowd. André scanned the line over and over, but his father was not there.

Firing squads entered the square and took positions facing the civilians. Several officers, Steeg among them, stood in the center of the square.

At this point André saw his father again enter the square. Albert walked directly towards Steeg and dropped to his knees. André could not hear what he said, and his father had never mentioned this to him, but instantly, inexplicably, André knew what his father was about to do, the unthinkable bargain he was about to offer. André started shaking uncontrollably, filled with anguish, with pity, and with helpless rage.

A sergeant waved and shouted at Albert to get back. But Steeg had never seen anything like this. He put up his hand.

"What is it?" he asked.

Albert spoke a little German. "Your Excellency," he said, "I beg of you…"

Surprisingly, Steeg answered in excellent French. "Don't beg. And get off your knees. What is it?"

"It's my wife. And my small daughter. Only nine months old, Your Excellency."

"Well, what about them?"

"Please, don't hurt them. Take me. Please kill me. Please! But let them go. For the sake of my small daughter. She is so young! For the love of God, I implore you."

"Where are they?"

Albert pointed to a spot not far from where he and Steeg were standing. "Over there."

"*Très bien. Ne vous inquiétez pas. Je vais arranger ça pour vous.*" Very well. Don't worry, I will take care of it for you.

"Oh, Your Excellency, God bless you. Thank you, thank you," said Albert.

"I want to make sure we have the right woman. Sergeant, go up to her."

The sergeant walked over to where Jeanne Laroche was standing, and then he turned to face Steeg.

"Is this her?" Steeg shouted to Albert.

"Yes, Your Excellency. God bless you."

Steeg walked over and stood in front of Jeanne.

"Thank you, Sergeant," he said.

Steeg pulled out his handgun. He killed the infant first. Then Jeanne.

A scream of agony rose from Albert. It expanded, filling the whole square, and seemed never to end.

Steeg turned to the Sergeant.

"The stupid fools! They don't understand our policy of *Schrecklichkeit*. That the more frightful it is, the more effective it is."

From the attic, André had not heard any of the words, but he had heard the shots, had seen his sister become limp and his mother fall, and had heard his father's screams. At first André felt absolutely nothing; what he had seen and heard was too absurd to have actually happened. It was a game of "Bang, you're dead!" played by small children, where the dead get up and everyone laughs. Then the reality struck him. The blood drained from his head. The sweat on his body turned to ice. André threw up and then collapsed on the floor.

Later he heard the firing. It went on seemingly forever. There were so many to kill, and so few doing the killing. He was still weak, and he did not want to look. But when the firing stopped, he knew that they had all been killed.

✠✠✠

André awoke to the smell of smoke. He got up and ran out the door of the attic. The landing was filled with the smoke. Holding his breath, André bounded down the stairs, several steps at a time. The ground floor was on fire, but he dashed through to where he remembered the door was, and suddenly was outside. It was nighttime. The town was in chaos and burning, filled with German soldiers shouting and laughing as they pillaged the houses, then set them on fire. There were soldiers running in every direction, some dragging women with them. André wasted no time studying the scene; restraining the impulse to run that might call attention to him, he just walked and headed downriver. German soldiers were everywhere, but they did not seem to notice him. After walking for a considerable time, he reached a spot along the Meuse River where his father kept a small rowboat. Although there were no houses nearby, the whole sky was lit by the fire that now engulfed the town; André caught sight of the boat some time before he reached it.

Although he heard the sounds of artillery fire in the distance, the immediate area was relatively quiet, at least for the moment. André got in the boat and cast off.

Steeg had noticed André coming out of the house, and he recognized him from the morning as the young companion of the arrogant troublemaker who had dared to challenge his authority. To Steeg it instantly became a point of honor to punish him. He shouted, "Stop him," and started after him, along with two enlisted men who were with him. Steeg also had the impulse to run, but since André was only walking, the officer figured this youngster would probably get away from them if he heard them running, and decided it was best to walk as long as they could keep André in sight. But when they saw him get into the boat, the Germans ran until they reached the riverbank.

André planned to let the river take him downstream for some distance, using his oars mostly for steering. A mist had begun to form over the water. As he pulled away from the shore, his figure started to become indistinct, and then seemed to disappear. André had been unaware of anyone following him, but he dropped to the bottom of the boat when he heard the firing.

There were several other rowboats tied up near this spot. Steeg and the two others got into one of these. While the men rowed, Steeg sat at the end of one of the benches, peering in the direction where he had last seen the youngster. At first Steeg saw nothing. Then he thought he saw a shape off to the side, stood up on the bench, pointed in that direction, and shouted, "There, there, quickly!" As the two enlisted men swung their oars to turn, the boat listed to the side where Steeg was standing. Thrown off balance, he cursed, struggled to regain his balance, and fell over the side. He went under for a moment, then came up and continued cursing his men for their clumsiness and ineptitude. Steeg did not know how to swim. Although his thrashing about did not ease the task, they soon got him out. At this point he decided it was best to drop the chase and get back to town.

André, who had remained below the gunwales of his boat all this time, had heard some cursing, the banging of the oars in their oarlocks, and a lot of splashing, but did not realize what had happened. He heard nothing more. After a long time he sat up. There was no sign of anyone. Before long, he had drifted a good distance down the Meuse.

✛✛✛

After he had drifted downstream for a long time, André came to an area where there was no sound of any fighting nearby. He beached the boat and struck out across the countryside. André had received a bicycle when he was ten and, like many Belgian boys of the period, had spent most of his spare time since then bicycling. By then he had become thoroughly familiar with the countryside for many kilometers in every direction from Dinant.

He walked around the towns and villages, and crossed over fields whenever possible. To get away from the fighting, he kept moving further into the areas already occupied by the Germans, which were mostly to the north. There were refugees everywhere; the Germans he saw paid no attention to him. Shortly before daylight, a farmer gave André some food and told him he could sleep in the hayloft. In the evening the man gave him some bread and cheese for the road, and sent him on his way.

After five more nights, André reached a farm which he knew was owned by a cousin of his father. The farmer was away in the Belgian army. The only persons on the farm were the cousin's wife and an older man who helped with the farm work. The woman had heard about the massacres; when André told her everything that had happened in Dinant, she was horrified. The wife told him that if he was willing to help with the work he could stay there until the end of the war. At that time, it was generally believed this would happen within four weeks.

1936

*A*NDRÉ AND RAOUL were sitting in a tiny room in a public library in Brussels. André squinted into the viewer, and saw a projected reproduction of the years-old front page of a local newspaper. The headline of the lead article read: "Dinant Massacre Trial Starts in Leipzig." The lead said: "After many delays, it was announced today by the clerk of the supreme court of Leipzig that the trial of those accused of the frightful massacres of August, 1914 will begin this week. In Dinant as in numerous communities throughout the country, the news aroused in the relatives of the martyrs both the agony of reliving the unbearable and the consolation of knowing that justice is about to be done."

Next to the article were photos of three of the accused. André immediately recognized the one on the right. It was his man, not as he had looked in the embassy hallway, but just as he had looked in Dinant. The same scar, the same eyes, the same man. His name was printed underneath the photo: Josef Steeg.

"'Josef Steeg.' Raoul, how did you find this?"

"It was nothing. All I had to do was go through about ten thousand pages."

André got the joke, but was still impressed with what Raoul had managed to come up with.

"But I can't believe this. Leipzig? A German court?"

"Yes."

"But why? How did this happen? The Treaty of Versailles said those accused of war crimes were to be turned over to the Allies for trial. What happened?"

"The Germans didn't want to turn them over. They promised to try them themselves."

"So?"

"So the Allies accepted their promise."

"You mean they caved in."

"Yes."

"By what right? These were not unintentional shootings. These killings were planned and ordered by men like Steeg. They had a name for it."

"*Schrecklichkeit.*"

"Yes. Ordinary murder is a threat to others, and murderers are punished for it. Yet those who plan and order mass killings are a threat to civilization itself, and they go unpunished. What right did the Allies have to agree to this?" André had turned livid with rage. "Letting these killers be tried by killers? Did they ask the victims? My father, my mother, did they ask them?"

"André, we don't even know what happened in Steeg's case."

"No, we don't. But I know all about Versailles. The punitive measures, the demilitarization and disarmament measures, which the Germans flout and the Allies just 'enforce' with a wink. And now this. They did it all backwards. I'd be very surprised if anything ever happened to Josef Steeg."

"Well, we don't know."

"But you're going to find out?"

"I've been working on it. Now that we have his name, it shouldn't take long."

✝✝✝

It didn't take long.

Raoul's business took him frequently into Germany, where

he had many contacts. He was back from a trip to Leipzig within a few days.

He called André.

"You were right. He was tried and acquitted."

There was a long silence.

"I know you want to hear more."

"Why don't you come over here?"

Raoul was there within twenty minutes.

"Almost all the others were also acquitted," said Raoul, "even though the evidence was overwhelming."

"They were acquitted."

"And treated as heroes. It makes no sense."

"No, it makes perfect sense. The innocent are killed; the guilty are heroes. It's a sort of joke."

"It shouldn't have been left to the Germans. It should have been done by the Allies." Raoul paused. "But on the other hand, if it had, would there have been justice, or just vengeance?"

"I had hoped there had been justice. Now, what's left, except vengeance?"

✚✚✚

Not long afterwards, André and Raoul were having lunch together, as they did at least once a week. They usually met in the same restaurant, on a narrow street near the busy Rue Neuve. The establishment was unpretentious, its décor simple: small tables set for two or four with white tablecloths and cane-back chairs. The fare was likewise simple, but delicious, the service attentive but not intrusive. Like most of its customers, André and Raoul favored it because it also provided a quiet midday respite from the bustling business district just outside its door.

"I was speaking to Charles Leblanc," Raoul said.

"Who is Charles Leblanc?"

"An old friend of mine. Works here in Brussels, at the German embassy. In some sort of minor position. All the important jobs are filled by Germans, of course."

"And?"

"Seems that Steeg works for the Germans in some capacity. It's not clear what he does. His main office is in Germany, in Münster specifically, but he comes to Brussels from time to time, usually for short periods, and always to the German embassy."

"What else did Leblanc tell you?"

"He doesn't actually know Steeg, but has a passing acquaintance with a fellow who works at the embassy. His name is Erich Behrndt. Leblanc is not sure what Behrndt does, but it's pretty clear that he's one of Steeg's subordinates. There are a lot of people working at the embassy, and the Germans are pretty tight-lipped about what they all do. After all, they are a dictatorship."

"I'm sure they were not sent here to run a charm school."

"Oh, but I do think they want to charm the Belgians."

"Yes. They're cultivating a presence here. Preparing for the day when they will take Belgium over."

"Oh, Degrelle's part of that." By this time, Léon Degrelle's political movement in Belgium was receiving considerable support both from the Nazis and from their Fascist friend, Mussolini. Degrelle had recently formed the political party called Rex, which, in this same year of 1936, would unsuccessfully challenge the existing Belgian government in a national election.

"Yes. Interesting, but where does all this lead us?"

"Straight to Steeg."

"Oh?"

"There's going to be a big reception at the embassy. There will be many Belgian guests. Leblanc said that Steeg will certainly be there, and he can arrange for one of us to be invited. I was sure you would want to go. That way you can dispose of any last doubt as to whether this is really your man."

†††

There were no flags or swastikas, no uniforms or salutes, no pictures of Hitler. The considerable attendance included hundreds of the most influential people in Brussels, but the room was so spacious that it did not seem crowded. The women were elegantly dressed, the men in white tie. The fare was not German but Belgian food, which was outstanding. Except for a few of the best German wines, only French wines were poured. The orchestra was small and accomplished, its music noncommittal; it made no attempt to compete with the conversation, which swirled gently about like a breeze. Everything had been done in good taste.

André spotted Steeg before Leblanc pointed him out. The German was standing five or six meters away, speaking with a handsome young man and an exceptionally beautiful young woman. The way Steeg was standing gave André the impression that he was on his best behavior, as if his life depended on it. However, André was not misled by Steeg's current demeanor. If André had had any remaining doubt about whether this was the man he had been looking for, it was now gone.

"The young man is Erich Behrndt," said Leblanc. "The other one is Josef Steeg. I don't officially know Steeg, so I'll just introduce you to Behrndt."

"Mr. Behrndt, Mr. Laroche."

"Delighted," said both of these men, as they shook hands.

"Lise, Mr. Steeg, I present to you Mr. Leblanc and Mr. Laroche," said Erich. "Gentlemen, Miss Hermann and Mr. Steeg."

"Delighted," was said on all sides.

The waiters had not yet started to come by with trays of drinks, but Steeg had already managed to start drinking at the reception.

"Mr. Laroche," said Steeg engagingly, "do you live in Brussels?"

André had the feeling that this could not be happening. The idea that the smiling middle-aged man he was speaking to there and at that moment was also the young officer who had killed his father, his mother, and his sister at another place and moment was a challenge to his mind's abilities to grasp. For Steeg, in contrast, it must be easy; he obviously had no idea who André was, or that they'd had an earlier encounter, and thought he was looking at just another Belgian.

André was having trouble staying with his current view of Steeg's face. What André saw were actually two images, juxtaposed like the print of a double exposure: one of the faces was before him now; the other remembered. The face before André appeared sporadically, smiling and composed, only to give way instantly to the other, deformed by cruelty and hatred. André felt overwhelmed by the contrast in these images.

"Yes," André said, staying outwardly composed, "I live in Brussels."

"It is such a lovely city. A beautiful country also, I must say."

André could not resist a small reference to the past. "Have you traveled much in Belgium?" he asked.

"Oh yes, I was telling these young people just the other day that I have been here before. It is such a lovely country, and the people are so friendly."

André had a sudden strong impulse to pursue this further, to rip open the wound and expose the corruption inside. This would, of course, have been insanity, and André had no intention of yielding to it. Not until the timing was right. So he just continued with the babble.

At one point in the conversation, as Lise was smiling at André, he noticed Steeg looking at her and saw a strange expression briefly come over Steeg's face. That look seemed to André to be full of anguish. The look worried him; André felt his chest knot up briefly with a vague feeling of anxiety for her.

After a couple more comments, André wandered away from the group.

✝✝✝

At first glance, André seemed to Lise to be just another man among the many at this gathering whom she perceived as too old for her. But as she watched André and listened to him speak, she sensed something comforting about him, although she could not have said what or why.

It was not unusual for Lise to go strongly with her first impression of men; she had found Steeg likable when she had met him, and still saw him that way. Perhaps this tendency was the result of never having had a father to measure other men against; perhaps it was just the result of youth and inexperience. Perhaps in André's case it was because the things he had lived through in his thirty-six years had made him tough yet not cynical, seasoned yet still full of life and optimism, and this showed. Lise didn't give these things much thought; she just knew there was something very appealing about André.

✝✝✝

Steeg was indeed on his best behavior. He had plans for this evening. The man was wise enough to know that with a prize like Lise it would not do to move too quickly, and old enough to be able to restrain his lust, at least for the time being. When he and Erich had taken the two women for a night out, and when Steeg had danced with Lise, he had had the impression that she liked him. Lise's amused but sympathetic tolerance of his clumsiness with the tango, and her cheerful attempts to help him with it, had encouraged him. But he thought he still would first have to gain her trust before attempting to go much further; accomplishing that would gain him capital he could use later on. Steeg knew that he would also have to get Behrndt out of the way, but at this point it was too early either to order him to keep away from Lise or to approach her directly.

As soon as Steeg had learned of this reception, he had seen it as an opportunity to advance his scheme. He would devote the evening simply to getting Lise to feel more comfortable with him and more trusting. His plan was to escort her home, to her own place of course, after the reception, and nothing more. Steeg had come to the reception without a companion; he had also arranged for Erich to be summoned away from the reception on urgent business at an appropriate time.

As the evening progressed, and Steeg basked in the warmth of this marvelous party and feasted his eyes on Lise, he felt good. The champagne and other wines were abundant, and by now he had had a few glasses. He began paying more and more attention to Lise, and he repeatedly had to check himself as the plan resurfaced in his thoughts. But as the evening proceeded, he nevertheless continued to drink and became louder and more effusive. As before, Erich, who stayed close to Lise throughout, could only watch helplessly.

†††

André continued to observe all of this, seemingly casually, at some distance from where Steeg, Lise, and Behrndt were standing. This very young woman, who was obviously Behrndt's companion, evidently knew nothing of Steeg's past or true nature; it was not clear whether Behrndt, who worked for Steeg, knew all of it. In any case, it seemed clear that as his subordinate Behrndt was in no position to do anything about Steeg's behavior. André became increasingly concerned about what might happen to Lise.

At one point, Steeg pulled a handkerchief out from a pocket, lightly patted his forehead with it, and put the handkerchief back. A moment later a waiter came up to them.

"Is there a Mr. Behrndt here?" the waiter asked.

"Yes, I am Mr. Behrndt."

"I'm sorry to interrupt, but there is a telephone call for you."

"Please excuse me," Behrndt said. "I'll be back in a moment."

Steeg and Lise went on chatting, although as before Steeg did most of it. Within a couple of minutes Behrndt was back.

"I must apologize," he said, "but an extremely urgent business matter has come up unexpectedly, and I must excuse myself. I will have to be gone for the rest of the evening. Mr. Steeg..."

Steeg broke into his most ingratiating smile.

"Mr. Behrndt, it will be my pleasure to escort this charming lady home at the end of the evening."

"Thanks so much, that is very kind of you," said Erich. "Lise, I am sorry. Good night." And he was gone.

A moment later a waiter came by with a tray of drinks.

"I think I'll have another," Lise said.

When he saw Behrndt leave the second time, André had been standing close enough to hear Erich say he would not be back. André decided to move closer to Steeg and Lise, still unobtrusively. The room had become more crowded, and he had to wind his way, glass in hand, among the guests. At one point André accidentally bumped very lightly into a woman standing very near Lise and Steeg. As André turned to apologize to the woman, Lise took a step backwards, and bumped into him.

"I'm so sorry," Lise and André said at the same time. Both of them smiled.

But her glass had spilled, spattering red wine on the front of her pale beige gown.

"Oh, I'm sorry," André said. "How clumsy of me."

Lise laughed. "Oh, it's nothing at all," she said.

"But just the same... I should have been more careful. Really, I'm sorry."

"Please don't give it another thought. It's really not important. Besides, I'm the one who backed into you."

They stood silently for a moment, while Steeg was distracted by a passing colleague.

"On further thought," she said finally, glancing down at the stains, "I did make a mess of my dress. I think I had better go home now, before any more disasters strike."

André was aware that Behrndt had not come back. "I can take you home," he said.

"Well…"

"I'll be happy to do that, and it will ease my conscience."

"Miss Hermann…" Steeg began, overhearing André's offer to Lise.

"Please call me Lise."

"Lise, I promised Mr. Behrndt that I would take you home, and I think I should keep my promise."

Lise thought this over for a few seconds. She liked them both, and felt she could trust either one. But she knew Steeg better. He worked at the embassy, and she had gone out with him and Behrndt. She had only met Mr. Laroche tonight, and she knew nothing about him.

"Mr. Steeg…"

"Please call me Josef."

"Josef, I accept your offer. And Mr. Laroche, I'm sorry but I'm sure you will understand…"

"Of course."

✝✝✝

As he drove away from the embassy with Lise in the seat beside him, Steeg thought about the evening so far, and about what had just happened. He had never heard of this Laroche and didn't know who he was. But Steeg knew there must have been some reason for what André did. You don't offer to take a woman home whom you have never met before, especially one at an event with someone they seem to know, just because of some spilled wine. There had to be a reason.

All at once, Steeg grasped it. The answer was both obvious and simple. Steeg had noticed the way she had smiled as Laroche spoke this evening. Any man would have jumped at the chance to give her a lift, and if she smiled at you like that, well… that explained it.

Lise did her best to make up for the awkwardness of Steeg's conversation. When they arrived at her house, he got out of the car with her. At the front door, he said he had enjoyed the evening, bowed, and said good night. Lise said she had enjoyed it too. Then she shook his hand warmly and said good night. As she did, she smiled, the same way he had seen her smiling at Laroche.

Everything had gone well. That smile was reward enough for now.

✝✝✝

The next day, André found himself going over the events of the previous evening. It was one thing to know that Steeg was at large, quite another to observe him enjoying the favors of unsuspecting society. André had noticed the attention Steeg had been paying to the young woman, Miss Hermann. Despite the fact that she had come as the companion of Erich Behrndt, developments had occurred that led to Miss Hermann leaving with Steeg. André had surmised that she did not, could not, know the Josef Steeg he knew—if she had she would have fled the room. He had felt concern for her safety as she walked out of the reception with Steeg. Now the whole incident was still on André's mind. He called her.

"This is André Laroche. We met last night…"

"Yes, of course, I remember." She sounded surprised.

"How did you get my phone number?"

"Well, I knew your name, and there the number was, in the telephone book. I want to apologize again about your dress."

"Oh, there's no need to apologize. No harm was done."

"Well, it was clumsy of me. Also, I wanted to make sure that you got home safely."

"That's kind of you. That nice Mr. Steeg saw me to my door."

"I was not sure whether he was someone you had met before last ight."

"Actually, I had met him, but only once. But this is very thoughtful of you. How about you? Did you know him?"

André didn't want to say no, but knew it would not be a good idea to say yes. If Miss Hermann was not going to have any further contact with Steeg, she was presumably not in any danger from him; if she did see Steeg again, André would not want her telling Steeg that Mr. Laroche mentioned that he knew you.

"I had never met him before the reception." This was in fact true. "Anyway, I'm glad that all is well."

"So nice of you to call. Thank you so much."

✝✝✝

The day after the embassy soirée, Stoeffler was in Steeg's Brussels office.

"About Lise Hermann, *Herr Hauptsturmführer*."

"What now?"

"As you mentioned, it's good to check everything."

"Get to it, Stoeffler."

"There's just one additional thing. She was not born to her present parents. She was adopted. Her birth certificate shows Viktor Hermann as the father and Margot Hermann as the mother, so we would never have known, but as you said, it never hurts to be thorough, so I decided to cross-check the records of the hospitals in the area…"

"For God's sake, Stoeffler. You're an even greater incompetent than I thought. Why in the devil's name didn't you do it in the first place?"

Stoeffler just withstood Steeg's glare of outrage as best he could. What could he say?

"Well all right, go on."

"Well, none of the hospitals had easily available records going that far back. It took a bit of work, but I went through the archives of all those hospitals for the year of Lise Hermann's birth. There was no hospital record of any such birth. I kept digging in various ways, and eventually found out where her natural father is. He's now a physics professor at *Ludwig-Maximilians-Universität* in Munich. He's also a decorated war veteran. Severely wounded in the war. The natural mother died giving birth to Miss Hermann. That's it."

"What's the father's name?"

"Stefan Mueller."

"You're sure that's not Jewish?"

"No. Protestant."

"The mother?"

"Also Protestant."

"So there's no change?"

"No, *Herr Hauptsturmführer.*"

"Stoeffler, I don't like this piecemeal approach. You should have caught this the first time."

"Yes, *Herr Hauptsturmführer.*"

"But since the result is no different, I suppose there has been no harm. But I don't want this to happen again."

Stoeffler saluted and headed towards the door.

"Stoeffler, you didn't say, but I assume you did check all the ancestors of these natural parents all the way back."

"Well no, it didn't seem…"

"What is wrong with you, Stoeffler? To not check the ancestors?"

Stoeffler stood there mute.

"Stoeffler, if this did not have to be kept absolutely confidential, I would surely report you and make sure you were severely disciplined. But..."

Stoeffler did not move.

"Get out of here, Stoeffler, and finish the job!"

Steeg was not worried. Stoeffler had given him proof of her racial purity. True, the university thing bothered him a little. The Jewish influences. But that did not change the fact that her parents, her natural parents, were both Protestant. And the natural father was a decorated war hero at that. Besides, her looks were the best proof. As he thought of this, a vision of Lise Hermann in her full Aryan beauty flooded his brain.

✞✞✞

Soon Stoeffler was back once more.

"What is it this time, Stoeffler?"

Stoeffler knew there would be hell. He did not know how to begin.

"Well, I checked the ancestors, just as you suggested."

"And?"

"Well..."

"Out with it, Stoeffler!"

"Stefan Mueller's mother was Jewish."

The idea that this obviously racially pure woman could have Jewish blood seemed preposterous to Steeg.

"What in hell are you talking about? he roared. "You've made another mistake!"

"The birth records."

"I don't believe it."

"I saw the mother's birth certificate myself. There is no question about Mueller's mother being Jewish."

As the truth began to sink in, Steeg's first impulse was to take it out on Stoeffler. His face became a monstrous grimace.

"Stoeffler, you've ruined everything."

"*Herr Hauptsturmführer*, I admit I was very careless. I deserve punishment." Stoeffler paused for just an instant. "But respectfully... well, it is the truth."

"What about Mueller's father? That name. Are you sure the father was not Jewish also?"

"He was not. I had that double-checked again. Mueller's father was baptized in the Protestant church. I saw the certificate."

Steeg was quiet for what seemed to be a long time. He wanted to lash out at Stoeffler again. But angry as he was at him, Steeg realized that the fix he was in had resulted from his own stupidity.

"Just get out of here."

"Thank you, *Herr Hauptsturmführer*."

✝✝✝

Steeg went out that night and got drunk. The next morning he lay in bed thinking about his predicament. The idea of fulfilling his dreams of sex with Lise— after all, that was the nub of it —was in jeopardy, but much worse, his ambitions of success within the Party and the SS could be as well. When his superiors found this out...

He sat up with a start. *If* they found it out! But his superiors need never find out. The only persons who knew of the adoption were Stoeffler and himself. And Professor Mueller, of course, but he obviously would never disclose it. Stoeffler, whatever his faults, would never talk, and besides, he was aware that Steeg knew enough about him to insure that he did not. So they would never know. Steeg suddenly felt much better.

The other answer dawned on him during breakfast. As a diligent member of the SS, Steeg had kept up with the racial laws, the Nuremberg laws, as one had to in these times; these laws were at the center of everything. Complex as they were, he knew their every detail.

So Mueller's father was a Protestant, his mother Jewish. Because he had two Jewish grandparents on his mother's side, Mueller was a half-Jew, a *Mischlinge*, or half-breed. However, he was treated as a Jew, because for many purposes, a *Mischlinge* was the same as a Jew. For example, a law had been passed expelling all Jewish professors from universities, but originally exempting all war veterans. A few months ago, both full Jews and half-Jews had lost the exemption, and all of them were now being expelled.

Odd as it might seem, even German Jews were not Germans anymore; only Aryans were Germans. Persons with two Jewish grandparents were *Mischlinge* of the first degree; those with only one Jewish grandparent were *Mischlinge* of the second degree. *Mischlinge* of the first degree were forbidden to marry Germans, yet *Mischlinge* of the second degree could marry Germans. Not only that, but if a *Mischlinge* of the second degree married a German, that *Mischlinge* became a German. The rationale for this remarkable metamorphosis was that their offspring would only be one-eighth Jews, and that in view of their very small numbers the Nazis had decided that this would not be enough to compromise the racial purity of Germany. It also had the advantage of bringing more certainty to the determination of who was a Jew and who was a German.

As Steeg ate his breakfast, and the full impact of how fortunate this all was hit him, he smiled. Since Lise was only one-quarter Jewish, she was not forbidden. Even if they found out about the adoption, it wouldn't matter.

When he thought about the fact that on top of that Mueller was a *Mischlinge* of the first degree, he could hardly contain his joy. The daughter was not forbidden, yet the father was available to be persecuted at Steeg's pleasure. Despite being a war hero, Mueller was subject to dismissal, and had probably already been dismissed from the University. Also, as a half-Jew, he was subject to further persecution. The way to the daughter was through the father. This was the best news.

But Steeg needed to have all this confirmed. He would assign that task to Stoeffler.

✝✝✝

Stoeffler had done a thorough job. The story was more complex than Steeg had thought, but Stoeffler had nevertheless found out all of it, and gave Steeg a full report.

The Nazis were in a conflicted position with respect to Professor Mueller. On the one hand, he was a Jew and a physicist who believed in Einstein and his Jewish physics, and hence a justified object of hatred and ridicule. At the same time, Mueller had become well-known and respected abroad, and the Party, as well as Hitler personally, did not want to be perceived as engaging in persecution, beyond such relatively mild measures as dismissing Jews from their university positions, even those, like Mueller, who were war veterans. And Professor Mueller—paradoxically, although the Nazis reviled him as a Jew, they still referred to him by that title—had in fact been expelled from the University.

This did not mean that Mueller was to be spared persecution, only that if he was to suffer anything more severe, it must be as the result of the "understandable," "spontaneous," and "uncontrollable" actions of "certain elements," and of course contrary to Party policy.

Professor Mueller had applied for permission to leave the country. Although the Nazis at this time were generally quite pleased to see Jewish scientists leave the country, in this case they considered it important to keep Professor Mueller from leaving, to prevent him from exploiting his dual position of decorated war hero and renowned scientist, portraying himself as a martyr, and becoming a world-wide witness and spokesman against Hitler's new order. Mueller's application for permission to leave the country had therefore been denied.

The Nazis were well aware that even then a tiny number of Germans, obviously at great personal risk, were giving aid to the "Jewish conspiracy" by keeping Jews in hiding, and in some cases helping them escape. The risk of escape was particularly high in the case of someone as famous as Professor Mueller; the Nazis were therefore determined to take every measure to prevent him from leaving the country, but without actually harming him or exposing themselves to blame for those measures.

All of Stoeffler's news confirmed to Steeg that this was an opportunity both to gratify his yearning for Lise and to achieve his ambitions of personal advancement. His work in connection with the Party's activities in Belgium had already received favorable notice, and he had continued his practice of keeping up his Party connections. Steeg now once more approached his superiors, this time with the request that he be given the assignment, in addition to his existing duties, of stopping Professor Mueller if he should attempt to leave the country.

Steeg's request was granted, but with several conditions. He would continue to appear to be a civilian, would have no official authority, and would receive no official help. When Steeg asked what was meant by official help, he was told that although the Party wanted Professor Mueller kept in Germany, it would take no blame for anything that was done to keep him there. Steeg might call on SS personnel or the police for some limited help, but his superiors would insist that he had done so entirely on his own. And Steeg alone would be held responsible if he failed. Finally, there was to be no violence or physical harm to Professor Mueller.

This arrangement pleased Steeg greatly. His plan was simple, yet beautiful. He would tell Lise all about the father she didn't know even existed; once her curiosity was sufficiently aroused, he would induce her to go to Munich to meet Mueller. He was sure that the gentle creature that Lise was would quickly form a bond with this new-found parent. Once she had, Steeg felt sure Lise would do anything to save her father from persecution by the Nazis.

Steeg knew this would work; he had done this sort of thing before.

CHAPTER 6

THE RESTAURANT was in the Hôtel Métropole, on the Place de Brouckère, right in the center of the city of Brussels and not far from where Lise was currently working. It was a magnificent hotel in the grand style of former days. For years it had been the place to stay in town, and it still was. The restaurant was lavishly decorated; the chairs and drapes had been done in shades of red plush, and the columns, in red and gold. Steeg had called Lise and said he had just thought they might have lunch together. She saw no reason why they should not and agreed.

He saw Lise as soon as she walked in, lovely in a pink dress. She had mentioned that her one o'clock work engagement had been canceled and that they would not have to rush through lunch. They ordered some appetizers, and the conversation began with small talk. Already knowing that Steeg was awkward at conversation, she compensated for it as she had when he had driven her back home after the reception.

Steeg knew that he would have to broach the whole subject of her father with caution, as casually as possible, to avoid raising suspicion. At some point Steeg said that since she was German, he assumed she had relatives in Germany.

"No," she said. "I don't think so. My parents... well, I never knew my father. He was killed in the war when I was only three."

All of this was of course already known to Steeg, but he did not let on.

"I'm sorry," he said.

"And my mother never mentioned any relatives, although of course I suppose… So if there are any, they are probably distant relatives."

This was the opening that Steeg had been prepared to exploit; he had planned to say—falsely—that the embassy had from time to time helped members of the German community get in touch with long lost relatives back home. Steeg thought that this line of approach might pique Lise's interest enough that she would eventually agree to his making such a search for her.

But at this very point he thought again.

Steeg knew more about himself than his unpolished ways suggested. He knew that his manner put many women off, especially women of the "nicer" or "gentler" kind. In his earlier years, this had not been a problem, in fact quite the contrary, as many of the most desirable women were attracted at that time to this very roughness. Evidently these women were drawn by its raw power, which seemed then to arouse passion in them, perhaps as some people are irresistibly aroused and attracted by danger. The response of those women had been magical, but he knew now that the magic no longer worked; Steeg had long since learned to confine his advances to women whose coarseness more closely matched his.

Steeg realized that he somehow lacked the "gentle side" that tempered other men's sexual impulse with the tenderness that was so appealing to women. Perhaps this had to do with his upbringing, but Steeg did not know how. He had often thought it was related to his relationship with his mother. However, in fact, he had only the haziest recollection of her. Steeg had not even a single image in his mind of himself as a small child being held in a mother's arms. He had been raised in an orphanage from a very early age on, and even his earliest memories of that were only of hard work, harsh punishment, and no love.

Steeg had thought of the problem of his rough manner many times before, and it flashed through his mind in the brief second or so between Lise's last comment and his next. But in that same instant, he looked into her eyes. Lise was looking straight at him, her eyes lingering on his for an instant just as they had in the restaurant when she and Steeg had first met. Now as then Steeg noticed how the pale blue of those eyes seemed to tint the black of her pupils, now as then how the so-slight myopia of her gaze mysteriously, miraculously, accentuated her perfection and made his heart stop. Now as then that look reminded Steeg of something he had long ago blotted out of his memory. But now it came back to him.

Her name was Maria. He had only been seventeen, Maria sixteen when he originally caught sight of her. He had never seen a creature as beautiful. The moment Steeg looked at her, he had for the first time in his life seen absolute perfection and fallen completely, insanely, and helplessly in love, as only the very young can. It was as if all the desperate, hopeless, unbearable longings of those interminable teenage years had in that one glimpse been requited.

Steeg was then already the raw bully that he would remain later. But that encounter with Maria changed all that, if only outwardly and only for a while. When he had first beheld her, some instinct brought forth by his desperate longing for the perfection that he saw in her made him realize that his usual uncouth, insolent manner was not the way to court her. What Maria needed was gentleness, kindness, and tenderness. So Steeg had put aside, or at least covered over, his bullying manner, and approached her with warmth and affection.

Almost to his surprise, Maria had responded in kind, returning his warm advances and caresses with her own. While this lasted, Steeg felt transformed, pure, free, and amazingly happy. However, like most such passions of the very young, this one did not last long. But unlike most such passions, its end was hastened by the return of his own usual coarseness and brutality, which resurfaced and swept away all the tenderness. At first he had blocked out of his memory the details of their breakup, except that he felt it had been his fault; racked with guilt, he had brooded over it for some time.

Then one day he had drunk himself into a stupor, had cursed her, vowed to forget her, and laid the first woman he was able to get his hands on, who happened to be a prostitute. Gradually the memory of Maria began to fade; by some strange inversion, he convinced himself after a while that the breakup had been her fault after all, not his. Not long after that, his hatred of Maria expanded into hostility towards all women, and it became the basis of his relationships with each and every one of them. After a few years he had forgotten her altogether. Until now.

Steeg determinedly redirected his thoughts to what he was going to say to Lise next. It was time to put his plan into action. It would lead right into his plan. He would emphasize that the embassy helped members of the German community find lost relatives only when asked to do it, and that it was done with great discretion, without alerting or contacting anybody, as that was strictly up to the parties. Steeg had gone over the exact words. He would not put any pressure on Lise; instead, he would wait to see if she showed any interest in this. When Lise did, he would "find out" about her father, and give her the information as one dangles bait before a fish. If she took the bait, as Steeg felt sure Lise would, the rest would be easy. In the end, Lise Hermann would be his.

However, before Steeg could speak, more memories of Maria came flooding back as he gazed at Lise. These were not the bitter, hateful memories Steeg had ended up with, but the tender memories of the first time he saw Maria's exquisite face and fell under her enchantment. It had been a moment he had never thought could exist; later, after their connection had been destroyed, he had been sure that such a moment could never exist again. But as he drank in Lise's loveliness, he thought of Maria. Then, smitten as he had thought he would never be again, Steeg felt that what had been true so many years ago could be true again. That Lise, like Maria, was the rare woman who could only be approached with tenderness, and that this would succeed better than the heavy-handed methods he had used on others. However, this time he would not repeat the blunder that had led to his breakup with Maria. Steeg was no longer an inexperienced teenager. He was a mature adult, and this time he would not let his thoughtless, even brutal, ways take over again. This time he would stay in control of himself. This time he would not lose her.

Steeg dropped the subject of Professor Mueller for now.

Lise was easy to talk with. Even though Steeg's conversation was always prolific, he knew how awkward it could be. Yet Lise made him feel that she was fascinated by it, and made their chat effortless for him. Steeg was surprised to find himself engaged in small talk, which was normally impossible. Lise mentioned that she loved the cinema, especially American pictures. She brought up a new one called *San Francisco*, with Clark Gable, Jeanette MacDonald, and Spencer Tracy. It was about the great earthquake of 1906.

Steeg had half-decided that before they parted he would ask to see her again. But after the waiter had brought the check he became so afraid of the possibility that she might turn him down that he lost his nerve. Steeg, whose impulses usually knew no restraint, was surprised to find such fear inside himself. At first he did not grasp the reason for it. Later he decided that it had to do with the memory of Maria that Lise had awakened. As Steeg thought about it some more, he also realized that it had to do with Behrndt. It was not just about Behrndt himself, but also about the clear reality of Lise's attachment to his young subordinate.

He would have to deal with that; it would take some time.

✝✝✝

Steeg had wanted to impress Behrndt with the importance of what he was going to tell him, so he had made Erich travel all the way to his regular office in Münster to hear it. Had this been before Hitler came to power, when Steeg's office had been a mere cubbyhole with walls of unpainted plaster, linoleum on the floor, and hard-backed wooden chairs for furniture, Steeg would not have done it this way. But now all that had changed. The room in which he now sat was much larger and more impressive; its walls were paneled, the floor was parquet, and the seats were leather armchairs.

When Behrndt walked in, Steeg did not invite Erich to sit down. Nor did Steeg waste any time.

"Behrndt, I will speak plainly."

There was a slight pause.

"I have been thinking about your mistress." Steeg placed the emphasis on that last word.

Erich was stunned. He knew how blunt Steeg could be, but he would have thought that he might continue to evince at least a modicum of grace in their social relations. Steeg had met Lise, but as far as Erich knew, that was all there was to it. What could Steeg possibly have to say about her? Behrndt braced himself for whatever it was.

"I like her," Steeg said. He paused. "And as it turns out, she likes me," he added.

Erich watched Steeg in disbelief. Disbelief at what he was saying, and disbelief that this could be why he had had him come all the way to Münster.

"I'm quite a bit older than Lise, of course, but I have found that many women find a more mature man much more attractive than a young one. Especially a man who radiates the kind of power that I do."

Erich could not conceive of what had led Steeg to think that anything could develop between Lise and himself. No doubt he might be correct in saying that she "liked" him, but if Steeg meant by this that she was romantically taken by him, the idea was ludicrous. True, Lise had mentioned that she found Steeg "powerful," and "harmless," but this was hardly the stuff that affairs are made of. Besides, the way Lise and Behrndt had kept each other busy every night ever since before Steeg had even met her could not possibly have left time for much contact between Steeg and her, let alone a love affair. Steeg was obviously engaging in fantasy. In any event, why was he telling Erich this stupid story?

"I would like you to break off your relationship with Miss Hermann."

"You are asking me..."

"Yes. I'm sure you won't mind."

"How soon do..."

"Immediately. I don't see any point in delay."

Erich was puzzled as to what had brought this on. Steeg was obviously confused. He was so much older than Lise and Erich that perhaps he had forgotten how hot the passions of the young can be. Perhaps Steeg thought the two young lovers were just friends. In any case, Steeg was completely out of line.

"My relationship with Miss Hermann is entirely private. It has nothing to do with my responsibilities in Brussels. I cannot accept..."

"You need to think about that."

"*Herr Hauptsturmführer*, may I speak to you as a friend? When you asked me to arrange for that evening at the restaurant, you yourself made it clear that it was a strictly social matter. I recall your saying that it would make for a pleasant evening for the four of us."

"Yes, and indeed it was. Of course, our conversation was also before I had met Miss Hermann. I must say I did not foresee how well she and I would—let me put it this way— hit it off."

It was amazing, Erich thought, how some people's perception of how they appear to others is so at odds with the reality.

"In my job, I am of course prepared to follow instructions from you as my superior," Erich replied, barely hiding his impatience. "But surely there is a line between my professional and my personal social life. Ultimately my allegiance is to..."

"...the Party."

"That's just what I was going to say. Also to our country, and..."

"...to Adolf Hitler. You took an oath."

"That's precisely my point. And I..."

"Behrndt, you seem to be forgetting that oath."

"But what has the oath got to do with this?"

"The oath has everything to do with it. As you just mentioned, you have sworn absolute loyalty to the person of Adolf Hitler. Surely you know what this means. You belong to Adolf Hitler, body and soul."

"I do understand that. But nothing I have done has... "

"Everything you do, everything you have ever done, must conform to that oath."

"I would never violate my oath."

"You apparently have also forgotten that you have already violated it."

A false accusation. This was going too far.

"But I have never violated my oath. I never would."

"No?"

Where was Steeg going with this? Something was wrong. Erich didn't answer.

"Does the name Christine mean anything to you?"

Christine. There had been so many. Christine. Obviously, someone named after Christ. Erich scoured his memory. Ah, she had been a nice young woman. But there was more. Something unusual. Yes. He had only found out later. Her mother. Christine had mentioned her mother, that her mother was Jewish, or had been before her marriage. But Steeg couldn't be thinking of that. It was so long ago. How would he know? How could he know?

"A Jew, Behrndt. A Jewess!" The words "Jew" and "Jewess" flew out like spit.

Erich stood silent.

"You defiled yourself with a Jewess!"

"But that was a long time ago. I only learned it after…"

"A long time ago, yes. Even later, nobody knew. Not even when you got this job."

Steeg stopped speaking. For what seemed to be a long time, he just looked at Erich, in whose mind it all now started to dawn.

"Look, Behrndt. I'm not proposing to make a big thing out of it; that's not my intention at all. You are a patriotic young man. You have a great future before you. But you need to think of your career."

That was it. This was not what Erich had joined the Party for, what he had sworn the oath for. When Behrndt had heard Hitler's call that day, he had been ready to follow him into the great battle against Germany's enemies and for Germany's glory. And that was still his dream. Yet…

Erich found anger flaring within him, but at the same time something in him restrained it. The thought of his father flashed through his mind. Steeg was his superior and for better or worse Erich respected his authority, as he respected his father's memory. Steeg could not be defied. Challenged perhaps, but not defied. He felt powerless.

Behrndt thought of Lise. Of course she would call him. What would he say to her?

It was as if Steeg read Erich's mind. "If she calls you, you can plead business. But I would appreciate your not making any reference, however indirect, to this conversation we're having. I'm sure you can understand that."

Erich did. "Yes, of course."

"That's all I have to say to you, Behrndt."

After Erich had turned around and was headed for the door, Steeg said one more thing.

"I knew you would understand."

✝✝✝

Steeg was certain that Behrndt was unaware of the facts of Lise's ancestry. In this he was correct. Furthermore, even if Behrndt had known about it, he was hardly in any position to use that information against Steeg. Nevertheless, Steeg had not mentioned it.

✝✝✝

Erich's loyalty to the Party and to Hitler himself was unquestionable and absolute; he would never betray it. As he had told Steeg, this business had not the slightest thing to do with that. Yet here Behrndt was, rendered powerless by this man who had just demonstrated that he would turn to blackmail without shame or hesitation. Yet, even after forcing Erich out of his way, how did Steeg think that he would then conquer Lise?

As Erich thought about this, he remembered his own conversation with Lise on the dance floor. He had taken it for granted that Steeg's obnoxious behavior, so embarrassing to him, would have been annoying, if not offensive, to Lise, yet she had seen nothing wrong with it; she had said it annoyed her "not at all." Could it be that, once he himself had stopped seeing Lise without any explanation, she might turn her affection to this man? Erich could not believe it. Lise was too fine a person, too intelligent and perceptive. Surely she would soon see what Steeg was really like.

Erich could not let Lise go. First, he knew her well enough by now that it was obvious that his dropping her suddenly, without any warning or plausible explanation, would hurt her deeply. Second, his fury at Steeg for forcing him not only to drop Lise, but also to deceive her by withholding the truth from her, made Erich's blood boil. Had Lise been any of the countless other women he had known, he might have given her up with hardly a thought. But Lise was somehow different, although he could not have articulated why. Perhaps a certain gentleness, an innocence, that none of the others had. All Erich knew was that he did not want to let her go.

Erich knew he could just plead pressing business, as Steeg had suggested. That would work for a few days, but what about after that? It would only be postponing the problem. What if he simply told Lise the truth, that he had been ordered not to see her? Of course that would only be part of the truth, not the whole truth, and without the rest of the truth, it would simply sound ridiculous and childish. Without knowing more, how could Lise possibly believe the idea that the "harmless" old man she saw in Steeg would give Erich such an order and the idea that Erich would obey it?

Revealing the rest of the truth as to why these restrictions were placed on him would mean disclosing the nature of his job and, inevitably, its *raisons d'être*. In Erich's eyes, this would be too close to treason; he would never do it.

There was no way out; Steeg had him completely trapped!

Erich stayed awake late into the night, thinking about this intractable problem. By the time he finally fell asleep, Behrndt still did not know what to do. When he awoke in the morning, he was no further ahead. There must be a way out of this dilemma, he told himself. He decided to do nothing for now except to go on with his daily work routine. Perhaps a solution would come to him soon.

†††

There was no call from Erich the following day, or the next. Maybe he had tried to reach her while she was out. The following morning Lise rang him. There was no answer. Perhaps he had already left the apartment. She wondered about this lack of contact. Aside from his many other good points, Erich had always been reliable.

Lise thought of not calling until Erich called her. But that was too much like a game, and she didn't want to play. The next day, she dialed his apartment. Erich answered.

"I've missed you," she said. Lise knew that she could have sounded less needy, but decided to opt for candor.

"Me too." This was the truth, but not the whole truth.

"How about tonight?"

"Lise, I know this sounds unusual, but it is. There is this… it's not a crisis, but it's urgent and it's taking all my time."

"Even at night?"

"Well, there are people here from Germany. They have to be entertained; there are functions to attend. It's hard to explain."

"There's no need to explain. I think I understand."

"I'll call you as soon as I can."

Erich's explanation only added to Lise's growing doubts.

†††

After Erich had hung up, he was overwhelmed by a jumble of conflicting emotions. He felt self-hatred at having put himself in this humiliating position, shame for the lies he had been forced to tell Lise, anguish at losing her, and just under the surface, a helpless, suppressed rage at Steeg himself. Behrndt had a sudden impulse to call Lise back, to say that he had misspoken, he had never meant to say that, it had been a mistake, that his business commitments could wait, he would put them aside because she meant too much to him. Perhaps he would come right out and tell Lise the truth, tell her how Steeg was treating her as if she were a mere object to be taken or given between one man and another like a farm animal.

But as soon as Erich had thought all of that he realized it was not possible; he could not do any of it. He would have to bear the pain of being an obvious liar without the release that only the truth could bring.

†††

More days passed. He never called. Lise was perplexed. If Erich had not just been making excuses, he would have called by now. And if it had been just excuses, she was not going to chase after him.

Suzanne had no explanation either. She said that sometimes people, especially men in important positions like him, did get tied up in their work; maybe Lise would hear from him before long. But as the days went by with no word, Suzanne became increasingly skeptical, although she didn't disclose this to Lise.

Lise was more than skeptical. She was becoming discouraged. She still was not sure whether what she felt for him could develop into love. A large part of her attraction to him was simply physical, but Lise had become used to her nights with him, and she missed them. When she came home from work, she spoke little and went to bed early. After a few days, Suzanne spoke to her about Erich again.

"Look, Lise, you can't let this man, any man, control your whole existence. So he has not called you. There might be a reason; I admit I don't know what. But in any case, why stay

home moping about it? Why not go on with your life? Let's—
you and me—go out and have a good time."

At first Lise was not interested. But after a few more days
of this, Suzanne again brought of up the idea of going out. This
time Lise agreed.

†††

When the phone rang, it was Steeg.

"I just wanted to say hello… I enjoyed our lunch."

"Yes, it was lovely," Lise said.

"I was wondering…I would like to see you again. I thought
maybe we could see that film, *San Francisco.*"

Steeg had seemed to her, and still did, in one sense a strange
sort of companion. However, she found him amusing, as she
had from the start. She also liked what she perceived to be his
forthright manner. Because of Steeg's advanced age, any
romantic notion of him was completely absent from her mind;
Lise figured that Steeg was just looking for some innocent com-
panionship.

Erich had never called. The complete silence both puzzled
and angered her. Lise had nothing to lose.

"Yes, I would like that."

"How about tomorrow? We could have dinner afterwards."

"That would be lovely."

"I'll pick you up."

†††

Lise liked the movie. She especially enjoyed Spencer Tracy,
who played a priest. His character made her think of the nuns
she had known, but Lise liked him better; he didn't follow doc-
trine blindly but adapted it to the real world. Lise was especially moved by the scene at the film's end, when San

Franciscans, seemingly by the thousands, marched forward to the crest of a hill, singing the "Battle-Hymn of the Republic," and beheld all of San Francisco lying in ruins below them, smoke still rising from the great fire that had followed the earthquake and consumed what remained. The scene climaxed in a fade-out of this desolation and a fade-in of the magnificent city that arose from its ashes, the San Francisco of 1936. As this reborn city filled the screen, the music swelled into a reprise of the movie's title song, "San Francisco." This was the sort of vision that made her heart glow. It also made Lise think of her own vision, which the nuns had shattered: the vision of a career in science, a field that others saw as mere disconnected facts and rules, but in which she saw nature itself, a nature filled with beauty.

They had dinner in a small restaurant. It was not as fancy as where Lise and Steeg had met, but it was cheerful and the fare excellent. Someone at the embassy had recommended it to Steeg; he would not have known where to find such a place. Steeg told Lise that he had traveled all over Germany, and that in his view it was the most beautiful country in the world. She did not think to ask him what other countries he had visited, and Steeg did not mention that most of his travels in Germany had taken place shortly after the war when he had joined the *Freikorps*. This was a collection of violent armed bands made up of men who had fought in the war, and later roamed all over Germany, spreading their violence and wearing the *Hakenkreuz* and the Death's Head, precursors of Nazi emblems, on their old Army uniforms.

He did tell Lise stories about Germany. Some of his stories amused her, but with others the point seemed entirely meaningless to Lise. Nevertheless they uniformly caused Steeg to burst into heavy laughter as he reached their punch lines.

Steeg continued on his good behavior. If he had wanted her less, he would have moved sooner. But with Lise, Steeg wanted to be sure of success, and he knew that the more restrained he was the better his chances would be in the long run.

✝✝✝

Steeg called again the next day.

"How would you like to take a short trip, just for the day, to the seaside? Ostend? Or I'm told Le Zoute is more in fashion now. By car, it would not take long. Tomorrow, if you like."

"It sounds interesting. But have you been to the seaside here?"

"No. That's actually one reason I thought of it."

"Well, the only thing is that the weather at the seaside is always touch-and-go, and in winter it is quite unpredictable. Rough seas and all that. The Channel, you know."

"Well then, perhaps somewhere else."

"Yes. Look, I have an idea. There's this charming town in the Ardennes that I love to visit. It's a lovely drive and there is an ancient castle that towers over the river. Also I found a little place there where you can have coffee and marvelous pastries, and it has a nice view of the river besides."

"Where is it?"

"It's called Dinant. Not far from here."

"Oh."

"You've been there?"

"Not recently." Steeg had not meant to say that; it had just slipped out.

"Oh, so you have been there."

Lying would only complicate things.

"Yes."

"Well then, what do you think?"

"It would be fine."

"All right then. What time?"

"How about ten?"

"See you then."

"All right."

✝✝✝

That night Steeg had a dream. In the dream, he was a young man, riding in the back seat of a car. Lise was seated next to him. She took his hand and placed it over one of her breasts, which he then realized was bare. He felt a rush of excitement. At that moment, the driver turned around and looked at them, and Steeg saw that it was an old man. He had never seen this man before, and could not tell who he might be.

All at once, in the way dreams change from one thing to another, Lise produced a baby from somewhere and began breast-feeding it. Steeg immediately withdrew his hand, and now looked at her. With a shock, Steeg saw that it was not Lise, but a plain woman, neither young nor old, dressed in simple clothes. She seemed to him to be a farmer's wife. As Steeg watched, the woman's expression turned to horror, as if she had glimpsed some frightful apparition, and she pulled the baby away from her breast and held the child out to him. Her face then became a silent plea to take the baby and save it. She thrust the baby forward, closer and closer to him. Steeg tried to back away, but couldn't. The baby now was practically touching his face. He felt on the verge of suffocating. He was sweating, and he did not know what to do. There was nothing he could do. Then Steeg awoke.

He was out of breath, and soaked in his own sweat. During the short interval between sleep and wakefulness, he had still been frightened. As Steeg became aware that he was now conscious, he became filled with relief that the ordeal was over; it was just a dream, he was safe. Then he began to think about it.

He had never had any dream of this sort. Steeg knew that he dreamed, like everyone else, and on some mornings, he had awakened with the slightest intimation of a dream just past. However there had never been any details, never any specifics, nothing that his conscious memory retained any awareness of. But this time he remembered the whole dream.

Steeg quickly saw that the dream was pure nonsense, nothing else. As he lay there, the absurdity of it overwhelmed him, and he began to laugh, first to himself, silently, then out loud, the way he so often laughed at the end of his own jokes.

By the time Steeg had climbed out of bed and was shaving, he had set the matter aside. "Just a bad dream," he told himself, resuming his laughter. But then he realized he would have to stop laughing or he would cut himself with the razor. It was the old-fashioned type of razor with a hinged naked blade that was longer than his hand was wide.

A small knot, not of breath-stealing, sweat-inducing fear, but of a subtler but still discomforting anxiety, began to form inside Steeg's chest. As he finished shaving and moved into the day, it did not go away. He did not ask himself why; he just tried to ignore it.

✝✝✝

He picked Lise up in a long, low, open, supercharged 5.4 liter 1936 Mercedes 540K. Its engine took up two-thirds of the car's length, and the front fender formed one long slow curve clear back to the rear wheels. Lise, though oblivious of these details, enjoyed its luxury.

Steeg tried to forget the dream and concentrate on enjoying the day, which had all the ingredients of the most marvelous kind of dream. There was the car, the beautiful countryside along the broad Meuse River, and of course Lise. He knew there was no rational reason why that other dream should continue to intrude instead. It was an absurd dream, in which the most corrupt elements of the wartime enemy, the civilians who had turned themselves into killers of unsuspecting soldiers, now turned on him. How salutary it was that he had in fact eliminated them; how many more atrocities would they have committed if he had not obeyed orders and done that! Steeg was proud of what he had done. Also, the courts had recognized the merit of it; he had been called a hero. Last night's dream was a vicious inversion of reality. Steeg decided that he would enjoy this day at all costs.

By the time they got to Dinant, Steeg and Lise were both hungry. They found that her little pastry shop served a light lunch, and they ate there. Lise had visited the town several times before. She asked Steeg if he would like her to show him around.

"I remember the town well enough from before," he said, "and I don't need to see it again. But I wouldn't mind a short walk. Perhaps along the waterfront."

Lise thought nothing of Steeg's response. She had no great interest in sightseeing as such. At one point along the way, they came to a small monument on a street corner, a sculpture on a pedestal. The sculpture was of a woman holding a tiny child, a girl. The work of art would not have been much different from many similar sculptures of mothers and infants, except for two significant features. In most such statues, the woman usually held her child to her bosom, but in this one, the woman was holding the child in her extended arms, in fact in her hands. It was as if she were offering the infant to the spectator. Also, here the mother's face was contorted into a grimace of horror, pain, and supplication all combined, as if she were begging the spectator to take the child from her grasp to save it from some horrible fate. The sculpted scene caught Lise's attention. She stopped.

"Oh, how terrible!" she said.

She noticed a plaque below the sculpture. It read "In memory of all the children who were among the men, women, and children shot to death—'*fusillés*'—by German soldiers in this town on August 23, 1914."

Like many young people her age in Belgium, Lise had heard that the Germans had killed civilians during the war, but she had never thought much about it or learned of any details. She had never heard of any specific massacre in Dinant or other places. As Lise read the inscription, she gasped and cried out, but Steeg did not hear her. A surge of sweat had begun to soak his body, while paradoxically his intestines were turning to ice. And the knot of anxiety in Steeg's chest was flaring up into a near-panic. He was overcome by an urgent need to defecate, and he started trembling. Lise turned to him.

"My God, what is happening to you?" she said. "You are so pale! You look terrible. Are you in pain?"

"No, I'm fine. Probably just the lunch." Steeg was afraid he would actually soil his pants. "Please excuse me." He rushed away.

Steeg was terrified by what was happening to him. He had of course been struck by the eerie resemblance between the sculpture and the dream, particularly the way the infants in both were thrust upwards towards him on the ends of their mothers' arms in that unusual yet identical way. But what made it so amazing was that he had never seen anything like that before. How could the author of last night's dream, who-ever that was, have foreseen what he, Steeg, would be seeing the next morning? And if it was not premonition, then what could have brought that coincidence about? Steeg knew that this sculpture referred to that August day when he had given the orders and fired the shots. However, on that subject not only was his conscience clear, but also his own country had not merely vindicated what he had done, but praised him for hav-ing done it. Search his mind as he would, Steeg simply could not come up with any rational explanation for his body's sud-den exudations.

"Are you all right?" Lise asked when Steeg got back to her.

"Yes. I'm fine."

Lise made no connection between his malaise and the monument. From his comment, she assumed that it was just one of those upsets that everyone gets at one time or another. But she was concerned about his discomfort.

"Maybe we should head back?"

"Yes. That might be best."

They got back to the car and left Dinant. At the touch of his foot on the accelerator, the Mercedes surged forward with a roar, pinning Steeg back in the seat. As the power of the engine flowed from the pedal into his foot and spread to every part of Steeg's body, the anxiety that had tormented him all day vanished, replaced by an exhilarating feeling of omnipotence, which stayed with him all the way back to Brussels.

When they had set out that morning, he had had in mind that today would offer him a suitable opportunity to make a small advance, just a kiss. But now, on the return trip, despite his exhilaration, he decided this was no longer a good idea.

✝✝✝

Steeg and Lise saw each other again a couple of days later. They went to another film, then to dinner. He drove the more conventional car that she had seen him use on previous occasions. The big Mercedes had evidently been borrowed just for the excursion to Dinant.

Steeg continued his pattern of telling stories about Germany. Some of them were in the nature of legends. Several involved Jews, who were invariably depicted as despicable creatures, and whose discomfiture or punishment he seemed to find amusing. Lise did not consider the idea of their being punished as amusing, but she had no problem with the view that Jews were somehow inferior; this was the way she had often heard them portrayed.

As usual Steeg drank a lot of wine. At dinner Lise had two glasses with the meal, and as he drove back to drop her off at the apartment, she felt pleasantly relaxed. They were both in a good mood.

He pulled up to the curb a short distance from her building. Before either of them said anything, Steeg put his arm around her. Almost instinctively, thinking to protest, Lise turned very slightly towards him. Seizing the instant, he started to lean over.

"Oh, no!" Lise said.

Steeg stopped. Even so, she could smell the alcohol on his breath. His actions had taken Lise by surprise, but had not offended her. She found the notion that at his age Steeg would have that sort of interest in her slightly amusing.

"I'm so sorry," he said. "I didn't mean to…"

He expected an answer from her, some more protest, but Lise made none. Her mouth was still close to him. Steeg kissed her.

The kiss evoked no emotion in Lise at all one way or the other. His mouth was just hard against hers; Steeg did not put any tenderness into it, and she felt none. She reacted very little, remaining passive, neither clamping her lips tightly shut nor opening them.

But the feel of her lips against his had excited Steeg, and he went to kiss her again. This time Lise brought her hands up against his chest and pushed, hard, and at the same time said, almost shouting, "No! You mustn't!"

Despite his excitement, Steeg remembered what was at stake, and he struggled to restrain himself. As soon as Lise had pushed him, he had pulled back. Now Steeg shifted his body away from her, and sat just looking straight ahead through the windshield. He was bewildered. Here he had been patiently biding his time, fighting every urge in his body, being almost unbearably patient with Lise, sensitive, he thought, to her every wish, holding back the overwhelming desire for her, the desire to grasp her, to have her immediately and completely. Holding all that back, for her sake, and waiting until Lise was ready, for her sake. Why had she let him put his arm around her? Why had she let him kiss her? Why was she now suddenly putting the barriers up, rejecting him? Lise was being unreasonable.

"I'm sorry," he said. "I thought..."

"No, Josef!"

"But I just thought..." He paused "...you liked me."

"Yes, I like you, Josef. Can you accept the idea of two people, you and me, just being friends, nothing more?"

"No, I can't. With some people, yes. But not between us. I have feelings. Feelings for you. I don't think of you as just a friend. When I think of you, I only think of love."

The idea of him as a lover appeared absurd. But as a friend, she could still feel comfortable with Steeg. If it could be just that.

"Josef, this is a real problem. I don't want to hurt you, but it looks as if I already have. You talk about love, but I have no such feelings for you..."

"All I ask is that you give me a chance. We've really known each other for only a few days. If you would just..."

"Josef, it's not going to work."

"Why not?"

"What you want is not possible."

"How do you know it is not possible if you won't even give me a chance?"

"Because I know myself, and... I'm sorry to put it this way, but I just don't have any of those kinds of feelings towards you."

"That can change. You'll see."

"No, Josef, it won't change."

"Lise, please give me a chance."

Despite her anger, Lise felt sorry for Steeg, sorry that she could not, could never, have any romantic feeling for him. Yet she knew only too well how it felt to lose someone you loved. She did not know what to say.

Steeg had not expected this stubbornness. He did not view Lise's rebuff as outright rejection, only the natural first response of a well-bred woman like her. He did not believe it meant "no," but more likely "yes," or if not "yes," at least "maybe." Steeg was familiar with idea that most women meant at least "maybe" when they said "no," and always "yes" when they said "maybe," and he actually believed this to be true. It was a little game they liked to play, a sort of tease, he had told himself. Steeg was sure that Lise would in fact be disappointed if he took her behavior as an outright "no" and abandoned his pursuit. But what Lise was saying aroused Steeg's anger, not because he thought she was just telling him the truth, but because he believed she was refusing to admit the truth.

"Lise, you're not being reasonable."

"All right, maybe you think I'm being unreasonable. Maybe so. But if so, it's because I can't help it. Because I do like you, and in a way I wish I felt more than just friendship for you, but I don't. I feel nothing, nothing that way, just the friendship. Now we have gone over this long enough. I'm sorry, but we have to end it here. I don't want to ruin our friendship."

The blood rushed to Steeg's head and he had the impulse to grab her. But he had vowed at all costs to stay in control. If he could just stay in control for these few more seconds. Even with all the strength he could muster, this effort was almost unbearable. But Steeg knew that if he didn't stop his frenzy then, he would do something terrible that would ruin everything.

"I understand," he said finally, almost managing to hide his disappointment.

Steeg got out of the car, walked around to Lise's side, and opened the door. He escorted her up to the front door. She unlocked it and opened it. By now, it was very dark outside and his face was in shadow despite the nearby lamppost, so Lise could not see that Steeg's expression was blank and frozen.

"I did enjoy the movie and the dinner," Lise said. "Good night."

"Good night," he answered quickly.

As he walked back to the car, his heart dropped. He had handled things very badly. But he still knew that underneath it all, she was playing that little game.

1917

*A*NDRÉ STAYED ON THE FARM owned by his father's cousin for three years. He had arrived there in 1914, at the age of fifteen. The war had been raging during this entire time. Except for a tiny corner in the west, the Germans had occupied all of Belgium since soon after the war had started. The area where the farm was located was a considerable distance from the front and was in German hands.

When it became apparent that the war was not about to end, the cousin's wife decided to enroll André in the local school. André opposed this vehemently, saying that school was a waste of time and that he wanted to join the Belgian army and fight. She told him he was too young, and that going to school would be much more important to him in the long run. André obeyed. When he was not in school, there was work to do on the farm. With time, André showed a facility for languages. Through daily contact with German soldiers, which was unavoidable, he soon learned to speak German. In school, in addition to Belgium's two languages, French and Flemish, which were mandatory for all Belgian schoolchildren, André also learned English.

For the most part, however, André had little interest in his studies. He tended to neglect his homework. As a result he was set back a year, but then still got poor grades. One subject, however, did interest him— history. André's classes covered European history right through the first years of the century.

One day, in an after-class conversation with the history teacher, he learned that the massacre he had witnessed at Dinant had been committed as a matter of national policy, which the Germans called *Schrecklichkeit*, and that the Germans had also carried out the same policy on previous occasions, notably in the war of 1870 against France. He spent a lot of time thinking about this, wondering how the senseless savagery that had killed his immediate family and his parents' own goodness could both exist in human beings at the same time. Hard as André tried, he could not think of an answer.

In the course of those three years, André's face had filled out and he had grown from a fifteen-year old boy into a tall man with a powerful build. He could lift fifty-kilogram—one-hundred-and-ten-pound—sacks with ease, and had become increasingly useful on the farm.

But André still wanted to join the Belgian army. Despite the fact that he had not finished school, the cousin's wife could no longer keep him back. An underground network guided him, as it had many other young men, to the Allied side. To join them he had to travel a perilous route, a portion of which involved a night trip at sea in a small boat. Within days, he arrived somewhere behind the Belgian line, where he was enlisted, given a uniform, and sent to the front.

The place where André was sent was known as the Ypres salient. The British, who also fought at Ypres, at first had pronounced it as "wipers," but had soon started to say it correctly as "ee-pruh."

✝✝✝

André had wanted to fight. Instead they made him a medical orderly. He had no qualifications for this. They gave him a few days' rudimentary training, and then he was assigned as a stretcher bearer, to recover the wounded.

At the first glimmer of dawn a few days after he had arrived at the front, as André was recovering some wounded from a trench, a German attack began. From this trench the ground rose gradually to the north, to a low ridge a few hundred meters away. The Germans came over the top of that ridge in successive rows, spread out over a wide distance on both sides.

Once they reached the top, they had to cross the long downward slope, straight into the withering fire of hundreds of machine-guns. From the moment each row began to appear at the top, the men in that row instantly began to fall in appalling numbers, those still standing then being further cut down as they advanced, with the process repeated with each successive row, the whole advancing force being rapidly and continuously reduced to a geometrically diminishing mass.

The continuing destruction of the entire attacking force did not slow in the slightest the flow of oncoming humanity behind it. It appeared that the Germans had an unending supply of young male bodies to feed into the Allied machine-guns.

But the attack ended as suddenly as it had begun. No more men appeared at the top of the ridge; no ground had been gained, or lost. All that was left were the dead and wounded.

André did not yet know this, but the process of evacuating the wounded often became disrupted in the enormous confusion that constantly reigned over the battlefields. This now happened, and André found himself marooned in this trench.

Three days later, the great British offensive at Passchendaele began.

✝✝✝

On the map, Belgium has the shape of the left hand held out flat, kept palm down, and rotated to the left as far as possible. The tips of the three left-most fingers are roughly the English Channel coastline. And the tiny corner of Belgium that became the focus of four years of the most massive assaults is the fingernail of the little finger.

Within that fingernail lay the small town of Ypres, a major objective of the German high command. Again and again from the war's start until its end, the German army hurled millions of its young men against that small fingernail, the Ypres salient. The battle of Ypres, actually four gigantic battles, went on for four full years. In all that time the town of Ypres, though leveled out of existence, never fell.

✝✝✝

The generals on both sides had completely disregarded recent developments that had tipped the balance between offense and defense conclusively in favor of the latter. The first was rifled artillery of vastly longer range, and much greater precision, than anything ever seen before. The second was the machine-gun, with which one man facing advancing infantry-men could kill or maim dozens of them, even hundreds, within seconds. The third was the fact that a combination of trenches, embankments, and barbed wire, supplemented by artillery and machine-guns concealed in underground concrete pillboxes, was simply impregnable to infantry charges.

Their minds unable or unwilling to grasp these facts, the generals of the First World War stuck to the infantry charge. When they were faced with the consequences, the generals decided that the only way to win was to keep pouring men into more such charges until the enemy had no more men left to feed into the slaughter.

As a result, casualties in the Ypres salient during the battle of 1914, known as First Ypres, alone, totaled more than two hundred thousand on both sides. Those in Second Ypres, in 1915, exceeded one hundred thousand.

In May of 1917, Field Marshall Douglas Haig, Commander in Chief of the British forces, obtained approval for a major new offensive to recapture the devastated village of Passchendaele. He said that this would bring about a decisive victory, but that if it did not, the offensive would still be worth it because of the number of German casualties it would cause. The casualties in the battle of Passchendaele, also known as Third Ypres, turned out to number over four hundred and forty thousand on the British side alone. The total for both sides numbered nearly seven hundred thousand dead and wounded, all within a period of three months and ten days, with almost no ground retaken.

In Fourth Ypres, in the last year of the war, there were nearly six hundred thousand casualties, within a period of six weeks.

This deadlock did not break until the end of the war in 1918.

✝✝✝

So many millions of giant shells had hurled their exploding steel onto the Flanders earth that the landscape in every direction consisted of nothing but thousands of craters of all sizes, which were now filled with the waters from the endless rains, from the sluice gates that had been opened and then flooded the region, and from the destruction by the unending bombardment itself of what was left of the drainage system in the area. The men in the trenches stood almost constantly in water at least half-way up to their knees.

Spread throughout this desolated earth lay all the crushed debris of war: demolished guns, cannons, gun carriages, shells, helmets, canteens, casings, picks, shovels, mess tins, boots, and clothing, and thousands of bodies, some still recognizable as bodies, but thousands more reduced to mere pieces, some still entwined with tatters of clothing, some naked, some on top of the mud, some wholly or partly buried in it. All these human fragments were what remained after previous recoveries had been completed; there simply was no way to recover more than a small portion of them.

✙✙✙

Most of the Ypres salient was nearly flat. However, the trench where André had become marooned was on a slight rise; the ground around it dropped away in every direction except north. As a result, there was a nearly unobstructed view for thousands of meters to the west, where the British forces were. It was now dawn, and as André looked in that direction, he saw British soldiers advancing to the north. They seemed to be moving in slow motion. This was only partly because they were so far away; the main reason was that the sixty-six pounds, or thirty kilograms, of gear that every British soldier was required to carry into battle slowed them considerably and caused many of them to slip down into the mud-and-water-filled craters of all depths, many deeper than a man's height, that were everywhere.

The advancing line, a long row which extended to the west directly away from André, consisted of many thousands of men. But coming up behind these was an unending series of further rows, each containing more thousands, the whole moving mass extending west and south for as far as he could see. Enemy shells exploded continuously throughout this entire mass in great numbers, raising clouds of earth and smoke, which when they receded revealed fresh craters filled and surrounded with more dead and wounded.

The first of the British troops in the distance were struggling with the barbed wire obstacles. Many, caught on their sharp edges, became captive targets for the German machine-guns. Those who managed to get through started to fall in the same horrendous numbers as their German counterparts had done. More British youth, coming up behind them in seemingly endless numbers, now marched into the same fire that mowed down those in front of them, only to be mangled in the same barbed wire obstacles and to be cut down in their turn.

Within a few hours, an immense cloud of dust and smoke began to drift over to the Belgian positions, reducing the entire battle to a faint glow. But the furious sounds of the battle did not abate until dusk.

✝✝✝

That night, André heard a voice coming from outside the trench. It was very close by, pleading for help, in English, with a British accent. Any of the other men would have ignored it; usually these things were traps, to be followed by a grenade lobbed into the trench. But André, totally inexperienced, climbed silently out of the trench, found the man, lifted him clear out of the hole he was in, and carried him back into the trench.

✝✝✝

His name was Trevor Exenby. Earlier that morning, he had been running forward in the British advance when he had been hit in the leg and fell. He had seen the others continue forward, but they were apparently headed straight into machine-guns, because they started falling in great numbers. More came in successive waves from the rear, going around him. Soon most of what had been a large group of his fighting mates had turned into a heap of dead and broken bodies. Those who died right away were the lucky ones; many of the others lay scream-ing or writhing in pain until morphine came or they died.

With so many injured, there was only a remote chance that Exenby would get any help soon. He had heard that if you could, your best chance was to try to get medical help, not to wait for it. He didn't think his injury was serious, but it hurt like hell. A sock he had tied around his leg seemed to have stopped the bleeding. After many tries, he had managed to stand up, and started walking, towards the rear.

Because of the fog and the smoke, Exenby soon was not able to see anything beyond a few yards. He went by the sound of the fighting, trying to keep it behind him. He fell many times, and needed to stop often to rest.

Night fell, and it became strangely quiet. For the first time, Exenby had the impression that he was all alone, although he knew that there were thousands of men all around him. He decided to keep going for a short while longer. Then he fell into a hole and called for help.

✠✠✠

The man in command in this part of the trench was Corporal Raoul Maartens. When Maartens awoke he immediately saw what André had done. This was the same man who had been a thorn in Maartens' side from the moment he had appeared, first because of his stupidity in getting stranded and second because it was obvious that he had no medical training or experience whatever and was therefore a fraud. Now, on top of all that, he had violated the rule of never leaving the trench except when ordered. Maartens screamed at André for his stupidity, his incompetence, and his insubordination. If Laroche wanted to get himself killed, that was all right with him, but he had no business endangering the lives of everyone else. At the first opportunity, he would report him and do what he could to have him court-martialed. In the meantime, Maartens forbade him to leave the trench, and said that if he attempted to, he would stop him by force and would add the charge of desertion to the other charges.

André did what he could for Exenby. He had given him morphine right away. It appeared that the bullet had gone clear through his leg, but by pure luck had not touched any artery or bone. André cleaned the wounds with what he had at hand, bandaged them, and gave Exenby more morphine. Within a couple of days, it became apparent that the wounds were healing, without any sign of infection.

The anger that Maartens had directed at André was far more than pique; he had some injured men in the trench, and the same battlefield confusion that had brought Laroche to this trench was evidently keeping other medical help away. Since there was no other help around, André had started to treat some of the wounded. Inexperienced as he was, Laroche was not able to do much. Nevertheless, what André did provided some relief, and in one case had actually meant the difference between life and death. Maartens noticed this, and was surprised that such an inexperienced idiot could be of any help at all.

By a happy coincidence, there was now a lull in the fighting. Such lulls were infrequent, and both their beginnings and their ends were completely unpredictable.

Exenby had been amazed to find out that he had wandered into the Belgian lines. Now, however, he was anxious to get back into the fighting. He did not want to be sent to a hospital. He said that he would rejoin the British forces by himself. André told him that this idea was insane. He added that with this injury Exenby would surely qualify for medical repatriation, and in any event would not be fit for combat. Exenby was more terrified than ever at the prospect of battle. However, for some reason that he himself did not stop to analyze, he also felt guilty for having survived while almost all the others in his unit were dead. He felt he ought to have died too, and now was willing, almost eager, to accept death.

✝✝✝

Trevor Exenby was twenty-five years old, married, and the father of a four-year-old boy. He told André that he had interrupted his graduate studies at Oxford to volunteer. He had only arrived in France a matter of days before. When they had sailed from England, he and the other young men in his unit had been almost to a man optimistic and full of patriotism and of the glory of the coming battle. Within days they had been thrown into this offensive. Within hours of that, thousands of his companions were already dead and more were wounded. Within a week virtually none of them were left.

Exenby told André that upon arriving in France he had learned that the casualties had become so enormous and so never-ending that the British Government was simply with-holding the worst of the news as much as it dared. But mean-while, each day thousands more mothers and new widows received the terrible news. At the same time Exenby had also heard of the endless streams of railroad cars unloading their mangled human cargoes, now almost always in the middle of the night to spare the population excessive alarm.

✝✝✝

André was impressed by the fact that Exenby had gone to Ox-ford. The young Belgian had never known anyone who had not only completed a university education, but also gone on to post-graduate studies. At first this, and the fact that Exenby spoke with the distinctive accents of the well-educated British, intimidated André. However, he soon found that underneath all that, Exenby was a real, down-to-earth fellow who was saying things that André had often thought. Like André, Exenby was interested in the causes of things. The two quickly became friends.

He was also the first man who had really talked with André. Laroche realized that this was because Exenby had been in combat long enough to have seen some of the worst of it, but not long enough to have developed the cynicism of the others. The little conversation these men conducted was mostly among themselves. But they did not seem to mind André's being there as long as he kept quiet; as a result, André had begun to find out what some of them were like, and to learn a bit of trench humor as well. He had discovered, for example, that underneath Corporal Maartens' curt manner lay a man who deeply loved the small village in Flanders where he had been born and where for centuries his ancestors had been born and died and been buried. When Maartens said that he wanted to be buried there, one of the others had answered that this should be no problem if they could just find the pieces.

André was certain that after this war, there would be another.

Exenby disagreed.

"The whole world will have learned that this kind of war has no winner," Trevor said. "They will never start one again."

"There's too much barbarity in mankind."

"Barbarity? Look at all these poor bastards, mowed down here. Nine hundred and ninety-nine out of a thousand were just plain blokes. Good chaps. On both sides. Except for the bad luck of having been born at the wrong time and in the wrong place, they would be home now, making love to their wives, raising families, working, living peacefully." Exenby looked down and grimaced. "They never asked for this."

"There is savagery in human beings," André said.

"But there is so much good!"

"There is! There *is* so much good! But there is also that savagery. I have seen both. And the tragedy is that the savagery of one man sometimes outweighs the goodness of a thousand. A hundred thousand!"

For some seconds neither spoke.

"I think savagery has the advantage," André continued, "for the very reason that it is savagery. I'm not saying that savagery always wins, just that it has the advantage. And violence breeds violence. Ancient hatreds, revived and perpetuated generation after generation and century after century. When this is over, there will be millions of widows, a generation of orphans, this beautiful, rich earth turned into desolation. The loser will sink into misery and hopelessness. Don't you see that all of that is just the seed of more war?"

"The people will know better."

"The good, common people, even when desperate, might. But when the people are desperate, brutal men, human monsters, always arise and play on that desperation. That's where the savagery comes in. These men pretend to care for the people, but they don't give a damn about them; all they are concerned with is their own power over others. And if the others, the good, stand by and let these men gain power, they will once again plunge all of Europe—perhaps the whole world—into war and more desolation. If we win this war, we had better make sure it doesn't happen again."

"I think we will make sure." Exenby paused, deep in thought .

"But just in case I turn out to be wrong," he finally said, "I have a proposal." He continued looking over at André.

"What?"

"We can agree that it is unlikely that either of us will survive this war."

"Yes, that's one thing we can agree on."

"Here's my proposal. If either of us does come out of it, he will do everything in his power to prevent another."

"I accept your proposal."

"Done."

The two men shook hands on it.

✝✝✝

Exenby left, on his feet, a few days later, to rejoin what was left of his unit. He would start by making his way towards the rear, in part through a system of connecting trenches as far as it took him. As André watched him go, he felt some small joy in the belief that, if he himself died, there was at least one man who might devote himself to making sure that nothing like this would ever happen again.

✝✝✝

Shortly after Exenby had left, the word spread that there would be an attack on this part of the front the next day. As soon as he heard that, André asked for a rifle. He told Corporal Maartens that he realized medical personnel were not allowed to fight, but that he thought it would be appropriate in this case since it was impossible for him to resume his regular duties. Maartens told him this was another example of how stupid he was, that as an untrained greenhorn he wouldn't last two minutes, and that it would not be allowed.

André then disclosed that his parents and sister had been among those massacred at Dinant. He said that all he wanted was one chance out there; he didn't care if he got killed; Maartens said nothing, but André saw that he was staring at him as if he had not noticed his presence before. Later that evening, Maartens approached André.

"About what you asked for earlier... this makes me as much of an imbecile as you are, but all right." André would be given a rifle and would go over the top with the rest of them the next day.

✝✝✝

Maartens had been at least partially right. The attack did not get far, and all those who were able to do so retreated back into the trench. When André got back to within about thirty meters of the trench, he was hit and fell. There was no question of rescuing him; anyone who tried would have been an easy target.

André's pleas for help could still be heard after nightfall, but gradually had become much weaker. Maartens knew from experience that the young orderly would not last long. Meanwhile, in the trench, life continued; everyone who could sleep was soon slumbering.

Later that night, when André's voice had grown still fainter, Corporal Maartens climbed out of the trench, found him, and half-carried, half-dragged him back into the trench. André's pain was such that he had not been able to stand or crawl. To the men in the trench in the morning, André's injuries looked survivable, but he had lost a lot of blood. Clearly he would not have lasted the night if Maartens had not brought him in.

In the morning litter carriers appeared, whether by plan this time or by another coincidence no one knew, and André was evacuated to a casualty center. Before he left, Maartens came over briefly and looked down at him.

"I want to thank you…" André began.

Maartens wished he had not yielded to the impulse to violate all rules and rescue Laroche. Maartens was not sure why he had done it; probably it was that he felt sorry for André because of what had happened to his parents and sister and because he was so obviously still green. But what nearly drove Maartens insane was that this boy—that was how the corporal thought of André even though he was only a few years younger than Maartens himself—was now about to blab the story of the rescue to the whole trench.

"I'm not interested in hearing about your gratitude."

"I just wanted to tell you…"

"Don't you understand anything? I said I'm not interested in what you want to say to me. And I have nothing to say to you."

"But you were right," André said. "It was stupid of me to leave the trench that time."

Maartens wanted to tell Laroche that he wished he'd left him out there. But the corporal realized with relief that it was really not that important; he was about to be rid of him once and for all. In the meantime, the best approach was to say nothing. Maartens kept his eye on Laroche, but kept his mouth shut.

"Especially at night," André said.

Nothing.

"At least now you won't have me to contend with anymore."

The corporal turned purple.

"It's good riddance," Maartens said, disgust on his face. "You are the biggest pain in the ass I have ever known. You are insubordinate. You are stupid and incompetent. You have all the judgment of a two-year- old. You are a menace to yourself, which wouldn't bother me at all, but you are a menace to everyone in this trench. You are the Boches' dream come true. You are the most useless man I have ever seen."

"I never expected..." André started saying.

Maartens interrupted. "Don't you have any brain at all?"

"But Corporal..."

"Shut up! One more word and I guarantee you will be court-martialed."

Neither of them spoke another word.

✝✝✝

One day, many years after the war, André was walking along the Boulevard Adolphe Max in downtown Brussels and he almost bumped into Raoul Maartens head-on. Maartens did not recognize him at first, as André was no longer the immature eighteen-year-old he had known. As these men exchanged the usual questions and answers, they each became curious about what had happened to the other since those long-ago days. There were two cafés next to where they were standing. They went in the nearest one, sat down, and ordered beer. The former antagonists quickly discovered that they shared the same views on many subjects, including the threat posed by the new Nazi movement in Germany; they talked for almost an hour. From that moment on the two were lifelong friends.

✝✝✝

André's injuries healed well; within two months he was nearly as fit as before. He asked to be returned to the front. Earlier in the war the request might have been denied, but now no one could be spared. A month later, he was back at the Ypres salient. There he stayed until the end of the war.

When the war finally did end the following year, André had a lot of difficulty finding a job that met his aspirations. He could have found employment as a laborer or factory worker, but such jobs paid poorly. Laroche found that better jobs required either experience or more education than he had. He thought of going on to higher studies in one field or another, but quickly learned that his poor school record foreclosed that. Now he wished he'd applied himself to his studies.

Almost desperate, André took a job in sales. He was given no customer leads; he would have to find customers and do everything else on his own. His only compensation would be a small percentage, and out of that he would have to pay all his expenses.

It soon became apparent that André had considerable talent in sales, and he began making money. A few years later, he opened his own business, which became successful. By the time was in his thirties, André was comfortable. Besides his house in the city, he had a small place in the country, an ancient farmhouse which he had equipped with modern comforts and conveniences. But he always regretted not having been more diligent in school, so that more doors would have been open to him.

André had liaisons with of a number of women; these partners invariably found him attractive enough that they were willing to accept the fact, which he always made clear at the outset, that he was not the "family type."

✝✝✝

Despite the passage of years since the war, André had frequent nightmares. The most common one combined the terror of having to plunge headlong into a fire or other holocaust with an overwhelming sense of guilt for some unforgivable failure, the nature of which was always concealed from him. He would wake up soaked in sweat. The terror vanished almost immediately, but the guilt stayed with him.

Meanwhile André had kept in touch with Maartens ever since they'd encountered each other on the Boulevard Adolphe Max. Raoul told André that among his German contacts, Raoul had found a man who was appalled by the resurgence of German militant nationalism, and who was anxious to work to prevent Germany from plunging the world into another war. Through this contact, Maartens had met another man who shared these views. From there, Raoul had gradually developed a group of Germans who shared his perspectives and who, in addition, had proved themselves completely trustworthy and reliable. They were keeping Raoul informed in considerable detail about Germany's rearmament, and Maartens passed this knowledge on to André.

It had started shortly after the end of the war. First there was the design of advanced weapons, in secret, inside offices with innocuous-looking names on their doors. Later, still in secret, Germany began construction and testing of tanks, giant guns, and other weapons, and eventually, under Hitler, the actual production of these weapons, all in violation of Versailles.

As André saw the rise of the Nazis and the rearmament of Germany, he often thought back to his conversation with Exenby, and the promise they had made to each other. That, and the nightmares, never stopped gnawing at him.

1936

$\mathcal{T}$HE DAY AFTER THE INCIDENT in the car, Steeg spent a long time thinking about where things stood with Lise. These thoughts were strongly colored by his attitude towards all women.

The only feeling Steeg had towards the opposite sex that was stronger than his desire for them was a deep-seated hatred. He didn't fully know why the hate was there, but he sensed it had started after the disastrous end of his relationship with Maria so many years ago. If he had been asked, Steeg would probably have said that it was because women were basically dishonest, hated men, and took pleasure in hurting them. He believed that women withheld their "favors" while desiring men on a deep level and wanting to have sex forced on them. He felt that the only women who truly liked him were prostitutes, and that these were the only honest women. Actually, the truth was that since the transactions with prostitutes were commercial in nature, the issue of whether or not they liked him never arose, nor did any other emotional issue; Steeg might as well have been purchasing a loaf of bread from a baker.

With Lise, Steeg had thought that, for the first time since Maria, he had found a woman who would love him, and a woman whom he could love. But after what had happened the previous night, he saw that Lise was like all the others. Like the others, she only knew how to tease, concealing her real desires.

Like the others, she was dishonest, and not even kind enough to give him the chance he had asked for, even begged for. Lise had said she liked him; however if that had been true she would not have rejected him so abjectly. She would not have humiliated him. Now there was no feeling for Lise left in Steeg's heart, only the desire to master her and release his pent-up lust on her. In so doing, Steeg could also take his revenge on Behrndt and quench the dual fires of his hatred and of his bitter jealousy.

Yet Steeg was glad that he had respected Lise's wishes the night before, and that in the heat of the moment, he had still maintained the needed perspective. He had fortunately realized that if he forced himself upon her then, it would not merely have ended the courtship, which was over anyway, but more importantly would also have made it impossible for him to carry out his plan. He would simply have lost Lise's trust.

Steeg dismissed almost instantly the idea of trying the gentle approach once more. It would just be a waste of time, and he had no desire to be humiliated again.

Steeg would proceed with the plan he had intended to carry out in the first place. He would wait a few days and then call Lise. As he decided that, he had another thought; before calling her, he would call Conrad Leist.

✝✝✝

It was three in the morning when Leist's phone rang. He knew it would be Steeg. Leist never had any business that actually required a phone call at that hour, nor did Steeg, but Steeg was the only one who called him at such a time. Furthermore, it was usually about personal business. Probably about Behrndt's girlfriend again.

"Leist, *Hauptsturmführer* Steeg."

Of course he would never think of apologizing for the early hour.

"Yes, *Herr Hauptsturmführer.*"

"Does your man still live on the ground floor in Hauser's place?"

"Yes."

"Anything new?"

"No, *Herr Hauptsturmführer.* As a matter of fact I spoke to him yesterday. There has been no change since my last report."

"So that visitor has not returned there?"

"No, *Herr Hauptsturmführer.*"

"Good. Let me know the minute that changes."

Of course "thank you" was not in Steeg's vocabulary.

✝✝✝

Later that morning, Steeg called Lise. He had to do this with as much delicacy as he could muster. She would naturally think he had not given up; she would be on her guard.

"I just wanted to see if you were all right."

"I'm fine." Her tone was guarded indeed.

"I wanted to apologize. About the other night. I behaved badly. I hope you're not angry with me."

"I'm not angry."

Of course. Steeg realized then that Lise had no way to know all of what he had been restraining himself from doing; she also undoubtedly had no idea of his outright hatred for her. From Lise's point of view, what had happened was simply that he had kissed her, and then backed off when she protested. Yes, then he had gone on to "argue his case." Still there was little reason even to expect that she would be angry.

"I promise you that it won't happen again."

She did not answer.

"Don't misunderstand me. I know you probably would rather not see me again, and I will respect that."

Again she said nothing.

"There is one thing though. That you still might just possibly be interested in." Steeg paused for a second, but she made no response. "Do your remember? You said you didn't know of any relatives you might have in Germany?"

"Yes."

"That's not unusual. I can remember a few times when we—I mean the embassy—have helped members of the German community get in touch with lost relatives back home."

Steeg paused; Lise had no reaction to that.

"Of course only if they asked us to. And very discreetly, without intruding into anyone's life."

Again he paused just briefly; again she remained silent.

"Of course, you may have no wish for that."

"No. Not right now."

"I fully understand. But if you ever change your mind, you know where to reach me."

"Yes. Thank you."

"Goodbye."

"Goodbye."

✝✝✝

During the conversation Lise had felt no interest in Steeg's offer to help locate relatives. But later that night she found herself thinking about it. It might mean unlocking the door to an unknown world, a world perhaps waiting for her but more likely unaware even of her existence. Perhaps this world would contain promise, perhaps not; there was no way to tell now. On the one hand Lise was curious; her school friends all had cousins or grandparents or aunts and uncles, yet her mother had never mentioned any relatives. Now Lise wondered whether she had any, where they lived, what they might be like, and why she had never heard of them. It might be nice to find them. At the same time, the thought of someone out there, totally unknown yet tied to her by blood, was somehow a little frightening; she could not have said why. As Lise lay in bed in the twilight before sleep, she tried to conjure these relatives into existence, to evoke images of them out of the void. However, no picture, no clue, appeared to her.

In the morning, Lise was still thinking about it. She knew that what was bothering her was simply the tension between curiosity and fear, not terror but only the slight uneasiness that always comes from the unknown. By the time she was up and dressed, she had made up her mind. She called Steeg.

"I didn't expect to hear from you this soon," he said.

"Well, I've been thinking about what you said. About relatives in Germany…"

"Yes."

"I might be interested."

His heart leapt.

"Just to find out about them," she added. "Nothing more, no contacts."

"Naturally. We are very careful. No one would be contacted. I could just make some inquiries."

"Yes, if you could."

"I will see what I can find out. I'll let you know."

"That's very kind of you."

He held off for several days before calling Lise.

"I have some information. About what we talked about."

"So did you find something?"

"Yes."

"Relatives?"

"Yes. I think it would be best if we could meet again; I'd like to tell you about this in person. To meet just for this, of course. Briefly."

They agreed to meet at a café downtown. It would be after work this time.

✝✝✝

It was one of the hundreds of cafés with outside terraces along Brussels' wide boulevards. Since it was raining, Steeg and Lise sat inside. After they had ordered their coffee drinks, Steeg got right down to the point.

"Here is what I have found out. Your parents, Viktor and Margot Hermann, are not your real parents."

"Would you repeat that? I'm not sure I heard right."

"Lise, Viktor and Margot are not your real parents."

"That's not possible. What are you talking about?"

"They adopted you."

"You are misinformed. You obviously have made a mistake."

"I'm telling you what we found. We made no mistake."

"You say 'we.' Someone gave you wrong information. I think you had better go back and check your information again."

"It has been checked. It's accurate. You were adopted."

"That's ridiculous. They obviously have the wrong person. Someone made a mistake, either you or someone else."

"I realize this information may come as a shock, but we have checked the records."

One part of Lise was angry at this obvious nonsense, but another part of her was angry at Steeg simply for throwing this at her just like that, without any warning or preparation. That was just like him.

"What records? Who checked the records? Did you do it yourself? If so, I think you should go back and see where you made the mistake. If it was someone else, I think you need to go back and talk to them. You might have thought of looking for my birth certificate. I have one, you know. If you had looked at it, you would have seen that your information is wrong. It says right on it who my parents are."

"I did see your birth certificate. But it does not tell the whole story."

"Josef, don't you see, this is not what I wanted. You said you would see if I had any relatives, not dig into my personal history." Lise broke into tears.

As always, Steeg had thought only of himself, of how he could use this information for his own ends. He saw Lise only as a vehicle for his own pleasure, not as the sensitive and compassionate person that she was. As he watched her cry, he was at a loss as to what to do. He could only wait until it subsided.

"I'm so sorry," he said then. "I did not mean to offend you. I know I am sometimes too blunt. I should have done this with more delicacy, more thought for your feelings. Please accept my apology."

She remained quiet.

"But in the process we did find out who your natural father was. It might interest you to know."

Up until this point, Lise had only thought about her own father, her own mother, the ones she knew. Certain as she was that Steeg was wrong, she had not even glimpsed at the possibility that if he was right it would mean there could be two other persons out there, another father and another mother. Now, his speaking to her of a "natural father" turned things around. Where Lise had not even wanted to hear what he had been saying, now she was at the same time curious to find out more and afraid of what there was to find out. She could not help asking the question.

"Who is he?"

"His name is Mueller, Stefan Mueller."

Hearing an actual name seemed to calm her. Besides, that name sounded vaguely familiar. Lise had seen it somewhere.

"Is he still alive?"

"Yes, but he's in danger."

"You expect me to believe all this?"

"You don't have to believe anything. Tell me you don't want to know any more, and I'll stop."

Lise thought for a moment. "No," she said. "Tell me what you know about him."

"He is German. Was in the German Army during the war. In 1915 he was seriously wounded. You were born that same year."

Lise nodded.

"What about my mother?"

"Your mother died when you were born."

Lise felt as if Steeg had slapped her. Why couldn't he have broken it to her more gently, at least first prepared her a little for the hard truth? This time the tears came out in a flood.

"Oh, that poor woman! That poor man!" Lise was not even thinking of herself, only of those two people who only a minute ago she did not even know existed.

"I'm sorry." Steeg couldn't think of anything else to say. He waited until Lise had regained at least a part of her composure.

"We think your mother's death is probably why you were adopted," he said. "After the war, your father returned to Ludwig-Maximilian University in Munich, where he had obtained a doctorate before the war."

"In what field?"

"Physics. He became a Professor at the University."

Now Lise remembered. From books about science that she had read. A famous scientist.

"And that is where he is now?"

"No. He has been expelled from his professorship."

"For what reason?"

"All Jewish professors have been."

"But he is not Jewish."

"His mother was Jewish."

"That's impossible. I told you this is the wrong information. It's about someone else. My family are good Christians, Catholic."

"We don't have the wrong information."

"How can you sound so sure? It's obvious that it's wrong. No Christian family would adopt a Jewish child."

"Maybe they were not told."

Lise hadn't thought of that. But Steeg was just compounding error with speculation; she didn't believe it.

"Do I look Jewish to you?"

"No."

"Isn't it more likely that you have made a mistake than that my parents were lied to? I never asked for this. Why did you bother me with it?"

He didn't answer.

"Why would my natural parents have lied?"

"Your father was Jewish."

"I don't believe any of this. Was his father Jewish too?"

"No. But half-Jewish is Jewish enough."

"What about me? Does that mean I am Jewish?"

"No. They draw a line between half-Jews and one quarter-Jews."

"Thank God!"

As soon as the words were out, Lise was mortified at what she had said. She paused and put a hand to her lips.

"But what do you expect me to do about all this?" Lise then said quickly.

"I expect nothing." Outwardly Steeg remained serious and calm, but inside he was excited with how well it was going.

"Where is he now?" she asked.

"He's still in Munich."

"Was that the danger you meant, being expelled from his position?"

"Not just that. Jews are simply being removed from their positions of excessive power all over the country. This is not being done to harm the Jews, only to protect them against the understandable hostility of the many who have been unable to find positions or have otherwise suffered at their hands. The government is even starting to separate them from the rest of the population. For their own protection."

"So then, what is…"

"The problem is that there are rogue elements in Germany who are openly aggressive. This includes the Munich area, of course, where your father is. Jews are being dragged out of their homes, beaten, and more, all directly against Adolf Hitler's orders, and despite the Party's disapproval."

Steeg paused for effect, inwardly looking forward to his next remark.

"My information is that your father is a very likely target of these elements because he is well-known."

Lise's eyes welled up again.

"But can't the authorities, the police, do anything about it?"

"They are doing everything they can. But the Jewish poison is so widespread that it's difficult. There are Jews everywhere, and these gangs roam about. They strike randomly. In some areas they are out of control, and the legitimate Party members have their hands too full to deal with all of them."

Steeg could see that Lise was disturbed by his latest bit of news. Tears were trickling down her face. It was time to ease up.

"I realize I have upset you," he said. "I didn't mean to make you cry."

Lise was at her wits' end. "This is too much for me. I need to go home. I can't handle it right now. Let me think about it."

+++

When she got home, Lise related to Suzanne everything Steeg had told her. They were in the living room having a before-dinner drink.

The subjects of politics and world affairs had rarely come up in Lise's previous conversations with Suzanne. Once, when Lise had told her that Erich had said that Jews were to blame for Germany's defeat in the war and for all the miseries Germany had suffered since, Suzanne had spoken out.

"I realize you were born in Germany," she had said, "and that you still think of it as your country. And I know that the people there have suffered a lot. But the people in this country have suffered just as much, maybe more. And as for the Jews, what he is telling you is wrong. I have known some Jews. Basically they are like most of the rest of us, no better, no worse. The idea that this tiny percentage of people is responsible for Germany's losing the war and all the calamities since is absurd. It is an old lie that people like Hitler repeat for their own purposes, to justify sending ruffians out to vent their hatred."

"This is the first time I have ever heard anything like what you are saying about the Jews," Lise had said. "My mother never said anything but good about Germany. She did not care for Jews. She never said much more than that about them, and I never gave it much thought."

Now when Lise had finished telling Suzanne about Steeg's news and comments, Suzanne spoke up again.

"The Nazis are just using Jews as scapegoats. 'Separating them out for their own protection?' What nonsense! It's persecution, like the Romans persecuting Christians. And 'rogue elements' beating Jews 'against Hitler's orders'? Let me tell you, no one disobeys Hitler's orders. I would be careful about believing everything that Steeg tells you."

"Maybe you're right. Besides, I still find the part about my being adopted and all that hard to believe. At the same time, if this man really is my father and he is in peril as Steeg says, then I want to help him."

"I know, Lise, you are Miss Compassion."

"But if Steeg turns out to be mistaken, I would feel like such a dunce!"

For a few moments neither of them spoke.

"Why not tell him you're still not sure," Suzanne said, "and ask for more proof."

"Oh Suzanne, I'm scared."

"Of what?"

"I don't know. The whole thing. Here I thought my life was, maybe not perfect, but simple. Now this man calls me, and suddenly everything is so complicated. This talk of Jews, of beatings, people being dragged out of their houses, of a father I never knew about."

"Lise, if he is your father that would be exciting news."

"Suzanne, I don't want anything exciting. And I certainly don't want anything as frightening as what Steeg is telling me about. If it's not true, what's the point, and why is he telling me these things? And if it's true…"

Still stunned, Lise looked blankly into the living room, as she searched her mind for answers. "Oh God, Suzanne, I'm so sick of this!" she continued. "You are sweet to me, Suzanne, you are my best friend, but you have no more experience than I do with these things."

"You're right about that."

Lise broke into loud sobs. "I wish there were someone that I could turn to right now."

✝✝✝

André had never stopped thinking about Steeg. Since he had found out that Steeg knew Lise, Laroche had thought about the two of them together, and the thought worried him. He had felt sure from the beginning that Lise could not have known what Steeg was like, and when she had referred to him on the phone as "that nice Mr. Steeg," he knew she did not.

André still felt he had been justified in saying that he had never met Steeg before; however at the same time he had begun to feel guilty about it, and had become increasingly concerned for Lise ever since.

André decided to call her again. He thought about what to give as an excuse. He could say that since Lise had asked he wanted to tell her that he did remember after all that someone had told him Steeg worked at the embassy. That shouldn't ring any unnecessary alarms. Or maybe it would be better to say that he had dialed her number by mistake. From there, André knew he could start some sort of a conversation. As it turned out, none of this was necessary.

"This is André Laroche."

"Yes. You called me before."

"I did. But…"

"How funny that you called. I was just thinking about you."

"You were? But we only spoke once, and so briefly."

"That's true. But something has come up, and you came to my mind."

André could not have guessed what, and certainly not that it would turn out to be the very thing that he had been concerned about.

"Yes?"

"Please don't think me forward."

"I would not have thought of accusing you of that."

"Well, this is a little unusual. But since you have called me, I would like to talk to you about something."

"Go ahead."

"It's a little too complicated to explain over the telephone. If I'm not imposing on you, perhaps we could meet briefly? When I explain it to you, I think you will understand."

"Gladly. If you work downtown, why don't we meet for lunch? That way you would be safe."

She couldn't help smiling; those had been Erich's precise words.

Lise told André this would be fine. He mentioned a small restaurant where the specialty was steamed mussels, potato *frites*, and beer. Lise said that she knew the restaurant and that it was one of her favorites.

✝✝✝

The restaurant was on a narrow, twisting street, a remnant of Brussels' medieval past. The street was barely wide enough for one car, although nowadays it was limited to pedestrian use.

They both ordered mussels, which were served in huge bowls in hot broth and butter.

"I really am embarrassed," Lise said. "Normally I would not discuss this with someone I have known so briefly. But I just had a feeling that you might be able to give me some advice on this one. I couldn't tell you why, except that it has to do with Mr. Steeg."

"Probably it's my honest face. Plus my age."

"Plus you have met Mr. Steeg. And this is not really about him, anyway. It's only about something he told me. I don't see what harm there is in my telling you about it."

André was amazed at her naiveté. Lise did not know who he himself was, or what he might or might not know about Steeg, yet here she was about to reveal what he assumed were some sorts of confidences.

"Since you mention being older," Lise continued, "I'll admit that most of my friends are about my own age, which is twenty right now. However I do think that you may have some wisdom that would be helpful to me, and I don't know why, but I feel I can trust your judgment. Besides, I don't consider you old at all."

Lise didn't mention that she had also been impressed with André's gracious manner throughout the whole incident at the embassy and his phone call the next day.

"I'm flattered on both counts," André said with an encouraging smile. "Go ahead."

"As I said, I have not known Mr. Steeg very long. Since you were at the reception, I assume you may also be aware that he works for the German embassy in some capacity. I'm not sure what."

"Yes, I've heard."

"A few days ago, I received a call from him. Oh, I should mention, I was born in Germany, and I'm a German citizen. Both of my parents were German Catholics. Mr. Steeg had called me previously and somehow the subject had turned to whether I had any relatives in Germany. I told him there weren't any as far as I knew, but that I couldn't be sure."

Lise did not say anything about her other contacts with Steeg, their afternoons and evenings together, or the trip to Dinant.

"Mr. Steeg then offered to look," she went on, "very discreetly he said, into whether I might in fact have any relatives in Germany. Only if I was interested, he said. I wasn't. But later I kept thinking about it, and... well, since my mother's death I do feel very alone in the world, so eventually I said yes. Within a few days he came back with the most amazing story I have ever heard."

"Yes?"

"According to Mr. Steeg, I was adopted, and my natural father was a physics professor at the University in Munich, but he has been fired from his position because he is half-Jewish. By the way, I thought the part about being a physics professor was odd. I always wanted to go into science. I was very good at it."

"Why didn't you?"

"Couldn't afford it, and it's not a profession seen as

suitable for a woman. But I think I am beginning to bore you. Surely you have no desire to hear this long story."

Lise would have had no way to know, but by now André found the story riveting.

"No, you've got my attention. But I am trying to visualize how you must have felt as you heard Steeg tell it."

"I felt terrible. It was contrary to everything I knew. I was puzzled as to why Mr. Steeg was telling me all this, and annoyed that he had dug into my personal life far beyond what I had had in mind.

"And, I didn't believe it."

"I can appreciate that."

"Yes. But there was more."

"And what was that?"

"He said that Adolf Hitler doesn't approve of persecuting the Jews, that he just wants to separate them from the rest of the population for their own protection, that there are some people who are out of control who are dragging Jews out of their homes and beating them, against Hitler's own orders, and that my father—this professor—is at risk of further persecution. Now, Mr. Laroche, do you know whether what he said about Jews being beaten and all that is true? Because if it is, and if the rest of what Mr. Steeg tells me is true, then my impulse is to want to come to the help of my poor father. That's just how I am. But I don't have any idea of how I would do that, so I am turning to you for help."

What Lise was saying deepened André's concern for her. Her conversation with Steeg rang false. He was not sure precisely why, but he knew that Steeg had a reason for saying what he did, and with Steeg the reason could only be something nefarious.

André's amazement at Lise's naively trusting him, virtually a total stranger, with all this information, was now intense. The thought briefly entered his mind that Steeg might be using Lise to draw him into... But into what? What could it be?

Although André felt certain that Steeg did not know who he was, anyone who inquired could easily have linked him to Raoul Maartens. As far as André knew, Raoul's German network was secure, but one could not rule out the possibility that Steeg knew of it. And in any case Laroche could not take the chance of telling Lise what he knew about Steeg. On the other hand, if Steeg was simply telling Lise the truth, then, from all that André knew about him and from his behavior towards Lise at the reception, he began to suspect that Steeg either had delusions about his ability to attract a woman as stunning and charming as Lise, or else was simply planning to coerce this trusting young woman into sex. Such extortion involving relatives was a not uncommon practice of the Nazis, though not usually for sex. Here that possibility fit Steeg perfectly. And André felt sure that Lise had not the slightest suspicion of such a prospect. He would have to be careful about how to answer her.

"Miss Hermann, you're confiding all this to me, yet you've barely met me. You don't know anything about me."

"Well, as I said, I'm turning to you because I feel that I can trust you and your judgment."

"I have no way to know how much of what Steeg has told you is the truth, or even why he has told you all this. You might want to be a lot more skeptical about what someone you hardly know tells you. For one thing, he is asking you to believe all of it just on his own say-so. Did you ask him how he found out about your relationship to this man?"

"He said he had checked records."

"You might ask him what records he is talking about. Ask Steeg to show them to you. I can't give you any other advice, except not to be too trusting of people you have just met."

Lise burst out laughing, and he joined in. She really liked André.

"Well, that's still the best advice I can give you," he said. "But if you find out anything more, I want you to let me know." She made no immediate response.

"Promise me you will do that?"
"Yes. I will."

✝✝✝

Lise told Suzanne about her lunch with André.
"You never told me about him before."
"There was nothing to tell. He was just someone I met at the reception."
"But he must have made some kind of impression on you."
"Yes."
"You liked him when you met him?"
"Well, yes."
"Ah! I thought so. Tell me about him. Is he good-looking?"
"I never thought of him that way."
"Well of course, after Erich…"
"André's much older. In his thirties, I think."
"Do you think of him as sort of a father type?"
"No. I wouldn't say that. What is this, a cross-examination?"
"Yes," Suzanne said, then laughed. "Seems to me this man may be interesting to you," she added.
"He is. André's someone I feel comfortable enough with to confide in, but of course I don't think of him in romantic terms."
"Not really what you're looking for in a man."
"I don't know what I'm looking for anymore."
"But you did enjoy the mussels and *frites*."
Lise couldn't help laughing now too. "Yes, I did."

✝✝✝

André knew that the part about the adoption needed to be checked out. So did the part about the threat to Professor Mueller's safety. He wanted to figure out what Steeg was up to;

if it was extortion, as André suspected, then Mueller faced not only the same persecutions as other Jews, but in addition Steeg's personal brand of cruelty. If Lise were to fall into Steeg's hands and were to succeed in rebuffing his advances, André knew only too well the kind of vengeance that Steeg was capable of inflicting on Mueller. And if not...

André spoke to Raoul about it. Maartens agreed to press forward with an investigation; he said he would get back to André as soon as he had something.

CHAPTER 9

AFTER THE LUNCH with André, Lise kept thinking about her problem. She wished the search for relatives had never started, that the whole issue would go away, that she had never met Steeg. But André was right; she needed more proof.

The next day, Steeg called.

"Look," Lise said, "I just don't believe it. You've been very kind, but this is not what I was expecting. I think we should just let this go."

"Are you sure?"

Lise didn't know what to think. According to Steeg, Lise had another family besides the only father and mother she had known. To her, "family" was not the pleasant word it was to so many others; the only family Lise had known died when she was still a child. Her life was just now beginning to become acceptable, and she had no desire to change it, not this way. The idea of this different father conjured up nothing but complications and troubles. She did not want any more of these.

"I feel sure that my mother would have spoken to me about this. I really can't believe it. I don't know. I would have to see more proof."

"Let me see what I can do."

✝✝✝

Two days later, Steeg called again.

"I have the proof," he told her.

Lise doubted him. "What proof?"

"Letters from your mother, Mrs. Hermann, that is."

"Just what letters are these?"

"It's a little complicated to explain on the telephone. Besides, I think you would want to see them."

That was in fact what she had said.

"Can you come to my place? Now?"

Steeg was on his way. Suzanne would be there.

✝✝✝

Steeg arrived a half-hour later. He was dressed in a business suit. Lise pointed to an armchair and Steeg sat down. She sat opposite him. Lise wondered whether she should offer him a drink, but she remembered how he was with liquor and thought better of it. For this occasion. Suzanne came out into the living room just long enough to meet Steeg; then she said there was work to catch up with, excused herself, and left the room. Steeg stood up when Suzanne came in and sat down after she left.

"Well, I'm sure you're anxious to see the letters," Steeg said as soon as he and Lise were alone again.

He took an envelope out of his pocket. He didn't open the envelope, but just held it in his hand. Lise kept looking at it.

"These are two letters from your adoptive mother, Mrs. Margot Hermann. One is to a lawyer. The other is evidently to your father. I mean the man who gave you life."

Lise didn't reach for or ask to have the letters; instead she just stared at him for a long time. Steeg appeared puzzled, as if he didn't know what to do next.

"If you look at them, you can see whether you recognize the handwriting," Steeg said after a while.

A thousand thoughts flew through Lise's mind. She wanted to look at the letters, point out the absurdity of what Steeg was saying, and put his nonsense to rest. At the same time, Lise was afraid of what she might find, afraid that somehow, against everything she knew, what Steeg was telling her might turn out to be true. This was not what Lise had asked for. She should never have told him to go ahead.

Lise thought of getting up, telling Steeg to leave after all. But it had gone too far. She had to know more, one way or the other. She held her hand out. In that moment, for Lise, her hand seemed to weigh ten kilograms.

"Let me see them," she finally said.

Steeg came over to where she was sitting, handed the envelope to her, and remained standing there. She took the letters out. They were in German. She recognized her mother's handwriting immediately. At the sight of it Lise's eyes welled up.

The first one read:

Dear Sir,

Today your precious little daughter was handed over to my husband and me. Despite our prayers, until now we have never been blessed with any children, but today those prayers have been answered. It is the happiest day of our lives. I want you to know that your daughter will always be loved and cared for by us as our very own.

We admire you for the courage and selflessness it took to recognize that, under the circumstances, your decision, painful as it must be for you, is in the best interest of your child. We will be forever grateful for your trust in us. You can rest assured that we shall be worthy of it. God bless you.

With all our gratitude

The letter was not signed with any name. It was dated shortly after the date of Lise's birth.

From its contents, it was obvious that the second letter had been written for the lawyer. This letter was also in Margot Hermann's handwriting, and asked him to have the first letter delivered to Lise's natural father. Margot had signed the second letter in her own hand, using her full name.

Steeg was still standing, right in front of Lise, watching her.

"Where did you get these?" she asked him.

"From the office of the lawyer who arranged the adoption. They were in his files."

"Well, these letters don't say anything, do they? They don't show who they were sent to. If they were sent."

She knew the letters were genuine, but at the same time she wished to undo what had now been irreversibly set in motion. Perversely, against all logic, she wanted to discredit the letters, as a child caught misbehaving may try to discredit the clear evidence of it.

She waved one of the letters at Steeg. "So that one wasn't sent, was it? To anyone? Did you ask the lawyer about them, about why it wasn't sent?"

"He is no longer living. But the handwriting? Do you recognize it? Is it your mother's?"

"It looks like it. But there must be some other explanation."

"Do you think someone forged the signature?"

"How should I know? You're the one who came up with all this. Anyway, we don't even know who this letter was intended for."

That was all Lise said. But the tears were rolling down her face. She handed the letters back to him.

"Thank you for bringing these."

"I realize I have upset you. I didn't mean to make you cry."

"I cry because I care," she said defiantly.

"Of course."

"If this turns out not to be true, I will never forgive you."

"I'm sure there is no mistake."

"Well, I think it would be best if you left now."

Steeg put the letters back in the envelope, put it in his pocket, bowed, turned, and left.

✢✢✢

After Steeg had left, Lise knocked on the door to Suzanne's bedroom, and Suzanne came out. Before either of them had sat down, Lise told her about the letters. Lise had been so moved by the one to her natural father that she remembered it almost word by word. As Lise told her what it said, Suzanne's face changed; she sat down and dropped her arms into her lap.

"Oh, my God! Are you sure it was your mother's handwriting?"

Lise, filled with both excitement and apprehension at the same time, could not sit down.

"It was her handwriting, her signature. And why would anyone have forged it, anyway?"

"Well, now that's beginning to persuade me. Maybe it's true after all."

"That was my exact reaction when I read them."

"I've never met this man, Mr. Steeg, before now. He's a friend of Erich's and he works for the embassy, right?"

"Yes."

"I would think that would be credentials enough. Why would he have volunteered to look this information up for you, and then not told you the truth?"

"It sounds logical. But I still don't believe it. I wish I had never opened this door."

✢✢✢

Steeg's order to stay away from Lise was constantly on Erich's mind. He knew that her predictable hurt at being "dropped" without any explanation would destroy—quite likely had already destroyed—their relationship, as Steeg obviously intended. Steeg had said Erich could plead business if she called; she had called, and he had pleaded business. Yet Behrndt knew that was not enough; it wouldn't explain this continued silence. He wished there were some way he could at least make the situation understandable to Lise without disobeying Steeg. Since he was allowed to plead business, wasn't the question of who did the calling rather a technicality? As long as he still gave business as his excuse, what was the difference? This time it wouldn't be just explaining the original silence.

✝✝✝

The phone was ringing. Lise figured it was probably for Suzanne. There hadn't been many phone calls coming in for Lise lately. She picked it up. It was Erich.

"I'm sure you must be wondering what happened to me."

"Not really." Lise's voice was cold; she had given up looking forward to Erich's call some time ago.

"I can't blame you for that. How have you been?"

"I've been fine." Lise was not going to give Erich the pleasure of asking him the same question.

"I want to apologize."

What kind of apology would work for what he had done? Lise felt a part of her harden and rise against him.

"I don't see what that would do."

"Lise, my feelings for you have never changed."

"Why, of course. I knew that was the explanation."

"I know it sounds ridiculous."

Lise was afraid that the earnest way Erich sounded was about to throw her off balance. Maybe that was what he was trying to do. But he was just angering her.

"You're right. It's ridiculous. Goodbye Erich. Don't call me back."

He didn't call back. Not that day. He called the next day.

"I told you not to call me."

"I didn't. You didn't say ever. Could we begin a new day?"

That was the Erich Lise remembered. Disarming. But she wasn't going to let down her guard.

"Is there even a remote possibility that you would listen to my explanation?"

What kind of explanation could there be for not giving any explanation? Lise felt increasingly irritated.

"I don't think so. Some things are so unkind and thoughtless that there is no acceptable explanation."

"What if I just groveled pitifully?"

Lise was amused now despite the irritation she'd been experiencing, but she was determined not to laugh.

"Please?" Erich said. "No, don't answer now. Please just think about it. I'll call you tomorrow."

Lise was silent.

"That's all right," he said. "You don't have to say anything. I'll call you. Goodbye."

She didn't reply.

The feelings Lise had for him—not love, but an odd combination of friendship and raw passion—had never faded. But those feelings were now mixed with anger at being taken for granted and betrayed. She had mourned the end of the affair because it could not survive the recent loss of her trust in him. That was why even Erich's most clever, disarming remarks could not rehabilitate him in her heart. She could not, she would not, give him another chance.

✝✝✝

Erich was perceptive enough to sense the change that his long neglect had brought about in Lise's heart. He could tell not just from the tone in her voice when she answered the phone, but also from the fact that that tone had never changed.

This was in spite of what he knew from long experience to be his winning manner. Even that short telephone conversation had been enough to intensify Erich's feelings for Lise, but he sensed that it had not been that way for her—Lise had remained cold and distant throughout.

As Erich thought about it further, he realized that his judgment might be amiss; perhaps more than just his neglect might be at work. He began to feel that there must be another explanation. He could only think of one: that Lise was in fact having an affair with Steeg. After all, that was essentially what Steeg had said. Revolting as the very thought was to Erich, he had to recognize that it might be the explanation.

He needed to make one more attempt to find out whether this was true.

✝✝✝

Erich called again the next day.

"I don't think you understand," Lise said. "I am not interested anymore."

"Steeg," he thought. But what Erich said was "I don't blame you. I am ashamed of how I have behaved."

"You apparently have no concept of how you hurt me. Obviously I am just someone you can turn away from, not call even once, but who will always be there, patiently waiting for you. Well…"

"…Lise, I wish I could make you understand that I got into a situation where it was impossible for me even to contact you."

"Oh, was someone keeping you from the telephone?"

Her almost precisely hitting the mark sent a wave of pain and frustration through Erich; he could not tell Lise the actual truth, and he was almost sure that nothing short of the truth could sway her.

"All right. Will you at least give me this chance? Let me explain as best I can?"

She thought about it for some seconds.

"All right. Go ahead."

"Not on the phone. I need to sit down with you and tell you."

"Oh no! Tell me now or not at all."

"What are you afraid of?"

She was not afraid of anything. Except the way that Erich looked, the way he smiled, his winning manner, all her memories of their times together.

"Nothing. I just don't think it's a good idea. And in any case I don't think you can come up with an explanation that I can believe."

"If you don't let me tell you, how will you know?"

This was almost word for word what Steeg had said; for Lise, this thought cast a shadow on what Erich was now saying. A thin shadow, but it was there.

"I won't. And frankly at this point I don't care. I'm through with waiting."

"Lise, I understand completely how you feel. I will even admit that the explanation may not convince you, even though it's the truth."

"Well, what is the explanation?"

"I was on a confidential assignment and could not call anyone, even you."

Lise didn't answer. For what seemed a long time, neither of them spoke.

Then he said, "I swear that my lack of contact had nothing to do with you. There is no other woman. I have not seen any other woman. I am not interested in any other woman."

"I'm sorry, Erich, but I just no longer want to see you."

"Lise, please… can't we just talk?"

Now she thought Erich might be telling the truth; certainly there was a chance that he was. And it made sense that it might have been impossible for him to talk about his work; she knew that diplomatic work is often carried out in secrecy. She was perhaps being too harsh. If Erich had committed an offense, it was only a first offense. Although Lise had serious doubts as to whether she loved Erich, she still felt that at heart he was a decent person.

"Here's an idea. Why don't we meet?" he said.

"Erich, you know..."

"Just for coffee."

Lise wanted to say no, but she couldn't bring herself to do it.

"Well, all right. Where?"

"How about the little restaurant?"

"All right. But just for coffee. Nothing else."

That was all he had suggested. But she was making it really clear.

"Yes. Nothing else."

✝✝✝

It was the same small restaurant they had gone to all those evenings. The friendly owner greeted Lise and Erich with a smile as they came in.

When they had finished their coffee, and a second cup, Erich said, "This place brings back many fond memories for me."

Lise did not answer, but wished she had not agreed to this place. It held memories for her too.

Erich reached for Lise's hand. She let him hold it for a moment, then withdrew it.

"No, Erich, I don't want to start..." Lise began.

Erich interrupted. "As I told you, the fact that I neglected you so badly doesn't mean I don't care. It only means I'm rotten."

Lise was quiet, deep into her thoughts. For the first time, Erich's charm, the very thing that was so attractive, seductive, about him, she saw as a deception, a way of covering up his thoughtless neglect of her. There was no explanation possible for why he had failed to call her, when it would have been so easy. But that didn't matter so much to her now. More importantly, she was annoyed that he knew he could always rely on his ineffable charm to seduce her back to him. She didn't like this, and for the first time Lise felt cheapened by it, because it was proof of how much Erich took her for granted.

"I think you're just afraid," he said, noting her silence.

"Afraid? Of what?"

Erich broke out into a huge leer but said nothing. They both knew this leer was implying that if she let him get too close, Lise wouldn't be able to resist.

"That's not going to work. Not this time," she said.

It had to be Steeg. Erich considered asking her about this point blank, but then thought better of it. If it was true, Lise might not tell him, and in any case Erich didn't feel he had the right to ask, not after the way he had behaved. And if it was not true, then it would mean that the problem had been his own conduct, and it would be better to deal with that at some future time.

He looked at her; Lise was staring down into her empty coffee cup. She glanced up and their eyes met.

Just then the waiter stopped by with the check. Erich paid it. Erich and Lise then left the restaurant.

When they reached the street, he took her hand. Before Lise could think, she squeezed his. Then she wished she hadn't, but she quickly realized that deep inside she didn't want to let his hand go, and she didn't let it go. Unexpectedly, Lise felt her heart pound and a surge of warmth course through her.

Still holding Lise's hand, Erich started walking. Lise knew where Erich was taking her but she didn't hold back. Neither of them spoke. The restaurant was not far from his place. They were in front of the house now. Erich let go of her hand while he took out the key. Lise didn't speak, she didn't turn, she didn't move. He was equally silent, seemingly focusing on the mundane task of unlocking the door. But his heart was pounding too.

Inside, the two walked up the stairs they had walked up so many times before. Inside his apartment Erich shut the door quickly and they clutched each other. They kissed with abandon. They headed straight for his bedroom and started undressing. They had now moved into that familiar yet magical territory of the most intimate of lovers, swept forward by the flood of passion that enveloped them both, unencumbered by coyness or even conscious thought. As Lise removed her blouse and her bra and flung them aside, images started flashing in Erich's mind one after the other, like stills in a slide show, but much faster. Images of holding her, his palms against her back, running his lips over her breasts, around her nipples, of being in bed, their hands all over each other, their mouths melting together, then her legs in the air...

At that instant, without warning, an image of Steeg, a single, misplaced, obscene slide in the show, appeared before Erich. Steeg replacing Erich in this identical, intimate moment. Steeg, naked, looking at Lise, wrapping his arms around her.

It was as if someone had struck him in the face. He thought again —having been thrown back into the world of thoughts— of Steeg telling him how well he had "hit it off" with Lise, asking Erich— it might as well have been an order—to get out of the way. Erich was convinced now that she had been seeing Steeg.

From Steeg, Erich's mind shifted to his father, who although only a hazy, formless memory, was still the dominant force in his life, someone to whom any disobedience was all but inconceivable. These two, Steeg and his dead father, now filled his brain. To disobey the one was to disobey the other. And to disobey by committing this particular act, defying their authority in this way...

Erich had let go of her. He just stood, naked and flaccid.

"I'm sorry," Erich said.

Lise showed no disappointment, only nonjudgmental sympathy.

"Don't worry," she said. "These things happen."

He fleetingly wondered if she knew this from experience, or had just heard about it.

"Do you just want to wait a while?" she said.

"I don't think so. I don't know what came over me. I'm so sorry."

"Don't be. It's not important."

After they had put their clothes on, Lise came over to him and gave him a warm, sweet hug.

She was really an exceptional, thoughtful, admirable person. But this only made him feel worse.

✝✝✝

Lise remained troubled for some time afterwards. Not over Erich's little failure. It was the shabby way he had handled everything else ever since they had left off before. Other things also bothered her, such as the mystery about his job. Also, while she had not thought much of it at the time, the recollection of Erich's sudden departure from the embassy reception now added to her vague but persistent unease about him.

What Erich's leer in the restaurant had implied was true. She had not been able to resist; she had given in to such easy temptation. Lise now wished she hadn't. She decided that if Erich called again she would tell him it was over.

✝✝✝

Steeg picked up the phone. "Yes. Steeg here."

"*Herr Hauptsturmführer*, this is Conrad Leist."

"What is it?"

"About Hauser."

"Well, what about him?"

"The visitor was there again."

"When?"

"Last night."

"What happened?"

"The same thing as always."

"Are you sure?"

"Yes, of course."

"God damn them both!"

"I'll keep you informed, *Herr Hauptsturmführer*."

"Thank you, Leist."

Leist was surprised at the thanks, if not at the outburst. But what he had no way to know was that Steeg's shock and envy at the news were mixed with pleasure, the pleasure of realizing how useful this information would be.

✠✠✠

What Leist had told him had so stunned Steeg that he could think of nothing else. He could not see why someone as ambitious and intelligent as Behrndt—his own dislike of Erich did not blind him to either of these qualities—could be so lacking in common sense as to risk his whole career by disregarding the warning Steeg had given him. Nor could he believe that Behrndt did not grasp the gist of what Steeg had told him; surely he had made the point clear enough. From what Stoeffler had reported, it was clear that Behrndt could have almost any woman he wanted; why, therefore, would he risk so much for this one? Behrndt was either deliberately disobedient or completely stupid, or perhaps he could be both; in any case this showed weakness, the worst flaw of all and the one that Steeg had recognized in Behrndt all along.

As Steeg thought about it some more, he began to wonder how useful Leist's revelation would actually be after all. To use it would require disclosing, or at least threatening to disclose, Behrndt's relationship from his university days with the Jewess who had the remarkable name of Christine. That threat could have worked, if Erich had been deterred by it. But since he had not, it only brought to Steeg's mind his own pursuit of Lise, who was after all also a Jewess. True, Steeg had found justification—and still did—in the fact that she was only a *Mischlinge* of the second degree. Just the same, making an issue now of Leist's information in Behrndt's case could prove to be a double-edged sword.

Steeg also thought briefly of abandoning his pursuit of Lise. But by now his own lust for her had reached the point where Steeg had convinced himself that the defense of *Mischlinge* of the second degree would work for him. That is as long as he did not raise any issue of religious defilement in Behrndt's case. Besides, since no one other than Stoeffler knew of Lise's Jewish ancestry, and since Behrndt himself could never use it against him, the issue would never arise.

Of course, this meant that he would have to use a stronger weapon against Behrndt. This was not a problem; he knew what to do.

╬╬╬

Steeg had surprised him so many times that Stoeffler never knew what to expect when he asked him to step into his office.

"Stoeffler, this fellow Behrndt. I'm afraid it's just as I suspected. He's not working out well."

Stoeffler was used to Steeg's occasional roundabout way of getting to the point, whatever it might turn out to be; it was always best in these cases to let him get to it on his own.

Steeg looked towards the empty corner of the room behind and to the right of Stoeffler, as if speaking to someone there.

"Loyalty, Stoeffler, loyalty."

He shifted his gaze back to Stoeffler.

"Loyalty is not just about taking the oath, if I dare say so. It's not just about performing his job. That proves nothing, except that you're glib, suave, educated." He said the last word with almost a sneer.

"Behrndt's shown in the past that he is sometimes careless. You know what I'm referring to."

Stoeffler now began to have a pretty clear idea of where Steeg was heading.

"These youngsters today. Not the same as in my day; in yours either, is it?"

"Not the same," Steeg repeated.

"In the war you learn, we learned, the breaking point," he went on. "We experienced it. By being tested."

Steeg paused. "Tested. I want him tested. Blooded." He put the emphasis on the word.

Now it was clear what Steeg had in mind, but still only in a general, not a specific, way. But Stoeffler knew that this would be next.

"I want you to send Behrndt out with one of those groups of new recruits that they break in. They can show him a few things. Take care of a few Jews. I know that the Party does not officially approve of such activities. I think it's unfortunate, although, heaven knows it's hard to restrain the widespread healthy enthusiasm for such actions."

"*Herr Hauptsturmführer*, these activities are usually for the armed groups. As a civilian…"

"Stoeffler, you forget the importance of the position Behrndt holds. Adolf Hitler himself believes that these positions abroad can only be filled by the most loyal, those who have proved themselves to be the most loyal. Of course, as you know, if it had been up to me he would never have gotten this job. Behrndt's too soft. I don't think he could hold up under pressure. That's why he has to be tested. Do I make myself clear?"

"Yes, *Herr Hauptsturmführer.*"

"And, by the way, you'd better make sure he passes the test."

Stoeffler almost laughed at the absurdity of the contradiction. But he instantly recognized it as pure Steeg. If there had been any doubt left of what Steeg was up to, it was now gone.

"But what if…"

"Stoeffler, do I have to spell everything out for you? Do what you have to do. I don't care if you have to alter his file. Do you understand?"

"Yes, I do."

"Also, this is just between us. So if what you do is ever questioned, I will deny that we ever had this conversation. Is that clear?"

"Yes, *Herr Hauptsturmführer.*"

✠✠✠

Back in his office, Stoeffler picked up the telephone.

"Connect me to *Unterscharführer* Kramer. Hello, Kramer? I'm sending someone to you. Yes, for field training. Erich Behrndt. See that he participates in your little activities. We want him blooded. Yes, that's correct. No, a civilian. But listen, Kramer. I have seen his type before. They may be dedicated, but they need a push. Yes, Kramer, I know that you know how to handle them. But you need to understand that this particular fellow I'm talking about is thought of very highly by some people of importance. Yes, a special case. Thank you, Kramer."

1933

THERE WAS NOT A SINGLE EMPTY SEAT among the several hundred in the auditorium at Munich Ludwig-Maximilian University, also known as Munich University. That was always the case whenever Professor Stefan Mueller gave one of the lectures in his popular series. This might have seemed surprising, given that not even the entire student body of the Physics Department would have filled more than a fraction of that number of seats, and that the topic of these lectures was usually physics, a subject not known for its popular appeal.

After his release from the military hospital in 1915, Stefan Mueller faithfully stuck to the program that was prescribed, including at first warm baths, then aquatic exercises. Despite his small stature, Mueller had been an athlete as a youth; determined to regain his former strength, he exercised seven days a week. Before long, Mueller was able to walk again, though at first slowly and with a cane. But soon he found his greatest strength while swimming. In the summer, Mueller had access to a pool; at other times, he swam in a nearby river. He became accustomed to the river's cold temperature, and was able to swim in it for a good part of the year.

After the end of the war, Mueller had resumed his research work at the University, where he had received his doctorate in physics just before the world conflict had begun. This University was well known for its Physics Department, which had produced a number of Nobel Prize laureates, including among others Wilhelm Röntgen, Wilhelm Wien, Max von Laue, and Werner Heisenberg. Mueller's published papers were well received, and resulted in a continuing exchange of letters with other well-known physicists, both in Germany and in several other countries. Among these correspondents were several who, like Mueller, were in the 1930's studying what happens when uranium atoms are bombarded with neutrons. These physicists included Enrico Fermi and Otto Hahn. This work resulted in the discovery of nuclear fission, for which Fermi and Hahn would later receive Nobel prizes, Fermi in 1938 and Hahn in 1944.

But in addition to Mueller's brilliance in both mathematics and theoretical physics, which was sufficient, his colleagues knew, to have placed him among the candidates for the Nobel Prize on at least one occasion, the Professor had the gift of bringing esoteric science within the grasp of the average person while making it entertaining. True, there were some on the faculty who took offense at what they saw as the vulgarization of science, and considered it to be inappropriate on the part of a university professor, but these were few. The large attendances at all of Mueller's lectures spoke for themselves; the crowds usually consisted almost entirely of students and not a few faculty members.

Mueller's lecture on this particular day, in March 1933, was entitled "Albert Einstein and The General Theory of Relativity." He was explaining the part of the theory which, put simply, said that space is not the familiar rectangular three-dimensional framework we all think of, but something curved, and that large objects in space, such as stars, are actually what cause that curvature to occur.

"As I said, I will not give you any rigorous proof, in fact any proof at all, of these things," he said. "If you want that, enroll in one of my physics classes." There was laughter. "I don't even expect you to understand intuitively what this means, because it is not intuitive." Mueller paused here. "At least to most of us." There was further laughter at this point. "Frankly, I myself have always had considerable difficulty grasping the concept, for that same reason. Of course Einstein saw it, but I will tell you a secret. I am not Einstein." There was still more laughter. "But let me try to explain it to you as best I can."

The audience became quiet now.

"Suppose just for a moment that the whole universe were only two-dimensional, meaning that everything in it were confined to a single surface. Suppose further that this surface were a sort of fine mesh, stretched tight yet flexible, suspended by the edges like an acrobat's net. Now visualize heavy objects, like billiard balls, resting at various locations on this net. The net would of course be curved at these locations by the weight of the objects. Now visualize a source of light somewhere on this net. Remember, this net is the entire universe; that means that the light is constrained to run entirely along the surface of the net. Since the net is curved in the vicinity of the objects, the light will likewise curve near them.

"This is a rough intuitive analogy to Einstein's universe. The net is space, although space is three-dimensional, not two-dimensional. The billiard balls are the stars. One of them is the sun. The source of the light in our analogy is a distant star. Just as the net becomes curved in the vicinity of the billiard balls, Einstein's Theory of General Relativity says that space itself becomes curved in the vicinity of large, massive objects such as the sun. And as a result, the light from the distant star will be deflected by that curvature when it passes near the sun.

"Einstein published his Theory of General Relativity seventeen years ago, in 1916. Like all theories, it means nothing unless what it predicts actually happens. Remember, the theory predicts that light will change direction when it passes near the sun, just as the light in the net changes direction near a billiard ball. And from the theory you can calculate by how much the light should change in direction.

"Because this universe seems so different from common experience, and perhaps also for other reasons I will not go into here, Einstein's theory came under considerable attack from many quarters. Some people still don't accept it even today. Nevertheless, as you probably know, there was a total eclipse of the sun three years later, in 1919. The stars near the edge of the sun's disk, which usually can't be seen because of the sun's corona, become visible during a total eclipse. Observations of those stars were made during that eclipse, and lo and behold, the light from them was found to be deflected, as predicted by the theory. The theory was confirmed."

That was how Professor Mueller made a very abstract theory understandable. The lecture continued for some time more, covering other aspects both of Einstein's life and his work. When Mueller finished, the auditorium burst into lengthy and enthusiastic applause. The professor smiled broadly, waving his appreciation.

When the applause had died down and the audience was filing out of the hall, Professor Mueller left the podium. Although he no longer needed a cane, he still walked slowly. Two of his colleagues accompanied him out the door.

✝✝✝

They were waiting right outside. There were six of them, all students. Several of them carried large placards, one reading: "JEWS GET OUT!" another: "EINSTEIN AND MUELLER—TWO STINKING JEWS," a third: "WE DON'T NEED JEWISH PHYSICS."

Professor Mueller had to go past them to get out. As he came near the picketers, one of them shouted: "That's the last lecture you'll ever give here." Another added, "One more and you'll need a wheelchair."

✝✝✝

Professor Mueller's regular Wednesday morning class in thermodynamics would start on the hour. It was now about five minutes before the starting bell. By this time the classroom was always at least three-quarters-full with thirty or more students, but today there were only four or five of them in the room. Professor Mueller was not aware of any unusual campus activities that might account for that fact, and he was puzzled.

Had he stepped outside the door to his classroom, he would have understood. About five or six meters down the hall in each direction stood several students carrying signs. Among them were the students who had picketed outside Professor Mueller's popular lecture in the auditorium the month before. Their signs now read, "JEW'S CLASSROOM" and "JEW INSIDE." A small number of Mueller's students had turned around and left the area as soon as they saw the signs. As the others got near the door, they found themselves facing several more students, standing to the left and right of the door, pointing cameras at them. At that point most of Mueller's remaining students turned around and left. As the few who continued on went through, they were greeted with "Welcome, Jew-lover," and their pictures were taken.

The bell rang. The Professor was still none the wiser.

"We seem to have a rather small attendance today," he started. "Does anyone know why?"

There was only silence.

"I will wait a few more minutes before beginning."

No more students came in.

"All right then," Mueller said finally, "we will continue with our discussion of the second law of thermodynamics."

1936

CHAPTER *11*

STEEG HAD BROACHED the whole subject of Lise's relationship to Mueller with considerable trepidation as to how she would receive it. However her tearful reaction when he had told her that Mueller was her natural father, and again when she read Margot's letters, persuaded him to continue with his plan. Only at the end, when Lise said she would never forgive him if he was lying, did Steeg have some doubt as to how whether to proceed. But the doubt had only lasted a moment.

✦✦✦

Steeg's phone rang. It was Lise. He was surprised. He had just shown Lise the letters two days before.

"Josef, I have spent a long time thinking about all this."

He waited for her to say more.

"About the information you gave me. The letters."

"Yes?"

"I can't do this over the phone."

"Tell me where."

"That café, where we had to sit inside because of the rain."

"All right. When?"

"How about twelve today?"

"I will be there."

✝✝✝

This time it was not raining. At least not at the moment. It was Lise's lunchtime. Steeg suggested leaving and going to a restaurant. Lise said no, she would just have a small bite at the café.

"As I said, I've been thinking about the letters," she said directly.

Steeg was pleased that Lise had saved him from having to bring the subject up.

"I recognized my mother's handwriting, and I know that those letters tell the truth, but at the same time... well, I just don't know..."

It had been her idea to meet. He waited for more.

"I'm very curious about this professor," Lise said.

"Of course." Steeg was trying to keep his expression from revealing how excited he was at this whole development.

"But it's more than curiosity. If he really is my father and if his life really is at risk as you say it is, then Professor Mueller is someone I would need to know."

"I can understand."

"What it amounts to is that my mind is convinced, but not my heart."

He paused for a long time, as if lost in thought.

"What if you could meet him?"

Lise looked as if this took her by surprise, as if she did not see how that could be possible.

"How?"

"I could arrange it. You could see for yourself."

"But where? I thought you said..."

"In Munich. He's still there."

"But you said he's in danger. Wouldn't my visit, a stranger seen going in and out, somehow make it worse?"

"No." Steeg's words were tumbling out. "No, he will be all right. I have some connections. I will make sure they take extra precautions. I'll have the house watched, things like that. Anyway, he does have visitors now and then, administrative matters left over from his position at the University."

"I could never afford that trip."

"I could have you driven there. By someone from the embassy. Some friends of mine who live somewhere else own a house there, where you could stay for a few days."

She seemed to be thinking about this.

"There is a housekeeper who lives in it. She could prepare your meals and look after you. I often go to Munich on business. I could arrange to meet you there during that time."

"That's very kind. But I don't know. Let me think about it."

"Of course."

"I'll call you."

✝✝✝

A few days later André and Raoul met again, at André's house. They were sitting in his library. It was really an office, but Laroche had had one whole wall of the room lined with shelves. These shelves were gradually getting filled with the many books André had been reading, a good number on history.

Raoul's cognac stood on a small table next to his chair; he took a sip and put it back down.

"Our people worked as fast as they could, but it took a while," Raoul said. "The story about the adoption turns out to be true."

"How did you find out?"

"It was not too hard to locate Lise's birth certificate. It shows Viktor Hermann as the father and Margot Hermann as the mother. But because of the story that Steeg had told her, we cross-checked the records of the hospitals in the area. Nothing there, but of course they only keep records in the hospital for so many years."

"So we went to the archives," he continued. "That's where we got our first break."

"What did you find?"

"That's just it, we found nothing."

"Nothing?"

"Nothing. No record of Lise's birth there. That fit the adoption theory, if we want to call it that, perfectly. One where the parties want to make it look as if there had never been an adoption, so they arrange to have the birth certificate show the names of the adoptive parents as the birth parents. But no hospital record of her birth."

"How do they manage that? I mean the birth certificate."

"There are always ways." Raoul paused.

"Then we got our second break."

The two men knew each other very well. André knew that Raoul would complete the story in his own way, so he restrained the impulse to ask more questions. Sure enough, after another momentary pause, Raoul continued.

"We got the whole story on Professor Mueller."

But this time André was unable to restrain himself.

"How did that...?"

Eager to share what he had learned, Raoul interrupted. "It turns out that this Professor Mueller is one of the people our contacts have been keeping track of as a particularly likely victim of persecution."

"Even without Steeg's entrance onto the scene."

"Yes, even without that."

"That's unfortunate," André said. Raoul nodded in agreement.

"Some of our people," Raoul continued, "already knew that Mueller had been dismissed as a physics professor at Ludwig-Maximilian University. He is quite well-known, not only in Germany, but all over the world. When one of their sources reported that there was a rumor about Mueller having a daughter, our people started looking for her. Starting from that end of the puzzle, they had already found out about the adoption and had located a file at that time from the office of the lawyer who had arranged it."

"And?"

"There were only a handful of documents in the file, but they included two handwritten letters, both of them in the same handwriting. One of them just concluded with the words 'With all our gratitude.' There was no signature. It was obviously intended for Lise's natural father. The letter assured him that Lise would be in good hands, et cetera. The other one was signed by Margot Hermann. It was addressed to the lawyer and asked him to send the first one on to the natural father, which the lawyer evidently never did."

"Ah!"

"There was one more thing," Raoul went on. "I asked them to go back and get the letters out of the file so they could show them to me. I wanted to be absolutely sure. Our people said they would. But they came back to me shortly afterwards, empty-handed. They said that when they got to the file, the letters were no longer in it."

"How long ago was that?"

"Three days ago."

"The records."

"What?"

"Steeg told Lise he had checked records, and I suggested she ask him to show them to her."

"And now he has."

"She asked for my advice. Obviously I couldn't tell Lise what we know about Steeg. So I just told her to be skeptical of what strangers tell her."

Raoul's face broke into a whimsical grin.

"Interesting, coming from you."

"Well, yes, it made her laugh. We still can't tell her about Steeg. But now with the letters gone from the file…"

"We need to warn her."

"Just what I was thinking. Before it's too late. I'll call Lise." André stood up.

"Meanwhile," he said, "about Behrndt…"

"My people are already investigating him."

✝✝✝

André called Lise after Raoul had left, but there was no answer. He called again later in the day. Suzanne answered the phone.

"Hello, this is André Laroche. May I speak to Miss Hermann?"

"She's not here now."

"Could you tell her I called?"

"Yes, when I see her."

"Thank you. Do you expect her back soon?"

"Lise is out of town, Mr. Laroche, and I don't know when she will be back."

"Well, it's important that I reach her soon. Is there some other place where I can call her?"

"No, I don't know where she is."

"Are you sure? It's urgent."

"I'm sure."

"Well, thank you."

✝✝✝

As soon as he had hung up, André called Raoul.

"Lise has left town. We need to talk."

Raoul came over to André's house right away.

"The woman Lise shares an apartment with says she doesn't know when Lise will be back, and she doesn't know where Lise is," André said.

"Or maybe she won't tell you. Lise probably told her not to tell anyone."

"The question is what do we do now?"

"Lise told you that if what Steeg was telling her was true, she would want to help her father. We know that Steeg has shown Lise the letters. That confirms what he told her, at least about the adoption."

"I think knowing that the Professor is her father is enough to motivate Lise to try to help him," André said, thinking out loud.

"Well, we know that the rest, about Professor's dismissal and the persecutions, is true. This means that whatever Steeg is up to, both Lise and the Professor are already in peril. And it points to Munich as Lise's destination. She may be on her way there right now. She may be there already."

"And she may not," André said. His concern showed on his face.

"Yes. It may simply be that Lise has gone to some completely different place. Not likely, perhaps, but…"

"…but in that case going to Munich might simply be a waste of time."

"It might be worse than that," Raoul warned. "It could throw us off the track. What if Steeg's not in Munich, but somewhere else, waiting for Lise to be brought to him? Or what if she went somewhere else, to wait for Steeg?"

"I suppose you and I could split up, one to Munich, one to… where?"

"André, on this one we need to go together, as a team. Neither one of us can do this alone, and neither of us can be replaced by someone else."

"That means we wait."

"One thing my people are good at is tracking people down. Let's let them track both Lise and Steeg down, her first. Once Lise is located, we'll leave."

"The delay could be costly."

"True, but that can't be avoided."

"I hate to say it, but I think you're right." As so many

times before, André was grateful for Raoul's insight and resources.

✝✝✝

Raoul called the next day. The two friends met again.

"You're not going to believe this," Raoul said.

"What is it?"

"Steeg is an SS."

"But he's a civilian."

"His attire is just a cover."

"Are you sure?"

"Absolutely. Cross-checked two different ways."

"Look, Raoul, it doesn't make any sense. He has a civilian job, as far as we can tell."

"As far as we can tell. That's just the point!"

"But what for? Why would the Germans have SS working in their embassy?"

"I have no idea."

"And if he is an SS, why is he wearing civilian clothes?"

"I don't think SS uniforms in Brussels would give the impression Hitler wants to make on his dear friends the Belgians."

"But you say you're absolutely sure?"

"Absolutely."

"An SS! My God, poor Lise!"

"We need to know more. About that young man."

"Erich Behrndt. I've asked my people who already investigating him to look into whether he has any connection to the SS. We should know soon."

André rang Lise's apartment again, but there was no answer. He tried repeatedly over the next several days, without success in reaching her. The woman Lise shared the apartment with was evidently away.

✠✠✠

When Lise had returned home in the evening after she had met with Steeg in the café, she told Suzanne of Steeg's offer to have her driven to Munich.

"Suzanne, I don't know what I should do."

"It's not what you ought to do, it's what you want to do."

"Well, that's just what I don't know. I feel the way I did before; I wish this whole thing had never come up, never happened, but now that it has, I'm scared for this poor man, and for myself. If all this is true, I would like to go to him, but I don't know whether that would help or perhaps even hurt him somehow by calling attention to him. And if it's not true… Suzanne, I'm lost in all this. What are your thoughts?"

"Well, let's see if we can break this down. First, there is the question of whether it's true, or some kind of mistake. Because if it's a mistake, that would be the end of it."

"Of course, that's the rational way to approach it."

"Now, what if it turns out not to be a mistake? Well, you can't make any decision, whether to help him or not, until you find that out."

"Yes, of course. And…"

"To find out, you need to go there."

"Yes, to end this uncertainty, one way or the other. That's enough right there to make me want to go to Munich. To see him."

As Lise said this, the idea of meeting face to face with this father she had never known, unsettling as it was, also seemed almost irresistible.

"That part boils down to whether you can trust Steeg. You know him better than I do. But he does work for the embassy, after all. Surely that's some guarantee."

Lise thought of the incident in the car when Steeg had kissed her, and felt a rush of anxiety for just an instant. But then she remembered how Steeg had kept his promise that it would not happen again. She had understood, and still did, how difficult it must have been for him to keep his promise; yet Steeg had kept it.

"You say he's even arranged for a car and a driver from the embassy," Suzanne said. "It seems to me that ought to remove any concern about your safety."

"Yes, I think so. If I'm safe, what is there to worry about?"

"Besides, it should be fun. They say that Munich is such a beautiful city. Romantic Bavaria. Near the Alps." Suzanne rolled her eyes up and broke into a gleeful smile. "A handsome driver, no doubt. Who knows what might happen?"

Lise ignored that last remark.

"I think you're right; it would be safe," Lise said, feeling somewhat relieved to have reached that conclusion.

She would accept Steeg's offer. If anyone called, Suzanne would say Lise was away for a few days, but not tell anyone where.

✝✝✝

She had been told that it would be a long drive, and to be ready to be picked up at seven in the morning. She was traveling now to Munich in a big Mercedes, but not the same one that Steeg had used on the outing to Dinant. This one was a closed sedan. Lise's driver was polite, but not a conversationalist. At the border, as they left Belgium, the two German officers looked at the license plate, seemed to recognize the driver, and waved them right through. Around noon the driver stopped in a small village for lunch. Lise didn't know whether the driver would be sitting with her; it turned out that he did not. The driver just said he would be at the car whenever she was ready to leave. The owner of the little restaurant was courteous and attentive, and said that Lise could order whatever she wanted, that everything had already been taken care of.

The restaurant was about half full. The fare was traditional German food. They made an overnight stop at an inn in another small town. She had a comfortable room, and again ate by herself in the dining room. The next morning they were on the road by seven once more. It was twilight when they reached Munich, so Lise was able to catch glimpses of the city as they drove through it. At one point they went through what looked like a large park, then immediately drove onto a bridge and crossed a river. Not long after that they pulled up to the house.

✝✝✝

André and Raoul were at André's house in Brussels again. There was more news.

"Here's the story on Behrndt," Raoul said.

"You're not going to tell me he is an SS too?"

"No. A member of the Party, but just a civilian. He's well-educated, started working at the embassy right around the time when Steeg began to be seen there. My people are still not sure what the relation is between the two."

"Well, from my short observation at the embassy affair, it seems clear that Behrndt is Steeg's subordinate."

"As is consistent from their respective ages and their near-simultaneous appearances on the Brussels scene. All of which would suggest that Steeg may be planning to use Behrndt in his scheme against Miss Hermann."

"Except for one thing, Raoul."

"What is that?"

"Behrndt was her escort that night."

"Ah, yes, and one of the things we also know is that Lise had been Behrndt's girlfriend, at least up to then."

"But it was Steeg, not Behrndt, who escorted her home that night," André pointed out. "True, Behrndt had been called away from the party on 'urgent business.' However, from what you and I know about Steeg, it's not hard to figure out that this may have been arranged by him."

"So either Steeg is not using, or not planning to use, Behrndt in his scheme, or if he does so, Steeg will be doing it against Behrndt's will."

"But what would Steeg need him for?"

"I'm not sure. As I just said, it may be that Steeg is not planning to use Behrndt. If that's the case, we don't need to be concerned about him."

"I agree. But knowing you…"

"…I'll have someone find out what, if anything , is happening to Behrndt. Where he is, for one thing."

"You took the words out of my mouth."

✝✝✝

Raoul first did the easy part; he asked his friend Leblanc whether he had seen Behrndt lately. Leblanc told him that Erich had just left town a few days earlier. This proved nothing, but might have meant that Steeg, wherever he was, had summoned him. Or it might mean nothing in particular. But Leblanc also mentioned that Erich had already gone out of town some time before, no one knew where. There had been a rumor at the time that Behrndt had been sent away for some "training." He had come back a few days later, but now had left again.

This information was cryptic enough that Raoul had had his German contacts, the same ones who had been so skillful in finding the Professor and deciphering Lise's ancestry, track down what sort of "training" Behrndt had undergone.

Raoul and André were stunned by what they learned. They were aware that anti-Jewish violence and cruelty, like some virulent disease that never stays far beneath the surface, had broken out of late in cities throughout Germany, Munich among others. Storefront windows had been smashed; their trembling, terrified owners were dealt with as the whim of the mob dictated. This meant that men, and sometimes women, were beaten, with some people being dragged away into forests or other places and killed. Now one of Raoul's contacts was saying that Erich Berhndt had taken part in one of these killing parties, in a forest not far from Munich, and had killed a Jew.

Raoul, who did not know Erich, could not reconcile this report with what he had heard about Behrndt. André, who had met Erich and had formed some concept of what he was like from his own acquaintance with Lise, simply did not believe that the report was true.

They decided to have Raoul's source look into the story.

✝✝✝

Raoul had been told by his contacts that the initial information on Behrndt had come from Erich's own file (the Nazis' compulsion for documentation of everything they did would later become enormously useful in the war crimes trials). Within a few days, at Raoul's insistence, his sources confirmed that the report of what was in the file had been accurate. However, the contacts had uncovered further revelations that would surprise both Raoul and André even more than the original story.

"One of my contacts spoke to a man who was at the so-called training," reported Raoul. "Besides the obvious purpose of killing Jews, the type of expedition Behrndt went on is apparently a means of probing the limits of the participants' commitment by ordering them to perform some brutal act, commonly a killing. My contact would not give me the name of the man he spoke with, but it was one of the leaders of that night. The leader stated that he was still upset about Behrndt's file. It seems the file had originally stated—accurately—that Behrndt had demonstrated cowardice and disobedience—meaning that he actually disobeyed the order to kill—but that the file had almost immediately afterwards been altered to state the opposite. The man said this had been done on orders from 'higher up,' but he could not, or would not, say whose orders."

"When did all this happen?"

"Recently. But some time before Behrndt left town again a few days ago."

"'Disobedience? Orders?' Why is a civilian ordered to kill?"

"André, I don't know why. But I do know that the German people, not just those in uniform, have been incited to the point where atrocities are being committed by them, the ordinary people, every day."

"I'm willing to believe that, but civilians being *ordered* to commit them?"

"André, once again, I don't know either."

"Maybe Steeg had a hand in that. I'll bet when they find Steeg, they'll find Behrndt."

For a moment neither spoke.

"I see this as a good sign," André said, "if Erich in fact refused to comply with that order. Especially if it was Steeg's idea to send him out there."

"Hard to say. How do we know Behrndt didn't want to comply but lost his appetite for it?"

"Maybe like this, Raoul. Steeg has taken Behrndt's girl-friend away from him," André surmised.

"We don't know that."

"No, we don't. But if that's what happened, it's not likely to have heightened Behrndt's loyalty to Steeg. And even if it's not what happened, Steeg then has him sent out to kill some Jews, and what does Behrndt do, he disobeys the order. Now I don't care whether that was the result of deliberate disobedience, which would be defiance, or lack of stomach, which would be cowardice—as they see it—because in either case it's a black mark for a young man with ambition within the Nazi Party. Maybe even, in the Nazis' eyes, treason. And that would explain why Behrndt's file was altered to remove the record of his dismal failure to meet the great standards of the Nazi Party. There's one person we know of who could have easily arranged that. Steeg. To give himself…"

"…one more weapon."

"I'd bet on it."

Raoul thought about all this for a while.

"A nice theory, André, I must say. If it's correct."

"And if it is, I think it means that Erich Behrndt could become quite helpful to us."

"Once again, maybe yes and maybe no. If Steeg's conduct towards him, including this potential threat of blackmail, makes Behrndt more obedient, then no. But if it turns Behrndt against Steeg, then maybe yes. But I don't know whether Behrndt would have the guts to do that."

"Look at one more factor, or potential factor, Raoul. We believe that Steeg is about to extort sex—at least try to—from Miss Hermann, Behrndt's former girlfriend. Add that to the mix. Do you think Behrndt would actually help to bring that about?"

"Depends on whether Behrndt actually knows that this is what he's helping to bring about."

"All right. We don't know. But if Erich finds out what he is really being asked to do, he could become an ally in our endeavor to get Lise away from Steeg."

"I'm still skeptical."

"That's all right, Raoul. It's healthy to be skeptical. Why don't we keep an eye on Behrndt?"

"I think we can do that."

"Does that take care of your skepticism?" André said with a smile.

"No. But it takes care of your optimism," Raoul shot back.

CHAPTER 12

*T*HE HOUSE STOOD in what was at that time a relatively sparsely inhabited area, across the Isar River from the center of Munich and some distance from it. In the fading twilight, Lise could see that, like others nearby, this was a large and imposing three-story dwelling. The place had obviously been built in another century.

The driver pulled away right after walking Lise's bags up to the porch. Lise watched the Mercedes leave and then took the steps that led up to the front porch. The housekeeper, a tall, thin woman, stood there waiting. Lise would later learn that this woman's name was Hilda. The woman wore a plain black dress, and her blond hair was tied in a bun. Though she had a good face that must once have been beautiful, the housekeeper now looked drawn, as if from hard work or a difficult life. The type of person whose age seems indeterminate, she looked to be anywhere from her early twenties to nearly forty. She said nothing to Lise, but obviously had been expecting her. The woman simply signaled to Lise to follow her, picked up the bags, and led the way up two floors, then passed through a door leading from the small landing into a long hall, and to a bedroom, on the right side halfway down the corridor.

The bedroom that would accommodate Lise was very large, with a high ceiling and prominent ornate moldings; the furniture consisted of two single beds with thick eiderdown comforters, two accompanying night tables, matching dressers, a dressing table with chair, two stuffed armchairs, a small table by each of the two windows, and sitting chairs. All the furniture was of dark, heavy hardwoods, elaborately carved. Looking down from each of two pairs of large, framed portraits on the walls was a stern-looking man and an equally stern-looking woman, from an older era. Lise guessed that these two couples were ancestors of occupants of this house. The window drapes were at the moment closed.

A double door through the wall on the left side led into a sitting room, which was as wide as the bedroom, but longer. The furniture in this room was arranged into two groups. Near one end of the room were a dining table with four chairs and a small sideboard. On one side of the rest of the room was a large couch flanked by armchairs; facing it was a massive marble-topped sideboard with a large gilt-framed mirror above it. Slightly to each side of this sideboard, and forward of it, were two more armchairs. Arranged throughout were small tables bearing lamps with pink shades. There was a second door, to the hallway.

The table had been set for one person. Hilda showed Lise a small dumbwaiter outside her room and explained that her meals would either be sent up to her on it or brought up. She also showed her a small stocked pantry and kitchen down the hall, which Lise was free to use if she needed anything else.

The bathroom was also down the hall. Lise asked her whether Mr. Steeg was at the house. Hilda told her that he would be coming later. She added that Steeg wanted to know whether he might join Lise at eight for dinner in the sitting room. Lise said that would be fine.

✠✠✠

At two minutes to eight, Lise closed the double door to the sitting room, came out to the hallway through the other door, and went into the sitting room. Steeg walked in at eight on the dot. He was effusive and overflowing with attention. He grasped both Lise's hands and called her "my dear." Had she had a good trip? Did she find her room satisfactory? If there was anything she needed, Lise should just ask for it. No, he was not staying in this house, nor were his friends who owned it.

Steeg did not mention that the real owners were in fact Jews who had been removed from the house by the SS. Nor did he tell her that the SS had then turned the house over to the Nazi Party, which now used it for its own purposes.

Steeg said he thought Lise had been very wise indeed to decide to come. Lise said yes, she was anxious to meet her father and asked when this might occur.

"Why, tomorrow morning. I knew you would want to meet him right away, so I have arranged for the driver to pick you up at eight-thirty."

"How far is it?"

"Oh, not far. Less than a half-hour by car."

"Does he know I'm coming?"

"I am sure he doesn't."

"You mean he knows nothing about this?"

"No. We are quite sure he is there, but no one has spoken to him."

He didn't explain who this "we" was, and Lise did not ask.

"I thought it best to leave that to you, Lise. This whole visit is still entirely up to you. I've brought the letters with me, in case you would like to show them to him."

"Yes, I would. Thank you."

"After you have shown the letters to your father, be sure to return them to me. I should add that we will have to be very careful. Some precautions are necessary."

"What kind of precautions?"

"Remember, I mentioned that your father is in considerable danger."

"Yes, you did."

"The rogue elements I mentioned are going against the policies of the Party. Of Adolf Hitler himself. It is a bad situation. The authorities are doing everything they can to stop all this, but frankly it is not easy. In fact, it is almost out of control."

Steeg paused. He noticed that Lise seemed very attentive, her expression serious. However she said nothing.

"Your father, while he was... until he lost his position at the University, had lived in a house he owned. Well, for his safety, it was thought best for him to move to another location."

"Where is that?" She sounded anxious, as if that news disturbed her.

"Oh, he is in another house. You will see, it is quite nice, but in another part of town where he is completely safe. Your father has all his books with him. The main thing, you see, is that everyone knew that this professor—he is well-known, of course..."

"Yes."

"...everyone knew where he lived. Other members of the faculty lived in the same area. But where he is now, no one suspects that this is where he lives. For his safety, as I said. So naturally, we have to be very careful, to keep that secret."

"So how does that affect me?"

"Not at all, really. You will just have to be careful too. I'm sure you can appreciate that."

"Yes."

"But we are friends, aren't we?"

"Yes, Josef, we are. I want you to know, I am grateful for what you are doing for me, for my father...That word sounds strange as I say it. Anyway, I do appreciate it. But tell me, what are these precautions?"

"Not that much, really. For one thing, the car you will be taken in will be an ordinary-looking one, not the luxurious limousine you came in. Less conspicuous. And there's no need to mention my name. I'm sure it would mean nothing to your father, and, again, because of those dangerous elements, it will be safer."

Steeg paused and studied her. Lise didn't seem to be bothered by any of this. She just continued to look attentive.

He continued. "Also, I think it would be best for you not to leave the house... this house, by yourself, while you are here. If you need to go out we... I will have you driven."

"Josef, my father's well-being is the important thing to me. I know you have thought all this out carefully. I will do as you think is necessary."

Steeg was relieved that Lise had voiced no objections; she evidently saw nothing wrong with the arrangements.

✝✝✝

Lise awoke early. She opened the heavy drapes. It was a bright day, but this side of the house was in the shade. She felt a mixture of pleasant anticipation and great anxiety. There was no sign of Steeg.

The car arrived promptly at eight-thirty. The driver, a different one, said good morning, but nothing else. When they got there, he opened the car door and told her he would wait nearby until she needed him. Lise got out and found herself standing in front of a small, attractive-looking house.

She rang the doorbell. After a little while, the door opened. In the opening stood a short man in a cardigan; he had a cautious smile on his face. Lise was struck by how small he was, and how old he seemed.

"Professor Mueller?"

"Yes?"

He stood looking at her for a little while, not saying anything. Lise realized that she had not planned what to say.

"Oh, please come in."

She stepped inside. Professor Mueller closed the door. He pointed to a chair near one side of the small fireplace.

"Please sit down."

The room was furnished simply, but looked cozy. There were a couple of framed pictures and a few other knickknacks on the mantel, and similar items on the small tables and the breakfront on one side of the room. Shelves lined one wall, and they were filled with books. He walked slowly over to an armchair on the other side of the fireplace, and sat down. She could not envision him as her father.

"You'll have to forgive me," he said. "I was thrown off for a moment. But of course I realize now that you're from the University. You're about the third person they've sent out here. I don't know why they keep doing that. After all, since I am no longer..."

"But I am not from the University."

"You're not? Then why are you here? Who sent you?"

Lise didn't know where to begin. He looked so vulnerable. She thought about what Steeg had said about Jews being dragged out of their homes and beaten. Lise did not want to hurt him, yet she didn't know how to tell the Professor her story without causing him a shock. Or perhaps angering him. If Mueller didn't believe what she was about to tell him, he would probably be annoyed; if he did believe it, he might be upset at her sudden and uninvited intrusion into his life.

"My name is Lise Hermann."

Lise was not an uncommon name. Any connection to the daughter he had never even seen was the furthest thing from Mueller's mind in that moment.

"I don't know anyone by that name. I think there has been some sort of mistake. Who sent you? Where are you from?"

"If you will give me a moment, I will try to explain, then I think you will understand."

"All right."

"You once had a daughter."

The Professor had often thought about the little girl he had never seen, had wondered what had happened to her, where she was, what she was doing, whether she was happy. But this woman obviously was not referring to that. She had been sent here by someone, apparently not by the University, but clearly by someone. The way everything had been arranged for the adoption at the time, there was no way anyone, let alone this woman, could know anything about it. And besides, that was so long ago.

"No. As I said, there's been a mistake. They sent you to the wrong place." He started to get up.

"No one sent me."

"But then why are you here?"

"I know I must seem to be a total stranger to you. But if you will give me a chance to explain, I will tell you about myself, and you will see that I am not a mere stranger."

In his youth, Mueller had had less patience. His father-in-law's ways in particular used make his bile flare up. Years ago he would have asked this woman, politely but firmly, to leave. But what he had gone through over the years had, paradoxically, made him more patient and accepting.

"All right."

"I was born in this country, in 1915. My mother died when I was born. I know that you were injured in the war that same year, and that you... well, very soon after I was born, I was adopted. You are the person I am talking about, aren't you?"

A strange expression came over Mueller's face, reflecting both recognition and disbelief. This young woman was reciting things that he knew were true. She obviously had come across them somewhere. But how could she know, how could anyone know, that she was in fact his little girl?

"It sounds like me. There must have been thousands like me." Mueller's voice was beginning to sound annoyed. "But it doesn't sound like you. That's where you are mistaken. Who told you all this? Your parents?"

"No. They are both gone. My father was killed in the war. My mother died a few years ago."

"I'm very sorry. But then who told you?"

It was not surprising that the Professor would be skeptical. But she remembered what Steeg had said, and she would not go against it by mentioning him or how he had arranged all this.

"*Herr* Professor, the person who told me is a friend of mine, a very nice person, the same person who arranged for me to come here, but warned me that, in view of your... situation, it would not be safe to talk about that. I think maybe you can appreciate that."

Up to a point, this made sense to Mueller. But he was still unconvinced.

"Yes. I think you are wise not to tell me. But how can I be sure, how can you be sure, that you are the little girl you are talking about? Because, as always in these cases, everything was kept very confidential, very secret. I never knew the names of my daughter's new parents, and they never knew mine. I am sure you are mistaken."

While the Professor was speaking, she had noticed one of the photos on the mantel, a picture of a young woman, in a silver frame. She stood up and went up to it. The silver was tarnished. The hairdo and the dress were obviously out of date. But the resemblance was startling; it could have been a photo of herself. She looked at it for a long time. Then she turned to him.

"Look at me," Lise said.

He was looking at her, but remained quiet .

Lise nodded towards the picture. "Who is that?"

"That's my dear darling wife. So beautiful. She was everything to me, and then..."

"Do you see any resemblance?"

"It struck me the minute you walked in," the Professor said, his eyes welling up. "It gave me a terrible shock. But of course it never occurred to me that you actually... I still can't believe it."

He had never considered himself emotional, but tears started running down his face.

The full realization that this man was her father was still sinking in. But Lise found him lovable quite apart from that. She could sense the terrible loss he was still mourning, so many years later. Lise knew how her father must feel; she had felt that same way herself too many times. She wanted to comfort him, to hug him. Lise went over to him, half-knelt by the side of his chair, and put one arm around his shoulders. She was weeping too.

"This is ridiculous," he said after a while. "Here you walk in, a total stranger, and within minutes we are both in tears." Lise saw the humor and laughed. They both went on laughing and weeping at the same time.

After a moment Mueller was collected again, like a child who had come out of a crying spell.

"But I still don't know. Logically it can't be."

"Does the name Lise mean anything to you?"

The Professor had never known anyone named Hermann, but he remembered now. He looked at her, his eyes red, nodded very slowly, and broke into a smile.

"'Lise,' yes. Yes, I remember. 'Lise.' That was the name the lawyer said your new parents were going to give you."

He had said, "you."

Lise stood up, got out the letters, and handed them to him. He unfolded them, and glanced over the correspondence.

"I recognize the name on this one," Mueller said. "It's to the lawyer who arranged it."

"They're both in my mother's handwriting," Lise said. "The signature, 'Margot Hermann,' on that one is hers. The other, to 'Dear Sir,' was obviously intended for you."

"But I never saw it."

"That's because the lawyer apparently never sent it on."

"Unfortunately."

"Or maybe fortunately. After all, it's that letter that brought me to you."

✟✟✟

Lise and the Professor were both emotionally drained. Lise told her father that she had to leave. Mueller said he understood, adding that they both needed time to get used to the idea of being related.

"But I want to see you again," Lise said.

"Yes, of course, we'll see each other again. Come tomorrow."

Professor Mueller stood up. Lise went up and hugged him.

"I will," she said.

✟✟✟

When Lise got back to the house, Hilda told her that Steeg would be there again for dinner. When he arrived, he was at his most genial. Before he had the chance to ask Lise how it had gone, she already had begun to thank him.

"Oh, Josef, I am so grateful to you for arranging all this. For bringing me to my father! Thank you so much."

Everything was going marvelously. Steeg was in a great mood. He had Hilda open some fine French champagne. He loved French champagne. Steeg and Lise drank, toasting "to the future."

"I plan to see him again tomorrow," Lise said.

"Of course," Steeg said.

✟✟✟

Erich Behrndt had tried to call Lise several times, but there had been no answer. This time he heard Suzanne's voice on the other end of the line. After they had greeted each other, Erich asked for Lise.

"She's not here, Erich."

"Would you ask her to call me when she gets back? Or I can call her later. When do you expect her home?"

"She's not in town."

That explained why Lise had not been home when he had called at her usual times.

"When do you expect her back?"

"She didn't say."

"Well, when she gets back, please tell her I called."

"I'll be glad to."

Erich suspected that Lise had been seeing Steeg. But he couldn't bring himself to believe that she would have gone out of town with him. Steeg was in and out of town so often that, although he worked for him, Erich was not always aware of his comings and goings. When Erich got to his office, he checked; Steeg was not in town, nor at his regular office in Münster.

✝✝✝

Until now Behrndt had been of little use to Steeg, and besides, it had been crucial to keep him at a distance. But now that Steeg had lured Lise to Munich, he had plans to use Erich. He had Behrndt contacted and ordered to Munich. Erich did not know why Steeg had called him to Munich. Erich's old friend Helmut Stangl had told him to be sure to let him know in advance if he ever made a trip to Munich. They decided to meet for dinner downtown on the evening of Erich's arrival. During the meal, Erich mentioned that he was to report to Steeg the next morning.

"Yes, I remember Steeg," Helmut said. "He started coming to Brussels, on and off, right around the time you were posted there. But I also knew him from before. I heard he's in town, here, again."

"Again?"

"Yes. Of course, I don't suppose you would know."

Erich looked at him with a quizzical expression.

"Comes here quite often. It's become a bit of a joke among the fellows, in fact."

Erich's interest in what Stangl was telling him must have shown, because his friend continued.

"There's this house—it's become known as 'Steeg's love nest.' Of course it's not Steeg's house—I think it belongs to the Party. Across the Isar River from here. The area is only partly built up, but there are a number of old houses. This one is quite beautiful, they say. Anyway, Steeg brings women there. There have been a few. There's a sort of built-in housekeeper, so it's very convenient. I heard he has one there right now. Most of them are just—well, you know—but this one is supposed to be different. A real beauty, classy, not his type at all. Arrived there in a big Mercedes, from Belgium or somewhere, just a couple of days ago, as a matter of fact. Isn't it amazing how much the gossip mill knows? But I think I'm boring you."

"Not really, since I'm supposed to report to Steeg in the morning.

But don't worry, Helmut, about what you just told me. My lips are sealed."

"I know. Oh, I should add, there's this inn in Meersburg. I think you know the town."

"On Lake Constance?"

"Yes. Well, Steeg has been taking his women—that's how the fellows refer to them—there. For little 'holidays.'"

✝✝✝

Erich was to report to Steeg's local office, which here in Munich was just a room that Steeg was allowed to use when it was not needed by someone with a higher rank. Behrndt arrived punctually at eight.

He was not sure of what to expect. It ought to have to do with business, the business he had joined the Party for. However as before Erich had an uneasy feeling that it had nothing to do with that.

The room to which Behrndt was directed was small, and not nearly as impressive as the setting to which Steeg had summoned him at his regular office in Münster. About half of the room seemed to be used for filing purposes. The only desk was plain and well-worn. Steeg was sitting behind it.

Erich got the impression that, despite these rather shabby surroundings, Steeg felt pleased with himself.

"Behrndt, please sit down."

An unusual courtesy.

"I have a new assignment for you. It has to do with Miss Hermann." Steeg paused, apparently, Erich decided, to let it sink in. "As you may have heard, she is staying with me."

This last amazing statement was followed by another "significant" pause. The air of camaraderie, of two close friends sharing confidences, annoyed Erich.

"But I don't want to give you the wrong impression," Steeg continued. "This is not just about pleasure, not at all. It's very much about business. Important business."

Erich was curious to find out what business there could be that would involve Lise.

"I'm not in a position to tell you the details right now. But at the appropriate time, you will know. You can rest assured of that."

"I need more of an explanation. How do you expect... What can I possibly..."

Steeg cut Erich off. "As I just said, when the time comes it will all be made clear. You will be told what to do. But for now, this is all you need to know. Until then, please remain where I can reach you."

Erich was more confused than ever. What was Steeg talking about? What was he planning? This was the second time that he had given Erich an assignment that was clearly unrelated to work. First that incredible demand about Lise. Backed by the threat of blackmail. But what could it be this time? Steeg already had Lise. And, implausible as it had seemed, it was clear that he and she had become lovers. Steeg was now sounding delusional.

He had had enough. Whatever this was, Erich wanted no part of it.

"You are speaking to me as if I were an SS, under your command. You apparently forget that I am a civilian."

"A civilian, yes. But a loyal civilian. One who can be depended on without question. One who has sworn absolute loyalty to his country and to Adolf Hitler." Steeg leaned forward, resting his forearms on the desk.

"It is rare, almost unheard of, for a civilian employee, not just to take the oath, but to volunteer, to insist, on taking it, as you did. I can assure you, the Party was impressed with that. And so was I. Here was someone who can be counted on, even for the most difficult of assignments."

Steeg's mind was always on the same track. Erich still could not make out what Steeg was going to have him do, but he knew that it would be equally obscene.

"The last time we had such a conversation, it was about that woman..." Erich said.

"...Christine, yes."

"One innocent mistake..."

Steeg righted himself in the chair. "That time it may have been, as you call it, a mistake. This time it was not a mistake."

Erich was more puzzled than ever.

"Since that time, you have again violated your oath." Steeg's eyes were hard and cold.

Of course, that was it. The forest.

"No," Steeg continued, "not a mistake. This time it's cowardice, disobedience, treason. You have placed yourself under a great cloud."

"But what has that got to do…"

Steeg interrupted him again. "Behrndt, everything you have now, your cushy job, your standing in the Party, your career, your whole future, you owe to me."

"I don't understand."

"Let me explain. Did you for one moment think that you would have kept your job after your shameful conduct in the forest? Do you think you would still have your position in Brussels? Don't you understand that your failure to obey orders to kill was removed from your file?"

Erich had been astonished when what had happened that night in the forest had never been mentioned again by anyone. When he had just returned to his job, there had been no adverse consequences. He had never understood it.

"It can at any time be brought to the attention of the authorities. There is evidence, there are witnesses. Your career would be finished, and probably much worse."

Steeg stayed quiet then for what seemed to be a long time.

Finally Steeg sat back in his chair and said, "So you will await my instructions. And when you receive them, you will do as you are told."

Erich was seething with rage. When Behrndt had heard Hitler's call at that rally, he had been ready to follow him into the great struggle against Germany's enemies and for the restoration of Germany's glory. And that was still his dream. Instead he had somehow fallen into the clutches of this petty martinet, a man obsessed with personal power and immersed in his own lusts.

Erich wanted to strangle Steeg. He wanted to stand up and do this now.

But Behrndt knew he was powerless.

✝✝✝

On the morning after the day of Lise's first visit to the Professor, some time after the driver had picked her up for her second visit with Mueller, Steeg dropped by and went into the small office he had set up for himself on the ground floor of the house. On his way in, he stopped in the main kitchen and asked Hilda to bring a pot of coffee and rolls with butter and jam to his office. He kept some papers there and had some work to do.

Steeg's heavy wooden desk faced the wall. He was sitting at the desk, his back to her, when Hilda entered the room. She put the tray on one side of his desk.

"She's very pretty," Hilda said.

She was still behind him, a little to one side. Steeg did not turn around or speak. He just grunted.

"I don't think this one is going to be as easy as the others," she said.

"How would you know?" Steeg had turned slightly to one side and started to butter one of the rolls, but still was not looking at her.

"You've never had anyone like her. She's in a different class altogether."

Steeg's only answer was to shove the roll in his mouth and grunt again.

"Besides, many of the others were a long time ago."

He had put the roll down and was pouring cream into his coffee.

"It wasn't that long ago that I had you."

"Women want more than you have to offer."

Steeg swung his chair around and faced Hilda. He took a sip out of his cup.

"You have this good job."

She pushed her lower lip up into a sneer. "Days of menial work so that you can entertain your 'friends.'"

He smiled. "You've never complained."

Her face was taut with rage now. "A lot of good that would have done."

"Besides, it's better than the way you earned your living before you found me."

"You filthy swine!"

"You never even thanked me."

Hilda felt like screaming, but she wasn't going to give him that satisfaction. She kept her voice low, but very firm, emphasizing every word. "You fool! You know you only did it because of what I could have done to your career if you hadn't."

Steeg laughed. "Nonsense... besides, as I recall, those squeals of yours were not exactly squeals of displeasure."

"That, you will never know."

As she left Hilda wanted to slam the door, but curbed the impulse.

†††

Lise's father answered the door right away. He was wearing a jacket and tie. He had coffee ready for her.

Their conversation started with a question; it quickly became a feast of exchanged memories. She wanted to know everything about her mother. He told her how beautiful her mother had been, not just outwardly, but from within also, as a person. He had been the luckiest man in the world to win her. Their marriage had been the perfect romance; it had from the start seemed to him almost too good to be true. When Lise asked him about his injuries from the war, he told her about this, briefly.

"They didn't think I was going to live. It was many months more before I could walk. I knew that when I got back I would have my career. But I couldn't have... You know that your mother died..."

"Yes, I know that..."

"My mother was no longer living. Your mother's parents, your grandparents, were over sixty, and my father, almost seventy. I could never have raised you, any child, by myself."

"I was torn in pieces," he continued. "But I wanted you to have parents, the family you needed, people who would care for you, love you."

Lise's eyes were moist.

"So there was no other choice. My greatest regret..." Now he started weeping. "My greatest regret was... that I never even saw you."

Lise wept.

"I'm so terribly sorry," he said, "but there was no way..."

"Oh, no, no, don't be sorry, don't be sorry. What you did was the greatest act of love ever possible."

"Lise, it crushed me. Absolutely crushed me. To lose your mother, and then you. Although it was a great comfort to know that you now had new parents, a new family, who I knew loved you. But there has never been a month since, not a day, when I have not thought about you. I would see a little girl who would have been about your age somewhere, in the street, in a store, at a playground, and I would wonder... And later, seeing young women who looked to be about your age, made me wonder where you might be, and could this possibly be you. I had a fantasy of seeing you somewhere, and knowing it was you. In that fantasy I would watch you, from a distance— I would not have wanted to intrude—just to look at you, briefly from a distance, to see what you looked like, how you walked, how you laughed."

"But look," he said, "I'm just rambling on. We should be happy. You are here. That in itself is a miracle. You have grown into a lovely woman. So much like your mother."

"I'm thinking... here I am, barging into your life, completely uninvited, without any thought of how you feel..."

"No, you're wrong. Remember? I asked you, yesterday. I asked you to come back today, and you said you would."

"Well, that was very nice of you."

"'Nice,' no, I wasn't being 'nice.' I wanted you to come back. I could have said goodbye, it was lovely to see you. Why, I could have said why are you barging into my life..."

Her tears had given way to a sly grin. "You would never have done that."

The Professor picked up on this and smiled, a teasing smile that looked oddly like hers. "Oh yes I would. You don't know me."

"But you didn't."

"No, I didn't. But enough of that. I've told you about me, but I want to know more about you. What were your parents like?"

"I was only three when my adoptive father was killed. So I never..."

"You never knew him."

"No. My mother was of course the person I was closest to. She was lovely, worked hard all her life supporting herself and me. She died when I was fourteen."

"That must have been awful for you. So many losses."

For a few moments neither of them spoke.

"Where do you live now?" he asked. "Tell me about yourself."

"I live in Brussels. My mother moved there after the war. Let's see. I went to school with the nuns."

"Yes, I remember now, a Catholic family. Very nice. So you see, I know a few things about you, not much of course."

"Oh, but I have to tell you, I know a lot about you. I've read about you."

"Where? What do you mean? How can..."

"Why, physics..."

"You've studied physics?"

"Yes. Just one year. I wanted to go on to university after graduating, but my mother had died by then and the nuns wouldn't let me. I always got my best grades, the best grades in the whole class, in physics, chemistry, and mathematics. Even in high school, I wanted to know more about these subjects than they taught. I used to go to the library and read books about science. But they said there wasn't enough money, and that it wasn't a field for women anyway, that I should become a bookkeeper instead. That's what I do now."

"Amazing!"

"That's how I learned about you. I never dreamed it was you, I mean your being my father, but I read a lot about famous scientists, Einstein, Heisenberg, many others. Fermi, I read about Fermi, Otto Hahn, the unexpected and unexplained appearance of those different elements when they bombarded atomic nuclei with neutrons."

"You know about all that?"

"I know it's a little unusual for a woman…"

"Well, maybe, but some women are involved in it. For instance…"

"…Lise Meitner!"

"You know about her?"

"Yes. Another Lise!"

"Yes, she worked with…"

"…Otto Hahn!"

"Yes!"

Her face was flushed with the excitement of it all. "And you! I read about you. I know that you worked on the same thing! I know about your correspondence with Hahn and the others."

Mueller was both surprised and completely fascinated. For her part, Lise was as excited as a child; she could no longer stay put. She jumped up from her chair and gave him a hug.

"I'm so thrilled," she said, "to find you, and then on top of that this other, this unexpected bond between us." She sat back down, smiling broadly at him.

"I have been crazy about science ever since I was a little boy," he said. "It started with the things all boys like, mechanical toys, kites, things like that. But as I began to learn about what made them work, and I realized one day that these are the same principles that govern the universe, well... I have never been religious, but the more I learn about the grand scheme the more I am awed by its magnificence. And that these tiny ants that we are have the ability to understand it, in a very modest way, of course, well, that's the greatest miracle of all. It has been a passion all my life."

Lise had never heard anyone else express those thoughts, and was pleased that they found an echo—though a much more humble one, she realized—in her own perceptions.

"I have this strange feeling," she said. "That I am in a dream. These are the same types of thoughts that I had as I grew up. And to hear them now, out of your mouth! When I first had these thoughts, the nuns did not encourage them. I suppose they were doing what they thought was best from their point of view. Later, I did what they told me I had to do. I had lost my mother and I didn't have any other choice. But I've never given that dream up."

"Lise, you should never give it up. You are still very young. You have your whole life ahead of you. Don't foreclose the possibilities. As for me..." He didn't finish the sentence. For a moment they were both silent.

Lise wondered how she should address him. "Professor" seemed too formal now. She thought about "Father" but that might be crowding him. And "Stefan" might be too familiar.

"Professor, I don't know how to address you."

"I am not a fussy person. Whatever you feel comfortable with. But I think we have become closer than 'Professor.' Perhaps..."

"Yes. How about..."

"...Stefan." They both had spoken the name at the same time. They laughed.

"Stefan, how is your health?"

"Basically, excellent. The only problems I have are from

these injuries. I still follow the orders the doctors gave me. Exercises. Swimming."

"Now that you've been… dismissed, from the University, what do you plan to do?"

"I'm quite satisfied to stay right here. I have my books with me; I can continue my work right here."

"But what about the experiments that are needed to test your theoretical conclusions?"

"Ah, my own experiments are mental experiments. That's the nice thing about theoretical physics; the physical experiments that will confirm or invalidate the theories are done by others."

"But I've been told that Jews are being persecuted all over Germany. Not just with dismissals. Terrible things. Dragged out of their homes, beaten, even killed. Aren't you still in great danger as long as you stay here?"

"What you've heard is absolutely correct. The Nazis are on the rampage all over the country. Many Jews are suffering horribly. But for me it's different. My work gives me considerable safety. As you know, I'm well-known abroad; I correspond with colleagues in several countries. Hitler would not risk harming me."

"But I've heard that the beatings and all those terrible things are only the work of certain elements, not of the Nazis. That they're actually contrary to Hitler's own orders. Is this true?"

"A scientist is never afraid to say he doesn't know. I don't know."

"But if it turns out not to be true, doesn't it mean that it is still very hazardous for you to stay here? Wouldn't it be much better for you to leave the country?"

"It might be. As a matter of fact, I applied for permission to leave. The request was denied. But Lise, for others, for you, it seems to me extremely unwise for you to remain in Germany."

"I don't believe it could be dangerous for me. After all, I'm a resident of Belgium, only here on a visit."

There was much more they wanted to say to each other. Lise and the Professor agreed that she would return the next day.

✝✝✝

The dinner at the house that night was excellent. Hilda—if she was the one who had prepared it—was a great cook. Steeg and Lise again had champagne. She drank several glasses; Steeg, even more. Lise was still exhilarated from her day with Stefan. By the end of the meal, she was feeling very relaxed. Earlier in the evening Lise had thanked Steeg for another marvelous day of getting to know her father. After they got up from the table, she turned to Steeg and thanked him again. He started to put his arms around her, and leaned over to kiss her.

Lise was stunned. Steeg's scrupulous behavior towards her ever since that night in the car had convinced her that he understood her feelings, that he would continue to respect them. Had she not been convinced of that, Lise would never have come here, never even seen him again. Now with a sudden shock she felt like a fool for having been so naive. She averted her head from the stink of his breath, brought her hands up, and pushed against his chest— this time with all the strength she could summon.

"No, no!" she said. "No, not again! I told you!"

Steeg's arms had not yet completely encircled Lise. He had the urge to clamp them around her, to find her mouth and force his against it. But for the briefest instant he again heard Hilda's words, "You never had anyone like her. She's in a different class altogether," and in that same instant he dropped his arms and pulled his head away. This might have done for another woman, but not for her. He was being too hasty, pushing too hard. He would wait.

But Steeg was absolutely sure now that, deep down, she wanted him. He could hardly control his joy. He had just moved a little too soon.

The door to the hallway was slightly ajar. There was a point in the hall from which they could be seen through that gap. Standing at that precise point, Hilda, unseen by them, had watched and heard it all.

✠✠✠

They didn't ring or knock. This was 1936, not 1932; Hitler now had absolute and unchallengeable power over every aspect of life in Germany. So they skipped the preliminaries. Professor Mueller awoke to the sound of the front door being forced in, the stomping of heavy boots, the shouting and laughing. His bedroom door opened.

"There he is, the Jew-swine," screamed the leader.

They dragged him out of the bed and into the living room. They started to beat him with their fists and their feet. Professor Mueller was sure they were going to kill him. But just at that point he heard a commotion at the front door, someone coming in, and, above the din, another voice.

"Halt!" the voice screamed.

All at once they stopped.

"Ah, Weigert," shouted the leader, "what is this?" All the others went quiet.

"I need you at the other place. There are a lot more Jews there than I thought. I need all of you…"

"But Weigert…"

"…now!" Weigert shouted.

"But we would have been finished with this one soon."

"You can come back another time. He's not going to go anywhere."

"The books, Weigert, at least the books?"

"Do what you want with the books. They're the venom these animals spread. But be quick about it."

"Good. Get those Jew-books!"

One of them went into the bedroom, pulled the sheets off the bed, and brought them into the living room. They spread one of the sheets on the floor. All working together, they swept the books off the shelves with their powerful arms, sending the books tumbling onto the sheet. They dragged the whole outside, and dumped the books into a large heap on the sidewalk. They continued in this way until, minutes later, the shelves were empty. One of them got a can of kerosene out of the truck and poured it on the pile. A moment later it burst into flame.

He heard their truck as it drove off.

✝✝✝

In the morning, when Lise got out of the car, she noticed a pile of ashes on the sidewalk on her way to the front door of Mueller's house, as if there had been a bonfire there. Although the sight made Lise wonder briefly what could have caused such a fire, she gave it no further thought, focused as she was on her visit to the Professor. Lise continued on up to the front door and rang the doorbell. This time there was no answer. She rang again, but still no one answered. The door appeared to be closed. However, when Lise pushed on it, the door swung open.

She called out, and heard her father's voice. It was faint, as if it came from a distance. She found the Professor in the living room, on the floor. As Lise rushed over, kneeled, and bent over him, thoughts flashed through her mind. At first she thought her father had just fallen. But when Lise saw his face, she let out a shriek. It was swollen and bruised. There was some blood on it, but the bleeding seemed to have stopped. He was looking up at her. His eyes seemed alert, but she saw fear and hatred mixed in them. Lise remembered the door. Steeg had spoken of beatings. But he had said that Professor Mueller was safe here. How could this be?

"My God Stefan! What happened?"

Lise didn't wait for an answer. She got up and rushed into the kitchen. She wet a towel under the warm water faucet, came back to Mueller, and patted and wiped his forehead, his face, and his neck with it. After that she ran back into the kitchen, ran cold water over a different towel, and used it as a compress on her father's bruised face. Lise wondered if there were injuries she could not see, and whether he could move.

"It's all right," the Professor said. "I hurt all over, but I don't think they broke anything. They stopped almost as soon as they started."

"You poor darling," Lise said. "Shall I move you?"

"I think I can get up. Just help me a little."

"Not too quick, now. Do you think this is wise?" Lise said as she gave her father support.

"Yes, fine. That's it. I'm up, you see?" She had her arm around Mueller's back, but he was standing now. Lise helped him over to a chair.

"I'm getting a doctor."

"No, you mustn't. I don't want to call attention. Besides, I don't need one."

"But you do. In your condition. Surely there must be some doctor who…"

"No, they can't be trusted. Don't worry; I'll be all right. Just some coffee, please. It's in the cupboard on the right."

His voice already sounded stronger. To Lise's amazement he was smiling, although the horror still showed in his eyes. Lise was surprised at how composed his mind seemed to be after this terrible beating.

"Lise, I've lived through much worse than this. From the way you are looking at me, I know you are worried. But underneath, I am still a strong man. Anyway, I'm not as old as I look. I'm only fifty. That's only four years older than Hitler."

He was smiling, joking.

"The secret is theoretical physics," he said, as if Lise had spoken the question. "It keeps the mind active."

"I am so relieved. Just now when I walked in, I thought... But you mustn't overdo it. You need to rest."

"Yes, dear Lise, my daughter, you are right. I promise to be good."

Neither of them spoke for a while.

"But the dirty scum did take all my books."

"Oh, God!"

"Don't worry, those can be replaced. Anyway, the most important stuff is safe." He touched his finger to his head.

Lise said goodbye and left almost immediately. She had not said anything more, but she was in a fury.

+++

Professor Mueller hadn't mentioned that the men had said they would be back. He didn't want to frighten Lise any more than he already had; besides, she would have no way to help him. However, there was someone he could contact; up to now he hadn't felt there was any need.

Later that night, there was a knock at the back door. Mueller got up and went to answer it. He walked more slowly than usual because of the beating. He opened the door. The man standing at the doorway had helped the Professor on several occasions before; Mueller knew him well. The fellow had in fact been there earlier in the evening; he had told Stefan at that time not to bring anything with him except the clothes he was wearing, and to leave everything in the house as if he had simply gone to bed.

The man led Mueller through the backyard garden, to the rear fence, which was a brick wall with a tile top. When they reached it, a man's face appeared above the top of the wall in a gap between two tall bushes. The man who was with Mueller lifted the Professor until the other one reached down and lifted him further and over the top. Then the second man helped the first man over.

The area on the other side was a large vacant lot. The men led Mueller to the right until they came to a second wall. The Professor was then lifted up and over this wall too, and taken from that garden into the house at the front of it. Stefan was then left with an old lady who showed him to a small bedroom upstairs. She told Mueller that she and her sister shared a bedroom downstairs, and that he would be staying in this room. The old woman also said the room had not been used in years. She pointed to a small iron bed and the small sink that was in the room, and said that the toilet was across the hall. She told the Professor that she would bring him his breakfast in the morning, and that he was not at any time to go downstairs.

When the woman brought breakfast the next day, she opened a small closet built into one of the walls, and stepped into it. When she pressed on what appeared to be part of a molding at the back of the closet, that back swung open. Beyond it was a smaller space. Except for the panel at the rear of the closet, this space had no walls; it was just a void under the roof. She said that if it became necessary he might have to hide in there. She pointed to a pipe that came up through the floor. She tapped out on the pipe a signal that they would use as a warning. If he heard that signal, he was to go into the space.

CHAPTER 13

STEEG WAS SMILING when he walked in the house. However as soon as he saw Lise he knew it meant bad news, though he couldn't have guessed what.

"Lise, what is the matter?"

"When I got there today, he had been beaten. It was awful!"

"Beaten?"

"Yes. Bruises all over him. Thank God he is alive."

"But that's not possible."

"That's what you told me before. I thought... How could this happen?"

"I wish I knew."

"But you said you would have extra precautions taken. That the house would be watched."

All Steeg could see were his plans crumbling.

"I did, yes. The house, watched. Yes."

"That was the one thing I was afraid of. That because of my visit, somehow..."

"Oh, I'm sure it was not your visit. I did tell you about the risk. But this had nothing to do with your visit."

"Yes, but..."

"It's just the basic situation. The danger, I mean. I also told you there are these rogue elements."

"Yes, you did, but you said it would be all right."

"Obviously, I was wrong. But it didn't happen because of your visit, I can assure you."

"I hope not. Because meeting my father has opened up a whole new world for me. It has truly been wonderful. But this worries me terribly. I'm frightened. About what may happen to him next. Josef, isn't there anything you can do to help?"

"I think there is."

"Maybe you don't have as much control as you think. Over these rogue elements, I mean. I just wonder. Because you told me before, that it was going to be all right. And now…"

"Lise, you are right. I did make those promises to you. And I had received assurances. That the house would be protected, watched. Instead, someone lied to me. But I beg you to believe me; the last thing I would want to do is to fail you. Yet it seems that's what happened. I am terribly disappointed."

Lise didn't know whether she could believe Steeg or not. But this sounded plausible. He had brought her all this way, arranged for her to be reunited with her father, sent her there again this morning, and then this. Obviously what had just happened must have been beyond his control.

"Josef, I know how much you have tried. It's obvious to me now that my father is at best still in great peril. I'm wondering. Wouldn't the best thing be if he could get out of there, even out of the country?"

"Now that's strictly forbidden by the authorities. I don't see how…" He paused, as if to think for a moment. "But perhaps…" Steeg's voice had trailed off again.

"Oh, do you think you could help him do that?"

These were the words Steeg had been waiting to hear.

"Yes there may be a way," he said slowly.

"Oh, thank God! I felt sure you could."

"Now, I will try. You must understand, I will try, but you see the kind of people we're up against. I can't guarantee that I will be successful."

"You said you had the right contacts."

"Yes. This time I will go higher. I should have done that the last time."

Lise was skeptical about what Steeg was telling her. She just kept staring at him.

"You have my word."

She felt torn. Steeg's personal behavior towards her had been revolting, yet he had done this marvelous favor of connecting her with Professor Mueller. She could not reconcile the two. The little experience she had had with men did not equip her for this. Erich, while he had been with her, had been the essence of tact. Although Henri and the others had had only one thing on their mind, they had never done anything against her wishes.

"Josef, you are a puzzle to me. What happened last night…"

"Lise, what happened last night will not happen again. I should have known better. Please forgive me. I only want what is best for you. Surely you can see that."

She could not deny it. But Lise was not going to admit it to him.

"And I know how you must feel, with your father… the terrible things that happened today. I sympathize with you, and I will do everything in my power for you. I assure you, you can count on me."

What Steeg was saying now had the ring of truth.

"I'm leaving immediately to start on this," he told her. "I will work on it all night if I need to. I hope to have some news for you in the morning."

"I am grateful."

"And I hope to earn that gratitude."

"You already have."

"I hesitate to say it, but do I dare hope for more?"

Lise could not believe Steeg had said that. She was furious. She did not answer.

✝✝✝

The only time André had seen Trevor Exenby since the war was in October 1935. Trevor had called André and said he needed to speak to him. Laroche had known it was something crucial. The two men had agreed that André would go over to England so they could talk face-to-face.

Although they hadn't seen each other during all those years, André and Trevor had been in touch for almost the whole period. Laroche was the one who had originally re-established the connection. He had known that Trevor Exenby had planned to complete his graduate studies at Oxford. Laroche had been greatly relieved and pleased when he in fact found Trevor there shortly after the war. From then on, the two had communicated from time to time.

From Oxford, Exenby had gone on to the Foreign Office, where he had been employed ever since. He was not working there as a policy-maker, but was one of the many civil servants who were the strength of the Foreign Office. For his part, André, without disclosing any compromising details, had kept him informed of what his contacts in Germany were accomplishing.

Trevor's work had kept him fully informed of Germany's unrelenting preparation for war; he had therefore given up the view that no country would ever want to start another such war. It became clear that Germany now presented an enormous and increasing threat to Britain and its allies. André had been right, and Trevor told him so.

However, Trevor was still in the minority in Britain. His generation was sandwiched between two others, both of which remained equally paralyzed in the face of the growing threat presented by Germany. Despite the calamity of the First World War, the faith of Trevor's father Alistair Exenby in the supremacy and imperishability of the British Empire remained unshaken. He believed that what Hitler was doing was good for Germany and good for the Empire; he also had substantial investments in Germany. Trevor's son Roger Exenby, on the other hand, had grown up a pacifist and was one of the university students who, two years before, had adopted a resolution vowing never to fight in a war.

Trevor felt he understood the totally different reasons why those two generations took such similar positions. They both genuinely grieved for what the war had done to Trevor's generation. However, his father Alistair's generation foolishly remained blind to the threat that Germany presented. On the other hand, Roger's generation saw that threat, but believed that they could make it go away by passing resolutions.

To Trevor the great tragedy was that the ruling circles in Britain, and the government itself, showed little if any concern about the worsening developments.

There were, however, a few outside the government who held the opposite view. Foremost among these was Winston Churchill, at that time a Member of Parliament. Churchill, working from his home in Chartwell about twenty miles south of London, had become the center of a group who secretly supplied him with reports of what was going on in Germany.

Trevor was one of the participants, albeit a minor one, in this process, and he had on a few occasions been given the task of driving to Chartwell to inform Churchill in person of certain recent developments. Exenby had driven down the steep winding driveway leading to the ancient house, and had been taken to Churchill himself. On two of these occasions, Churchill had asked for further details, which Trevor had provided as best he could. Through this process, the two had become somewhat acquainted.

Before André's visit, Trevor needed to obtain clearance from Churchill, through one of his confidants, for the limited information he wanted to communicate to Laroche. Since André was already known to Churchill's unofficial intelligence group, and had on at least one occasion provided useful information obtained through his contacts, he was considered very safe. Within a few days, Trevor was told that he had permission for this.

✝✝✝

André decided to make the trip to England by plane. There was regular service now between Brussels and the Croydon airfield in London. The new Instone Air Line biplanes were roomy, fast—with speeds of one hundred miles an hour—and believed to be safer than the earlier planes, two of which had crashed on this same run only two years before.

Trevor met him at the airfield around noon and drove him directly to his father's great house in Kent. What Trevor had to tell André could be said very briefly, but the visit would be a good excuse to catch up on everything else. André and Trevor both had agreed that this house would be the ideal meeting place. They would be pulling into its graceful driveway at about two o'clock. As they were both anxious to take care of business, they had decided that they would get to that almost immediately. Later they would have a leisurely dinner and a quiet evening. André would fly back to Brussels the next morning.

The clock had just rung half-past-two when both men sat down in the imposing main living room. Like his father, Trevor loved this particular room, mainly because of the views it afforded both of his family's estate and of the Kentish countryside beyond.

They said very little about the war itself. What had happened was too dreadful to relive. Besides, nature's healing process had intervened, shrouding even the most painful recollections. It had also put a deceptively benign gloss on the memories of the few small, consoling things, like the warmth of a cup of coffee, or the rare and brief reprieves away from the front. Without mentioning this, both Trevor and André realized that it was best to leave these things alone.

Trevor was impressed with how well-informed André was; he was as aware of Germany's rearmament and preparations for war as Trevor was, at least up to a few months ago. They were both distressed by the Allies' perverse insistence on looking the other way.

"Hitler's now begun the production of aircraft," Trevor said. "Aircraft, for Christ's sake!"

This was news to André.

"And he has started war games—all over the country," Trevor continued. "People in Germany are bragging that their country will soon be at war."

"And the Allies remain indifferent."

"Hitler's about to test them."

"Where?"

Trevor got up, went over to the large window, and looked out. Immediately before them lay the garden. Beyond it, and separated from it by a very low hedge, a broad, perfectly-groomed lawn stretched gently downward, stopping in the distance at a line of trees which ran along the banks of a small stream. Beyond that stream, the ground rose to a low crest, but the great height at which the house stood enabled Trevor to see over the top of the crest to the lands beyond and to the distant horizon in the direction of the Channel and, beyond it, of France and the Continent. As his mind traveled across the Channel, Trevor saw again the bloodied trenches, heard again his comrades' shouts at their anticipation of glory, remembered again their screams of agony and despair. As he looked at the gentle scene that now lay before him, Trevor knew that there could be no greater glory than the glory of peace, not the coward's peace of denial, but the peace for which their comrades had paid such a terrible price.

As certainly as he had ever known anything before, Trevor also knew that from beyond that horizon, beyond the Channel, and beyond France, the despot was at this moment preparing once more to violate that country's soil, and that this time he would strike across that Channel, and, bloodying England's own shores, would assault these very slopes. Unless he was stopped in time.

Trevor knew that André, like him, had long been concerned about the Rhineland. This was a fifty-kilometer-wide strip of land located inside Germany and running along the Rhine River, which separates Germany from France. After World War I, fearful that Germany might at some future time once again attempt to invade Belgium and France, the victorious Allies included in the Treaty of Versailles a provision making the Rhineland a buffer zone. The Treaty of Versailles forbade Germany from ever maintaining any military facilities or armed forces in that buffer zone, this despite the fact that the Rhineland remained in all other respects an integral part of Germany. To put teeth into this provision, the parties also entered into the Locarno Pact, which provided that if Germany ever did attempt to reoccupy the Rhineland with armed forces, the Allies were not only allowed, but also obligated, to march in and expel the German forces from the Rhineland.

Trevor was still looking out the window when he spoke. "Mr. Hitler has had his high command draw up plans for the reoccupation of the Rhineland."

"How did you find that out?"

Trevor turned to face André.

"I can't tell you. But I can also tell you that German troops are preparing for it at this moment."

"Same question."

"Same answer."

André smiled at his friend's discretion. "I thought so." He then paused, growing serious at this news.

"I predict," André said, "that the Allies will continue to display their same blind, suicidal indifference, and let him get away with it."

Trevor had moved away from the window, and now sat down in a large armchair near André. He was looking straight at Laroche, and his face became more animated as he spoke.

"There's a big difference," Exenby said, "between building weapons and occupying forbidden territory with them."

"The Allies will do nothing."

Trevor's voice rose. "You may be right. If they indeed do nothing, they will have missed the chance to stop Hitler while he's still inside Germany. If they do nothing now, he will go on to the next step. And that..."

"...that will no longer be inside Germany."

"Exactly. His next step will be to invade another country. If they let him do that, he will go on to the next step, and then the next, until it's too late and there is another World War. But if they make a stand this time, I mean if they *fight*, there and then, they will stop him."

"Isn't it already too late for that?"

"André, it's not too late." Exenby was speaking vehemently now. "Hitler has been building weapons for some time, but he has only started conscription within the last few months. His total forces are still minuscule, a few tens of thousands of men at the most. But France alone has an army of more than half a million men, not counting its reserves, an enormous superiority over the Germans. Plus there's France's massive tank forces and artillery, of which Germany has very little. And that's only France. If you add Britain and the others..." He left the sentence unfinished.

"So the big question remains, will the Allies strike back at him?"

"It's the only question. Because Hitler is no fool. He is well aware of how powerful we are, and how weak he still is. His plan to reoccupy the Rhineland is nothing but one colossal gamble. If we fight, he'll just retreat."

"I still think it would take a miracle for the Allies to decide to fight."

"I am working on that miracle. And in the event that it should happen, then Hitler's whole system could collapse."

"If it does happen, that would surprise me, but it would be great news."

For a few minutes neither of them spoke. André stood up.

"In any case," Laroche said, "before I leave, I want one more favor from you."

"You shall have it."

"I think you know how dangerous the work is that my contacts in Germany are doing." Exenby nodded. "But it's proof that there are Germans who abhor what Hitler is doing, brave Germans who are risking their lives. How soon do you expect that Hitler will give the order to reoccupy?"

"It will not come for several more months."

"Is your information that precise?"

"Yes. I am very close to the center of things. And I will know when it's imminent."

"That's what my contacts will need to know."

"When it is actually about to happen, and I say '*when*,' not '*if*,' I will be one of the first to know. And I will let you know, immediately. Can you have someone contact me?"

"Raoul Maartens…"

"Your old corporal!"

"You remembered! Yes. He is actually the one with the contacts.

He and I work together like this." André held up his index and middle fingers, twisted together. "I'll ask Raoul to get in touch with you for the arrangements."

✝✝✝

That had been in October 1935. It was now early in 1936. Trevor, through Raoul, had kept André informed all along. During the rest of 1935, things had remained essentially the same. But after the start of the new year the situation began to change. In early January, Hitler moved four divisions up to the edge of the demilitarized zone. The French and the British spent the rest of the month, and into February, "consulting" over it.

╅╅╅

When André and Raoul discovered that both Steeg and Lise had left Brussels, they immediately knew what had to be done: get Professor Mueller out of the country. Until that was accomplished, the Professor would continue to serve both as lure for Steeg's entrapment of Lise and as Steeg's prey himself. Within a few days of this discovery, word came from Exenby that Hitler's reoccupation of the zone was now imminent.

This presented André and Raoul with a difficult decision. Risky as it was for Professor Mueller to remain in Germany, any attempt to get him out of the country now would be that much more dangerous; the Germans would certainly patrol all borders with heightened vigilance from this point on. The alternative was to get Mueller to a secure hiding place, and keep him there until after the reoccupation had taken place. If the Allies did nothing, Professor Mueller's situation would still be critical, but no worse than right now; in fact it would probably ease up, at least for a while, once the Germans realized that the Allies would not fight. If, on the other hand, the Allies did come to their senses and attack the invading troops, and if, as Trevor expected, Hitler's whole system were to collapse as a result, Mueller could be saved without the peril of an attempted escape. The best alternative was clear—locate Mueller, take him into hiding, and wait.

All of this assumed that they would be able to locate all three of them—Steeg, Lise, and Mueller— in the first place. Until that was done, all the rest was speculation.

Their first break came with a report that Steeg had been located. He was in Munich. This confirmed what André and Raoul had both suspected. It was time to leave for Munich.

✝✝✝

Before leaving, André arranged to speak to Trevor once more. They both felt that meeting in person would be safer than the telephone for what they had to discuss. This time Trevor flew to Brussels. Both short of time, the two met in a small restaurant not far from the airfield.

"Trevor, our contacts are working on one case right now. I can't say that this case is more important than the others; no life is worth more than another. But this one involves a man who murdered innocent children during the war, and is now free and prowling for more victims."

André hesitated. He knew that he had told Exenby about Dinant. It might look as if he were just asking for help with his personal revenge. But then, Laroche thought, this was not just personal.

"This is the man who killed my father, my mother, and my sister. I actually saw him kill my mother and sister. We have tracked him down. He is about to strike. His prospective victims this time include a well-known scientist, one who is admired and respected throughout the world. We are planning to get this scientist out of the country, and the Nazis want at all costs to prevent him from leaving, to keep him from attesting before the world to Hitler's horrors. So you can appreciate the risks involved.

"If the miracle should happen, then this man could be saved without the risk of an escape. So we would much prefer to wait. Here is what I need. There's no need for you to tell me when the reoccupation takes place; that will be big news everywhere. But as soon as you know whether the Allies will fight or not…"

"That you shall know the minute I know."

"Trevor, you are indeed a true friend."

"Yes, I am. And so are you."

Trevor flew back to London the same day. André and Raoul left for Munich that evening.

✝✝✝

They had decided that the best way to get from Brussels to Munich was by car. Raoul had recently driven across the border numerous times; the car he used, which had German license plates, had become familiar to the customs men at one particular crossing point. His papers and André's were in perfect order, and when the two got to the border, they were waved through. Some distance inside Germany André and Raoul stopped at a farm, where they switched vehicles and drove on in a car that the farmer had ready for them.

CHAPTER 14

*L*ISE HAD BEEN SO FILLED with anxiety and distress that she had hardly slept at all. She was up long before breakfast. Instead of waiting in her room, Lise dressed and went downstairs. The last of the night's darkness was still fading when Steeg arrived. She went up to him as soon as he walked in. Her face was pale and drawn.

"What news have you got?"

"Not good, I'm afraid."

"What now?"

"I am terribly sorry, but…"

"He's dead." Lise was sure of it.

"No. He's not. But he's gone."

"Gone?"

"From the house. I found out only a few minutes ago."

It was as if Steeg had struck her. Lise felt weak, as if she were going to collapse right there. But within an instant her strength returned. And her anger.

"But you promised me! You said you would do everything in your power! Instead, you tell me he's gone. I thought you were going to have the house watched."

"But I did. Our people saw them take him from the house."

"Your people saw it, and they did nothing?"

Steeg had a moment of panic. If he told Lise the truth, that Professor Mueller had not been seized by rogue Nazis, but instead rescued by Mueller's own sympathizers, Lise would realize that Steeg had lost the one thing that actually kept her in his power, namely his own power to regain control over the Professor. He could not tell her the truth.

"Lise, you have to realize…It's not that simple. There were a lot of them, big strong thugs, enraged, armed with guns." He was trying to talk to her as one talks to a child, in soft, consoling tones. But as he spoke, Steeg realized that those roles were becoming reversed.

"If our people had tried anything," Steeg went on, "they would have been killed, maybe your father too. We can't do it that way. But our people saw it and followed them, and we know where they are keeping him. That's the good news."

"But they might kill him any time." Steeg was pleased to see that Lise sounded even more desperate than he felt. He might still be able to see his plan through to the end.

"There is that possibility, but I think it's remote. If the men had wanted that they could have done it right there and then."

"But why would they be holding him?"

"I don't know. But the important thing is that we will rescue him."

"How can I believe it?"

"Lise, I am telling…"

She broke in. "I am beginning to wonder about what you tell me. I only know what has happened. First that awful beating, and now this…"

"I know how distressing this is. I don't blame you for being upset. Not at all, believe me. Lise, I am dedicated to helping your father, rescuing him. But, as I said, if we had tried at that moment, it would have been too soon. It would only have backfired on us."

Lise didn't answer, but Steeg saw that he had her attention.

"It was just last night that you and I spoke about the attack on your father. That they struck so soon is only bad luck. There was no way I could have prevented that. It happened too soon. But my fondest wish is to help you, and I will use my contacts to make this rescue. However I must tell you that doing so will put me at great risk, because there are all kinds of people out there. One can never be completely sure where someone stands, even some of the people I know. But I will do it, I will do it for you, and I beg you to be patient just a while longer. I will not disappoint you."

Lise was skeptical. Too many things had gone wrong. The repeated promises to help her father, to keep him safe, then the repeated disappointments. Hope, elation, had given way to doubt.

✝✝✝

At André and Raoul's next stop along the way, one of Raoul's contacts gave them a further report on Steeg's where-abouts. A house had been located, one that Steeg was known to have used in the past. It did not appear that he was staying there, but a young woman had arrived there within the past few days. Since then, Raoul's people had seen her leaving and coming back to the house several times, each time by car. The fact that Steeg, and apparently Lise also, had been located was good news; however at the same time the fact that he evidently was holding Lise captive was alarming. Taking turns at the wheel, they drove through the night.

✝✝✝

Underneath his almost cloying appeal to Lise's patience, Steeg was boiling with rage and frustration. Here, just when his most fervent desires were within reach, they were in danger of being snatched away. It was as if thugs from his own revered Nazi movement by their neglect were conspiring with the Jews to undo him. Lise would have been shocked and sickened if she had known that the noble "rescue" Steeg had promised would in fact be a merciless hunt for those who were trying to save Professor Mueller.

From the house Steeg went directly to SS headquarters, where he gave a high-priority order— find the Jew Mueller.

✝✝✝

Steeg had arranged for champagne and appetizers to be brought up to Lise's sitting room at seven, with dinner to be served later. He seemed to be in a very good mood. He was standing in front of the large sideboard, where the champagne and appetizers had been set up, holding a half-empty glass. His eyes lit up when Lise came in.

"I have good news," he said. He seemed bubbling with enthusiasm.

"We have had good news before, and it has turned to disappointment."

"Ah, but this is different. This morning after I left you I reached the person I wanted." Steeg filled a glass and handed it to her. "Do have some champagne."

Lise was in no mood for champagne, but she took the glass. He refilled his.

"The people before were lower-echelon," Steeg said. "That was my mistake, I already told you, *my* mistake. But I learned that lesson. I can't give names, I'm sure you can understand that. But this time it is, let us say, someone very high up." His manner told Lise that she should be impressed.

"So I can safely say," he continued, "that you can look forward to seeing your father freed."

"That would be good news."

"But, my dear Lise, it *is* good news. You see, you were so skeptical. I can't blame you, but you needn't have been. As I told you, I want nothing more than to help you. And you must admit I have been of more than a little help to you."

Lise had to acknowledge the truth in what Steeg was

saying. He had brought her here, had arranged the meetings with her father. Perhaps she had been too harsh.

"Yes, you have. I admit I was skeptical yesterday. But really, Josef, what you have done for my father, and for me, has been splendid."

They were both still standing near the sideboard. Lise had put her glass down after a few sips. Steeg was on his fourth glass of champagne. He moved closer to her.

"I'm so happy that you realize how much I have been able to do for you. Because it has not been easy. It has turned out to be much more difficult than I ever thought. You saw with your own eyes how vicious they can be."

Lise thought of how pitiful her father had looked when she last saw him.

"To tell you the truth," Steeg said, "had I known, I probably would never have undertaken it, and let me add, for anyone else I would have given up by now. But for you…" He stopped and took a quick breath. "As we have spent more and more time together, I feel we have become even closer. I know that you like me. I am not insensitive to that."

"Don't start again. I thought I made this clear to you. I am grateful to you, and I like you as a friend. But that's all."

"Lise, I remember, and that's all I'm saying. But sometimes actions speak louder than words."

"What actions?"

"For example, when we danced, the way you laughed so kindly at my clumsiness. And the way you looked at me when we first met, in the restaurant. I could see it in your eyes."

"Could see what?"

"Lise, don't be coy. That certain look in your gorgeous blue eyes. You looked at me again in that exact same way at the Métropole. And in the car…"

"In the car!"

"Oh I know what you said then. But looks, just like actions, tell more than words. When you turned towards me that time in the car, and let me kiss you. Your lips spoke for you."

"I can't believe this!"

"And when you got here and you spoke those lovely words and said how grateful you were, not once, but on at least two occasions. And after dinner just the other night when you stood tantalizingly close to me, with that look in your eyes, and thanked me again, and I started to put my arms around you…"

She shook her head. "But Josef, I told you right then…"

"Yes, yes, I know what you said. And I respected it. I understood. I had just moved a little too soon. It was bad judgment, I admit. But it is only natural that I should be looking forward… I genuinely like you, much more than 'like,' dare I say love you?"

Steeg had gradually been moving still closer to her, but now he stepped back, just a little.

"Lise, I know you have just been teasing me."

"Teasing you! Is that what you think? Are you crazy?"

Lise's mind went back again to the other night, to Steeg's arms almost clamped around her, his foul breath in her face, his mouth searching for hers. Lise had been taken aback, as she had been in the car. But then, as in the car, she had been reassured by the fact that when she had said no, Steeg had backed off immediately. But Lise realized now that he had no perception of how unwelcome his advances were or how repulsive she had found them.

"Oh, not necessarily on purpose," he went on. "You probably don't even realize that you're doing it. It's so natural for women. But if you knew how terrible it is. To want you so badly, and to be so teased."

"You're out of your mind. Let's end this right here."

"Lise, when one takes as many risks as I have, one is happy to get some appreciation for it." Steeg had gradually come closer again.

"But, Josef, I do appreciate it. But that doesn't mean..."

"Well, I must say I am extremely disappointed. I had expected a little more appreciation from you."

She was amazed. A minute ago Steeg had been speaking of love; now it was "a little more appreciation." More appreciation? He sounded like a waiter complaining about his tip. Did he really have any concern at all for her father's plight? For that matter, did he have any concern at all for her plight? Up to now Lise had thought of Steeg as a friend. But these were not the words of a friend.

"I've already expressed my appreciation. And now that you tell me that my father will be freed, I am more grateful than ever, as you have made my dream, and my father's dream of being free, come true."

Steeg had once more refilled his glass. He took a gulp from it. "Oh, but dear Lise, I think you have misunderstood me."

"How so?"

"I didn't say that he *will* be freed, I said that you can *look forward* to his being freed."

"You're being ridiculous. What's the difference? You said you had arranged everything, at high levels."

"I have. I have." Steeg's voice had now become much softer, almost a whine. "But it's not going to happen automatically. I'm sure you can understand that there are some steps I have to take first."

"What steps?"

"I can't disclose the details, except that those steps will put me at great personal risk."

"Well, that's what you're going to do, isn't it? I don't know what you're saying."

"Simply that if I am to risk everything, before I do take that risk..." He moved very close to her now. "Well, as I just told you, I think our relationship is much more than just friendship."

What was taking place now was altogether different from anything Lise had ever imagined. It frightened her. She took a full step back.

"Are you saying that you will not help my father unless I submit to..." Lise could not bring herself to finish the sentence. "Is that what you just said?"

"Well, I would not put it exactly that way..."

"How would you put it?"

"Lise, I've just told you..."

"And I heard you. 'A little more appreciation?' Is that what all this is about? All your talk about helping my father, all your promises, all those twists and turns, all that has just been so you can lure me in? You've staged this whole sordid show. And you're still at it. What kind of person are you?"

Steeg was moving towards Lise again, but she kept backing away.

"Lise, your father has nothing to do with this. I am not a monster. I am the same man you have known all along. It is just that I like you so much; is that so bad? Do you have any idea of how attractive you are, what effect you have had on me? I lie awake at night. I can't think of anything else but you."

So it was her fault. Lise had seen enough bullies in her young life to recognize this telltale sign— that it's always the victim's fault. It was her fault, and therefore she deserved... what? To be coerced into sex, perhaps raped?

"You liar! Now I see the real you for the first time. You invoke this helpless old man's torments in order to force yourself on me, then blame me in order to conceal your lust. Yes, my eyes have opened for the first time, and I see you clearly, just as I see clearly the evil that is loose here, that unleashes gangs of armed thugs against the most innocent and helpless of the helpless."

Steeg had her backed up all the way to the table. Lise might have been able to escape at the beginning, and she wished now that she had tried. But it was too late; he was between her and the door now, and she would have no chance of reaching it.

"Stay away from me!" Lise said this slowly but firmly, her voice almost a whisper.

"You don't fool me," Steeg said. "Behind all that teasing I see the passion in you. I hear you talking about coercion, but what I see is a magnificent, passionate woman, who pretends anger only to conceal her desire to be mastered."

While Steeg got nearer, Lise reached behind her, as if to support herself on the table. She had earlier spotted a knife there, and now she seized it, keeping it behind her. At that moment Steeg lunged and put his arms around her. He had a firm grip on her now, but her hand, unseen by him, was still holding the knife. Steeg dragged her, as she screamed, to the couch and fell on top of her. Somehow she managed to keep the hand with the knife underneath her.

Lise stopped screaming.

"Don't be in such a rush, Josef. Just give me a minute. It will be much easier that way."

He let go of her and stood up. Lise could see his opened fly, the bulge in his shirttail.

With one quick motion she brought her arm around and held the knife up. It was a large, pointed meat knife.

"You bastard! I will die before I yield to you!" Lise was shouting and her eyes were aflame.

Until a few minutes ago Steeg would have thought her incapable of such an act, but he was now convinced Lise might do it. Even with that sharp knife, she would be no match for him. If she struck at him Steeg felt sure he could disarm her. But Lise's screams, her face, and her eyes told him that she would put up a terrible fight. Steeg's main fear was that in the scuffle she might get injured, even killed. There were certain people, Jews or other enemies of the cause, whom Steeg could harm, even kill, with impunity. But not this young woman, who, although a German national, was a permanent resident of

Belgium, and who would be seen as a guest in this house. It would be one thing to have forced himself into her, quite another to have to deal with the consequences of her being injured—the blood, or killed—her corpse. There would be an inquiry; it would get back to the embassy in Brussels, and to other places. It could destroy his whole career, and ruin all his ambitions. Crazed with desire though Steeg was, his instinct of self-preservation prevailed. At least for this moment.

Steeg was ashamed of himself—not for the ordeal he was inflicting on her, not for what he had tried to do—but for having bungled it. Steeg didn't care one whit about Lise; he hated her for depriving him of what he wanted. Perhaps there might still come a time. A more propitious opportunity might still arise. But for now he stepped back.

"There is no need for that," he said. "I only want to make love to you."

"Come near me and I'll gouge your eye out," Lise screamed at the top of her lungs.

He said nothing more. As Steeg walked out, he slammed the door.

✢✢✢

Lise stepped out of her room much later. She would leave. She had placed all her most essential things in a small bag that could be carried. She would find a telephone and call Suzanne, André, someone. Lise walked to the end of the hall and turned the handle on the door to the stair landing. It was locked. There was no other exit from her floor. She looked out the window; it was a drop of at least seven meters, far too high to jump. Lise pushed and pounded on the door, shouted, then screamed, for a half-hour. No one came. The house was completely quiet.

✢✢✢

The more he thought about it, the more Steeg hated Lise—"this woman," as he now thought of her—for endangering his career. It never occurred to him that Lise had had nothing to do with that, that the problem was entirely his own total lack of perception and his inability to control himself. Instead Steeg saw himself as the victim. After all, if Lise had been reasonable and accepted his advances as the others had done before, the affair and his career could both have gone forward. But he had not reckoned with her blockheaded obstinacy.

It would be best to try to forget her for now, to get his focus back on the more important goal of his career. Steeg comforted himself with the thought that until now he had managed to keep his career and his pursuit of her separate from each other. He would have to make absolutely sure that they stayed that way. He was comforted by the thought that he had managed to keep secret her relation to Professor Mueller, and by the knowledge that the letters from Margot Hermann, that were a key link in the chain of proof of the adoption, were safe among his papers.

As Steeg thought of this, a small wave of concern rippled through his mind. He went into his small office downstairs. He unlocked the desk drawer and pulled out the folder in which he kept the two letters. They were not in it. Frantically, he looked through all the other folders, turned over every sheet in the desk. The letters were gone.

✠✠✠

Erich remembered André from the embassy reception and from the fact that Lise had casually mentioned him a few times since then. As a result, he did not hesitate when the man said that Mr. Laroche was in town and would like to see him. The man gave Erich directions to the proposed meeting place—one of Munich's many beer gardens—and a time for the meeting. He told the man that he would be there. Erich made his way there on his own and, as he had been directed, walked around to a building in the rear of the beer garden, which Erich took to be the proprietor's residence. There he found André and Raoul sitting at a large table. André introduced Erich to Raoul, invited their visitor to sit down, and asked if he would like a drink. Erich sat but declined the drink.

"It was nice of you to come," said André. "I'm sure you must be wondering why we asked for you. I wasn't even sure whether you would remember me."

"From the embassy, of course," Erich said. "I remember you well."

"I'll tell you why we wanted to speak to you. It has to do with Miss Hermann. We are concerned about her."

"I don't know what you have in mind, but I should tell you that she and I no longer have anything to do with each other."

"We would not have bothered you, but we assumed—and I realize we may be wrong—that you and she are at least still on friendly terms." André spoke those words as a statement, not a question.

Erich gave no answer but it was obvious that the statement was true.

"We have some information about her, and because we know that she and you have been friends, we thought we should tell you about it. But please don't misunderstand me. We have no wish to intrude into your private life. If you would rather not have us talk about it, or if you would rather leave, you are obviously free to do so."

Whether it was the words that André was speaking, his tone of voice, or some awkwardness that Erich sensed in the air, he did not know which, but something was making him nervous. But what André was saying also aroused Erich's curiosity, and the curiosity was just outweighing the nervousness.

"Of course, even if you don't want to hear about it," André said, "you are also welcome to stay. We can find other things to talk about. Better things, I would say."

"No, I'm prepared to hear it," Erich said evenly. "But before you tell me anything, I have a question for you."

Both men's eyebrows rose questioningly.

"I'm aware that you must know a few things about me," Erich said. "For one, you know that I work for Mr. Steeg. Since you are concerned about Lise, I assume this has to do with him. So why would you be telling me these things?"

Neither of the others spoke.

"Aren't you afraid that I would tell Mr. Steeg what I have learned from you?"

"No," said André. "We're not."

"I've also told you that Lise and I no longer…" Erich paused.

"Do you know where Miss Hermann is at the moment?" said André, getting past the awkward moment.

"It's of no concern to me."

"We understand that she is with Mr. Steeg."

"I am aware of that."

"You are not concerned about that?"

"No."

"If we told you that her life, her safety, is at risk, would you not be concerned about that?"

"She is not in any danger."

"How do you know?"

"I don't believe I am giving any secrets away here, but—it's pretty well known—she and Mr. Steeg are having an affair."

"Is that what you think?"

"I know that it's true."

"Mr. Behrndt, there are certain facts, facts that we ourselves have learned only recently, that will completely change your view of what has happened to Miss Hermann. But as I said before, if you don't want to hear about them, we can end this conversation right now."

To Erich all of this still sounded like nonsense, and he was tempted to stop the conversation then. But his curiosity, even further aroused now, again prevailed.

"No, go ahead. I'll listen."

"You say you are aware that Miss Hermann—Lise—is with Mr. Steeg. Do you know where?"

At this point Erich was not interested in playing hide-and-seek or any other games. "I've heard reports about a certain house," he said.

"Our information is the same." André paused and looked kindly at Erich, then said, "Perhaps you already know this, although that would surprise me, but Lise is partly Jewish."

These two men were so obviously misinformed that Behrndt felt sorry for them. He made no answer, and his face showed no reaction.

"I know that this information may come as a surprise," said André.

"It might have if it were true."

"I can understand that you might find it hard to believe. We had the same reaction. But I can assure you it is correct."

"Who told you all this? And why?"

"I can't tell you that."

"And I suppose that you have no proof of these accusations."

"They are facts, not 'accusations,' as you call them, but we can't prove them to you."

Erich was shaking his head in disbelief.

"Lise often talked about her parents. If this is so, why didn't she ever mention it?"

"She didn't know about it."

Erich smirked.

"Lise was adopted, but she was never told."

"Anything else?" Erich was getting impatient.

"Yes. Her father is a professor. He's being persecuted."

"Let me assume all this is true. Why are you telling it to me?"

"I told you. Because we are concerned about Lise."

"I don't... What is there to be concerned about?"

"Steeg is planning to use this information against Lise."

"Planning to use...?"

"That's why she has come to Munich. We have reason to believe that Steeg has used extortion in the past."

Although Erich was in no position to tell them what he knew on that subject, this hit home.

"And we doubt that Steeg will react well if you tell him what you learned here," André continued. "And it doesn't matter whether or not you believe that what we have told you is true. If it is, you would be telling Steeg that you know he is having an affair with a Jew. And if it's not an affair, you would be demonstrating to him that you know enough to infer what he is planning against Lise. Affair or no affair, you must agree that Steeg would make sure you told no one else. I'll leave the details to your imagination. On top of that, in either case you would also be admitting that you yourself had a... friendship... with a Jew. I'll let you decide how he might use that information. Now if everything we have told you is false, I'm not sure how telling it to him would help you; however, most important, we don't think you would take that chance, the chance that it may be true after all, with all its consequences."

Erich wondered not only whether any of this was true, but also why they were telling it to him.

"You may ask why we are telling you all this," André said, as if Behrndt had asked the question.

Erich just stared at Laroche with an expectant look.

"I know you have told us that you and Miss Hermann no longer 'have anything to do' with each other, as you put it. And we don't know how close you are to each other. However let me just say that for her sake we think you will refrain from telling Mr. Steeg the things we have told you."

"*You* are taking *that* chance."

"Yes," André said confidently.

The subject had been exhausted.

"Now there's one other thing that we have not mentioned. One other chance that we are willing to take. We think that once you have thought about all this, you may decide that you want to help Lise. At least you will if you become convinced that what is going on between the two of them is not an affair."

Erich started to speak, but André cut him short. "There's no need for you to decide about this now," he said sympathetically. Why don't you think it over?" André scribbled something on a piece of paper and handed it to Erich.

"Memorize this number. If you ever decide you want to help her, call. They will know how to reach us. But just in case you are wondering, whoever uses that number will be thoroughly screened before being put in touch with us."

Erich stood up. "Thank you. I must be going," he said.

"There is one more thing you should know." Erich sat down again. "I'm sure you must realize that we would not have asked you to come here without making inquiries about you." Erich had assumed as much. "We know that you have participated in... I'll say it plainly. We know that you killed a Jew."

Raoul understood what André was doing.

"That shows how wrong your information is. I never killed anyone, Jew or otherwise."

"Our information comes from a very reliable source. You say that it is incorrect?"

"I just told you. It's completely false."

"But who would have given us such false information?"

"That's for you to find out."

After Erich had left, the two men spoke briefly.

"What do you think?" said André.

"Well, there's two things I noticed," said Raoul. "First, he seems to be very poorly informed. Second, I was impressed by his response when you told him that the record showed he had killed a Jew."

"I didn't tell him that."

"I know. If you had, you would have been telling him the truth. You told him our information showed he had killed a Jew. That wasn't true."

"So I concealed some of what we have learned. But I'm glad I did."

"Of course. Your little deception drew the truth out of him. I'm not sure whether Behrndt will ever risk helping us. However, if he should, it could help a lot."

✝✝✝

That same evening was one of the nights when some of the younger men employed in the office where Helmut Stangl worked went out for a few drinks. Helmut invited Erich to come along. Erich had participated in similar evenings in Brussels. There, as was the case in Stangl's office in Munich, these young men usually met in the same small beer establishment. In Munich as in Brussels, several of them considered the prime objective of these evenings to be inebriation, an objective which they usually managed to achieve in a remarkably short time. Some of the others usually drank more modestly, and actually concentrated on the conversation. On this particular evening in Munich, the conversation consisted largely of humorous remarks, some barbs, and the telling of jokes, and, as on other evenings, the accompanying laughter increased in exponential proportion to the amount of beer that had been downed.

In Brussels, although Erich had more education than most of the others, he never made a show of it. He spoke without affectation, and knew how to hurl a witty comment at one or the other of them that broke the group into rollicking laughter, while at the same time never hurting his target's feelings. As a result, they appreciated Behrndt's wit and his unpretentious demeanor, and he was popular with them. Here in Munich, however, Erich felt he was more of an outsider, and he listened more than he spoke.

At one point on this particular evening, just as usually happened in Brussels, both the conversation and the jokes started turned to the subject of Jews. One man told a joke at the Jews' expense, then another did. At this point in Brussels, Erich would have come up with a new joke that the others had not heard. But on this evening, Behrndt remained uncharacteristically quiet, in part because of Erich's status as a guest, but also because his mind was preoccupied with what had been said at his meeting with André and Raoul earlier in the day.

His expression did not show it, but Erich's mind was in fact pondering the revelations that André had made concerning Lise's ancestry. André's disclosure had put Erich into a turmoil. Until this moment the path that his life had followed, like the course of a ship, was based on certain assumptions— reefs and shoals on each side, the familiar channel between. But now everything had shifted; where there had been deep water, rocks now lurked just below the surface. Everything he had ever known told him that Lise Hermann was an Aryan, pure and untainted, but now he was to believe that she had Jewish blood in her veins. As the others went on with their chatter, Behrndt struggled to absorb the idea that Lise was Jewish, in order to sound out how it would feel and what he would do if she were.

Aside from the neighbor who had helped his mother in her time of distress, Erich had never known even a single Jew, except for Jacob Grunberg and the others that night in the forest, and their pitiful appearance had only filled him with compassion. Sitting in the Munich beer hall now as the others laughed, Erich—for the first time in his twenty-three years— began to wonder whether everything he had ever heard about Jews, about the evil conspiracies and the filth, might not be true, and whether it even could be true. He knew that if Lise was Jewish, everything he had ever heard about Jews had to be false. But he also thought about Steeg. Whatever could be said about Steeg, his loyalty to the Nazi cause, and to Adolf Hitler himself, was beyond question. Womanizer though he was, Steeg would never have any association with a Jewess. Erich was aware of Steeg's extensive connections within the Party, and of his practice of having everyone and everything investigated. Steeg surely would have had Lise investigated before getting involved with her, perhaps even before he had met her that first time in the restaurant. Yet Steeg had since then, as he had made plain to Erich, become deeply involved with her.

The conclusion was clear. The story about Lise being Jewish was just that, a story. André Laroche and his friend Raoul were simply mistaken. And although it made Erich's skin crawl at the thought, what remained absolutely indisputable was that what was going on between Lise and Steeg was a love affair.

✝✝✝

Munich had been designated by Hitler as the Capital of the Nazi Movement, and it was there, on Meiserstrasse, that the Nazi Party had its national headquarters. As Steeg arrived, he was not unaware of the symbolism of having been summoned to appear at this place. The room to which he had been ordered to report was large, and seemed to be a sort of courtroom. About half of the seats in it were occupied, the front third of them with SS men, the rest with civilians. Only four of the SS besides Steeg were officers, and they were all sitting in the front row.

In the chair from where one would have expected a judge to be presiding sat a civilian; he was apparently some sort of functionary. A stack of files as high as the top of the man's head filled the left side of his desk. For what seemed to be a long time this man sat doing nothing. Then a telephone, which

Steeg noticed for the first time, rang on the man's desk, and the functionary answered it. Two seconds later he hung up, and picked up the top file in the stack, looked briefly at its cover, and called out a man's name. That man stood up and identified himself. The functionary held the file up in the air.

The man went up to the functionary, took the file, and left the room; the functionary went back to doing nothing.

Things continued in this fashion for the entire morning and into the afternoon. Either there were only a few rooms available or the proceedings were lengthy, because the phone calls were far between. Steeg was quickly disabused of any expectation that being an officer would get him preferential treatment; none of the three groups—officers, ranks, or civilians—seemed to have any priority over the others. The process appeared to be completely random. At lunchtime the functionary was relieved by another, but all those who were waiting were required to remain in their seats and the process, such as it was, continued.

At mid-afternoon Steeg's name was called, and he picked up his file. Room 187, to which he was assigned, was long and narrow. It was completely empty except for a small desk at the far end, behind which sat an SS officer, and a smaller desk to one side and in front of the other, at which sat a man who turned out to be a clerk. Behind the officer were the obligatory oversized Nazi flag and portrait of Hitler.

"Come forward!" barked the officer.

When Steeg got to within about five meters of him, the officer ordered him to halt. The officer was a young man, with a boyish face; he did not look over thirty. To his surprise, Steeg now saw that he was a *Standartenführer*, a high rank, a colonel. A small plaque on the officer's desk identified him as *SS Standartenführer* Theodor Klecker.

"Identify yourself." The voice that issued from the boyish face was peremptory, the look both insolent and icy. Another immature youngster in an important position; Steeg sensed that this man was not about to display the kind of respect that had bound fellow-officers together in the former days of the SS and even before that in the even wilder days of the *Freikorps*. Steeg soon found out that he was right.

"*SS Hauptsturmführer* Josef Steeg, *Herr Standartenführer*," Steeg said.

"Hand the file to the clerk."

After Steeg had complied, the clerk handed the file to Klecker, who looked at it for a few moments.

"Steeg, you face serious charges," he said. "Racial defilement, specifically by having sexual relations with the Jewess Lise Hermann, in violation of the racial laws and of your oath and duties as an SS officer. Also dereliction of duty, in that you failed to prevent her father, the Jew Stefan Mueller, from escaping into hiding. What is your defense, if you have any?"

Steeg was stunned. He had been dismayed upon discovering that the letters were missing from his desk but, knowing how slowly things usually moved, he had not suspected that a case would be brought against him so soon. Steeg wondered whether he had perhaps been under suspicion, and observation, for some time, and whether, in fact, these charges had even been the result of the disappearance of the letters from his desk. He also wondered whether for some reason he could not fathom, his case had been given special attention, and if so why. Steeg stood dumfounded.

"Do not stand there like an idiot. Your defense, Steeg."

He would have to focus better. "First, *Herr Standartenführer*, as to this woman…"

"Do you deny that charge? I warn you, the evidence is clear. Do you deny that you know her?"

Steeg was used to engaging in this machine-gun style of questioning when he was the inquisitor, and had always enjoyed doing it. Now, on the receiving end, his reaction was not the same; under the barrage he began to feel weak, almost helpless.

"I know her, *Herr Standartenführer*."

As soon as Steeg said it, he wondered whether he had blundered. Was it wise to admit anything? Or would a certain candor, a willingness to admit some things, but not the crucial, damning ones, work to his advantage? Steeg wished he had a lawyer, someone who understood these cases, to tell him what to do. But he knew that was out of the question here.

Klecker looked again at the file. "You have had her transported to a residence in this city frequented by you, and are presently harboring her there. Furthermore you have entered this house at various times of day and night, and remained there for various lengths of time. Do you deny that?"

How could he answer that? There were so many questions rolled into one. Once again, should he, could he even, admit part of it, without destroying his case? And what about the things that some of those questions, like "remained there for various lengths of time," implied? Steeg wanted to explain, but he knew he wouldn't be allowed.

"*Herr Standartenführer*, this woman..."

"You cannot deny that, can you?"

"No, *Herr Standartenführer*." Once again, that terrible dilemma, that doubt.

"Do you deny that you have had sexual relations with her?"

This was better. This was where he would stand and fight.

"I deny that."

"What evidence do you have?"

How could you prove you didn't do something? How unfair if he were to be punished for what he had not even done!

"Answer, Steeg! Do you have any evidence?"

Evidence! How could one stand and fight without any weapon?

"I will swear..."

"I said, what evidence?"

"*Herr Standartenführer*, I cannot prove a negative…"

"So then you admit you have had a sexual relation…"

He had forgotten. He was a small boy. In the orphanage. All those questions. A barrage, like this one. One question, one accusation after the other, over and over. The helplessness. Then the beating. Everything was now crumbling.

"But this woman…"

"Don't interrupt me, don't argue. Just answer. Do you deny that she is Jewish?" Klecker looked at the file again. "I warn you that evidence was found in your own desk."

Steeg said nothing.

"Do you have any defense to that charge?"

He knew his defense was gone. Except for one other thing.

"The woman is not a Jew." He knew, of course, that this defense was not a defense at all; that there was almost no chance that this young SS colonel would not be familiar with the intricacies of the Nuremberg laws. But he could think of nothing else.

"What nonsense is that?"

"Her mother was Aryan, all the way back. Her father was an Aryan, a Protestant…"

"We know all that. You are just being evasive, stalling. You will admit that her father's mother was Jewish, was he not?"

"Yes, *Herr Standartenführer*."

"So she is Jewish, a *Mischlinge*."

"Only of the second degree, *Herr Standartenführer*. And under the racial laws, Germans are not prohibited from having sexual relations with…"

"Steeg, you take me for a fool. You forget that you are an SS, and as such you must meet the highest of standards. You forget that racial purity is our strength. Absolute purity, that is our only standard."

"I have not forgotten, *Herr Standartenführer*."

"Then why have you violated it?"

"I didn't think…"

"Do you have the impertinence to suggest that your oath of loyalty to Adolf Hitler permits you to wallow in that filth like a beast? You have no defense."

The case was lost. It might be hopeless, but there was one thing he could still try.

"If I may, *Herr Standartenführer*. There is just one other thing."

"Yes?"

"It relates to the other charge."

"Well, do you deny that Professor Mueller has disappeared?"

"No, you are correct in that, *Herr Standartenführer*."

"My report will reflect that you are fully responsible for his escape."

"*Herr Standartenführer*, as you have pointed out, the woman in question, Lise Hermann, is in fact Professor Mueller's daughter."

"Yes, but what of it? Steeg, you are just wasting my time."

"Respectfully, *Herr Standartenführer*, if you will hear me out…"

"Get to the point."

"The reason I have sequestered the daughter is to put pressure on the father."

"Ah! Well, I see. Go on, Steeg."

"I plan to tell Professor Mueller that if he attempts to escape…"

"Ah! I must say, Steeg, that sounds creative, almost brilliant. Except for that fact that Mueller has already escaped and you have no idea of where he is."

"Yes, *Herr Standartenführer*, I understand. However, I have been working on that, and I expect to be successful very soon."

"The horse, maybe here we should say the pig, that has left the stable is not usually recovered. I warn you that if you fail to recapture him, you will suffer further consequences.

"Now, as to the matter of the Jewess," *Standartenführer* Klecker continued, "I'm going to have to report your serious violation of the racial laws and of your oath. However, if you are successful, by using the Jewess or by other means, in getting this professor back into our hands, that would certainly be considered in my report. I will therefore suspend the report, but just for the time being."

"Thank you."

"One other thing, Steeg. If there is any evidence that you have even attempted to have sexual relations with this woman, the rest will not matter; your fate will be sealed."

"Thank you, *Herr Standartenführer*, but I can assure you that is not the case."

Steeg had tried every trick he could think of. He had lied. He had lost the case. He had been reduced almost to helplessness. But he had kept on fighting. All the ordeals he had ever been through for so many years, those he had endured and those he had inflicted on others, had toughened his body and hardened his heart. Steeg may have felt like a child but, unlike a child, had proved that he could withstand any punishment and still fight back.

He had only that one chance left. He had to capture Mueller. As Steeg walked out of the national headquarters of the Nazi Party, he felt a surge of excitement at the prospect.

✝✝✝

"How are they doing it?" Steeg asked from behind his desk at the house. One of his men had just told him that some civilians were watching the house.

"There is an abandoned car in the street," the man said, "or at least it appears to be abandoned. It actually comes and goes from time to time, usually staying only briefly, but it has that look. The windows have some kind of coating; you can't see inside, but they can see out."

"How can you be sure that's what it is? That it's not the SS?"

"My contacts checked that. It's not anyone working for the SS. It's probably the Jews, or more likely the vermin who help the Jews."

It could only mean one thing: these civilians knew that the Professor's daughter was in the house. Steeg's first impulse was to have whoever was doing the watching killed. It would be a violation of the strict orders he had been given to avoid violence, but at this point Steeg was desperate. Up to now, failure to keep the Professor from leaving the country would merely have stalled his career. But his disastrous appearance before *Standartenführer* Klecker had changed all that; now this failure would destroy his career, cause him to be imprisoned, and quite possibly cost him his life. With the stakes raised so drastically, it would be far better to violate the orders to refrain from violence and bring the Professor back alive than to obey them and fail. But almost immediately Steeg realized that these men in the car were probably only underlings, and killing them would only be counterproductive. It would be much better to seize this opportunity to make use of them.

"Whoever they are, tell them that if they want to hear from the Professor's daughter, we can be of help."

Steeg's man returned about ten minutes later.

"We are to watch for a signal on the windshield. And if the car is followed, they will not talk."

The next morning, there was a piece of paper on the windshield. Steeg's man went down to the car from the house; in about fifteen minutes he was back.

"They want you to let her go."

"Tell them we have no control over her, that Miss Hermann is free to do as she pleases, and she has made it clear that she doesn't want to go anywhere. They will say they don't believe it. When they do, tell them we would be willing to intercede if they will help us in return."

The man was soon back. "They want to know what you want."

"Tell them we want the Professor turned over to us."

The answer came later that day.

"He said I was to repeat this to you word for word. 'The whole world knows that the Professor has been persecuted and is waiting to see what happens to him, and you must be out of your mind.' That was the entire message."

"Tell them that the Professor is a Jew, that criminal charges have been filed against him, and anyone harboring or otherwise helping him is subject to punishment. But if they turn him over now, no questions will be asked."

There was no response to this message. Steeg thought about it for several more hours. He realized that he might have been too hasty, as was often the case. The reality was that unless he could produce the Professor, unharmed, his career was over.

"Tell them I will meet with them face-to-face, but only with someone who has full authority."

✝✝✝

They had agreed on a small restaurant, more a café actually, on Amalienstrasse, near the University. It was almost always crowded with students, artists, and others of all ages, and would be both convenient and safe. There was to be only one person from each side.

The front part of the café was crowded as usual, mostly with students, many of them drinking beer. Others sat silently and studied, while nursing cups of coffee. Steeg walked through this room into the smaller room in the back. It was still noisy there, but not so loud that they would have to shout. As soon as Steeg entered the room, a man saw him and stood up, smiling and pointing to a chair.

Steeg remembered the face immediately from somewhere, but for a second or two could not remember the place or the context. Then he recognized him, and was startled to see that this was the man they had sent; Steeg remembered him only as the man he had met at the reception, who had seemed very much interested in Lise and had offered to take her home. He had known nothing else about him. Steeg had assumed then that this man's interest in Lise was romantic; he knew nothing more now, and still made the same assumption.

Steeg sat down.

"I remember you," Steeg said. "You are the one who offered to take Miss Hermann home. From the embassy."

"Yes," André said.

"But I am surprised to see you here. I'm aware of your interest in Miss Hermann, but this involves much more than just that. I am at a loss as to why you are here. They sent the wrong person. I don't suppose you even know who Professor Mueller is? I specified someone with full authority."

"Full authority?"

"To decide about Professor Mueller."

"You are right. I don't have any authority to decide about the Professor."

"Do you even know him?"

"I know enough to tell you that no one has that power except the Professor."

"You seem unaware of the fact that he is a Jew, and furthermore has committed crimes."

"What crimes are these?"

"Using his position at the University to spread falsehoods. Communicating with persons abroad in furtherance of the Jewish conspiracy against the German people. Advocating false and pernicious theories under the guise of science. And so forth."

"Ah, 'Jewish physics.'"

"Yes. So you've heard about it?"

"Yes."

"Amazing, isn't it?"

"Yes. The whole notion is shocking."

"I'm pleased to find you to be so perceptive. That is becoming so rare in someone from outside Germany these days."

"Yes, the perception of so many outside of Germany, as you put it, is quite contrary to your perception here on so many things."

"You are so right. Well, this is a good start. Perhaps you and I will be able to get along after all." A waiter came by. "Would you like a drink?" Steeg asked.

André pointed to his mug of coffee resting on the table. "No thank you. But don't let me stop you."

"Some wine, please," Steeg said to the waiter. "French wine."

"I must say," said André, "you have a point there, about punishing those who commit serious crimes. But are you sure that the Professor fits that category? I have never seen the man, but from what I hear, he seems to be a small, quiet, intellectual sort of man, quite pleasant."

"Ah, but often these are the very ones who are the most vicious. Especially in positions of influence like that. They are the ones who spread the Jewish poison. Intellectualism is, how shall I say, not in fashion in this country. Hitler is not an intellectual. Never attended university. If a great man like that… But maybe I shouldn't be…You are not a Jew, are you?"

"No."

"Of course. I could tell. And do I understand you are a Belgian, just here on a visit?"

"Yes."

"I hope my frankness does not offend you."

"Not at all. I am a firm believer in frankness."

"I still don't understand what brought you here. I mean, to meet with me. Of course, as I said, I know that you are interested in Miss Hermann. But I don't know that I would have picked you to speak on the Professor's behalf."

"No, I'm quite sure you wouldn't have. And anyway, I just told you, no one can speak on his behalf."

"But you see why it is important to us—I mean to this country—not to allow him to leave."

"Yes, of course."

"So you can see why we want him turned over to us."

"Yes. You see it as a matter of crime and punishment."

"Exactly so."

"I'm sure there must be many others here who have committed serious crimes, and are still running loose."

"A great many. Thousands. I'm sure you have nothing like that in Belgium."

"Perhaps not. But there are some."

"Relatively few, I suppose."

"Actually, a great many."

"Really? In Belgium? The Belgians seem like such peaceful people. I love them. I spent some time there, you know."

"I know you work at the German embassy."

"I was also there long before that. During the war."

"Oh, the war."

"Yes. Painful. But I have some pleasant recollections from that time, also."

"How so?"

"The satisfaction of having done one's duty for one's country. It's a funny thing about wars, isn't it, but men who were shooting at each other from opposite sides during the war can agree afterwards that on both sides they did their best for their countries, and rightly so. And I have some pride in knowing that I did my best for mine. But you were saying, there are criminals running loose in Belgium too?"

"Persons who committed crimes there. Not all of them are still in Belgium. Some have taken refuge in other countries."

"But I would think the law…"

"As you know, there is very little by way of international law to deal with some of these crimes."

"Still, I'm surprised. So many crimes, in Belgium, you say. I wonder…"

"Yes. In Dinant, for example."

If Steeg was startled, he didn't show it.

"It's a small town on the Meuse," André said, "south of Brussels."

"I know."

"There were some murders there."

"Recently?"

"During the war."

"The war, of course. Tragically, there were millions of casualties. On our side alone, Germany and Austria-Hungary, over eleven million. But military casualties, terrible as they are, don't count as murders."

"But in Dinant, there were murders."

"Well, there are always murders. Even in the military, sometimes two soldiers get into a fight, as people might anywhere, over this or that, and the first thing you know…"

"These were civilians."

"Well, of course, civilians too. But only a few, I'm sure."

"There were hundreds."

"Unfortunately, modern warfare, even with the greatest care, some civilians get killed, and over a period of time, it adds up."

"This was in one day."

"One day? Civilians? During the war?"

"Yes, in one day. At the very beginning of the war, in August 1914."

"August 1914."

"They were all made to line up. And shot. Not a single one survived."

Steeg paused, then broke into a huge grin.

"Oh, now I know what you're talking about! I have heard those stories too. About hundreds being lined up, and all that. You mustn't believe all that nonsense. Those kinds of stories circulate after every war. But believe me, that didn't happen."

"Didn't happen?"

"Well, I feel sure it didn't. Of course, in every war, there are some misguided civilians who don't observe the line. They forget that they are civilians, they get a rifle, just like a soldier, they cross that line between the two and they become *franc-tireurs*, and kill unsuspecting soldiers, from behind, from the side. Those, of course, sometimes get killed. But that's just 'He who lives by the sword,' and all that."

"There was one account. About that day in Dinant. A woman and her infant were about to be shot. They say that the husband got down on his knees before the officer in charge. Begged him to save the lives of his wife and child. Offered his own life instead. The officer shot the infant, then the mother, then had the father shot."

"That's typical of what I was talking about. There are those stories, each more fantastic than the other. Usually there's some heartbreaking little detail in it, like a mother or an infant. That makes the rumor almost irresistible, but it's the sure sign that it's one of those fabrications. Just the typical propaganda that is used to incite hatred. But these things always turn out not to have happened."

"Well, they say this one did."

"But, don't you see, if all this had really happened, someone would have come forward. There would have been witnesses. And as you just said, this was just one account."

"Maybe there were witnesses."

"Well, I doubt it, or they would have come forth, and we would know. But no, there never are witnesses to these stories. Not if you were actually to check into it and dig for the truth. Because they are all fantasies."

"That's a comforting thought, isn't it?"

Steeg seemed to hesitate, as if confused. But only for the briefest instant.

"Yes, of course it is," he said, "because it never happened. You have to realize, there are always people who will claim that they saw this and that, or at least that they know someone else who did, or someone else who knows someone who does. That always makes the rumor spread more easily. And sometimes after someone has heard the same story enough times, they begin to think they actually saw it themselves. But have no fear, Mr. Laroche, I'm sure you will not find any witnesses. If you ever find one, I would like to see him. But now, as to the reason we came here…"

"I'm here to get the release of Miss Hermann."

"As I said, it's not a question of releasing her. She is a free person. But I'm certainly willing to do my best. Only I need some cooperation."

"Meaning you want the Professor."

"We understand each other perfectly."

"Yes."

"And you're telling me that you do not have any authority in this matter."

"That's correct."

"Even if I could get the lady to agree to go to you?"

"If the condition were to turn the Professor over to you, I know that she would never agree."

"I am terribly disappointed at your obstinacy—I am using the royal 'you.' I have been made to come here under false pretenses. I'm not accusing you of that. It's not your fault. You seem to me like such a reasonable man. And, besides, you are not a Jew. You and I could have got on quite well, I'm sure. You had no way to know. It's the others, the ones who sent you here. They are the ones who committed the deception. I should have known better."

André said nothing.

"Now, Mr. Laroche," Steeg went on, "I still feel that things could be worked out. Miss Hermann is such a charming person, I would hate to see anything... Why don't you talk to those people? Would you do that?"

"I will."

"Oh, one more word, Mr. Laroche, before we part. Please don't make the mistake of having anyone follow me when I leave here. I am being carefully guarded."

"So am I."

✝✝✝

It was well past midnight when Hilda walked out of the house and down to where the car was still parked. She knocked on the window. Somewhat to her surprise, it rolled down immediately, revealing a driver with a rather fat-looking face and a small brown beard. A skinny young man with blond hair and a mustache sat in the passenger seat.

"Yes, what is it?" said the driver.

"Second floor, second window from the front, on this side," Hilda said. This meant the second floor above the ground floor.

"Tomorrow night at this time. She will be there. The window will be open. There's a ladder next to the shed in the back."

"How do we know this isn't a trap?" said the man with the blond hair.

"You don't. But if the idea is just to kill you... well, you're right here, aren't you? And if she weren't going to be there, what would be the point?"

"Who are you anyway? Who sent you?" the blond young man asked.

"Too many questions. But no one sent me. Will you come?"

"Yes," said the driver.

"Unless the light at the side door is on. That will mean canceled."

As she turned to leave, Hilda wondered whether they would come. At almost the same moment the driver spoke again.

"Wait." He handed her a small piece of paper.

"What is this?" she said.

"Memorize it and throw it away."

She looked at it. It was a telephone number.

"You have helped. If you get any more information, call. Identify yourself as Ursula, the maid. When they ask you where you are working, say room 526."

"Why are you giving me this number? Aren't you worried about the danger?"

"With that number you won't be able to hurt us. Or her."

✝✝✝

When Lise picked up her breakfast tray in the morning, she found a hand-printed note sticking out from under the coffee pot. It read: "Tonight at a quarter to one, open the left-hand window in your bedroom. When they come, go with them. Bring nothing with you. Don't ask me questions."

Lise was puzzled, and she thought about it for a long time. As far as she could tell there had never been any sign of anyone else but Hilda in the house, except the times when Steeg had come. The question was, if the note had been written by Hilda, as it must have been, why had she done it? Certainly Steeg was not the one who had instructed her to do this. Why would he have? To induce her, Lise, to attempt an escape? Why? So she could be caught? She was already his captive. If Hilda was doing this on her own initiative, she was risking her life. Why? Any way Lise looked at it, Hilda's leaving of the note made no sense. Lise could only think that it must be part of some elaborate plot by Steeg, although she could not picture any of its details. Any other explanation would be a fairy tale. She decided to think it over, but at the moment Lise was inclined to ignore the note for now.

In the evening Lise found her dinner on the dumbwaiter. There was another note under the soup plate. When Lise read it she understood. It read:

"I know what he tried."

✝✝✝

Lise had opened the window and was waiting ahead of time. She saw no light, but heard them after a while. She heard the ladder being put up against the house, then saw it reach up to the window. A man climbed up on it. He didn't speak to her, except about the mechanics of it, of grabbing hold of the ladder and getting on it. "Here, hold on here—yes—now this foot here," and so on. Lise had no trouble getting down to the ground.

Both men from the car were there. They took the ladder back to the rear of the property, then walked with Lise to the automobile. They moved quickly, but quietly. The man with the large face and the small brown beard again drove. Lise sat between the two rescuers in the wide front seat. As they moved along she looked out through the windshield, but saw only empty streets lit by a few lampposts.

A BMW sat in a driveway near the house. Seconds after Lise's car passed by, the BMW pulled out into the street and followed at some distance. After about twenty minutes, Lise's car stopped and the man with the brown beard got out of the car with Lise. The building before which they were standing was almost completely darkened, but through the glass in the front door Lise saw a dim, recessed light. The man rang the doorbell. In a few seconds a man's voice from inside asked who was there.

"It's me," the driver said. The door was opened by a middle-aged man.

"Ah, our guest has arrived, I see," he said.

The man with the beard left. After the middle-aged man had let Lise in, he led her down a long hallway to a room at the back. The hallway was unlit except for light spilling out from the open door to that room. Once Lise and the man were inside this room, he shut the door to the hallway behind them.

"There's a letter waiting for you," he said. "'I'll be right back with it. In the meantime, please sit down and make yourself comfortable."

Lise was now in a small dining room, which she took to be part of an apartment. Its furnishings were modest—a small stove in one corner, the red glow of its coals visible through a small isinglass window; the table and chairs in the center; a deep red couch framed in cherry wood along one side of the room, and a breakfront on the opposite side. The only light other than the fire was a small crystal chandelier over the table. To Lise it all looked crowded but cozy, an island of warmth and security from the horrors outside.

The man came back holding an envelope, which he handed to her.

"Here's the letter," he said. "He said you would know who it's from."

Lise opened it. There was no salutation. It read:

> *Just a short note to explain. You are safe where you are. In the morning we'll move you to another place. From: Your friend who remembers the mussels and frites.*

Lise smiled both with amusement and a feeling of relief at being free.

✠✠✠

When Lise's car had stopped, the BMW had been a block away. Its driver had pulled over to the curb and parked. The driver of Lise's car had never noticed that he was being followed. The man in the BMW watched Lise go into the house. He waited for a few minutes, then drove off.

✞✞✞

The middle-aged man asked Lise if she would like some food. It was well past one o'clock in the morning, but Lise was too keyed up to feel fatigue or hunger. The man said that he had a bedroom ready for her whenever she wanted to sleep. She thanked him and said she would just like to sit for a while if that was all right with him.

Lise had spent a great deal of time in the past few days thinking about André. As her feelings about Steeg had turned from gratitude to disillusionment, then to dismay, and finally to loathing, she had thought more and more about what André had said to her. It was André who had suggested she have Steeg show her the records proving her adoption. She had followed that advice. But he had also cautioned her not to be too trusting of Steeg; now, looking back, she regretted having ignored that advice. Most important of all, again in retrospect, was the fact that André had asked her to let him know if she found out anything more and, instead, she had gone off to Munich without so much as a word to him. How foolish she had been, and how wise André was! The instant liking Lise had formed for him had now become a warm glow of admiration.

After a while Lise told the man she would like to retire for the rest of the night, and he led her to her room. There were fresh linens on the bed and fresh towels in the bathroom. After Lise went to bed, her mind went over the horrendous events of the past few days. She was physically exhausted and emotionally drained, but superimposed on that was an immense relief at having been rescued and being safe now. These things and the fact that she was about to see André filled her with optimism. Lise soon fell into a deep sleep.

✝✝✝

A bell was ringing, somewhat like a doorbell, but far away. Then some voices. It did not seem to concern her. Lise started to roll over, but the voices got louder. She recognized one of them as belonging to the middle-aged man who had let her in. She heard him shout, "You have no right!" Then a louder voice gave some sort of command which she could not make out. Then there were footsteps stomping down the hall, coming closer. Then a knock on her door.

"Who is it?" Lise said, through the door.

"It's me." She recognized the middle-aged man's voice. "You'd better come out."

"What is it?"

His voice sounded strained. "You'd better come."

She got up and opened the door. The man stood before her, looking to one side with a terrified expression. She followed his eyes. A couple of meters down the hall stood a uniformed policeman, his gun drawn and pointed at the owner. Behind him stood a second policeman.

"What is this?" Lise said. "What do you want?"

"Lise Hermann?" said the policeman with the gun.

"Yes?"

"You are under arrest. Come with us."

"What do you mean? What do you want with me?"

"Criminal charges. You will find out."

Everything—her miraculous escape, Hilda's unexpected but providential help, these kind people's efforts, the thoughtful note from André—it was going to be as if none of that had ever happened.

Lise turned to the policemen. "This is a mistake," she said, almost in a shout. Her face was flushed. They paid no attention to what she was saying.

"What is this nonsense?" she asked the middle-aged man.

He was staring at the gun still pointed at him. He looked helpless.

"Stop them!"

"I can't."

"You can't? Why not? It's a mistake. You know it."

"Can't you see? It's the police. I tried, but they have orders. I'm sure you can get it straightened out at the police station."

"I won't go. They have no authority. I'm just here on a visit. You have no authority." She was shouting.

The second policeman grabbed her elbow.

"Let me go! Let me go!" she demanded. She was struggling to get away from him. For a moment she almost seemed to break loose from him, but his hand tightened on her elbow like a vise. Her face had turned puffy and red, and she was kicking him.

At the top of her lungs Lise yelled, "Let me go! Let me go, damn you! You have no right!"

The policeman jerked Lise off balance, pulled her out of the doorway, and pushed her down the hallway to the front door. Lise never stopped struggling, but he kept his tight grip on her elbow. Finally the officer pulled Lise out into the street, as she still fought vigorously, and then he shoved her into the back of the police car.

From inside the house came a loud sound, like a gun being fired. Then the policeman with the gun came out, still holding the weapon. He put it back in its holster.

"What was that?" asked the other policeman.

"I took care of him."

"What in hell for? You didn't need to do that."

"He argued with us. People like that are dangerous."

✝✝✝

A car was parked a way down the street from the house that Lise had been in. There were two men in it. They had been watching the building before the policemen came along. A while later they were found dead, shot, evidently by two persons each firing into the car through one of the two front windows, which had shattered into a thousand fragments.

✝✝✝

Steeg had been up all night. In the morning he went to the house. As soon as he saw Hilda he exploded.

"Why did you let her out?"

"I didn't. She escaped."

His face had turned purple.

"Escaped? How could she escape?"

"Through the window."

"How do you know? You let her out, didn't you?"

"She got out by herself."

"Do you take me for a fool? She just flew through the air?" Steeg growled. "You're lying again. It was you, wasn't it?"

"What if it was?" Hilda was yelling back at him now. "I heard you. I heard her screaming at you. I heard *what* she was screaming."

"You bitch!"

"Your so-called little affairs are one thing. Rape is another. Did you think I was going to keep her here for you after that? This is lucky for you."

"Lucky!"

"Yes, lucky! I knew you would come at her again. Like a dog at a bitch in heat. You have no brains. The only brains you have are in your pants. You would have kept on until you destroyed yourself and her both."

As Steeg raised his arm, Hilda cut him short.

"Don't try that! You know it doesn't work. You know I'm stronger than you. What I could have done before, I can do now. You'd have to kill me, and…"

He dropped his arm.

"You whore!"

"Well, she's gone, anyway."

"She isn't. I've got her back."

He turned away from her and walked out.

✝✝✝

When André and Raoul found out about it in the morning, they were stunned. André was overwhelmed with feelings of guilt. Raoul, however, was not devastated; so much of his life had been punctuated by bad news and terrible losses that he had long ago learned to turn his grief into an inner force which enabled him to keep on fighting. Raoul knew that without this he would never have survived to this point.

Both he and André were particularly distressed that this was happening to someone as innocent and trusting as Lise. They felt sure now that they might have been able to avoid her recapture if they had left Brussels sooner. More immediately, it might have been prevented if they had moved Lise to another house the previous night.

✝✝✝

Among the many high military officers who had found Hitler and his Nazi ideas attractive from the beginning was General Werner Edward Fritz von Blomberg. He had been a general staff officer during the war, and after the war had risen to successively higher positions in the military. In 1932 he had been made head of the German delegation to the Disarmament Conference in Geneva. When Hitler came to power in January

1933, he appointed Blomberg Minister of Defense in the new government.

Blomberg always remained loyal to the Führer. The most important of the many steps through which Hitler consolidated his power was the Night of the Long Knives, also known as the Blood Purge, of June 30, 1934. During that night, Hitler had his SS troops brutally murder thousands of the SA's top leaders, including its Chief, Ernst Röhm. This eliminated both the SA's ambition of becoming a new German army and Röhm's ambition of becoming its commander. One of the essential factors that had enabled Hitler to make the decision to purge the SA was that Blomberg gave him the Army's consent to it.

The next year, in 1935, Hitler named General Blomberg both Minister of War and Commander-in-Chief of the *Wehrmacht*, Germany's army.

✝✝✝

The date was March 7, 1936. Rumors that something big was about to happen had been circulating everywhere in Germany; the most widespread guess was that it would be a reoccupation of the Rhineland. Because this was explicitly forbidden by the Treaty of Versailles and the Locarno Pact, these rumors aroused at once great expectations and great fear, and therefore high excitement.

André and Raoul had moved into a different house in Munich once more. They had arrived there separately, carrying nothing with them. Now André was on his way back to this new house from a short errand. As he crossed a nearby square, André found a large crowd gathered around a loudspeaker mounted on a truck. At first he did not pay much attention to it, since radios were not yet a fixture in every home, and such trucks were occasionally used to bring entertainment and announcements to the public. But as he got closer, what the announcer's voice said caught his attention; it said that at approximately eleven o'clock this morning the Führer had announced to the ambassadors of France and the other Allies that at dawn today German forces had entered the Rhineland.

At these words, the crowd in the square broke into applause, which then temporarily subsided as the voice continued. It said that Hitler had then made the announcement before the Reichstag, Germany's Parliament, which at that point had burst into loud and lengthy cheering. Hitler had then declared to the Reichstag that the Treaty of Versailles was henceforth null and void, and the Locarno treaty as well. When it heard this, the announcer continued, the entire Reichstag went wild with even more enthusiastic cheering, which did not end for many minutes. Now, at this news, similarly loud and prolonged cheers erupted from the crowd in the square.

At that very moment in fact, Germans throughout the country, some in their homes, some at work—it was a Saturday—went delirious with joy and broke into spontaneous cheering, shouting, and singing.

✠✠✠

The order to carry out the reoccupation of the Rhineland had been communicated to General von Blomberg by Hitler personally. Like almost all of Hitler's other top generals, Blomberg understood that if France were to oppose the reoccupation with force, the result would be certain disaster for the enormously outnumbered German force, and consequently for the Nazi regime and for Hitler himself. Blomberg had therefore asked Hitler for advance authority to retreat if any resistance were encountered. This Hitler gave him.

For these reasons, on March 7, 1936, at the very moment when ordinary Germans throughout the country were going wild with happiness and enthusiasm at Hitler 's announcement to the Reichstag, one small group of Germans reacted to this news with dismay and dread. These consisted of most of the top generals in the *Wehrmacht,* including Blomberg himself.

‡‡‡

French General Maurice-Gustave Gamelin had been a division commander during the war, where he had distinguished himself both as a skilled commander on the battlefield and as a brilliant strategist in the planning room. Over the years following the war he was promoted to ever higher military positions. Paradoxically, this rise coincided with a gradual but steady decline in the very qualities that had led to his earlier successes. Where Gamelin had been courageous, he became overcautious. Where his mind had been keen and adaptable, it became dulled and rigid. Where he had been daring, the General became hesitant to take personal responsibility and took refuge in placing conditions on his agreement to strategies.

In 1931, General Gamelin had been appointed France's Army Chief of Staff. In 1935 he was appointed president of the French Supreme War Council. As of March 1936, he was Commander-in-Chief of all the French armies.

Immediately upon receiving the news of Hitler's announcement from Berlin, French Prime Minister Sarraut convened an emergency meeting of the cabinet, in which he included General Gamelin. The reoccupation of the Rhineland was not in any way a surprise, and indeed it had been anticipated for weeks. Nor was there any doubt in Sarraut's mind as to what had to be done—comply with the Treaty of Versailles and the Locarno Pact and send in enough troops, backed by tanks and artillery, to hurl the small symbolic German force back out of the demilitarized zone. The forces required would not be large; a small fraction of the half-million-man army that France had available would be enough. Besides, thirteen French divisions—a force in itself many times the size of the German force

in the Rhineland, in fact larger than Germany's entire army—
were already in positions near the border. Gamelin, a brilliant
Généralissime, certainly had plans ready for this contingency.
Sarraut turned to him and asked him to set them forth.

Gamelin said that in his opinion France should order a general mobilization of the approximately one million men it
could call up, and draw up a plan and take all measures needed
to defend France against invasion. In the meantime, he proposed moving troops towards the border, but nothing more.
Prime Minister Sarraut asked why he could not simply attack
the Germans and throw them out. Gamelin replied that this
was out of the question; that if this were done, Germany would
retaliate with a major counterattack.

Sarraut could not believe what he was hearing. He told
Gamelin that he was talking as if an invasion of France by massive German forces had taken place or was imminent; there
was in fact no invasion of France, nor even any threat of one
at this time, and furthermore Germany had no such forces. But
Gamelin would not budge from his position.

The result was that France took no action, except the legal-
istic route of lodging appeals and other papers with the League
of Nations.

Although Hitler had several army divisions in place near
the Rhineland boundary, he had only sent in a few battalions.
He evidently believed that such a purely symbolic force would
be that much less likely to provoke France into attack. If
France did attack, the few divisions Hitler had would be no
match for France's mighty army in any event; and if France did
not attack, it would be easy enough for the Führer to send in
the rest of those forces within the ensuing few days. As things
turned out, that is exactly what Hitler did.

CHAPTER 15

STEEG FELT A SENSE of exultation from having Lise back in his grip. By now he had given up any plans to force himself on her; that was not why he had brought the sham charges against Lise. His objective at this point was to capture Professor Mueller, preferably without violence, and Steeg planned to use Lise for that. After she had been formally charged at the police station with crimes, the exact nature of which were left obscured by such terms as "conspiracy" and "espionage," he had her released to his custody. Steeg had also arranged to have her brought back to the house at a time when he would not be there. She was taken by the police up to the same room of the house, and the hallway door was locked again. As they took her up Lise started screaming, but one of the policemen told her to shut up, and this time she did.

But after the police had gone, Lise began screaming again. After a while, she heard someone come up the stairs.

"Hilda, is that you?" Lise called out.

"Yes, it's me." Hilda was on the landing, just outside the door.

"Unlock the door, please."

"I can't."

"For Christ's sake, what are you talking about? Open it."

"I can't."

"Why not?"

"I shouldn't have helped you before. It was a mistake."

"But you did. What was the point of it, if you won't help me now?"

"Miss Hermann, I did what I could. I gave you the chance. I took a great risk. The rest was up to them. They obviously wasted the opportunity. They should have made sure you were safe. Don't blame me for that."

"I'm not blaming you. I'm thankful for what you did. But you know what he'll do if you leave me here."

"I know what he'll do if I let you out. Besides, it would be a waste of time. They'd catch you again. Then where would we both be?"

"I beg you. It isn't just for me. It's my father."

"I don't know anything about that."

"Let me explain…"

"I don't want to hear it. I'm not interested."

"Hilda, please, let me explain. You'll understand."

"I don't want to hear about it. I paid enough of a price for letting you escape once. I will not do it again."

"Hilda, please, for my father's sake…"

"I told you, I'm not interested in hearing about all that."

"If you would just…"

"Save your breath. He'll be here soon enough. You can tell him."

✝✝✝

Later that day, Lise heard someone coming up the stairs. The steps were heavy. She went out into the hall, taking the long knife with her.

"Who is it?" she said.

He was still on the landing, outside the locked hallway door.

"It's me, Josef."

"Stay out. I'm holding the knife, and this time I'll use it."

Lise had been surprised that they hadn't come and removed it.

But Hilda may not have known about the knife, and Steeg may not have been worried about it that much. She had no way to know the reason.

Steeg laughed. "I only want to talk to you."

"I don't want to see your face. Do it from out there," Lise told him through the shut, wooden door.

"Lise…"

"Look, we have nothing to say to each other. I just want you to let me go."

"Let you go? You know I can't do that. The police have put you in my custody. I'm responsible."

She didn't answer.

"You should never have tried escaping. Now there are criminal charges against you."

"You know those are phony charges. They were invented by you."

"It's very simple, Lise," he said in a condescending tone. "You were only released because of my intervention, and I can have you returned to jail any time."

"You know as well as I do that those charges were completely fabricated," she replied.

"Well, we'll certainly see, won't we?"

"Besides, I am a Belgian resident and you, they, have no right to keep me."

"You're mistaken about that."

"Oh, I see. I forgot, I'm in Germany. Of course. You're the one who tried to rape me, and who is holding me prisoner, but I'm the one who faces criminal charges. Naturally! Well, let me tell you. Even if your corrupt government won't prosecute you for your crimes, the Belgians will hear about it. And when that happens, you know what will happen to your job at the embassy, whatever it is."

"My dear Lise…"

"I am not your dear Lise."

"…there are a few things you should know. You are a

German citizen, and I am a German citizen, and Belgium has no jurisdiction over crimes committed in Germany by German citizens."

"Well, once the Belgian authorities learn about all you've done…"

"Your concern about my job is touching, but frankly, I am not worried about my job. My government appreciates what I am doing."

She said nothing.

"So you're going to stay here, Lise. For now. Don't worry, I won't be bothering you up here. You'll be quite safe."

She heard him turn back and go down the stairs.

Steeg gave Hilda strict orders not to let Lise out of her floor under any circumstances. In addition, he arranged for guards to be posted at each of the doors to the house.

✝✝✝

As soon as Steeg had seen that the man who had come to the restaurant on Amalienstrasse was André, he had suspected that something might be wrong. Before the conversation had ended, he knew that something was seriously wrong. Steeg began to regret deeply that he had never had an investigation made of this Belgian. And Steeg knew that he should have at least suspected that there might be more to André's involvement than simply a romantic interest in Lise.

Their response to his demand that they "produce" the Professor was nothing more or less than what Steeg had expected. What he had never dreamed was that anyone, let alone this man, would bring up the Dinant affair. Steeg had long believed that the whole matter was as dead and buried as the skeletons of the six hundred-and-more who had died there. Yet once in a while during the intervening years since his acquittal, Steeg had experienced transitory fearful thoughts, usually during the night, that some soul from the past might some day stalk him, seeking vengeance. He had always dismissed these, as he had the nightmare on the day he and Lise had gone to Dinant. But as he listened to André, a storm of dread had swept through his whole body. Steeg didn't know how much André actually knew beyond what anyone could have gleaned from the newspapers of the time, nor how he had learned it. The details concerning the tiny child, its mother, and its father were particularly chilling to Steeg, not because of any belated remorse, but because of a feeling that some dreadful retribution was about to come this way. He would somehow have to fend that retribution off. Steeg didn't know where it would strike from, but he understood that André would play some part in it.

✝✝✝

The doorbell rang. The owner of the house answered. He came back and told Raoul that it was a man named Hector, who had a message for him from Rita. Raoul knew that Rita was an entirely imaginary person whose name they had agreed on. He told the owner to bring the man in. The fellow was tall, pleasant looking, and well-dressed. By the way he looked at Raoul, André could see that they were old friends.

"Hector, my friend, how good to see you!" said Raoul. "How are you?"

"Very well, thanks." Hector glanced briefly at André, then threw a questioning look at Raoul.

"It's all right, Hector, this is André Laroche. André, I've mentioned my old business colleague Hector."

"Of course."

"Sit down," said Raoul. "I take it you have some news."

"Yes, from Exenby."

"Tell us."

"You know the first part, that the Germans reoccupied the Rhineland?"

"This morning, yes. Great jubilation hereabouts," Raoul said.

"It's the same all over the country. They're hysterical with joy." Hector looked at his watch. "It certainly didn't take them long. Shall I start with the conclusion?"

"Please," said Raoul.

"The Allies are not going to fight."

"Shit!" said André.

"They haven't the stomach."

"What happened?" said André.

"It began at dawn. Some airplanes flew over Cologne and other places in the Rhineland. Just a few, for show. As you know, Hitler hasn't got many. Meanwhile the crowds in the streets there went wild."

"I'm sure," said Raoul.

"What about troops?" asked André.

"A few battalions. A parade, really. They got a noisy reception. Everyone smiling, laughing."

"Tell us the rest," said Raoul.

"It started badly. In Paris Sarraut convened the cabinet. But even before the meeting, Clark…"

"The British ambassador to France," said André.

"Yes. He relayed a message to the French not to take any action without first consulting with London."

"If your house catches on fire, don't do anything without first consulting with me," said André.

"No, not the house. Just a small piece of paper that can be snuffed out with your foot. However, if you don't, then the whole house will burn down."

André said nothing.

Hector continued. "I should add that it's Eden's…"

"The British Foreign Minister," André said.

"…belief that there is actually no support in Britain for any military action. Sarraut and Foreign Minister Flandin called the British Foreign Office. They had no luck. Of course today is Saturday."

"Oh, Christ, the British weekend," said André.

"Why do you think Hitler picked a Saturday?" said Hector. "Most of the important ones, the ones who could make decisions, are in their country houses. For the weekend. But you would think…"

"Exenby was in London, though," Raoul said.

"Yes, of course. That's how I know all this."

"By the way, how the hell did you learn all this without…" André started to ask.

Hector understood what André was asking. "Oh, it's very simple. Raoul knows the volume of cables that my business generates every day, many of them long ones."

"That's right," said Raoul.

"Everyone, the telegraph office, are used to it. So it was easy. This time we just used a code that Trevor and I agreed on and it went through some obscure address outside of London. Quite safe. Anyway, Paris has been told that no decision can be reached before Monday."

"Monday! God help us!" said André.

There was a pause while they all absorbed that.

"You were saying the French cabinet met," said André.

"With Gamelin."

"What happened?" André asked.

"It all came down to Gamelin. Sarraut wanted to throw the Germans out, but Gamelin said that it would start another war, and he would first need a general mobilization."

"But that's absurd!" said André. Why, France alone has an army of five hundred thousand men! Hitler's whole army is not a tenth of that!" He turned to Hector. "A few battalions, did you say? He only sent in a few battalions?"

"Yes."

"A general mobilization?"

"Yes," said Hector. "I have plenty of water to drown out this small fire, but I won't act until I have every fire truck in town at the front door."

As Hector's story unfolded, André had been growing more and more restless. He had stood up, started to walk back and forth, sat down again, repeated the sequence over and over—all the while focusing intently on the other two, looking from one to the other.

"So, it was all for nothing!" André finally said.

He paused, absorbed in thought. Raoul knew that he was about to say more. Neither he nor Hector spoke.

"The four years of blood, all the dead, the crippled and the maimed, the mothers and fathers, the wives, the orphaned children, all the bereft, all of it! For nothing. Everything gained, lost in one hour!"

André paused. No one else spoke.

"Gamelin's body may have been present in Paris today," André went on, "but his brain is still stuck somewhere in the mud and trenches of twenty years ago, unable to budge. He should have been retired, not put at the head of France's armies! In God's name, what were they thinking about?"

"By the way," Hector said, "his counterpart..."

"Blomberg, yes?" André said.

"Trevor's contacts in Berlin saw Blomberg, right after Hitler's speech to the Reichstag."

"Yes?" said André.

"Blomberg was in a state! Obviously terrified. And he wasn't alone. We—that is, Trevor—had it on reliable authority for some time that all the top German Generals were convinced that if Hitler reoccupied, the French would make short work of it. It would be the end."

"Of course," said André, "That was absolutely true. Those generals are not fools. They were only wrong about one thing: they didn't anticipate the apathy, the paralyzing fear and fatigue that would immobilize the Allies. That's the great tragedy! The mothers, sick with fear of the past's repeating itself. The youth, horrified at the prospect of another meaningless slaughter, and pathetically deluded about how to prevent it. The rich, so fearful of Bolshevism that they send their money to support this monster. The foolish in high British society who admire Hitler and consider swastikas stylish. The people everywhere, young and old, so weary of war, so hollowed out by it, so afraid of another, that they think they can prevent it by denying its possibility. The British ruling circles, the government itself, marching forward confidently, ears covered and eyes shut. That's the tragedy."

For a few moments, no one moved or spoke.

"But there are a few others," said Raoul.

"There *are*," said André. "Churchill, some others, even Exenby, of course. But today their hands are tied."

Again no one spoke.

"I feel like a preacher. I'm sorry," said André.

"No, you're right," said Raoul.

"I know I'm right," said André. "There will never be another chance like the one Britain and France gave up today."

"Oh, there may be," Raoul said.

"There will never be," André said. "Hitler is rearming at a furious pace, while the Allies do nothing. So the next time, their overwhelming advantage will be gone, and obviously they will be even less inclined to resist him. But bad as what happened today is, that will be infinitely worse. After all, he's still inside Germany. The next time he will invade another country."

"Unless they stop him then, "Raoul said.

"If they didn't do it today, I don't think they will then. They will do nothing."

"At some point they will," Raoul said.

"Only when they have no more choice in the matter, when their back is to the wall. By then Hitler will have assembled the mightiest army the world has ever seen, and there will be no other choice. We will all have to fight."

"Again," Raoul said.

"Yes, again."

"This time we may not win."

"Oh, we'll win," André said. "We'll fight Germany's army with even mightier armies, its air power with even mightier air power, its sea power with even mightier sea power. We'll do it because we'll have no other choice. Above all we'll need leaders, not the spineless men we have now, but men with greatness in them, who see things as they are and deal with things as they are. Such men will arise; they always do. And we will win. But the cost! That war will engulf the whole world. Again cities will be leveled, farmlands, whole countries, devastated, covered with the waste of war, the bodies of the dead. Millions more mutilated, blinded, maimed. And it all will have been so unnecessary; it all could have been prevented so easily… if the Allies had acted today."

"What a betrayal!" Raoul said.

For whole minutes, no one spoke. Raoul sat expressionless, staring at a point on the carpet beyond his feet. The other two men just looked at each other, also without expression.

"A betrayal," Raoul finally added bitterly, "of every poor bastard who died in that war. And of all the crippled and the incapacitated who didn't. The millions of them."

"A travesty," André said. "Do you remember 1918, when it all ended?"

"Of course. How could I forget it?"

"How the world was filled with hope?"

"Yes. The idealism! The cheers! There was never going to be another war."

"The whole world believed the storm of death was finally over," André said. "Oh how the sun shone! So many years ago, but it seems like yesterday." He paused.

"But it was only a break in the storm," he said.

✝✝✝

As soon as Hector had left, André and Raoul had to decide on their next move.

Now that the Allies' inaction had destroyed any chance that the Nazis would collapse, it was imperative that Professor Mueller's escape from Germany take place immediately. By now his escape had become important to the rest of the world; this made preventing it now even more important to the Nazis.

André and Raoul had planned all along to rescue the Professor if events took this turn. However, Lise's abduction now presented them with a dilemma. To rescue and get Mueller out of the country immediately would mean leaving her in Steeg's grip. But to attempt to rescue her first would mean leaving the Professor exposed to perils which would increase by the hour. Putting their personal feelings about Lise aside, the two men saw clearly that the more compelling choice was to get Professor Mueller out of the country as quickly as possible. Furthermore, although Lise was certainly Steeg's captive, André and Raoul did not think he would actually harm her physically now; from what they knew about him, they felt sure that he planned to use Lise as a pawn to get the Professor back. Besides, the reason Lise had come here in the first place was to help save her father; they were certain that she would want them to put rescuing him above her immediate safety.

After they had thought about it for a short while, the choice was clear.

✝✝✝

Erich Behrndt had received his instructions. He was to pick Lise up at the house. A driver would take him there. Erich wanted time to have a private talk with Lise; so when the driver called him the day before to confirm the arrangement, Behrndt told the man that he would get to the house on his own and be there by the time the driver arrived. The driver apparently did not see anything unusual about this, and he easily agreed to it without consulting with anyone.

Before hanging up, Erich asked if the driver could tell him where he had been instructed to ultimately take them.

"Meersburg. His favorite place. I'm quite familiar with the route."

If Steeg had intended the destination to be kept confidential, the driver had evidently not been told. Nor, apparently, did the driver think there was any reason why he should not tell Behrndt. Erich knew that Meersburg was a popular resort on Lake Constance, which was where Stangl had mentioned Steeg usually took "his women." It all tied together. True, Steeg had also said that this assignment was about "business, important business." But he had previously already demonstrated to Erich a propensity to place the line between business and pleasure wherever it suited him at the moment.

The demeaning assignment of escorting Lise to a waiting Steeg both galled and puzzled Erich. He wondered whether Steeg always had his women escorted in this fashion, and if so why. Perhaps he thought that this made these trysts seem less commercial. Or perhaps Steeg wanted to make sure the ladies didn't have a change of heart on the way. There was also the obvious question of why Steeg had chosen Erich. Here again, the answer was easy; in the past Steeg had not hesitated to make similar requests of Erich in the most debasing fashion, and he would undoubtedly derive pleasure from the humiliation that now pierced Behrndt's insides like a sharp blade. However, Erich decided that, like a true martyr, he would reveal no sign of this pain, either in his voice or in his demeanor.

Erich arrived early by car and parked around the corner. After he got out of the car and had turned the corner, he saw a woman come down the steps and walk in the opposite direction. Since Erich had been told that the only woman in the house besides Lise was the housekeeper, he assumed this was her. Erich had also been told about the guards, who, he also knew, had been instructed to let him inside.

When he got to the house, he rang the bell. At first no one came, and so he rang again. This time the door opened, and there stood Lise.

"Erich, what are you doing here?" she said.

"I was going to ask you the same thing."

She still looked puzzled.

"I am only joking," he said. "I knew you would be here. Steeg has sent me to pick you up."

"You?"

Erich assumed Lise must have been told that someone would be picking her up, but that no one had mentioned it would be him.

"I knew that a driver would come for me…" She left the rest of it unsaid.

"Can I come in?" he said.

"Of course."

Lise led Erich from the vestibule through an archway into the living room. They stood looking at each other. At first glance he had seen her just as the woman he knew, the recognition of the familiar making scrutiny unnecessary. But now he noticed how different she looked. A certain sadness, a distraught look, her eyes red, her face pale.

Erich didn't know what to say. He had a feeling of unreality. Not as if they had been lovers only a matter of days ago; more like old friends seeing each other for the first time in many years. He didn't know where to start or what to ask. He was also afraid to open a door that would disclose some unpleasant secret. He glanced around.

"I didn't know you were living in such grandeur."

Erich immediately wished he hadn't said it.

"Are you all right?" he said.

"I'm fine. Why don't you sit down?"

"I don't mean to pry, but you look as if you've been crying."

"It's all right, Erich."

He was still standing.

"Please do sit down."

"We seem to have disappeared from each other's lives."

"At least you from mine."

Of course. It was true that he had never really explained that.

"I tried to reach you. Just a few days ago. Suzanne said you were gone. She wouldn't say where."

"Yes. It was quite sudden."

"Me too."

"You *had* to come to Munich?"

"Yes."

She smiled. "I thought maybe you had followed me here. But you say it's just a coincidence?"

"Business."

"You still work for Steeg?"

"Yes."

"Well, is that why you came to Munich? To pick me up?"

Erich felt it would sound ridiculous if he said yes, and if he said no, she would want to know why he ended up being there.

"No."

"Then why are you here? Was it your idea to pick me up?"

"No."

"Steeg just asked you to do it."

His discomfort must have shown. He was grateful to her.

"Yes."

"I've never understood what it is that you do. I'm not asking. It's none of my business. Anyway, I suppose it doesn't matter; we're both here because of Steeg."

"But I was asked to come here. You chose to be with him."

"To be with him?"

"Well, it seems to be all over town."

"What's all over town?"

"Your affair with him."

"An affair? Who told you that? There is no affair."

"But there was?"

Lise looked serious, and sad. She didn't answer.

"Well, I don't understand it," he said. "I mean, if you didn't choose to be with him, why did you come to Munich?"

"It's complicated. I don't feel like going into it now."

Erich felt he understood. All Lise probably knew was that he had neglected her terribly, taken her for granted, then dropped her and disappeared from her life completely, without any explanation. And now here he was, asking *her* for explanations. What a cad he must seem!

"I believe I'm the one who should do some explaining," Erich said.

She was still as beautiful as ever. But the sadness in her face made her beauty seem darker, almost tragic. Erich felt her silence said more than any words. But to his surprise, it was Lise who spoke.

"The reason I came here was not what you heard, but it does have to do with Steeg. I can't tell you any more than that because you work for him."

"What there is between you and me has nothing to do with my job."

"Erich, there's isn't anything between you and me anymore. There hasn't been for a long time."

"I know that it's my fault. But you had no way to know why I didn't... why I neglected you so."

"It doesn't matter anymore."

"It was because of Steeg."

"You said it was business. That didn't sound like much of a reason, and it still doesn't."

"He forbade me to see you."

"But why did you obey him?"

"That's what hurt me so much. I realized it didn't sound like much of an excuse, and in a way it wasn't."

She didn't say anything.

"He threatened to destroy my career if I continued to see you."

"What gave him so much power over you?"

He was moved by the understanding this showed.

"I had had a brief relationship, while I was at the University, with a woman who I later learned was part-Jewish. He had found out. Steeg threatened to disclose it unless I stopped seeing you, or even calling you, or if I told you the reason."

"I find that very interesting. So you obeyed him."

"With one exception, of course. That time at the restaurant. Lise, you don't know him."

"But I do. I said I wasn't going to tell you why I'm here... it was because of my father," she finally said.

"Your father? You told me he was killed in the war."

"I was adopted. My—other—father is still living."

She paused for a long time.

"Where?"

She didn't answer.

"Here, in Munich?"

She said nothing, but her expression changed ever so slightly. It said yes.

"So you came here to see him. But why all the..."

"My father is Jewish."

"Who told you all this?"

Lise tilted her head slightly to the right and glanced in that direction.

"He did."

"Steeg."

"Yes."

The same story that André had told him. But Laroche had also said that Steeg was planning to use it against Lise.

"You believed it?"

"Yes. Did you really think there was... that there could be an affair between Steeg and me?"

"I didn't know what to think. Especially when Suzanne said you had left town. It seemed pretty obvious that you had told her not to say where. And then when I found out that he was gone too."

"My father is a university professor. He'd been dismissed from his job."

"How can you be sure that what Steeg told you…"

"I've met my father. That's why I came here. Steeg told me about him back in Brussels. He offered to help, to bring me here, to this house, so I could meet this father I never knew. Steeg seemed so nice. I was so trusting, so foolish. Then the problems started. He said my father was likely to be persecuted. Then some ruffians broke into my father's house and beat him up—I saw him the next morning. It was awful! Steeg said he had nothing to do with it, that it was just an example of the hazards my father faced. He told me that he could help my father, help him escape from this country. But there were conditions. Steeg is not subtle."

Erich did not need any further explanation. It all fit Steeg so well.

"But why are you still here, in this house? A guard at the door?"

"You said I don't know him. If you don't understand that, you don't know him. I didn't want to tell you. Erich, he tried to rape me. Upstairs. In this house. I fought him off with a knife. I am a prisoner here!"

"How did he… Oh, my God!"

Erich had turned pale and stared at her, speechless for a long time. There was a horrified look in his eyes.

"Lise, you have to get out. We are both his prisoners. Let's go away together."

"I told you, what there was between you and me is over."

"I wish it wasn't. But that's not why I'm suggesting this. It's because of what you have just told me."

"Erich, that makes no sense to me. I know how you love your country, that you believe in Hitler, that you are understandably distressed at your father dying in the war and the terrible things that happened afterwards, including how your poor mother suffered. And I know how dedicated you are. That's what you live for. You would never give that up."

"You're right. I'll never give that dream up. But there are many ways to do that. What I'm doing now, my work with Steeg, is only one of these, and if I disobey him, I would be destroying that. But I will still pursue my dream. Come with me, while there's still time."

"I don't believe you would do it."

"Lise, what difference would it make? We are both his prisoners. If he captures us, we would not be any worse off than we are now."

"Maybe not me. But you would be."

"I think what matters most to you now is saving your father. André gave me a number to call for someone who can reach him. He told me about your father. I didn't believe it. I thought he was mistaken. But I memorized the number."

"When did he do that?"

"Just a few days ago. André evidently had me tracked down, because he got hold of me almost as soon as I got here. My car is around the corner. As soon as we leave here, we can call him; at least you will then have a chance. If we wait for Steeg's driver to come, you will not have that opportunity. But it's getting late. We need to leave immediately."

Lise sat there, obviously undecided. Erich got up from his chair.

"Lise," he said.

She got up and stood in thought for a moment more.

"All right," Lise finally said. "My bag is packed. I'll get it."

She went upstairs. In a few minutes Lise was back, carrying the bag, and she put it on the floor near the door.

The doorbell rang. Lise opened the door. Erich had allowed a lot of time, but the driver, who now stood in the doorway, was almost a half-hour early. Beyond him they could see the car. It was a large four-door sedan. There was no more time for talk. Lise picked up her bag. At the door, the driver went to grab it, but Erich reached out and took the bag instead.

"She's not going with you," Erich said. "Come, Lise." As he said it, Erich took her hand, turned away from the driver, and started walking across the porch. It was then that they heard a voice. From behind them.

"You're not going anywhere," it said.

Turning around, Lise and Erich saw two men they had not noticed before, one on each side of the door. The men were holding guns, one pointed at each of them.

A moment later, Erich and Lise were going down the steps, the two armed men directly behind them. The guns were against their backs. Lise spoke in a near whisper, her head bent and turned part way towards Erich.

"Oh, Erich! I shouldn't have hesitated. I'm so sorry!"

"Keep your mouths shut, both of you," one of the men said.

They got into the car; Erich sat next to the driver, she, in the back seat. One of the two men with guns also got into the back, and he sat next to Lise. He pointed his gun at the back of Erich's head.

Hilda had come around the corner just in time to see them get in the car. She saw them drive off. Then she went into the house.

✝✝✝

A rumor had reached Steeg. Two old ladies, on the street behind Mueller's house. Someone, it was not clear who, had heard something, it was not clear what. No one had been seen going in or out of the Professor's house for some days. The rumor was that the ladies were hiding him.

It was mid-afternoon when the doorbell rang. The younger of the ladies, the one who had shown the Professor up to his room, opened the door. It was a policeman. He was middle-aged, rather portly, with a smiling face. He had obviously been a policeman for many years.

"Good afternoon," he said, politely. "We have information that someone, someone the authorities are looking for, may be in this house."

"You are mistaken," the woman said. "There is no one here."

"Would you mind if I looked?"

"Not at all. Come in and see for yourself."

He went in. It was not a large house. A corridor ran from the front hall to the back. A door on the left side of the hall led into a bedroom; another door on the right side opened into the living room. Stairs led up from the hallway. He went into the living room. The other sister was sitting by the fireplace, knitting. He touched his hat and nodded to her. An archway led from the back of the living room into the dining room, which faced the garden. He went into the dining room, then through a door on the left back into the hallway, and on to the kitchen on the other side of the hall. He went back into the hall, and from there into the bedroom. Then he came back out into the hall, opened the door to the basement, went down the stairs, and a few minutes later came back up.

"May I look upstairs?"

"Certainly."

She followed him up the stairs. The policeman was already at the top when she remembered the signal on the pipes. In her nervousness she had forgotten all about it. It was too late now to do anything about it. She felt faint.

She hoped he would first go into the other room, a smaller one, across the hall. But he didn't. The policeman knocked on the door to the bedroom. There was no answer. He opened it. For a moment he stood still, just looking in. From where the lady was standing she could not see into the room.

"No one in here, I see," he said. "Let me look inside."

He opened the closet and peered in. It was empty.

He went through the other room, came out, and glanced into the small toilet closet.

"Sorry to have bothered you," he said.

As he turned to leave, he stopped at the door of the first room. He was near the sink. He noticed that the soap bar on it was wet. He said nothing more, and left.

✝✝✝

The younger of the two ladies picked up the phone immediately and called her old friend Gisele. "Gisele, could I have a couple of eggs? I'm making a batch of those butter cakes. Thanks, that's lovely."

As soon as the woman had hung up, Gisele dialed another number.

"Hello." She recognized Raoul's voice. "The cake is ready. It's nice and fresh."

"Thank you. That's very kind."

They had planned to pick the Professor up the next day, but this news meant they had to do it now. Raoul called Dutrec. When the phone rang, Dutrec was on the bed, fully dressed except for his shoes, taking a nap. He jumped up.

"Richard, it's time."

"I'm on my way."

"Good luck."

Dutrec had studied the immediate vicinity of the ladies' house, and he knew his way through the vacant area behind and to one side of it. This was the same area through which the Professor had been brought there. Within a few minutes Dutrec was at the ladies' back door. By now it was almost dark. He didn't have to knock; the younger of the ladies had seen him coming and opened the door.

The other lady had called the Professor; he was downstairs by the time her sister opened the door. They all knew there was no time to waste in conversation.

Dutrec and the Professor went out the back door, followed by the younger lady. They went through the garden to the back wall, where a heavy wooden door, which had been locked on the previous occasion, had now been unlocked by the lady.

"I can't thank you enough," the Professor said.

"Good luck," said the lady. "We'll be praying for you."

Dutrec led the Professor outside, and the lady locked the door.

Dutrec and the Professor went through the vacant area to a door in the rear of what looked like a small shed. Dutrec unlocked it and they went in. It was a garage with a car in it.

"I want you to try lying on the floor in the back."

The Professor did as he was told. With his knees up, he just fit.

"How is this?" the Professor asked, looking up at Dutrec.

Dutrec nodded, and then handed the Professor some blankets. "Cover yourself with these. Good, you're invisible."

A minute later they were on the road. The car was a German-built 1934 Ford Rheinland sedan. It was just beginning to get dark. Dutrec kept his headlights off while he was still in the sparsely-inhabited neighborhood from which they had started. However he could not avoid going through a part of the center of the city, and there he turned the lights on to avoid being conspicuous. Then Dutrec kept the lights off again while he crossed the less crowded suburbs on his way to the road that led south to the Alps and to the Austrian border. Once he reached the open, unlit highway, he put them back on.

As soon as the two men had left, the ladies had begun to clean the Professor's room and remove from the house every scrap, every crumb, all evidence of his having been there.

✝✝✝

Lake Constance, or the *Bodensee*, is over sixty kilometers—thirty-seven miles—long and about six to twelve kilometers—four to eight miles—wide, running from northwest to southeast. A peninsula projecting out from its short northwesterly end divides that end into two forks. The lake is bounded by Germany along its long northeast shore—the peninsula itself is also part of Germany. The short southeast end of the lake is in Austria; and to the east beyond that end of the lake rise the Austrian Alps. The long southwest shore is in Switzerland, and to the south beyond that shore lie the Swiss Alps.

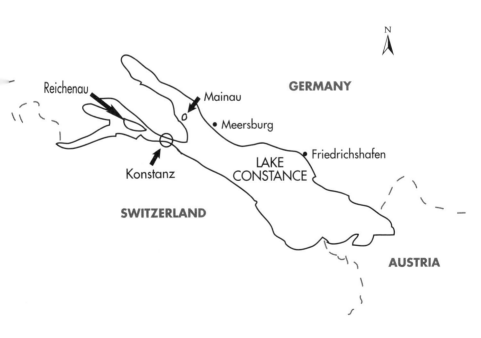

The lake is actually an enlargement of the Rhine River, which enters it at the southeast end and exits at the opposite end through the southerly of the two forks. Two small islands lie near the tip of the peninsula—Mainau, off its north side, and Reichenau, off its south side. Each of these two islands is connected to the peninsula by a causeway, so that it is possible to drive from the island of Mainau, through the peninsula, to the island of Reichenau.

A number of towns and villages line the shores of the lake. One of the most picturesque and historic of these is the small town of Meersburg, on the north shore, nearly opposite the tip of the peninsula. At that point the lake is at its narrowest, providing the quickest way to the other side. As early as the days of the Roman Empire, Meersburg had been a starting point for travelers and merchants headed south across the lake for what is now Switzerland and for the lands beyond.

The lake is blessed with a surprisingly sunny, warm and moist climate, in part because of its unique location. Exotic plants and flowers in Mainau's lush gardens and vegetables on Reichenau's farms grow in abundance, and the water in the lake is exceptionally warm.

✠✠✠

Richard Dutrec had obtained his doctorate in physics at Ludwig-Maximilian University in 1932. His graduate advisor had been Professor Mueller. Dutrec lived near Zurich, and was of Swiss nationality and French-speaking ancestry. He was a large man with red hair, a hearty appearance, and a cheerful disposition. Dutrec was now thirty years old. He respected the Professor deeply, and had been an admirer of his as long as he could remember. Dutrec, who was a Protestant, could not understand, and certainly could not stand, the idea of anyone being judged, let alone hated, on the basis of the race of his ancestors, or of his religious beliefs or those of his ancestors.

As he saw the Nazis starting to become a major force, around the time when he received his doctorate, Dutrec became very distressed. What Hitler and his followers stood for, and the things they did, were repugnant to everything he had ever believed in. When the persecutions began, Dutrec was appalled. When he saw what they were doing to Professor Mueller, he was outraged.

After making discreet inquiries of several friends of his who were also disturbed by these developments, Dutrec was put in touch with someone who knew Raoul Maartens, and eventually with Raoul himself. Before he had any idea that anyone was planning to get the Professor out of Germany, Dutrec had suggested that this be done; when he had learned that it was being planned, he had said that nothing could give him more satisfaction than to have the opportunity to help bring it about. Eventually, on a signal from André he had traveled to Munich, where he had waited for the further signal that would tell him that the time had come. Dutrec had traveled by train and bus, as he had so many times before. For the escape, he would be supplied with a car.

+++

There were three of them waiting in the automobile. Steeg sat next to the driver. The third man sat in the back. From the car they could see the front of the old ladies' house. They had someone watching every garage in the block in which the house sat; that way, if they took the Professor out the back door and left from any one of those garages, someone would see them leave. They also had men posted within view of every intersection in the immediate area, so theoretically it was impossible for them to escape without being seen. Of course one could never be totally sure. In the worst case some time might elapse until whoever saw them reached Steeg's car to tell him; however, with a little luck Steeg's car might be the one to spot them. From their informers they knew that a car, a 1934 Ford Rheinland, had recently been put into a garage that up to then had always been empty. With all this information, Steeg felt confident that this time they would catch the Professor once and for all.

A car drove by; it was a 1934 Rheinland. Steeg and the driver both recognized the license plate at the same moment. It was the number they had been given.

"That's them. Go," Steeg said, although the driver had already started the engine. The driver pulled away from the curb, then followed the Ford, headlights off at first. They were not gaining on the Ford but managed to keep it in sight. Just as Steeg had expected, the Ford headed due south on one of the roads leading towards the Austrian Alps.

They were going through a cluster of shops and restaurants, which they could see were open. The road, actually still a street at this point, was a straight stretch ahead of them.

"Get out here," Steeg said to the man in the back. The driver pulled over.

"Call them all along the line," Steeg said. "Tell them it's as we thought. Be sure they have the license plate number."

The man got out. The other two drove on. The Ford had moved along, but they still had it in sight.

+++

They noticed that the Ford ahead of them had kept its headlights off until it reached the busier parts of Munich, and had turned them off again not long after passing through these. When it had reached the open road the driver of the Rheinland had turned the lights on again. Steeg's driver had kept his lights off the whole time; however, when they had reached the unlit road, he had had no choice but to turn them on.

Less than an hour after leaving, they went through Starnberg, on the edge of beautiful Lake Starnberg, the

Starnberger See. Steeg had been to this place, but now, in the night, little of it could be seen, and besides, without romance these kinds of places did not interest him. Right now Steeg's mind was consumed by the excitement of the hunt.

A few kilometers further on, as they were going through a village, the Ford took a turn to the right, heading west. This meant that instead of continuing towards the Austrian border, it was now running roughly parallel to it.

A short while later, at the next village, Steeg and the driver saw the Ford go around a corner; but after they themselves had made the turn, Steeg and his driver no longer saw it. They looked into one side street, then another, then several other streets and some alleys. All of this wasted precious time. After a while the two realized they had lost the car. Most of the small village was already darkened, but after a while they found a café that was still open. They pulled over and both went in.

Steeg pulled a piece of paper out of his pocket and handed it to the driver.

"Read these out to me," he said.

The man on the first call must have been waiting by the phone, because he answered almost immediately. Steeg gave him the description of the Ford and its license plate number, and the name of the town that the Ford had appeared headed for.

"We've lost them," Steeg said, "but if they continue the way we last saw them, they should reach you within ten minutes to a half-hour. The instant you spot them call Munich. Yes, him. No, he'll call me."

Steeg hung up and dialed another number. When this second man answered, Steeg told him where he was located. "They were in front of me, heading west," he continued, "but I've lost them. Our people on that road are keeping an eye out for them. But it's possible that they have turned back and gone your way. Yes, south, towards the Austrian Alps. If you spot them, call Munich. Yes, a 1934 Rheinland. Here's the license number…"

After several more similar calls, Steeg called Munich.

"I've lost them for the time being, but everyone is on the lookout for them. They'll call you. As soon as you hear from them, call me here. Here's the number…"

Steeg could do nothing but wait. There were no other customers in the café. The minutes seemed like hours. After about fifteen minutes the phone rang. It was the man in Munich.

"They were just spotted. They're headed for Schongau."

This was a town to the west of where Steeg now was.

Thirty seconds later Steeg and his driver were back on the road. They would have to travel fast, but Steeg estimated that he could catch up with the Rheinland. In fact Steeg thought he'd even have time to stop somewhere for a minute to call Munich for any further information.

✝✝✝

Like the vehicle that Dutrec was driving, the car André and Raoul were driving was one that they had never used before. They had left right after the call to Dutrec. Because the house they left from was further to the south, they had an automatic headstart. They got on the road to Starnberg, and continued on past it. In a small village a few kilometers further on, they made a right-hand turn into a side street, then pulled into a driveway and into the opened door of a two-car garage. They turned off their headlights, got out of the car, and waited.

They had only waited a matter of minutes when Dutrec pulled in and turned off his lights, but it had seemed like an hour. There was no time for chatter. In the near-total darkness, the Professor got out of the Ford Rheinland.

Dutrec pulled out fast, turned into an alley that paralleled the main road for about half a kilometer, then turned left and then right again onto the main road. At first he saw no light following him. After he had gone several kilometers, Dutrec saw headlights in his rear-view mirror. There was no other car in sight. When he saw those headlights unrelentingly gaining on him even though he was driving as fast as he dared on this mountain road, Dutrec became increasingly certain that this car was following him. He had been heading west, but a short distance before Schongau, he turned left, onto a road heading south to the Austrian border and the Austrian Alps.

✝✝✝

Raoul, André, and the Professor were quite certain that there was no one nearby, but out of caution they did not speak or make any noise. After the sound of the Rheinland had faded and finally disappeared completely, they continued waiting in silence. Then, after what seemed to them like an eternity, André at last whispered "now." The Professor, got in the back of the car and resumed his position on the floor. André covered him with a blanket and got in the passenger's seat next to Raoul, and they drove off.

A few kilometers further on, at Schongau, they made a turn to the right and headed due north. This meant they were now traveling directly away from the Alps; they had made an almost complete reversal of direction, but were on a different road from the one they had been traveling on when they had been traveling south towards the Austrian Alps a while before. Some distance further on they turned left, now heading west again. After that they stayed on the same road, which veered to the southwest, away from the Austrian Alps and towards Lake Constance.

They saw no sign of anyone following them.

✝✝✝

For a while after Dutrec had made the turn to the south towards the Austrian border, he saw no lights behind him; he began to think that his pursuer had lost his trail, probably at the turn. It began to rain, a light shower at first, but soon afterwards a heavy downpour. After Dutrec had driven some distance further, a pair of headlights appeared through the blur of his rear-view mirror. Dutrec continued driving at full speed, his tires squealing on the sharper curves. There were still no other cars on the road, and the car behind him did not let go. Now he felt sure it was Steeg.

After a while the car came up close behind Dutrec. For a long time its headlights stayed in the same place, blurred both by the water pouring down the rear window and by the downpour itself. Dutrec sped up; the headlights kept their position in the mirror. He tried slowing down and got the same result. After a while the headlights came even closer, and Dutrec had the feeling the car was within centimeters of his bumper.

Dutrec had hoped to lead them far into the mountains before Steeg could realize that the Professor had gone somewhere else. However, with the car so close to his, he began to doubt that this was possible. He decided that he would have to take some additional action. When he came to a straight enough stretch of open road, Dutrec floored the accelerator. As he picked up speed, the headlights stayed at the same close distance, and before long came even closer. When the speedometer reached 110 kilometers per hour, Dutrec slammed his foot on the brake. His tires screamed. The car skidded and swerved, but Dutrec managed to keep it on the road. The car following him evidently hit its brakes, because its headlights dropped out of view and for an instant Dutrec saw the top of the car getting closer, the rain pouring down on it. Then he felt the crash. Dutrec's car spun to the left and turned almost sideways. Then there was a second crash, against the driver's side. Then everything stopped.

Steeg jumped out of his car and came up to Dutrec's. He could see Dutrec, but both doors on the left side of Dutrec's car were smashed in by the front of Steeg's car. He went around to the passenger's side, glanced at Dutrec through the front window, and then looked through the rear window at the back seat. He saw no one there. Steeg opened the rear door. He reached in and ran his hand all over the floor.

"*Scheisse*! He's not in there," Steeg said.

The trunk! Steeg walked to the back again. The trunk lid was smashed in, leaving a gap between it and the trunk bottom. Steeg got a flashlight from his car and peered through the gap. There was nobody in the trunk.

Meanwhile Dutrec could not move. The back of his car and its whole side had crumpled and he was pinned in. Dutrec's body hurt in many places, but he could not tell what his injuries were. Steeg took one more look in at him, then walked back to the other car. The whole front end of it was crushed in. He got in anyway and sat in the front passenger seat. The driver pressed on the starter. Nothing happened. They both got out of the car and started walking down the road.

Dutrec thought Steeg and the driver might come back, but they didn't. For many minutes he kept trying to pry himself loose, but it was hopeless. He felt a draft of cold air, and heard rain dripping into the car through a broken window or other opening, but he could not see where. Dutrec could do nothing except sit imprisoned, and hope someone would find him. He felt weary. Not long afterwards he dozed off.

✝✝✝

By now it was well into the evening, probably around half-past nine or ten o'clock. Steeg remembered that it was approaching full moon, but any moonlight there might have been was almost entirely obscured by the heavy overcast; for practical purposes, it was completely dark. Both Steeg and the

ARNOLD SIMON

driver knew only roughly where they were. Neither of them could remember having gone by any house or building with a light on it since they had made the turn near Schongau; at this time of night, many of the inhabitants of this mountainous area were undoubtedly already in their beds. And the two men had not seen any vehicle going in either direction except the one they had been following. Steeg discussed it with the driver; they both agreed that the only thing they could do was to start walking back north, towards Schongau. At least the rain had lightened, and it soon stopped.

During this walk, Steeg had plenty of time to think. He was sure that the Professor had been in the Ford Rheinland when it left Munich. From its sudden disappearance around the corner in that village, plus the fact that the Professor was no longer in that car, it was obvious that there had been a switch, coupled, Steeg suspected, with a change of direction. Steeg remained convinced that they had been headed for the border. From the road on which they had started out, he had surmised that they were headed south towards Austria. Assuming they had indeed changed their course, Steeg had to consider that they might now be headed for Switzerland instead. But where on that border?

The part of that border that was closest to Munich was along Lake Constance, which has its northeast shore in Germany and its southwest shore in Switzerland. That lake in effect *was* the Swiss border. And it was less than 200 kilometers from Munich, a relatively short distance. It had been his best guess all along that this was probably the actual area where the escape would be attempted, and this is where he had arranged to have Behrndt and Lise taken. The location had advantages for Steeg, and if he found out that the escape was to be attempted at another point, it would be relatively simple to have the two transferred then. Now, as he put everything together, he became convinced that his guess about Lake Constance had been correct.

As soon as they reached a telephone he would, as a backup plan, give instructions for someone to pursue the possibility that it might be Austria after all. However, as for himself he decided to head for Lake Constance. He would also arrange for a search to be made of its entire northeast shore.

✝✝✝

After about a half-hour, Steeg and the driver came to a small isolated house and knocked on the door. There was no immediate response. They kept knocking for some time, and Steeg shouted for the occupants to open the door, saying he had been in an automobile accident. After about five minutes of this, they heard some sounds inside and saw a dim light go on and a window curtain move. Steeg kept on shouting. A few seconds later they heard sounds again, receding this time, and the light went out. Whoever lived there was evidently not interested in opening the door to strangers at this time of night. Steeg and the driver moved on. Though it had stopped raining, they were both soaked. They tried knocking and shouting at several other houses further on, with similar results.

About a kilometer further on, they noticed a light ahead near the side of the road. As Steeg and the driver neared it, they saw that the light came from a single light bulb inside the open door of a barn. Inside the barn a man was working on some kind of farm equipment that was not familiar to Steeg. He explained that they had had a car accident and needed to use a telephone to call for help. The man said that he had one inside the house that they could use. Steeg asked the man how it happened that he was working this late; the man said that the equipment, which he identified only as "this Goddamn thing," had broken down again and that he needed it for work in the morning.

Steeg called a contact in Munich, told him what had happened, and gave him some orders. The first was to start the search of the northeast shore of Lake Constance. The second was to have the Ford's license plate traced. The man said he had already done this. The car was registered to someone in Berlin. They had checked the address given by that person, but there was no such address. The third order was to have a search for the Professor made at all the approaches to the Austrian border. Because of the very mountainous nature of that terrain, that border could be crossed only at relatively few points, which could only be reached by well-known roads. Although success could not be absolutely certain, Steeg knew that all the approaches were adequately manned for the task; it was mainly a question of supplying the right information to the right people, and he knew that his contact in Munich would be able to do that.

Steeg's fourth order had to do with a boat suitable for intercepting and capturing the Professor and his accomplices when, as he expected, they attempted to escape across Lake Constance. When Steeg had first guessed that the escape would probably be attempted there, he had made a request from his superiors for a boat with an armed crew. This had been denied out of hand; they said the last thing they wanted was an international incident on this lake, bordered as it was by three countries; if Steeg needed a boat he would have to make his own arrangements. He had then had someone locate a boat and an experienced pilot. Steeg had assumed that the owner of the boat would want to know what he planned to do with it; however the man had said he didn't care what Steeg wanted to do as long as he himself was being paid. The order that Steeg gave now was to have the boat ready for him when he reached the lake.

Despite the warning he had been given about avoiding an armed incident on the lake, Steeg had also obtained two high-caliber pistols—since, despite his civilian attire, he was an SS, this was easy for him—one for himself and one that he would have Behrndt use when the time came. His information was that the people who would accompany the Professor would be civilians, most likely those two Belgian businessmen. Steeg was sure that whoever it was would not be armed, and even if they were they would be no match for his highly expert marksmanship borne of years of battle and other military experience.

But the guns were not his main weapon. That weapon was Lise, and what Steeg could threaten her with if there was any resistance.

✠✠✠

It was still dark when André, Raoul, and the Professor reached Meersburg, on the north shore of the Lake. Raoul had been to this town before, and knew the way. From the highway they turned on to a street that led down the steep hill through the ancient town and to the shore. This was the very street that centuries of travelers had followed on their way to board the boats that took them to the part of Europe that lay beyond the opposite shore. But just part-way down towards the hill, Raoul turned to the right onto a street that ran parallel to the shore. After a short stretch of vacant land on both sides of this street they came to a lone house on the downhill side. The owner of the house had been waiting for them and had the garage door open; he closed it as soon as they were inside.

✠✠✠

Raoul and André had given it a lot of thought. At the entry to the lower of the two forks, where the city of Konstanz stands, the lake narrows to a small channel, then widens again. This narrow channel runs through the city, where it is spanned by a bridge. Because this bridge was sure to be closely guarded, it was obviously not the place to attempt a crossing. The relatively isolated and unpopulated island of Reichenau, on the other hand, lies further to the west, in the middle of the south fork, and is only about one kilometer from the Swiss shore. For these reasons, and because Reichenau could easily be reached from Mainau by taking the causeway to the peninsula, and from there the causeway to Reichenau, André and Raoul decided that Reichenau was the place from which they would launch the final leg of the escape to Switzerland.

An old and trusted friend of Dutrec who lived in Switzerland owned a suitable boat which he offered to bring over to take them across to the Swiss side. His name was Karl. They would first stay overnight on Reichenau at the farm of another old friend, named Bernard, again a Swiss who could not stomach the way the Nazis had treated Professor Mueller.

CHAPTER 16

*T*HERE WAS LITTLE CONVERSATION. André, Raoul, and the Professor told the owner they were not hungry, only tired. Their plan was to take the Professor to Mainau, the first leg of the journey, using a small boat that belonged to the owner of the house. To reduce the chance of being detected, they would land on Mainau at a point removed from the public landing. They had planned to do this in the morning. However, the owner said that he had arranged things so that they could leave immediately if they wanted. This meant they could land on Mainau while it was still dark, further lowering the chance of being seen. All three of them could have used a few hours' rest, but they agreed that reducing the risk was much more important than this inconvenience.

Their host called and alerted a contact on Mainau. Since the owner was roughly the same size as the Professor, just a little taller, he had easily found suitable clothes for Mueller. These he took from a shed in which he kept clothes for working in his garden. These included trousers and a shirt made of coarse materials, farmer's shoes, and a straw hat with a wide brim. The clothes fit the Professor well enough, although he had to stuff paper inside the shoes, which were a bit too large. Within minutes, the owner, the Professor, and Raoul left the house. The plan was that André would leave for Mainau in the morning.

The three men headed west along the street. After a while the street changed to a dirt path. Some meters further on, a narrower path took them downhill towards the shore and to a small boathouse. The owner unlocked the padlock and opened the door. The boat had a motor, but was still small enough that it could be rowed. They set out from the shore in almost complete silence.

Only a few lights shone in the distance, but the owner seemed to know where he was going. Despite his relatively small frame, his rowing propelled them at a good clip. After a considerable time, he let Raoul relieve him at the oars. Just before he did so, the owner pointed to something in the distance ahead of them.

"You see that light?"

Raoul, who at first could see nothing in that direction, eventually made it out. A faint yellow twinkle.

"That's them," said the owner. "They're waiting for us."

✝✝✝

Since nothing had been heard from Dutrec, one of Raoul's men in Munich called a man named Wilhelm who lived in the area near Schongau. He asked him to search for the Rheinland on the road between there and the Austrian border. It did not take Wilhelm long to find the two wrecked cars. He had brought an assistant along, and between them they managed after some considerable effort to pry the door open with the tools Wilhelm had in the trunk. They extracted Dutrec from the car. He was bruised and felt weak, but otherwise did not seem to have any serious injury. They drove Dutrec to Wilhelm's house, where he was given a bed and fell asleep immediately. Rising several hours later, Dutrec announced that he felt as fit as ever and was anxious to get back to Switzerland, as had been his original plan. Before leaving, he did agree to have a bite to eat, and ate like two men who had not had any food for an entire day. After that, Wilhelm headed out with Dutrec in Wilhelm's car.

✝✝✝

Steeg had said almost nothing to Lise, except that she must from now on obey everything he said, and that her father's well-being, his life in fact, depended on it. If she cooperated with Steeg, he would do "whatever is possible" for her father. Otherwise, he could not "answer for his safety." Lise did not know what was going to happen, only that Steeg knew "where he is" and was "making arrangements for his rescue." The only good part of it was that Steeg had evidently given up, at least for now, his pursuit of her "affections." Whatever happened, Lise had at least, apparently, achieved that not-so-small but undoubtedly temporary victory.

Steeg had also told Lise that he had decided she could see her father as soon as he was rescued; when the time came, someone would come to take her to him. Lise knew that almost all the things Steeg was telling her were lies, but she didn't know what parts might not be. There was nothing she could do about any of it.

Ever since Lise's escape, Steeg had become much more cautious about letting Hilda in on his plans. Before he sent Erich to escort Miss Hermann, he had simply said that someone would be coming to pick Lise up within the next day or two, that someone would call to let her know the night before, and that Lise should be ready to leave the following morning.

✝✝✝

When they reached Meersburg, their driver pulled up in front of an inn. The man behind Erich, the one who had kept a gun at his head, got out. Erich started to get out.

"Just her. You stay in the car," the man said.

Erich paused. The man had put his gun away. They were just outside the entrance. A couple, evidently guests at the inn, were leaving, and an attendant was putting their luggage in the trunk of their car.

Erich got out the rest of the way.

"If she's getting out, I'm getting out," he said.

The man stood directly in Erich's way, only centimeters from him.

"I'm sorry, sir," he said, "but I am under orders." The man dropped his voice almost to a whisper. "If you don't do as I say, I have orders to kill you."

Erich felt sure that the man was not about to pull out a firearm in this place.

"Not here," the man said. "My friend and I... You cannot resist us. We will take you and do it somewhere else."

Clouded as Erich's brain was with rage at this further humiliation, he saw one thing clearly enough—defying this man would accomplish nothing. This was neither the right place nor the right time. Besides, the man was probably telling the truth when he said that he was obeying orders; he was likely to be just as much in Steeg's grip as Erich was. On top of that, the real victim here was Lise, and trying to stand up to this man would do nothing for her. Erich got back in the car.

Lise was still inside the car.

"Where do you plan to take me?" she asked Steeg's man.

"Everything is arranged. You will be quite safe here."

The attendant, who had by now finished with the departing guests, had already taken Lise's bag and was waiting. She started to get out of the car. At the last moment, Lise turned her head and looked back at Erich. She wanted to say something to him, but everything had already been said.

She got out and followed the attendant inside.

✝✝✝

Lise was not actually a prisoner, but the effect was essentially the same. She had a beautiful room, actually a suite, with a magnificent view of the lake and the mountains. All her needs were taken care of. She could even come and go; however she knew that if she went out someone would follow her. So it was useless to think of leaving to get in touch with André, or anyone else for that matter.

None of this was satisfactory. Lise did not trust what Steeg had told her about her father—she no longer trusted him about anything. She was deathly afraid for her father's safety; Lise wished that she could be near him. She would also have given anything to find André. Lise had no idea of where he was, and was sure he didn't know where she was. But she felt certain that wherever he was, André was devoting all his energy to rescuing her father. And that was more important to Lise than being with her father, more important than her own life.

She would just have to stay here and wait.

✝✝✝

Hilda wore a well-worn plain black dress without ornament, and a good-sized hat whose wide brim drooped down to her eyes. Her blond hair was tied up in a bun as usual. The cloth bag she carried appeared to be stuffed with what one would have assumed were the ordinary belongings of an ordinary woman. Hilda looked for all the world like a cleaning lady, which in a sense was what she was.

A train would be departing just over an hour after Lise and Erich had left, and by rushing Hilda managed to get on it. Before leaving she had called the telephone number that the man with the fat-looking face had given her.

"This is Ursula," she had said to the male voice who answered.

There was only a silence.

"The maid."

"Where are you working?" the man asked.

"Room 526."

"Glad to hear from you. What news do you have for me?"

"The lady is being taken to Meersburg. They just left."

She gave him the name of the inn.

"I'm on my way there," she said. "On my own. If I can free her, I will call you. Don't do anything until then."

✝✝✝

Much of the scenery along the way from Munich to Lake Constance was spectacular, but it was wasted on Hilda, concentrated as her mind was on her self-appointed mission. The train did not go into Meersburg, but to a nearby town; from there she went by taxi the rest of the way.

When Hilda reached Meersburg, she had the taxi drop her off on the edge of town, and walked to the inn. Hilda knew from long experience that Steeg always took his women to Meersburg on beautiful Lake Constance for a "holiday," and she was familiar with the particular inn—it was always the same one—where he stayed on those occasions. Steeg also had a favorite room, and usually had Hilda make the arrangements with the inn for it. Actually, Hilda could not have been sure whether Steeg would follow the same practice this time, as he had not asked her to make the call. But when the inn had telephoned while Steeg was out, she had found out.

Carrying her bag, Hilda went around to the back of the inn, easily located the servants' entrance, and walked in as if she did this every day. She knew that although the inn was not large by big city standards, it was known for superb accommodations and service, and employed a good number of maids and other servants. Hilda passed other maids, all of whom were running about busily and looked at her but did not seem surprised to see her. At one point she passed by the door to a supply room, where a supervisor was handing linens out to several maids. When this woman saw her, she said, "Oh, so you are one of the new maids. Take these towels to room 209, and get rid of that useless hat and that bag."

Hilda took the towels, delivered them to the guest in 209, then walked up to 313— Steeg's lucky room. She knocked. The door opened, and Lise stood before her, looking puzzled.

Hilda said nothing. She put her index finger to her lips, then, with the index finger of the other hand—which was still gripping her bag—reached up and pushed her hat up. Lise almost let out a shriek but managed to stifle it. Hilda walked on in and Lise shut the door.

†††

No trace of the Professor or his accomplices had yet been found. Since there was not enough time to search the entire northeast shore meter by meter, Steeg would have to use the little information he had to guess at the most likely spots for an attempt to cross, and to position his few men at as many of these as possible. It was also out of the question to try to patrol the entire five hundred or so square kilometers of the lake. Steeg assumed that they would not attempt to use the steamers from Friedrichshafen or the other larger harbors, which he knew were tightly monitored.

Because it was the area of the shortest water crossing, Steeg's own best guess was that the attempt was likely to be made at the peninsula, but avoiding the German city of Constance, or Konstanz, which is located there, because it was so closely watched. Meersburg's location was strategic to that whole part of the lake, including the peninsula. He had arranged for watches to be posted in and around Meersburg, and all of his people were still searching for clues, or even rumors, that might lead to the Professor. But until this extensive search should turn up some other evidence, Steeg was still inclined to focus primarily on the fork of the lake south of the peninsula.

✝✝✝

When André awoke, he just took time for a quick cup of coffee and some bread and butter. The Meersburg house was built into the steep hillside that lined the shore in the entire vicinity of that town. André took his coffee with the owner and his wife in a large room facing the lake. Although it was still early, the mist that often covers the lake had already dissipated, and the lake and all beyond it reflected the dazzling morning sunshine. Not far beyond the opposite shore he could see a band of low hills. Behind and above these rose a range of mountains, the actual foothills of the Alps. Still beyond these towered the Alps themselves, their majestic snow-covered masses capped by peaks that pierced the highest clouds.

André hoped that their evasive maneuver, and particularly the last-minute decision to get the Professor over to the island of Mainau immediately, had bought them enough time to elude Steeg completely. It all depended on how far into the mountains Dutrec had succeeded in luring Steeg. But André was quite sure that no one had followed them here, and he believed that they had gained enough time.

To keep André from having to linger at the boarding area, they waited until the last possible moment; the owner then drove him down, dropped him off at the dock, and drove away. Although it was not quite yet spring, the boat was already crowded, in part with early tourists attracted by Mainau's spectacular floral displays, but also with quite a few locals, workmen and others as well. Almost as soon as André disembarked he was met by a young man in working clothes, who greeted him by name and led the way to private quarters where he found Raoul.

+++

They had originally planned to make the crossing with the Professor the next night, but decided to discuss the message from Hilda that had been waiting for them in Mainau. They knew that it had been Lise's desire all along to do all she could to help free her father; Raoul's man in Meersburg was already standing by to take her across to Mainau in his boat. Raoul called their man in Munich and instructed him to alert the man in Meersburg and to have Hilda, if she called, tell Lise how to get to his house. They had already decided that attempting to free Lise first was not worth delaying the Professor's escape, and would have diverted their efforts, probably uselessly and perhaps fatally. But now there was a possibility that Hilda might manage to free Lise soon; waiting for Lise might only delay the crossing by a few hours, or perhaps until the following night. André mentioned that it was Hilda who had engineered Lise's original escape from the house.

"Since Lise is already in Steeg's hands," André continued, "Hilda obviously did not come down here to give any help to him. It seems to me that we can trust her. At this point I don't see what we have to lose by waiting to see if she can free Lise."

"Except time," said Raoul.

"We know Steeg wants to use Lise as a pawn. I don't think he'll come after us as long as he thinks he could catch her again first," André said.

"All right, let's wait," Raoul said. "If Hilda signals that she has failed, or if there is no call from her by tomorrow, then we can go."

"All right," André agreed, "but if Lise gets free, we'd better make sure she doesn't lead them to us."

"We'll just have to be very cautious about that. Arrivals in Mainau, even by small boats, can be spotted. I'll make sure that she doesn't get any further than Mainau unless it's safe."

"I agree. There's risk either way, but this is our best choice."

✝✝✝

Raoul and André would get to Bernard's farm on Reichenau the following morning. But the two had decided they would get the Professor over to Reichenau that evening after dark. Mueller would stay in another house located near Bernard's farm but on a different road, until shortly before the crossing to Switzerland.

In the evening an enclosed truck, driven by Bernard, set out from Mainau for the peninsula. It did not seem likely to attract much attention; Bernard frequently made the same trip at all hours, carrying farm products and other items related to the island's castle and gardens. On this trip his truck was filled with boxes, bags, barrels, plants, tools, and equipment of every type. It was also carrying Professor Mueller, who was concealed among all these goods, inside a crate. When he reached the peninsula, Bernard turned away from the city, wound his way along the narrow roads to the causeway, and arrived on Reichenau. A small lane crossed the road a few hundred meters further ahead. A small horse-drawn wagon was stopped at the intersection, just around the corner. Bernard pulled over to the side of the road, left the engine running, jumped down to the ground, ran to the back door of the truck, opened it, climbed in, undid a latch on the crate, and swung its side open.

"Professor, this is where you get out."

"Thank you so much," said the Professor.

"We'll see you soon," said Bernard. "In the meantime, he'll take good care of you. Sleep well."

Two minutes later, the Professor was installed in the back of the cart, where he concealed himself as well as he could among the plants and produce that nearly filled it. Within a few more minutes, Mueller had reached the house where he would stay until their departure for Switzerland.

✝✝✝

A hundred meters further on, Bernard turned a corner and saw two bright lights in the middle of the road. As he got closer, Bernard saw that these were held by two men. The one on the left signaled for him to stop.

The man went up to the driver's window. Bernard rolled the window down.

"Oh it's you, Bernard," the man said, sounding surprised and somewhat relieved to recognize someone. "How are you?"

Bernard recognized both men. They were from the area. It was a small community.

"Very well, Martin," said Bernard, "and you?"

"Very well, thank you." The man paused briefly. "Did you just come from the Peninsula?"

"Yes."

"And before that?"

Bernard knew that this man was familiar with his routine. "Mainau."

"There's someone they're looking for. Supposedly near here. Someone from Munich, a Jew, I think, a fugitive. They asked us to help find him. Don't suppose you've seen anything unusual like that, have you?"

"No. Nothing at all."

"When we saw you coming, we didn't know who it was. Thought it might be a stranger, and here it turns out to be you." The man laughed. "You don't have him in that truck, do you?"

"No, I don't. But you're welcome to look."

"Bernard, I was just joking. I know you don't. If I'd known it was you, we wouldn't have stopped you."

"I know."

"But as long as I did, and since you came from Mainau, I'd better look. I'm sure you won't mind."

"Of course not. Go right ahead."

Bernard again jumped out and opened the back door.

Martin shined his flashlight into the doorway.

"You have a full load there, I see," he said. He was moving the beam back and forth.

"No Jews, though!" he said.

His flashlight caught the crate in its beam. He stepped up into the truck, went straight to the crate, noticed the latch and pulled it open.

"Empty," he said. "What's this?"

"I use that for chickens sometimes. Why, I just delivered a load a while ago."

"Well, sorry to bother you, Bernard."

"That's all right. One can't be too careful."

"Good night."

"Good night."

†††

The part about the wet soap bar convinced Steeg that the rumor had been true. He immediately ordered the house searched, but this time by SS personnel; they were more experienced and thorough in these things. The Professor would undoubtedly be gone, but Steeg hoped they would find an item of clothing, a pinch of tobacco, some small clue that would lead them further.

The SS men took their time, and they were meticulous. They took the bedding apart, looked for crumbs on the floor and in the crevices of the chair, examined the towels. The bed had been made up with fresh linens—which was either exculpatory or incriminating, depending on how one looked at it—and the only towel was dry and fresh. In sum, they came up with nothing. They never found the opening to the space behind the closet. All of this made no difference; the Professor was already gone. But they took the ladies away for questioning.

†††

Some time later, Steeg spoke with an SS about the ladies.

"The two women both said no one had stayed here."

"They're Jew-lovers. What do you expect? You should have arrested them."

"We did."

"What did they say."

"They wouldn't talk."

"Make them talk."

"They tried."

"And?"

"The first one didn't talk. She's dead."

"Fools! And the other one?"

"She saw the other one die, but nevertheless she didn't talk. She also died."

"Bunglers!"

CHAPTER 17

*R*UMORS THAT THE PROFESSOR had been seen on Mainau or on the Peninsula persisted, but they were not backed by any first-hand report or other hard facts. Steeg had people searching the general area of the Peninsula, with no helpful results so far. He knew that this might be in part because he had to work with little or no support from the authorities. Steeg suspected that someone on that island might be providing refuge to Mueller. In Steeg's eyes this of course would be criminal.

Steeg sent someone to the island to inquire about it. He instructed the man to say that the Professor was a fugitive, to ask whether he was on the island, and to request that he be turned over. When the man came back, he reported that the person he spoke to—he didn't get his name but had been assured that this fellow had full authority to speak on behalf of the island's owners—said that the Professor was not on the island, but that even if he were he would not be turned over to anyone without a warrant.

In theory Steeg could have sought a warrant. But Steeg was well aware that while the Party was quite anxious to prevent the Professor from leaving the country, it did not want him pursued like a common criminal. If the news of such a pursuit got out, it could provoke a reaction abroad; this would quite likely end up backfiring against Steeg himself.

The rumor nevertheless strengthened Steeg's growing conviction that the escape would be attempted across the south fork of the lake. To try to intercept the Professor before he set out across the water would require a tedious search of the shoreline, for which there was no time. To Steeg the best option would be to stand offshore and intercept Mueller on the way across towards the Swiss side. The fast and highly maneuverable boat Steeg had insisted on would give him control over a wide area, and he figured that would do the job.

✝✝✝

Hilda had left the inn sometime in the evening and called the man in Munich. He told her that if Lise could get away she should go to the house of Raoul's man on the northeast shore, and gave Hilda the instructions on how this would be accomplished.

Hilda was "on duty" most of the night. When her work shift ended, she returned to room 313. Lise was ready. They did not waste time in conversation; it took only a few minutes for them to exchange clothes. Hilda put Lise's hair up in a bun just like her own.

"Here's how they plan for you to rejoin your father. The regular boat may not be safe at this point. So a man who lives not far from here will take you over to Mainau in his own boat."

Hilda passed on the directions that the man in Munich had given her.

Within a few minutes, Hilda stepped out of room 313, went down to the lobby, and stepped out into the street. She looked as much like Lise as she was able to—Hilda was wearing Lise's dress, her hair was done like Lise's, Lise herself had applied Hilda's makeup, she had Lise's shoes on, and a pair of sunglasses blocked any view of Hilda's eyes.

She had walked some distance and was about to cross the street, when a car pulled up alongside of her. Two men jumped out of the vehicle and impeded Hilda's way. They were well-dressed and looked for all the world like some of the well-to-do visitors who often stayed in the town.

"We know who you are," the man on the right said. His tone was polite, but firm. "We are friends of Mr. Steeg." He opened the back door of the car. "Please get in." Uncertain as to what Lise would have done, Hilda hesitated for a moment. The other man was looking straight into her sunglasses, as if trying to see what her response would be.

Hilda decided that in any event nothing was to be gained by objecting. She would get into the car. One of the men told her to sit in the back behind the driver. He then sat next to her. The other man hopped into the front passenger seat. The car pulled away from the curb, accelerating hard, and disappeared around the corner, tires squealing.

†††

For Steeg the opportunity to see Lise again had been too tempting. They had known where to reach him; in the same sentence, the man on the phone had told him both that Lise had escaped and that they had caught her almost immediately. This news turned what would have been an explosion of rage into a double pleasure, combining as it did the gratifying fact that Lise had once again not been able to get away with the elation at having at last achieved complete power over her, if not sexually at least physically. He felt as triumphant as a lion who had just brought down a magnificent wildebeest; it did not cross his mind that it was more like a cat and a mouse. But Steeg had not been able to resist taking it one step further; he decided to interrupt his total concentration on the Professor's pursuit, and told them to have her back at the inn in exactly one half-hour, no sooner.

Now Steeg sat in room 313, waiting for her. The rush that he felt was of course not the anticipation of imminent sexual gratification that had flooded through him on so many other occasions, only the anticipation of seeing Lise—head bowed, at least figuratively—once again his captive, this time for good. Interestingly, this anticipation was just as intense, and even more intoxicating.

When the door did open, Steeg felt only the briefest surge of triumph which, as he realized that this was not Lise but Hilda, collapsed into a bitter mix of disappointment and mindless rage. He was angry at Hilda, and of course at the incompetents who had brought her here and now still stood right behind her at the door. He immediately began to shout at his men; however, Steeg quickly had to face the fact that no matter how long or loudly he shouted, it would change nothing, certainly not how they would perform their responsibilities in the future. These men were only bit players in the drama of which he saw himself the hero, and however much he would berate them, their deficiencies would never go away and their performances would never improve. After a few shouted epithets, Steeg waved them away, and they were gone.

Once again he vented his fury on Hilda. She did not respond; just sat there—she had not waited for an invitation from Steeg to sit down—looking impassive.

"This time it's over. This time you're going to help me."

She said nothing.

"You know where Lise went, and I want you to tell me."

No response.

"Tell me, damn it! I know that you know where."

"If I did, I wouldn't tell you."

Steeg pondered this for a few moments. He stood up and moved closer to her. Hilda did not follow his movements; she just sat looking straight at where Steeg had been. That irritated him as much as what she had said, because it told Steeg that what he had to say to Hilda was not important, that he was not important. Yet Hilda was just a servant, nothing more; it was her duty to obey him. What hurt most about these flagrant violations of that duty was that time and again he found himself unable to do anything about them. True, Hilda had fought back by using blackmail; there was not much he could do about that. Nevertheless there ought to be a way.

"This time I will make you tell me."

"You know you can't."

"That same old trick."

"It's no trick."

"My mistake has always been to take your threats too seriously."

"No one is forcing you to take them seriously."

Steeg continued to stand there, not saying anything, just thinking.

"Look, two can play this game. There are things I can do to you."

"I have no doubt."

"Do you think that I would do them?"

"I would not doubt it."

"Do you think I would be afraid to fire you? After you had done to me what you have always threatened, how would you manage? What would you live on? You're not young anymore, and even for an ordinary job, that's important. Besides, don't forget that I will make sure you never work again. And even that is just the beginning of what I could do to you. I can have you arrested—I have grounds—and if I did that…"

"Don't concern yourself too much for me. Besides, don't forget what I can do."

"Ah, Hilda, that's where you're wrong! After I accomplish the mission I have been given, nothing will be able to touch me. Not you, not anybody."

"You're dreaming. And you know it."

At these words, Steeg felt an unexpected shock, as if someone had punched him in the stomach. Steeg had begun to feel invincible, but now he wondered if it could be that he was allowing himself to get carried away. He wondered whether success tonight was really as certain as he was saying.

"Hilda, we were once friends. Don't you remember?"

"I remember."

"Why can't we be again?"

She made no answer.

"Don't you see that we need each other?"

"I find that idea very strange."

"I know that you don't want to help me." He paused. "Hilda, I know what you think of me, and to be honest I don't blame you. But this isn't just for me. What I'm doing here I'm doing for the Party, for our country."

"I know nothing about that."

"I know, I know. And that's just the point. You need to know. This is not about what I want for myself."

"Oh, I see. You've given her up. Do you expect me to believe that?"

"I know that may sound strange to you. But believe me, that's now over. I have to explain."

Steeg saw that Hilda was now looking up at him.

"What you don't know is that this is not like all those other times. And that I have been assigned by the SS, and the Party, to prevent someone, a dangerous Jew, from leaving the country."

She laughed. "You? Why you?"

"It's complicated. I can't tell you the details, but they consider it essential to keep him here, but without harming him. How I was assigned this job is a whole story. Let me just say that I have special qualifications for the job. Now, this woman is his daughter."

"She's Jewish?"

"No, no, of course! Just adopted. She's no Jew, you can see that. Anyway, she is trying to join him, and that's where she's headed now. This man, this Jew, is a professor, a scientist, known all over the world, and if he escapes he plans to exploit his fame by spreading lies about our country and our Führer. Our Party, Hitler himself, wants him stopped."

"And the Führer has assigned you to stop him?"

"Well, not him personally, of course, but… For God's sake, I told you it's complicated. There are things I can't tell you."

"I'm sure there are."

Steeg was looking down at her, looking for some change in Hilda's expression, but there was none; she had stopped looking at Steeg and was looking straight ahead again with a blank expression.

"Well, do you see now? Why I need your help?"

"Steeg, you never change, do you?"

"Don't you hear what I'm telling you?"

She kept up the same blank stare, and didn't say a word. "Hilda, please help me." He was pleading now. "This one time. I promise you, I'll make it up to you."

She still said nothing.

"Tell me where she was going. For God's sake, will you help me?"

"No."

"Do I have to force you to do it?"

"You can't."

"You know I can. And your threats won't stop me. Not this time."

Steeg felt humiliated and helpless. He knew he had completely lost control, that Hilda was the one in control. He had to change that, to make her do as he commanded. The blood rushed to his head. His hands started trembling. He rushed over to the small writing desk on one side of the room, opened the drawer where he had put his gun earlier, pulled it out, and pointed it at her.

"Now you will do as I say."

Hilda was looking at him, not at the gun in his hand, but into his eyes. Her face was completely calm, as if she didn't even notice the gun.

"Just tell me where she is." Steeg wished he hadn't said "just." It sounded so desperate.

"You know I'm not going to."

Steeg wished she had screamed this out at him; that would have matched his fury. But she had said it without the slightest emotion, and that only increased his sense of helplessness.

"I warn you."

She did not respond.

"Tell me, or I will kill you."

She just kept looking at him.

"You can do what you want, but I won't tell you."

Steeg walked up beside her and put the gun to the side of Hilda's head.

"Tell me, bitch, or I'll shoot."

"I will never tell you!" She was screaming it now. "You can kill me! Do you think I care? Do you think there is any threat you can make that will make me tell? You stupid bastard, go ahead. Shoot!"

He felt all his determination dissolve into uncertainty. Steeg knew that he would able to shoot her, but he also knew that she did not believe he would, and that she was not going to do what he wanted, and that even if she turned out to be wrong and he were to do it, she was willing to die, and she still would not have told him, and then…

Steeg knew that there was no way he could win. Hilda had already won. She had overcome the fear of death, and by doing so she had saved her life.

Defeated, his whole body now trembling with futile rage, Steeg stuck the gun in his pocket and stormed out of the door.

✜✜✜

Minutes after Hilda had left, Lise—wearing the hat with the drooping brim and carrying the large bag, to whose contents she had added one of her own dresses—left the room.

Hilda had told her which stairs and corridors to take to mini-
mize the chance of being observed. Lise's transfer would take
place after dark. In the meantime, a man named Fritz, who was
a temporary maintenance worker at the inn, would bring her
to the house of the man who would take her across to Mainau
in his boat.

Fritz was waiting for Lise in the inn where Hilda had said
he would be. He recognized her from the description he had
been given, down to the hat and the bag. He led Lise into the
service area at the rear of the inn, then through a door which
he had to unlock, and then through a further corridor which
led into another building, past a small bathroom and into a
storage room nearly filled with barrels. Fritz pointed to a stool
and told Lise to wait there. It might be some time, he said, but
everything was arranged and he would be back; she was not to
worry. If anyone asked Lise who she was or what she was
doing there, her story should be that she was his cousin Anita
and that Fritz was going to give her a lift when he left.

Before she even left the inn, Lise had realized that she
needed to give a great deal more thought to what she was
about to do. Anxious as she was to join her father, Lise knew
that, no matter how carefully this was done, there was a
chance that it would inadvertently lead Steeg to him. On the
other hand, she knew that Steeg would make every effort to
recapture her, and that if he succeeded he would use her to
coerce her father into giving himself up. This meant that she
had to choose between two courses, each fraught with enormous risk for her father.

Someone was coming down the hallway. For a moment
Lise had the urge to hide, but realizing it was probably Fritz,
stayed put. To her surprise it was Hilda.

"Hilda!" she said. "I thought you were far from here by
now."

Hilda told Lise what had happened, about having been
almost immediately captured, then taken to a private house

nearby, then returned to the inn, her confrontation with Steeg, and how it had ended.

"You see what you missed? He was waiting for you."

"You're so brave! He might have killed you."

"Somehow I didn't think he would, but of course I couldn't be sure."

Lise remembered again the iron grip of Steeg's arms around her. She recalled the feel of the knife in her hand and the appalling sight of Steeg as he had stepped back.

"I have to admire you," she said, looking respectfully at Hilda.

"Lise," Hilda said, "as I told you earlier, everything is arranged. But I'm beginning to wonder if it is really wise for you to join your father."

"That's what I've been thinking over also. Since you told me the plan."

"And that was before you knew that they would catch me."

"Yes. But either way, they'll be looking for me. And if I lead them to my father, all may be lost. The question is not what is safer for me. If I don't join my father, and Steeg captures me, I'm not worried about what he can do to me. My value to him is as a hostage, to lure my father with, nothing else. That was his plan all along. That's the only thing that really worries me. So I think I have made my decision."

"To not try to rejoin your father, right?"

"Your guess is correct. That way he at least will have a chance."

"They're expecting you. I can get a message to them."

"Yes. They will understand."

"I know they will. But remember, the minute Steeg realizes you're not leaving, in my clothes or not, they will come after you. And he will stop at nothing to do it. Of course they would have been looking for you anyway."

"But not in these clothes."

"But now they will be."

Lise sat in thought. She knew what Hilda was thinking; she had the same thought herself.

"Yes. Our clothes." Lise's face lit up. "Say, you don't suppose we could…"

"Yes, why not? It may not fool them, but I don't see how it can do any harm."

"All right. But first I have an idea. Before we exchange clothes, why don't I first go down to the dock and buy a ticket? For a later departure. If they are watching they will see me."

"And they'll assume that's the way you will leave."

"Yes."

"But they may grab you right there."

"I don't think they will, because they'll want to see me get on that boat first. I'm willing to risk it."

"I have a better idea. Why don't we exchange clothes now, and then I'll go buy the ticket. If they don't grab me, the result will be the same. And if they do, you will still be safe. Either way you'll be away from here by then."

"But what about you?" Lise said.

"I'm not afraid of Steeg." Hilda paused.

"Here is some money…"

"I've got money," Lise said.

"How much?"

"Plenty," Lise assured her.

"Good." Hilda handed Lise a piece of paper. "Memorize this. I'll go out right now and arrange for a taxi to take you to Friedrichshafen. It will be safer that way. When you get there, call this man at this number. He knows about you. You can trust him. Tell him that Hilda told you to call him. He'll take care of you."

A few minutes later, they both emerged from the little bathroom, each wearing her own clothes, and Hilda left. In a few minutes she was back.

"Any sign of life?"

"I didn't see any, but who knows? Go out this way. When you reach the street, turn right. The taxi is just around the first corner, on the right." She gave Lise the license number. "I paid him the fare all the way to Friedrichshafen. If he's not there or there is some other problem, come back here."

Hilda waited for twenty minutes after Lise had gone, then left too. She called Munich and told the man that the lady had canceled the cruise she had booked. Then Hilda headed down towards the lake and the ticket office for the boat.

✝✝✝

Lise's taxi ride to Friedrichshafen was uneventful. The taxi dropped her off at the train station, and she went into a telephone booth outside the building. She dialed the number that Hilda had given her. The man answered. He said someone would pick her up around the corner to the right as she came out of the station. He would be driving a Fiat and would say that his name is Leopold. She was to give hers as Anna.

Lise stepped out of the phone booth and turned to the right. She was halfway to the corner when a man in a military-style trench coat blocked her way.

"Excuse me," Lise said.

The man reached out to take hold of her, but she spun around and started running the opposite way. Almost immediately Lise ran head-on into a second man, this one coatless. This man grabbed her by the wrist. Lise tried to escape his grip, but then felt a pain in her arm so intense that she found herself unable to move.

"We don't want to hurt you," the first man said. "Just come with us." He said this with a big smile on his face. The man who had seized Lise relaxed his grip so that, while he still held her firmly, the intense pain had stopped. She started to scream and tried again to disengage herself. The intense pain came back. Several pedestrians passed by, but to her amazement none of them seemed to pay any attention to her struggle.

Both men were now dragging Lise towards the curb, where there was a car that she had not noticed earlier. One of its doors was wide open. They got Lise, still screaming and twisting despite the pain, into the back seat, where the second man maintained his grip on her. The first man got in the back on the other side of her and the car drove off.

✝✝✝

That night, after Hilda's last message had been relayed to them, the Professor made the short trip from the house where he had been staying to Bernard's farm, and they walked from there to the dock where the boat was tied up. Raoul, who earlier had gone down with Karl to see the boat, led the way. This was not a long walk; it was easily manageable even for the Professor. A slight breeze swept a few clouds across the sky, occasionally concealing and then revealing the nearly full moon.

The boat was not large. The helm and engine controls were in a shallow well amidships; further aft was a small deckhouse, into which they led the Professor. Karl started up the engine and they set out. The water was calm, the air clear. A few lights dotted the Swiss shore across from them. Karl set a steady, low speed; they had decided this would be the least likely to draw attention. The rush of the water against the hull could easily be heard above the rumble of the engine.

✝✝✝

To avoid being detected, Steeg reasoned, the Professor's boat would probably proceed at a low engine speed; once Steeg's boat was in pursuit of it, the greater power of his boat should make it impossible for the Professor to get away.

Steeg had his pilot head westward not far from the shore of the peninsula. There were two or three boats with their running lights on in the area, but none of these was headed away from the shore of Reichenau or the Peninsula. Besides, Steeg felt sure that the boat he was looking for would not have its lights on.

When they were approximately abreast of the eastern end of Reichenau, he had the pilot cut the engine off. The current caused them to drift very slowly westward, parallel to the shore. The wind had almost died; the only sound was the slap of the water against the hull. Steeg was standing next to the unlit searchlight. He ordered everyone to keep still, and he began to listen.

For a very long time, there was nothing. Then he heard it. A barely audible, soft rumble, as from an engine almost idling, nearly dead ahead of him. For a while Steeg did nothing, just strained to hear, wanting to be sure, to pinpoint where the sound was coming from. Then he swung the searchlight in that direction, and turned it on. There was nothing. Steeg started sweeping the beam over the water, to the right. Then he saw it, caught in the light.

✝✝✝

At first André thought he saw an indistinct shape in the moonlight, ahead of them, off the port bow. After a while, although he still was not sure whether it was his imagination, he saw a shadow, the faint silhouette of a boat. Like them, it had no running lights; it seemed larger than them, taller.

A moment later, a bright light came on from the same spot, a searchlight. Its beam hit the water some distance ahead of them. Then it glided over the water, towards them. A moment later it was pointed straight at them, illuminating the whole boat. Considerable light also spilled out from the searchlight onto the other boat, revealing a low deckhouse, with an outside ladder, a stairway, leading to an open bridge on top of it. They heard its engine start up; the boat soon started closing in on them.

As it got closer, they heard a man's voice, shouting. At first it sounded unintelligible. Then they made it out above the sound of the engine. "Halt!" It was Steeg.

The boat was now even closer. The searchlight was high up on it, the light aimed down at them. The light that spilled from it revealed the pilot on the bridge, helm in hand and, some distance behind him, as if frozen in the glare, three more persons: Steeg, Erich, and, standing slightly apart from the other two, Lise. She was an arm's length away from Erich, who had his arm hanging down at his side, a gun in his hand.

André, who, like Raoul, was unarmed, was surprised to see that Erich had a gun.

The other boat, now very close, had cut back its engine and turned to the left, so that it was running almost parallel to them. Both boats were barely making headway.

"Go!" André said to Karl. He had kept his voice low, but there was strength in it. Karl opened the throttle. At first nothing happened. Then the stern trembled as the screw began to churn the water.

Finally they began to pick up speed.

But slowly. This was no speedboat. Its small size was matched by its diminutive engine. But it was gradually beginning to move faster.

"Halt!" Steeg shouted again. They kept going. While they were still within hailing distance, Steeg shouted a series of orders to his crew. His voice carried over the water, and could clearly be heard on the small boat despite its own now louder sounds. The larger vessel quickly began picking up speed and easily caught up with them.

"Halt!" Steeg shouted again.

Their boat did not stop, but it was obvious that they could not get away. Steeg's pilot kept completely even with them.

"Give us Mueller! Hand him over!" Steeg shouted. His voice came through clearly over the other sounds.

"André!" shouted Lise. "Don't listen to him. Save him."

"Laroche, give me Mueller."

"Never!" André shouted. "You murderer!"

"You told me that story before, Laroche. Where are your witnesses?"

"I am the witness," said André, still shouting. "My father, my mother, my sister. You killed them all. I was there. I saw you do it."

"You stupid Belgian! Don't you even know? I was tried, and I was acquitted!"

Steeg shouted an order to the pilot, and more lights came on. The whole scene—the two boats and the water all around them—was now as bright as daylight. Steeg scampered down the steps to the deck. He shouted another order, and a young man, apparently a deck hand, came out of the deckhouse. The two boats had continued to come closer to each other. They were still parallel, even with each other, less than a meter apart. Some line lay coiled on the deck, one end made fast to a nearby cleat on the side facing André's boat. Another line lay further aft, made fast to another cleat. The deck hand quickly took one of the lines, jumped across the gap, and made the line fast to a cleat on the smaller boat. He jumped back to Steeg's boat, did the same with the second line, then jumped back again to Steeg's boat. The two boats were now lashed together, almost touching.

"Turn him over and I let her go," said Steeg.

The Professor, who had remained out of sight in the deckhouse, now came out.

"I'm going over," he said.

"Don't do it!" Lise and André shouted, almost at the same time.

"Stefan, don't!" Lise said again. "You can't trust him."

"It's my decision," said the Professor.

He moved surprisingly fast; an instant later, Mueller was on Steeg's boat.

"Here I am. Now let her go."

Steeg pulled out a gun and aimed it at the Professor.

"Welcome aboard," Steeg said. "I must tell you, you came over for nothing. She stays with me, and so do you."

"But you said…"

Steeg kept the gun aimed at the Professor, but otherwise paid no attention to him, because André had started towards Steeg's boat, with Raoul close behind him.

"Stop, or the Professor dies," said Steeg.

André stopped, only a step away from crossing over to Steeg's boat.

"You can shoot me; it doesn't matter," said the Professor.

Mueller took a few steps towards the rail, on the side away from the smaller boat. Steeg kept his gun pointed at him. All of his virulent hatred was now concentrated on this small figure; every fiber in him wanted to kill the Professor. But once again Steeg remembered the orders he was under, and thought of his career, his ambitions.

"Behrndt!" Steeg shouted. "The gun. Put it to her head. Now!"

Erich heard the words, but as a mere observer, not as himself. The Erich who heard the words was standing next to him, curious to know what would happen, but not otherwise involved.

"Put the gun to her head," Steeg said again. Then he added "Or her father dies."

Erich put the barrel of the gun against Lise's head.

André expected Lise to cringe, to cry out, to back away, but her expression didn't even change.

"Stop," Steeg now shouted to the Professor, "or she dies!"

The Professor stopped.

"Now, Behrndt! Shoot! Kill her!"

There was only a pause of a few seconds, but to everyone, and especially to Erich, it was an eternity.

"No!" Erich finally said.

"What did you say?" Steeg said, turning to look at Erich.

"I said no," replied Erich, looking Steeg in the eye.

Steeg knew he could do it himself. The Professor was still close enough to him; he could kill her and he would still have time to stop the Professor. He aimed at her. But at that moment his hand froze; he could not bring himself to do it.

"Kill her! Or I will," Steeg shouted.

This time there was no delay on Behrndt's part. In one swift move, Erich stepped in front of Lise, putting himself between Steeg and her.

Steeg could do this easily; in fact, it would be a pleasure. But the shot might go clear through him and... Seconds ago Steeg had ordered Erich to kill her; now he was still unable to do it himself. He wanted to kill Behrndt only, but he was afraid the bullet would hit Lise too.

The four, Lise and Erich up on the bridge, Steeg and the Professor below, stood immobile, as if captured on an old photograph.

At that moment, the Professor jumped over the side. At almost the same instant, André leapt onto Steeg's boat, Raoul close behind him. Steeg spun around and fired at Laroche. The bullet missed him but hit Raoul, who was still on the smaller boat, and fell.

"It's nothing," Raoul yelled. "He only grazed me."

Steeg whirled back and fired at Erich, but in the same moment André had got hold of Steeg. Although Steeg's aim had been thrown off, the bullet still hit Erich. Blood spurted out from somewhere in his middle, and the gun Erich had been holding flew out of his hand, fell to the main deck below, and bounced overboard.

André had his hands on Steeg, and the two were grappling with each other. From the bridge above, Erich started to make his way down to the main deck. He moved slowly, and as he did he left a trail of blood on the steps. Behrndt spotted Steeg's gun lying on the deck, but saw the two men were so tightly entangled in their struggle that it would be useless.

Although neither André nor Steeg had intended it, by now the fight had brought the two close to the rail. At this point, this barrier was merely a low cable strung between two stanchions. The two men seemed locked in a death grip; at first neither gained on the other, but then Steeg began to get the edge. Despite André's youth and stamina, Steeg, who seemed to have the strength of ten, managed to lock him into a position between himself and the rail from which he appeared unable to extricate himself. Erich now finally reached the bottom of the steps, and as soon as he did, lunged at Steeg and gripped him with both hands. For what seemed a long time, the combined strength of the two barely kept Steeg in one spot. But then his footing very gradually began to give way and the three moved, first away from the rail, then closer to it again, this time with Steeg against it. Still struggling mightily, Steeg lost his balance, rose slightly off the deck, and fell backwards over the cable and into the water.

Erich immediately picked up a long pole that he had earlier spotted on the deck, and raised it, ready to strike Steeg with it, but at that instant started to fall. He managed to hand the pole to André, then collapsed and lay on his back, motionless, his eyes wide open, all life gone.

Steeg went under as soon as he hit the water. He came up quickly, gasping and flailing his arms about, but before André could hit him with the pole he went down again. This time Steeg stayed under for what seemed to be a long time. He came up again, still thrashing, gasping, and coughing up water. He went down once more, and did not come up.

There was silence, broken only by the muted sounds of the engines, both of which were apparently just idling. There was no sign of the Professor.

They had Steeg's pilot sweep his searchlight back and forth over a wide area. They watched and waited, but at first saw no sign of the Professor or Steeg. After a while, however, they spotted Mueller. He was already some distance ahead, swimming vigorously and moving steadily towards the Swiss shore, which was now only a few hundred meters away. At a word from André, Steeg's pilot opened the throttle and signaled to the pilot of the other boat to do the same. The two boats, still lashed together, continued towards Professor Mueller.

✝✝✝

Lise had not been hurt, and had followed Erich down from the bridge. She now turned her attention to him. Behrndt was lying in a pool of blood; Lise fell to her knees and leaned over him. His eyes remained wide open, glazed in death. Lise was filled with a mixture of intense emotions such as she had never felt before. Gratitude mixed with admiration, and both of these tinged with sorrow. What Erich had done was unlike anything she had ever seen or could have dreamed. He, whom—despite his many good qualities—she had perceived as somehow indecisive and weak, more pursued by his dreams and loyalties than pursuing them, had now performed this inconceivably brave, generous, and unselfish act. Lise was moved as never before.

Lise wanted to cry, but could not. She was just filled with an infinite sadness. And with pity. Pity for what Erich might have done, but never did; for what he might have been, but never became. For the tragedy of his death. Lise admired Erich and would be forever grateful for what he had done. She was overcome with dreadful sorrow, but it was sorrow for the loss of the life he had sacrificed for her, not sorrow for the loss of love. She understood that whatever flame of affection might have developed between them had been snuffed out before it had had any chance of growing into love.

+++

All these events had been so intense and had come so fast one upon the other that there had not been even an instant to think about Raoul. André now for the first time looked over at him. Raoul was still down on the deck.

"Raoul," he said. Maartens did not answer. André ran and jumped over to the small boat. When André reached his friend, he saw that Raoul was unconscious. Fighting back panic, André bent over him. There was no breath, no pulse.

"Raoul, Raoul, say something," André said. "No! Raoul! Raoul, don't go!"

He paused, as if Raoul were going to awaken.

"Oh, God!" André now said, almost to himself.

And then grief and despair filled his heart and choked off his voice. Raoul, of all people! The best friend anyone ever had! Raoul, the strong one, the one who knew everyone, the one who took care of everything, the only one without whom it could never have been done. Why had it been him? Raoul, who had saved André's life, risking his own. Raoul, who had marched into death a thousand times, and never got a scratch. Why him? Why now?

André threw himself on the deck, put his arms around Raoul, hugged him and shook him, as if somehow this terrible, unthinkable thing could be undone. He began to sob and tears flooded out of him, born of the sudden release of all the unbearable, accumulated tension, and of this so sad death coming at the moment of such triumph. It seemed that those tears would never stop.

+++

The boats caught up with the Professor. André shouted to him to come aboard, but the Professor shouted back that he was fine.

"In the water, my legs weigh nothing, and I feel like a god," he said. Just the same André kept a close eye on Mueller as they followed him.

✝✝✝

After Lise had come aboard André's boat, the pilot of Steeg's boat sent his deck hand over to the small boat to help, and he and André finally placed Raoul's body on a bench near the stern and covered it with a blanket.

Steeg's pilot shouted across to them, asking what they were going to do about the body of the young man. André looked at Lise.

"What do you think he would have wanted?" André said.

Lise thought a long time before answering.

"I think he would have wanted to be buried in Germany. What he did was not against that country, but against someone who, in his eyes, was not faithful to it."

"I don't know whether the Nazis would see it that way."

"I don't think they would. My first thought was that for that reason he would not have wanted to be buried there, but I think the Erich we saw today wouldn't care how they buried him or in what grave. I'm convinced that the certainties in his own heart would be more important to him than all that."

André turned to the pilot...

"Tell them," he shouted back, "that he gave his life to save someone else's. Tell them they should bury Erich Behrndt with honors."

The lines were then let go and the pilot of Steeg's boat headed back to where he had come from.

After a while a multitude of tiny lights were seen ahead, bobbing up and down in the water. When their boat got closer,

André and Lise saw that these were small boats, just rowboats. It turned out that in each one was a scientist, in some two or three, all friends and admirers of Professor Mueller. Despite the late hour, a great party in celebration of Professor Mueller's escape was about to begin not far inland. In view of the great regard they had for the Professor, they had constituted themselves a welcoming committee and come out to meet him before he reached the shore. Professor Mueller did in fact accept the invitation of one of the boats to come aboard, and he was transported ashore in great triumph.

Once everyone was ashore, the greeters explained to the Professor how they had known he was coming. It was of course Richard Dutrec who had told them approximately where and when Mueller could, God willing, be expected. To be sure to intercept him, they had spread their rowboats out over a wide area.

✝✝✝

Karl was appalled at what had happened, and he felt guilty about Raoul.

"I should have come to his aid," he said. "I might have been able to save him."

"Karl, no one is more devastated by Raoul's death than me," said André. "He was my closest, dearest friend. But you would have endangered us all if you had left the controls. Besides, although he told us it wasn't serious, the bullet somehow did frightful damage; there was nothing you could have done. It's a dreadful loss, but it was certainly not your fault."

When they reached the Swiss shore, Karl offered to take Raoul's body to the Swiss authorities, suggesting that André could make whatever arrangements he desired for Maartens' burial in Switzerland. André said that this offer was kind of Karl, but declined the suggestion.

"Raoul deeply loved the small village in Flanders," André said, "where he was born and where for centuries his ancestors have been born and died and been buried, and it was his wish to be buried there. He has no immediate family, so I'm going to go with his body to that village and see that that is done."

✝✝✝

Much later that night, André and Lise took a walk down towards the lake. They reached a wooded area, and then came to a spot where the shore could seen through the trees. They continued walking down towards the water. Soon they reached a point where a few lights on Reichenau could be distinguished across the way. They stopped.

The storm of emotions that had been deluging Lise had begun to abate. She now felt drained, downcast, and filled with guilt.

"Those two die, and we go on living. Why?" she said. André had no answer, and gave none.

"I'm sorry to be bothering you with that thought," she said, looking over at him.

"It's all right. It's just that I have no answer," he said.

"I have the strange feeling that after all that happened today, you and I will never see each other again, and I some-how wanted..." She left the thought unfinished.

"You just wanted to talk to someone about it."

"Not just to someone. To you."

"You have a whole life still ahead of you."

"I feel I have already lived a whole life," Lise said quickly. She paused. "It's so unfair," she continued. "I don't mean to me, but to them, both Erich and..."

"His name was Raoul. We were at the front together during the war. He risked his life to save mine. When he had only known me for a few days."

"I had no idea," she said. "I knew none of that, of course.

I didn't know him. Just a while ago, when I saw Erich down on the deck... dead, I was devastated but no tears came. But when I saw Raoul lying there, and I saw you... as if you were trying to bring him back, I felt that somehow I understood your grief. That it became my grief. I was so moved that I cried with you."

She was quiet, remembering something.

"My mother died a long, lingering death," Lise said. "It would have been better if she could have just..."

"Well, there can be a time for death. But this was not the time for Erich, or for Raoul."

"I don't know how you have the strength to bear it."

"I don't. But Raoul always did."

"I don't know why I'm still living."

"It's the same with me. I feel that I should be punished for living now that he's... But then I think about what they— Erich, Raoul—would have wanted us to do."

"I think they would want us to live," she said.

"Yes. Living is its own reason," he agreed. "I think they would want us to live our lives to the fullest."

"I think you're right," she said.

Lise had been facing the lake. After a long time, she turned and faced him.

"I've never known anyone like you," she said. "You have been a rock for me. You've saved my life, you and Raoul both. I'm very grateful. I have a lot of admiration for you."

"You're very kind to say that."

Lise thought back to the time Suzanne had teased her about André after the "mussels and *frites*" lunch. "André's someone I feel comfortable enough with to confide in," Lise had said, "but of course I don't think of him in romantic terms." Now she had told André that when she saw him just a while ago, with Raoul lying there, she had understood André's grief. But Lise really understood much more, because she had discovered something in André that she had never found before in any man—tenderness. And that changed everything. Lise had told Suzanne that she was not sure of what she wanted in a man. But now Lise was sure. She wanted *André*.

"Yes, I am grateful but I'm not just being kind," she said, smiling. "It's that I've grown fond of you."

"You're very young," he said.

"I'll be twenty-one this year."

"You still have dreams to pursue."

"Yes."

"Science? Is that still your dream? Or have you given it up?"

"I will never give that up."

"I have a proposal to make to you. You pursue your career. University, post-graduate studies, the lot."

"I can't afford it, and my father…"

"I know. But I have money."

"I didn't mean it that way. I'm embarrassed."

"I know you better than that. You should pursue your dream, and I have plenty of money for it. I've always regretted not having had a better education myself. Now I can at least see to it that you have the means to complete yours. There will be no strings attached. Besides, by the time you finish, I'm sure you will have met the right fellow anyway."

Lise reached out and took his hand. While she was reaching for him, André thought of it as the gesture of a friend. But as they held hands, a shiver that surprised him coursed through his entire body. He squeezed her hand for some seconds, then let go of it. They started walking again towards the water.

"Remember," André said, "you still have your whole life ahead of you."

"And what about you?"

"There will be plenty of time. We can stay in touch with each other. I have my whole life ahead of me too."

"Yes, we'll stay in touch," Lise said with a pretty smile, as she looked straight into his eyes.

André and Lise had stopped walking. They were now very close to the water's edge, clear of the trees, at a point where the shoreline protruded slightly and the view in all directions was open to them. In the last glow of the setting moon, Lise seemed wrapped in softness, but André knew that fire and determination were also within her.

The breeze had died, and the sky had cleared completely. Across the lake, some lights on Reichenau still flickered. Far to the right towards the east, the first thin edge of dawn appeared over the distant Alps.

"How old are you?" she asked.

"I'll be thirty-seven this year."

"You know, that 'right fellow' you mentioned?"

"Yes."

"Actually, I've found him."

She took his hand again.

SOURCES CONSULTED

Chant, *Hitler's Generals and Their Battles,* New York, Chartwell Books, Inc., 1976.

Falls, *The Great War,* New York, Putnam, 1959.

Fodor's Germany, New York, London, etc., Fodor's Travel Publications, 2000.

Friedlander, *Nazi Germany and the Jews,* New York, Harper Collins, 1997.

Gilbert, *The First World War: a complete history,* New York, Holt, 1994.

Giles, *Flanders Then and Now,* London, Battle of Britain Prints International, 1987.

Keegan, *The First World War,* New York, Knopf, 1999.

Los Angeles Times, March 8, 1936.

Los Angeles Times, March 10, 1936.

Los Angeles Times, March 12, 1936.

Manchester, *The Arms of Krupp,* Boston, Little, Brown & Co., 1968.

_____, *The Last Lion: Alone* ("Manchester II"), New York, Dell Publishing, 1988.

_____, *The Last Lion: Visions of Glory* ("Manchester I"), New York, Dell Publishing, 1983.

Pertinax, *The Gravediggers of France,* Garden City, New York, Doubleday, Doran & Company, Inc.,1944.

Shirer, *The Rise and Fall of the Third Reich,* New York, Simon and Schuster, 1960.

Tuchman, *The Guns of August,* New York, Bantam Books, 1989.

Williamson, *The SS: Hitler's Instrument of Terror,* Osceoloa, Wis., Motorbooks International, 1994.

NOTES

290 Versailles, Locarno voided: Manchester (II), 173-174; Los Angeles Times, March 8, 1936, Sec. A, p. 1; Shirer, 291

290 Blomberg authorized to retreat: Manchester (II), 175; Shirer, 291

290-291 Generals' dismay: Manchester (II), 175; Shirer, 291

291 Gamelin's background: Pertinax, 34

291-292 Cabinet meeting: Manchester (II), 176; Shirer, 292-293; Los Angeles Times, March 8, 1936, Sec. A, p.6

292 Size of reoccupation force: Manchester (II), 179; Los Angeles Times, March 8, 1936, Sec. A, p. 1

298 Clark's message: Manchester (II), 178

298-299 Eden's belief: id. at 178-179; Los Angeles Times, March 10, 1936, Sec. A, p.1

298-299 British weekend: Manchester (II), 178

300 Blomberg's reaction: id. at 174; Shirer, 292

301 Swastikas stylish: Manchester (II), 188

316 Lake's climate: Fodor, 218, 237

ABOUT THE AUTHOR

ARNOLD SIMON was born in New York City, but his family traces its roots to the region where the events that form the background of this story occurred, and he lived in Europe at the time before World War II when they were unfolding.

Simon returned to the United States on the eve of the war. After graduating from Yale, he worked for some years in the aerospace industry. He entered law school at the age of thirty-nine, and became a partner in a Los Angeles law firm. He also studied creative writing at UCLA.

He and his Irish-born wife Nancy live in Los Angeles.

www.aBreakintheStorm.com

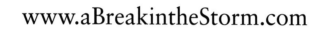
www.aBreakintheStorm.com